AF411927

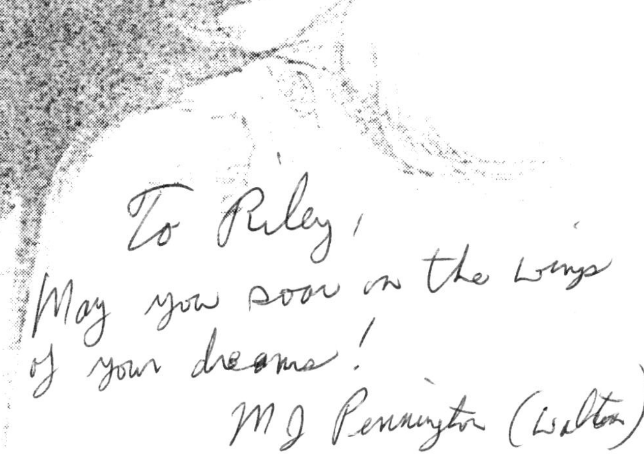

M.J. PENNINGTON

New Horizons Publications

ISBN 0-9648049-0-5

Library of Congress Catalog Number: 95-70928

Cover design and illustrations by the author

Photograph of the author by Phil Sensinger

This is a work of fiction. Characters and events described are imaginary.

Author may be contacted through:

New Horizons Publications
5403 Everhart Road, #282
Corpus Christi, Texas 78411-4895

Printed in the USA by

MORRIS PUBLISHING

3212 E. Hwy 30
Kearney, NE 68847
800-650-7888

*This book
is dedicated to all women,
and to the men who love them.*

MY HEARTFELT THANKS:

To Phil, for your love, unfailing support, technical advice and assistance, and for insisting we buy the computer.

To Kurt, for your support and technical advice.

To Jane, for always believing in me.

To the memory of Tom and Mary Davis, who gave unselfish love.

To Marian and Glenda, for your enthusiasm and encouragement and for motivating me to do it.

To the other two 'Cateers: Dorothy, for teaching me the way, and Cathy, for paving the way; and to both of you for reading and listening, listening, listening—and much, much more.

To Marty, Tanya, Rose, and Marilyn, for your encouragement.

To Dave, for your insightful editing and welcomed suggestions.

To the public libraries for research assistance and for creating an insatiable hunger in me for reading at a very young age.

To the National Multiple Sclerosis Society for information.

To Ray Bradbury, the absolute master of the short story, for sharing his talent with the world.

And to The Moody Blues, whose moving, musical poetry inspires whatever creativity I might have.

CONTENTS

PROLOGUE

She knew she wouldn't have to wait long before he would come to her. Although she didn't know what he looked like, she was certain that she would recognize him. She relaxed as she sipped her red wine and looked around. It was a pleasant little bar with excellent music on the jukebox. Some she hadn't heard in years. Nostalgia! Everyone seemed to be looking back to try to find a happier time from their past. This seemed very sad to her that, for so many, looking back on their lives had become more meaningful than looking ahead. Michael had become one of those people. That was why she was here; to try to save him, to try to help him move past that place, to move on with his life...as only she could.

Her eyes were magic; like deep pools of ebony.

THE EVE OF THE BEGINNING

"That's enough!" I thought as I snapped off the lights and walked out of my office. While locking the outer door, I looked at the impressive brass name plate on the wall. "Hatten, Berger, Levy and McGinnis: Attorneys at Law." I was the "McGinnis." Michael McGinnis.

As I rode the elevator down the fifteen floors to the lobby, a depressingly eerie silence seemed to echo throughout the deserted building. Well, what did I expect at 9:30 on a Thursday night?

I felt restless as I stepped outside into the sultry, South Texas October air, and realized that I really didn't want to go home yet. I had celebrated my fortieth birthday two weeks ago, and since then I had been having difficulty accepting the sudden awareness of how rapidly my youth had slipped away. So I decided to stop at my most recent second home; a quiet cozy little bar on Water Street named Anytime.

The guy who owns it is named Doug. He was a whiz kid on Wall Street until a year ago when he suddenly decided he hated his job and needed a drastic life style change. Since he had enjoyed several spring breaks here while attending college, he sold all of his possessions that wouldn't fit into a U-Haul, cashed in his investments (which had earned him a nice chunk of change), moved here and opened Anytime. He told me once that he had tended bar as a part-time job while in college, a job which he had thoroughly enjoyed and still did.

Although I like the guy (and he has some interesting philosophies he isn't shy about sharing with his clientele), I enjoy his juke box most of all. He has a large selection of the best music from the late '60s to the late '70s, which he rotates once a month so it doesn't get stale. I always look forward to hearing his current selections. Sometimes, hearing a particular song I had all but forgotten about, brings back such a flood of memories--so poignant-so visual, it almost takes my breath away. I guess that through the music I'm able to relive some of my happier memories. The place seems to give me some sort of comfort I'm apparently missing in the rest of my life.

Even though I'm a successful defense attorney, my personal life (or lack of it) is a disaster. I'm twice divorced, with no children. My first wife, Joy (she was born on Christmas, so her mother named her Joy Noel), and I met during our first year of law school. I fell in love with her instantly--the first time I laid eyes on her. With her thick mass of dark curly hair cascading down her back, and huge blue-violet eyes, she looked like a princess who had just stepped out a fairy tale. We went on our first date the night of the day we met, and were married in our second year of law school.

After graduation, Joy and I moved here to Corpus Christi; we had become enamored of the laid-back, three hundred thousand-populated "Sparkling City by the Sea" when we had spent our brief but romantic honeymoon here. We had reveled in the temperate climate of the South Texas Gulf Coast city, along with its lush tropical flora, its interesting blend of ethnic diversity, and its varied ambiance of jeans, boots, and barbecue--ranging to casual elegance. But most of all, we had been attracted to the unspoiled serenity of the hundred mile stretch of barrier island gulf beach, merely minutes away across the bay.

So, with a keen eye on my future (the cultural giants of Houston, Dallas and San Antonio being just hours away) Corpus Christi seemed the logical place for us to live. I joined a prestigious law firm and Joy got a job with the city as an assistant district attorney. Neither of us was making large salaries then, but with our combined incomes we had a comfortable existence, and after a year we had saved enough to buy a small attractive house on Del Mar Boulevard, in an older but up-scale neighborhood.

Unfortunately, the longer we were together...the more we grew apart. We always seemed to be at totally opposite ends of what we considered to be important in our lives. She wanted to take care of the poor, the downtrodden, the innocent victims. To me, there were no innocent victims, merely cases to win. She would frequently tell me I had an unusually lousy sense of justice for being born under the sign of Libra.

Three years later we split, with an amicable divorce and a sense of great sadness--mingled with relief; we had been destroying each other. Joy moved to Dallas where she again became an assistant prosecuting attorney and has been making quite a name for herself since. Unfortunately, I've never been able to completely get her out of my heart, and keep frequent tabs on her through mutual friends. She hasn't remarried and, as far as I know, doesn't have a special man in her life.

My second marriage was four years later to Karen, who had come to work at my law firm as a legal secretary and soon worked her way up to becoming my legal assistant. She was tall--five feet, ten inches--and model slender. Her deep tan contrasted handsomely with her platinum blond hair, which she wore cut very short. She was both ambitious and strikingly attractive. She was also a prize bitch!

She was calculating and shrewd. She soon convinced me that she was indispensable in both my professional and my personal life, and for a while I believed her. Eleven months--almost to the day--after she began working at our firm, we exchanged nuptials at one of the larger, more affluent downtown churches. The wedding cost a small fortune, which, since Karen and her parents were of middle class means, I paid for. By then I had risen to the position of junior partner in the firm, and was pulling in a very lucrative salary.

Karen picked out a large, expensive house in one of the exclusive older neighborhoods, quit her job, and began trying to elbow her way into the established network of old Corpus Christi society. I realized shortly after our marriage ceremony--with some degree of horror--what a terrible mistake I had made. That was when I knew I had never gotten over Joy, that I was still in love with her. I tried to make the best of a bad situation, but after a year Karen and I divorced. I gave her a large, more than generous settlement, just to get her out of my life. After that disastrous experience, I gave up on my personal life and concentrated solely on my career. Within four years I became one of two or three of the most successful trial lawyers in South Texas. I still am.

October has always been one of my favorite months. Besides being the month of my birthday, I had spent my childhood in the Midwest where October is the last warm month before the cold set in, and I fondly remember crisp, cold October mornings, which later evolved into golden, sunny afternoons. The crunch of the fallen leaves underfoot; the fun of raking them into large piles by the curb; and later in the evening they would be lighted into bonfires around which all of us neighborhood kids would roast wieners and toast marshmallows. Once I tried to bake a potato in the fire, and even though it turned out scorched on the outside and raw on the inside, I ate it anyway--every bit of it. And it was delicious!

However, probably the best was the anticipation of Halloween--which seemed to make the whole month exciting and mysterious. When I was a child, Halloween was an absolutely enchanting time for me and is still my favorite holiday--even in my present, chronically melancholy mood.

So with these reflections, on the nostalgia of Halloweens from my childhood, I entered Anytime to the sound of Justin Hayward's lamenting "Forever Autumn."

I sat at the bar and ordered a beer. Doug began to discuss federally mandated health care, and since I was tired and didn't really feel like getting into any kind of deep discussion or debate, my eyes began to wander around the room. When I spotted her, sitting alone at a small table in the back, I felt my pulse quicken. She was one of the most intriguing looking women I had ever seen, and for a few seconds she took my breath away.

Doug followed my gaze. "She's really something isn't she?"

I was already getting to my feet without bothering with a reply. It was as if she were a magnet--drawing me to her. I don't think I could have resisted even if I had tried. She was looking at me...watching me walk towards her. Her eyes were magic, like deep pools of ebony. Her hair was just past her shoulders and dark, with bangs cut straight across her forehead. Her lips were faintly curved in the hint of a smile, as if she was secretly amused by something.

For many years now I had considered myself quite sophisticated, articulate, and very able to hold my own with anyone, including some very distinguished judges. But when I reached her table, to my total embarrassment, I found myself unable to speak. I felt as if I was tongue-tied. So I just stood there--foolishly looking down at her.

"Would you like to sit down?" she asked softly. I nodded, pulled out the chair and sat down while I continued to stare--my eyes locked to hers. She took a sip of her wine, then smiled as she asked, "What is your name?"

I cleared my throat and, thankfully, was at last able to find my voice. "Michael," I said huskily. "Michael McGinnis."

"Nice to meet you, Michael," she said.

"Would you like to go have dinner someplace?" I blurted out.

"I've already eaten, thank you, but I do think it would be nice if we could go someplace a little more private and a little more comfortable," she said as she reached out and took my left hand in hers. In my astonished glee, before I could suggest my house, she said, "Why don't you follow me in your car?"

She dropped my hand, stood, and began to walk gracefully towards the door. I couldn't believe my good fortune. I found her completely fascinating! And classy! I wondered if she was a professional prostitute. What the hell! If she was, whatever she charged would surely be worth it. I quickly got to my feet and followed her out of the door to the melodic plea of "Love, Reign O'er Me," by The Who.

In the parking lot, I noticed in the mercury flood lights that her hair appeared to be very dark auburn, rather than black, and her eyes were deep violet. She had on black trousers, and a black tunic which reached almost to her knees, made of some soft, clingy material.

She walked to a white Mercedes 560 SL and stopped. "Follow me," she said again, then got into her car. She waited until I had gotten into my Porsche and started the engine before she drove out of the small parking lot.

She drove to Shoreline Boulevard and turned south. I could feel my excitement mounting as I followed her down Shoreline onto Ocean Drive. The moon, which lacked only one day of being full, loomed straight ahead, as if guiding me. I suddenly felt as if I was about to experience something new and totally different.

My heart began to beat faster and the palms of my hands became sweaty as I felt a thrill of desire surge through my groin. I had always been pretty straight as far as sex was concerned. Oh, I had read and heard of plenty of kinky things. However, they had never particularly interested me. But now I didn't know what to expect. And that excited me even more. I guess that from the rut of boredom I had been mired in for such a long time, I was ready for just about anything!

After several miles, she pulled into the parking lot of a luxurious, nine-story condominium on the waterfront side of Ocean Drive. I followed her through the security gates into the parking lot, and she waited for me while I locked my car. When I joined her, she took my hand and led me to the door of the building. Nearby palm trees rustled in the gentle sea breeze, as if in secret knowing whisperings of what was to come, and I suddenly felt like an adolescent schoolboy suffering the pangs of first love.

She led me inside and down the hall to the elevator. As we rode up to the ninth floor, her enchanting eyes seemed to pull me into her and I felt the delicious excitement of anticipation. By the time we reached the top floor my knees had become weak, and my legs trembled as she led me off the elevator and down the hall to her apartment.

When she unlocked her door, we were greeted by a large, handsome Siamese cat with eyes almost as mysterious as hers.

"Hello, Aladdin," she said, as it rubbed against her ankles.

"Yeow," it answered her.

She picked him up and stroked him several times, then put him down and he ran off to another room. A lighted wall sconce gave a soft glow to the hallway, and she took my hand. "Come with me," she said, as my legs continued to tremble.

At the end of the hallway we entered her bedroom. By now I had reached such a pitch of excitement my body seemed to tingle all over. I looked around at the exquisite taste and beauty of the room; it was just like her.

At the end of the large room was a fantastic bed made of verdigris finished metal in a filigree design, with the open canopy frame swagged in white filmy material. The bed was covered with a burgundy colored duvet and the headboard was mounded with pillows.

At the opposite end of the room was a large antique European armoire, with beveled mirrored doors. A small candlestick lamp on a bombe chest, next to the bed, gave off a dim light. Open French doors to a balcony overlooking the bay let in a refreshing breeze which made the filmy white curtains billow gracefully into the room. And I could see that huge moon suspended so close to the balcony railing, it was almost as if I could reach out and touch it if I wanted to. The effect had a magical--ethereal--quality. I shivered and closed my eyes for a few seconds, feeling as if I had somehow entered another dimension.

From a combination of the beer and the excitement, I suddenly had a need to use the bathroom. I asked, and she pointed towards the wall on the far side of the armoire. When I opened the door I saw that her bathroom was also large, and just as elegant as her bedroom. Three walls were covered with beveled mirrors, and there was a whirlpool bathtub big enough for two people, a separate glass enclosed shower, and even a bidet.

After using the facilities, I stared for several seconds into the large mirror over the sink, distressed at the reflection of my haggard face and haunted eyes.

When I returned to her bedroom, I saw that she had lighted small white votive candles in clear glass containers all over the room; the breeze from the open French doors caused their flames to flicker--casting dancing shadows onto the walls and ceiling. She was standing beside the bed, and when I looked into her eyes I could see the reflection of the flickering candle flames. I felt as if I had fallen under a spell. Maybe she was a witch, I mused; after all it was only three days until Halloween.

"Come," she whispered.

I did as she asked. I didn't think I could break the trance I seemed to be in--even I had wanted to.

"Lie down on the bed," she said.

I sat on the edge, took off my shoes, then lay down on her magnificent bed. I closed my eyes, not knowing what to expect, and felt her take my hand; she began to kiss my finger tips, then gently sucked on the tip of my index finger for several seconds, which I found wildly erotic.

Suddenly, I opened my eyes in surprise as I felt something soft and smooth being wrapped around my wrist. My God! She was tying my wrist to the headboard! First one--then the other. I again felt that thrill. As she gently tied my ankles in the same manner to the footboard, I looked at the material of my bonds; they were white satin scarves. Some of the deeply emotional words from that beautiful, classic song, "Nights in White Satin," immediately ran through my mind-- accompanied by fevered anticipation.

I had never had any experience with bondage; however, I was so utterly captivated, I really didn't care what she did to me. By now I was completely under her spell. As I settled my head comfortably against the mass of pillows and closed my eyes, I could hear mysterious, exotic music--with unusual instruments--playing softly in the background.

Then she sat on the bed and leaned over me. "Michael, this is going to be a night I hope you will remember always."

I opened my eyes and felt a rush of embarrassment as I started to reply. I realized I had been so lost in her magic spell that I didn't even know her name.

"I'm sorry," I stammered; "I never asked your name, or what you do, or where you're from, or anything about you." I stopped, abruptly, feeling like a fool.

She smiled that little Mona Lisa smile again. "You may call me Schere. I am all women, and I am from all places. I am wisdom through the ages, personified. I am going to teach you about love, about sensitivity, about how to recapture your spirituality. You've lost that, Michael--yet you had it as a child.

"We often experience such deep pain and disappointment associated with all types of love, because, being human, we are vulnerable. The more sensitive we are, the more vulnerable we become. In order to try to stave off some of our innate loneliness, we reach out for someone we hope will be like ourselves. However, if we cease to do this, in an attempt to try to protect and shield ourselves from our own vulnerability, then we might as well cease to live; for without love, there can be no quality of life. Michael! You must learn to open all of your senses so that you can find and receive love.

"From the time we are born we search the big, often empty, sea of life--whether we are sailing or foundering--for that one person who will be an extension of ourselves. The special someone who feels the same way we feel inside. Frequently, that person is someone who also resembles us physically. Someone who might even share some of our same quirky mannerisms and gestures. Someone in whom we might see a part of ourselves. Maybe, if we love a person who we subconsciously feel in some way resembles us physically, we can then be free to love ourselves. Therefore, we continue to search for that person, with hopes that when found, we will also find ourselves. That we will, at last, no longer be alone."

I felt confused. I wasn't sure what she expected of me, which I guess she must have sensed, because she gently placed the palms of her hands on each side of my face and held it as she said, "You must look deeply into my eyes, Michael, and soon you will understand. You will learn life's truths from the stories in my eyes. Michael! See the stories in my eyes!"

I was mesmerized. I did as she asked: I looked deeply into her eyes, and felt myself spinning into those vast dark whirlpools as I heard her voice softly say...

"One of the most important and greatest loves we experience, is that very first love: the love from our parents--which can help mold the rest of our lives; the love that helps to sustain our belief in ourselves. I am going to tell you the story of Andrew and the story of Joe: two stories of love between parent and child."

"Come," she whispered.

WONDROUS JOURNEY

He was abruptly awakened when he felt a gentle nudge--
a sensation unlike anything he had ever experienced before.
He sleepily rubbed his eyes with his fists as he listened for
the familiar slush-thump sound that always seemed to be
present. Hearing its steady rhythm always gave him comfort, sometimes it was faster, and sometimes slower, but
whatever the speed, it was always in a regular beat. Yes. It
was still there--soft and slow. Yet, for some reason, he had
a vague feeling that his world was about to undergo a drastic
change. He yawned, closed his eyes, and was almost instantly asleep again.

* * * * * * * * *

Jane felt a momentary feeling of panic, then laughed. It's
finally here, she thought: the time has finally come, after
all these months.

Now she felt light and giggly, even with the added weight
around her middle that seemed to throw her balance askew.
Sometimes, even walking had become almost precarious;
as if her ballast was off center. She felt another mild twinge,
like a dull ache in her lower back. This was the second one.
The first had been about ten minutes ago.

From the ultrasound they had done in her fifth month,
she knew she was carrying a son, whom she had already
named Andrew. She even knew what he would look like:
blond hair and brown, laughing eyes. She wasn't sure how
she knew this...she just knew! The same way that she had
known she was carrying a son from the first month she
had suspected she was pregnant--which she had been right

about--just as she knew she would be right in knowing how he would look.

She began to pat her tummy. "I love you, Andrew," she said softly. "I can hardly wait to see you." Then she began to sing the French lullaby ("Gué, Gué") which she often sang to him.

* * * * * * * * *

There it was again. That nudge. Only stronger this time. Maybe if he changed his position it would stop, and his sleep wouldn't be disturbed again. He tried to twist his trunk, but lately his space had become so confining that he was barley able to move.

There had been plenty of room in the beginning; but his environment had begun to shrink, gradually becoming smaller and tighter to the point that he was now only able to move his legs a bit and turn his head. In the beginning he had been able to twist and roll and float at will. Now he was cramped and uncomfortable.

He felt yet another nudge, stronger than the last. This one seemed to propel him downward, causing his environment to become even smaller and more constricting, and he began to feel uneasy. Then he heard that soft murmuring which was sometimes present, and the words "Andrew" and "Love," now familiar sounds to him. As he began to listen more carefully, he was barely able to hear that other sound he had also become aware of lately. The one that rose and fell in a soothing, continuous lilting flow. The one that made him feel contented and drowsy. He closed his eyes and felt himself drifting away into sleep.

* * * * * * * * *

"Rick, it's time to go to the hospital," Jane said, as she gently shook her husband who had fallen asleep on the sofa.

Startled, he opened his eyes. "Are you sure? Oh my God!" He jumped up, grabbed his jacket, and began to look for his car keys.

"Relax, silly; we have plenty of time yet. But I called Dr. Roth and he said to go on to the hospital."

As he looked at her standing in front of him, holding her small suitcase, looking so serene, yet so vulnerable, he felt his breath catch in his throat.

Thirty minutes later when Jane was in her hospital room unpacking her suitcase, she had her first really hard contraction. "Wow," she gasped, as small beads of sweat popped out on her forehead. She looked at the clock; it had been six minutes since the last one. She finished unpacking the rest of her things and climbed into bed.

Rick walked into the room, saying excitedly, "So this is finally it! How are you feeling, Jane? Can I get you anything?" His face looked pinched and the crease between his eyebrows was deeper, as it always was when he was under stress.

"Don't worry, Rick, this is normal and natural, and I'm in excellent condition. Just sit here beside me and hold my hand."

* * * * * * * * *

He didn't know what was happening but he did know that he didn't like it one bit, and that he was extremely uncomfortable! It was totally impossible to sleep now, and his environment was rapidly becoming steadily more confining. His movements were now so severely constricted that all he was able to do was flex his knees. He listened for the slush/thump sound. He could still hear it, but it seemed to be farther away and faster than usual.

He heard the soft voice murmur again, and even though he found it to be a pleasant sound, this time it didn't have its usual calming effect. However, it was still able to give him some small bit of comfort: he didn't feel quite so alone.

Then, once more, he was abruptly propelled downward, head first, and felt as if he was being squeezed.

* * * * * * * * * *

"Pant, Jane--that's good--now rest."

Damn! It hurt! Her body was soaked with sweat, plastering her bangs to her forehead. She had been here for more than eight hours and she was beginning to get scared. What if she died? It still happened sometimes--women dying in childbirth. What if something was wrong with Andrew? She fought back the feeling of panic that started to envelop her and tried to focus on the clock. The pains were now less than two minutes apart. Why--oh--why, had she refused to have that epidural? she thought, as she realized she had grossly miscalculated her courage.

"Good, Jane," Dr. Roth said, "You're almost fully dilated. Just a little while longer and you'll be ready to deliver."

"Thank God," she gasped. "I never dreamed it would hurt this much." Her mouth was so dry she could scarcely talk. She longed for a tall glass of ice water, or even better, a nice refreshing ice cream soda; yes, that would be nice! A big, chocolate ice cream soda--with lots of whipped cream. And she was so exhausted! She wanted to sleep so badly, but it seemed every time she closed her eyes she would have another contraction. She tried to concentrate on the ice cream soda, when suddenly she was hit by another avalanche of pain.

"Pant, Jane, pant!"

"Pant? Pant? I just want to scream!" she rasped. Poor Rick. He looked almost as bad as she felt.

* * * * * * * * * *

Adding to his increasing sense of alarm, the voice-noises had also become much louder--no longer calming or comforting like they had been before. They were now almost shrill at times, hurting his ears. And, besides the shrill voice noises, there was also a roaring sound in his head, preventing him from being able to hear the comforting slush/thump at all. Suddenly, he was again squeezed and constricted, as he was once more helplessly propelled forward--head first.

* * * * * * * * *

The nurse positioned Jane's feet in the stirrups. Thankfully, she was finally ready to deliver; she really didn't know how much more of this she could stand. Dr. Roth peered around her knee, looking so strange in his cap and mask that she could scarcely recognize him. "OK, Jane. You're fully dilated. Now with the next contraction, I want you to push as hard as you can."

She groaned as the next wave of pain came crashing down upon her. As she pushed as hard as she could, she heard a grunting noise and realized that it was coming from her. Now she knew why they called it "labor." She had never worked so hard in her life.

"That's good. Now rest until the next one."

"Yeah, right! That's a good one! Have you ever tried to rest in this position, Dr. Roth?" She was angry now. How could any man possibly understand what this was like? She must have been crazy to want to go through this. Then she was hit by the next pain. She gasped and pushed. Please, God! Just let this hurry up and be over with soon. She clenched her fists and pushed as hard as she could as the pain crested again. Then she heard herself screaming, not from the pain, but as an involuntary reaction to the force of her effort, as she pushed with all of her might and strength!

* * * * * * * * *

He briefly opened his eyes and could see light ahead, accompanied by a frightening cacophony, before he closed them. He felt fear; a feeling he had never experienced before. What was happening? Then, as he felt himself suddenly freed of his constriction, he opened his eyes again--to such glaring brightness--he felt pain, and quickly closed them. He also felt cold and dry. What had happened to the warmth and the wetness? Then he felt the familiar wetness again, as something soft was rubbed over him. He was tapped sharply on his foot, which caused him to gasp. A loud wail emerged from his throat--then another--and another----until it became a continuous noise which he was unable to stop.

* * * * * * * * *

This time when Jane pushed, she felt a sudden give, followed by a strange feeling as if she had been divided in half; then the pain was over. Soon she heard the first cry from her son. "Andrew! That's my baby! I want to see him!" She gasped.

* * * * * * * * *

He felt himself being laid on his stomach, against something warm and soft, and he ceased his wailing.

* * * * * * * * *

Now, it was almost as if none of the pain had ever existed. Jane felt light and dreamy. "Oh, Andrew, you're so beautiful," she said, as she looked at her son for the first time. He was lying on his tummy against her upper abdomen, and when she spoke he opened his small, bewildered eyes. Tears filled her own eyes as she looked adoringly into his, and she said softly, "Welcome to the world, Andrew. I love you."

* * * * * * * * * *

He heard that familiar, soothing voice-noise again, along with a faint rhythmic thump/thump, similar to the slush/thump he used to hear, and it gave him a sense of security to hear it. He opened his eyes; the light was still too bright, but not as bad as it had been the first time. As he looked up through the blur, he saw the most beautiful sight; a face with big green eyes, tenderly looking at him, and he instinctively knew this must be the source from which had come the voice-noise, as well as the slush/thump sound. As he looked at the wonderful face, he was filled with a flood of warmth--of peace and contentment, along with a new feeling, and he was certain that this new feeling must be the meaning of that other voice-noise he had been hearing with the word, "Andrew." The word, "LOVE."

CHILD OF MINE

A world to you I'd gladly give,
If I could only find the way,
A world of freedom in which to live;
A world of joy to fill each day.

To you I'd give the suns and moons
Of far off galaxies' shining stars,
Their crystal clear and cool lagoons,
Exotic music of flutes; sitars.

A life of enchanted innocence,
With fervent hope you'd never know
A world of intolerant violence
As to adulthood you'd begin to grow.

But alas, most precious child of mine,
I can not shield you from the seed
Of hate circling Earth: insidious vine,
Choking--destroying--in its greed.

I can only give you loving care
And truth, with hope that you may find,
Within yourself, great passion to share
Your inner beauty, and peace of mind.

FOR THE LOVE OF HELEN

I know Marie never believed my story of what really happened, or at least she hadn't until two weeks ago. I think maybe since then, the way she looks at me sometimes with a deep thoughtful look, that maybe now a part of her does believe my story. At least, I pray that by the time I die she'll know I told her the truth.

I'm an old man now and the years of heavy drinking have taken their toll on my body, but the memory of what happened forty-five years ago is as clear to me now as it was then, and I swear that what I'm about to tell you is the truth.

I was twenty-six and Marie was twenty-three when it happened. We had married young and were blessed right away with a beautiful daughter. Marie, being somewhat of a romantic, was fascinated with mythology and insisted we name her Helen.

Marie's pregnancy was difficult and Helen's birth was a nightmare. I almost lost them both. Since Marie was unable to have any more children, Helen was the light of our lives, even though she was born blind.

We live in New Orleans and Marie's parents owned a small club in the French Quarter. That's how we met. I play the piano; sort of a bluesy, jazzy style of my own. I've played the piano for as long as I can remember. I guess it was a God-given gift because I never took a lesson, but I can sit at the piano and play anything I've ever heard. I also compose my own music. I guess maybe I could have been more successful, maybe even famous, if it hadn't been for the whiskey.

I've been on my own since I left home at age fourteen, and when I was young and on the streets, before I started getting many gigs, one of the old-timers told me to drink whiskey on cold nights to keep me warm. I tried it and it seemed to work. Unfortunately, I came to rely on it for more than warmth. My parents and I had never really been close. I was the second oldest of nine children, and they just had too many mouths to feed. So when I took off, that left one less for them to worry about. I guess whiskey became my family.

I drifted around the country for a while, playing at small clubs, and finally ended up at Marie's parents' place. It was love at first sight between me and Marie. She was just seventeen, and four months later, on her 18th birthday, we slipped off and got married.

Since my music was bringing in the business, Marie's parents grudgingly accepted me as a son-in-law. Next to Marie and Helen, I loved music more than anything in my life--along with the whiskey, of course.

Helen began to play the piano as soon as she could reach the keys while sitting on a pile of books on the bench. To my delight, she had inherited my talent. By the time she was four I had been able to teach her some of my jazz chords, and we spent many happy hours sitting together at the piano playing duets.

Since Marie and her parents spent most of their time running the club, I did most of the taking care of Helen. Marie was very protective of her, but I wanted her to experience more of the world that just the inside of the club. So I started taking her to a nearby wooded area and began to teach her about nature, using her other senses; the smell of the magnolia blossoms in spring, the velvety feel of the leaves, the feeling of the warm sun on a crisp autumn day. I just wanted her to know more of the world. Unfortunately, I still had my craving for whiskey so it was always with us too.

That day I came home without Helen, I thought Marie would kill me. In fact, she tried. I still have the scar on the side of my head where she threw the heavy cast-iron skillet at me. Maybe if I hadn't still been half-drunk she would have taken it better. I just did what I thought was "best" for Helen.

That spring day was particularly beautiful. Helen had just turned five. We packed a lunch, headed to our favorite wooded area, and had just finished eating when we heard a rustling sound in the bushes. Suddenly, two figures appeared before us: a male and a female, but unlike any I had ever seen before. I gasped, and Helen said, "What is it Pappa?"

I hugged her close to me and said, "It's OK, sugar; just some people."

And what people they were! They were tall (well over six feet), extremely slender, with skin the color of rich honey, and with silky platinum hair. Their eyes were a shiny gold color, which literally glinted like metallic gold, but with no pupils. They were dressed in simple white clothing: the woman in a flowing dress to midcalf length, and the man in white trousers and a white tunic. They had silver boots on their feet, made of some kind of soft, mesh-type material.

They carried a small metal device, which looked almost like a version of what they now call notebook computers. It had a blank screen with a glowing metal bar on one side. The man-being held it out so that I was able to see the screen. Then put the palm of his other hand against the metal bar and the screen filled with words which read, "Don't be alarmed, we come in peace. We do not wish to harm you. We want to help. We live on the other side of your solar system."

My heart was pounding and Helen seemed to instinctively sense my fear. She clung to me. I wanted to pick her up and run, but I couldn't move. I just stood there--transfixed.

The screen then read, "Put your hand on the bar and it will translate your thoughts to us."

I stretched out my hand and reluctantly touched the bar. I felt a tingly sensation, but nothing worse. I put my palm against it for a few seconds, as he had done, and watched as strange looking symbols filled the screen. Apparently all that translated was my fear, because the man-being quickly moved my hand away and touched the bar. The screen again read, "Please don't be afraid; we are here to help you."

He stretched the bar towards me once more. My mind was a jumble of fearful thoughts. How could this device sort out what I was thinking when I didn't even know myself, other than that I was afraid my heart would bust a hole through my chest--it was beating so hard--and that I wanted to run as far as I could as fast as I could?

This time I tried desperately to calm my thoughts when I touched the bar, and again the strange symbols raced across the screen. Helen clutched me tighter and said, "Pappa?" in a fearful, questioning voice.

I swallowed and said, "It's OK, Helen. Really. I'm just startled."

I knew I had to get a grip on myself so that I wouldn't alarm Helen, and tried to compose my thoughts into a coherent sentence as I held my palm tightly against the bar. The symbols continued until, finally, the man-being gently disengaged my palm and, in turn, placed his on the bar. I had asked how he could help.

The screen read; "We can give your daughter sight. We can also triple her life span. One year of our life is equal to three years of yours."

My heart was still pounding and my mouth flew open. I couldn't believe this was really happening. Helen still clung to me. I patted her head and began to talk so she wouldn't wonder why we weren't speaking. He held out the bar towards me. This time I spoke my thoughts.

"How can you do these things?"

Helen began tugging on my hand saying, "Let's go, Pappa! I want to go!"

I told her it was important that I talk with the people. That they were friends, but that they were unable to speak, which made it necessary for them to have to write whatever they wanted to say, and that was why she didn't hear them. It was probably the first time in my life when I was glad that she was blind, because I could imagine the terror she would feel if she was able to see these beings. She relaxed and loosened her grip on my hand.

The man-being held his palm to the bar. The words read: "We can take Helen with us to our planet. She will be given sight and she will live three times her current life span. However, she will become as if one of us, and will have no memory of you or of her years on Earth."

I was overwhelmed. I grabbed the bar and yelled, "No! Never!"

Helen gripped my hand tightly and clutched at my jacket. I let go of the bar and patted her shoulder and said, "It's OK, Helen. I just got a little excited. There's nothing to be afraid of."

The man-being touched the bar and the screen read: "Think about what you would be giving to your daughter. We would also be able to develop her talent in a way in which you never could. That is what attracted us to her. We search the universe for unusual talent. Since she would have no memory of you, or of Earth, she would not miss you or be sad. It would be the supreme gift of love. You would be giving her a second life. We will allow you to think about our offer and we will return in thirty minutes." With that, he and the woman-being turned and walked back into the woods.

I didn't know what to think. I sat down and put Helen on my lap. I began to stroke her hair and think about the awesomeness of their offer.

Was I being selfish? Wouldn't it be better for Helen to have the opportunity to see? To live three times longer than what she would here on Earth? And to be able to develop her wonderful talent?

Helen interrupted my tumbled thoughts with the question, "Are the people gone yet, Pappa?"

"Yes, Helen, but they're coming back in a little while,"

Then I hugged her and asked, "Sugar, do you ever wish you could see?"

As soon as I said it, I thought what a stupid question it was. We had never discussed it before; it was something that none of us ever talked about.

Helen hugged me and said, "Oh, Pappa, yes! I would love to be able to see! All of these wonderful things you have shown me--I would give anything to see what they look like. And what you and Mamma look like, and what Grandmamma and Grandpappa look like. Oh, Pappa, yes! But why are you asking me this?"

"It's just something I need to know, my Angel."

"But why, Pappa? Please tell me why!"

"Helen, those people I was speaking with, they can make you see."

"Oh, Pappa, can they really? That would be wonderful!"

I thought for a few more minutes. I guess by then I had pretty much made my decision, but with one condition. I couldn't stand the thought of losing Helen forever.

"Helen, when they come back, I want you to go with them. And you must be very brave."

"But, Pappa! I don't want to leave you and Mamma!"

"Helen, it'll be just be for a while," I lied; "And when you return to us you'll be able to see. It'll just be for a little while, and they won't hurt you."

Helen was silent. She gripped my hand again.

I said, "It'll be a surprise for Mamma and Grandpappa and Grandmamma."

Finally, with a quaver in her voice, she said, "OK, Pappa; if you really want me to go with them, and if it'll just be for a little while, and it'll make Mamma and Grandmamma and Grandpappa so happy, then I will."

We just sat there. . .silent. Me holding her on my lap. . .waiting. Once again I was glad she was blind, so that she couldn't see the tears in my eyes.

In a short while I heard the faint rustling in the leaves and the two beings reappeared. I stood up and gently stood Helen next to me, holding her hand. "They're here, Helen."

She gripped my hand tighter, but only for a second. Her total trust in me about broke my heart.

I said, "I've made my decision. I have to let her go with you. It's her best chance for happiness."

They gave me a puzzled look and held out the translator device to me. I touched my palm to the bar and repeated what I had just said. They nodded, started to take the translator--and were startled when I roughly grabbed it back. I hastily tried to organize my thoughts, this time not speaking them. I watched as the symbols of my thoughts quickly filled the small screen: "Helen thinks she will just be gone for a while and then will return. She doesn't know she will become like one of you and forget me. I will let her go with you only on one condition. You must let me see her again before I die. I know she won't remember me, but I can't stand the thought of never seeing her again. So unless you can do this for me, she will not go with you."

They looked at each other for a few seconds, then nodded as if they had come to a simultaneous agreement.

They took the translator and turned the screen towards me: "Yes," it read. "We will honor your request. But it will not happen until the time of your ceasing to exist draws near."

I bent down and hugged Helen, my face wet with my tears. She hugged me back and said, "Please don't cry, Pappa. You don't need to cry. I'll be brave like you asked, and soon I'll be able to see you."

I put Helen's hand into the man-being's hand, then turned and lurched away as they escorted her back into the woods.

Well, since my whiskey was along with me, I grabbed the bottle and took a long swig. I stumbled around in the woods for several hours, drinking and crying, and proceeded to get very drunk. Finally I lay down on the grass and slept-- from exhaustion.

When I awoke it was dusk, and by then I was partly sober with the beginning throbs of a headache. As I began to walk home, it suddenly hit me! How was I ever going to explain this to Marie? I became more and more worried as each step brought me closer to home.

When I finally got there, Marie frantically met me at the door. "Where have you been?" Then she saw that I was alone. "Where is Helen?"

I just stood there, looking at her, and the tears started streaming down my face as she began to scream, "Where is Helen? Where's my baby?"

I put my arms around her and told her to calm down-- that Helen was all right.

"Then why isn't she with you?"

I took her inside, gently sat her on the sofa, and knelt in front of her. Then I took each of her hands in mine as I began to explain what had happened. Immediately, her eyes grew wide and disbelieving. However she didn't say anything until I got to the part about the offer to help Helen. Until then, I guess she had been speechless.

She started screaming again. "No! No! You're crazy!"

I held her hands tighter and forced her to listen to the rest of my story. By then she was practically hysterical, her body shuddering with each sobbing breath.

"You got drunk and lost her, didn't you?" she screamed.

"No, no! It's like I told you! I swear!"

She ran to the phone and called the police, and right afterwards, that's when she threw the skillet at me.

They searched the woods. They looked all over the city. They searched for weeks. When they found no trace of Helen, they almost accused me of murdering her and disposing of her body. But even, Marie, as angry as she was, knew that I would never have hurt Helen. Marie's the one who finally convinced them that I was incapable of hurting Helen, so they decided not to charge me with anything. However, Marie was still convinced that while I had gotten drunk, Helen had gotten lost somewhere. I know she would have divorced me if she hadn't been such a devout Catholic.

For months Marie kept hoping that Helen would be found. I tried to comfort her and convince her that I was telling her the truth, but she would refuse to listen to me. Finally, as she began to accept the fact that Helen was gone, she refused to even speak of her at all. It was almost as if Helen had never existed. Several times when I mentioned Helen's name, Marie gave me such a foreboding look that I instantly became silent.

We no longer had a husband and wife relationship; but as the years passed, we compensated our lives in other ways. Oh, we still lived together. We even developed a kind of formal politeness with each other as we went on with our lives, each in our own separate way.

Marie became very astute at managing the club, especially after her parents died. (Their deaths no doubt hastened by the disappearance of their only grandchild.) I continued to drink and became absorbed in my music. The club prospered.

Oddly, due to the notoriety of Helen's disappearance and my bizarre story, the club was packed every night for a while with curiosity seekers. But when many of these people (some to their surprise) discovered that they liked my music, we developed a large, regular clientele. We even expanded.

Marie began devoting all of her time to devising better and more efficient ways of managing the club, while I became somewhat of a local celebrity. I even had a recording contact for a short while, but that required too much sobriety, which I was unable to manage. It was too painful being sober. Besides, drinking helped the time pass more quickly.

As the years went swiftly by, eventually bringing with them the disabilities of age, I began to think more and more of the promise the beings had made to me. As I started to also feel the effects of all the years of whiskey, I wondered if they had lied to me.

Then, one particularly beautiful spring day, I was compelled to return to the woods where Helen and I had parted. I sat down in that special place where I had last held her on my lap, and as I prepared to take a big swig from my bottle I heard a rustling sound near by. When I turned my head and looked, it was as if the past forty-five years had suddenly dropped away. There stood the same two beings. My heart started to beat more rapidly as they walked towards me, and I noticed that they didn't have the little translator device with them this time.

They stopped in front of me and the man-being said, "We have learned to speak your language. We are here to honor the promise we made to you."

I swallowed and was only able to nod.

"Helen is now a talented jazz pianist. She is going to tour your country giving musical concerts, and she will play at your club in six weeks."

They told me a date. I nodded again. Then they just stood there, looking at me expectantly. I took a big swig of whiskey and started to speak. A funny croaking sound came out of my mouth so I cleared my throat and tried again.

"Is she happy?"

"Yes," they said, nodding. "Very."

"How can she tour on Earth without anyone knowing where she is from?" I asked.

They smiled. "There are many of us on your planet. We're involved with a large number of the various artistic endeavors on Earth. Therefore, it is no problem. Helen is just one of them. Do you wish to ask any more questions?"

I couldn't think very well, so I took another long swallow of whiskey, waited a minute, my thoughts still jumbled, then shook my head.

"In a few days you will receive in the mail the promotional material you will need." Then they turned and walked back into the woods.

I went home. Of course I didn't mention any of this to Marie.

Sure enough, in four days we received all of the information in the mail. I convinced Marie that having this pianist appear at our club would be a real boost to business. Oh, her name wasn't Helen anymore; they had changed it to Elena. The promotional material contained a photo, and when I looked at it I knew it was my Helen. She looked exactly like Marie, or rather the way Marie had looked the first time I saw her. Only, instead of having her previously dark hair like Marie's, Helen's hair was now platinum blond. But she had Marie's high cheekbones and delicate fine features.

Starting that day, I quit drinking. It was really rough some days, but when I was to get to see my little girl for the last time, I wanted to be sober. If Marie noticed, she never mentioned it.

Finally the day arrived! The day of Helen's (rather, Elena's) performance. When she arrived at the club, it was all I could do to keep from hugging her. She was beautiful, very confident, and charming. But best of all were her eyes; her wonderful, beautiful, golden-brown eyes. They could see!

She said she was familiar with my music and wanted us to play a duet together, with two pianos, as the finale of her concert. I was, of course, stunned, flattered, and delighted. When we practiced the duet together it was perfect the first time.

"I see I've done my homework well," she said. And I thought: "Oh, my angel; if you only knew!"

That night the club was packed. In fact, people who couldn't get into the club were standing outside in the street to listen. Helen's piano style was very similar to mine, only much better, and at the end of our duet she hugged me.

When Marie first saw Elena she got a funny look on her face, but then quickly assumed her businesslike role of the efficient club manager, which she now was.

As Marie and I sat together during the concert, I noticed several times she had tears in her eyes, and once she even clasped my hand, but only for a brief moment. After the duet, Marie looked at me and said, "Oh Joe!" And I nodded.

After everyone had gone, and Marie and I were closing up the club together, I went to her and put my arms around her. She started to push me away, then relaxed, but didn't return my hug. Even after all these years, she was still so beautiful.

I started to speak, but she briefly covered my mouth with her hand and said, "Hush."

When she took her hand away I said, "All I want to say is that they kept their promise."

She trembled and started to cry, then pushed me away.

I still haven't touched any whiskey, although I know it's too late to undo any of the damage resulting from all those years of its abuse. But somehow, I just don't seem to need it anymore. I'm still playing the piano, of course, and, like I said, Marie looks at me differently now. I think deep down she knows. At least I hope she does.

It's been a little more than two weeks now since I saw Helen. I know my time is very near. It's something I feel. I'm planning to go back to that special place in the woods again tomorrow--without my whiskey this time.

I still think I did the right thing for my little girl. Maybe on this visit to my special place in the woods it'll be my turn to go. That's where I want it to happen...where I want to leave this life behind...in that same special place where I gave my beloved Helen her second life.

THE EVE OF THE BEGINNING (CONTINUED)

I felt myself spinning. Pinwheeling. I was dazed and groggy; similar to the feeling I had when awakening from an extremely realistic dream.

Schere's voice said softly: "You were fortunate, Michael. You had that first love from your parents--which is so important--some of us do not. You must draw on that. You must use that resource now!"

I blinked. They were stories--not dreams--I thought, as I realized where I was. I looked at Schere. Now her eyes were green--emerald green--with flecks of gold.

She knelt beside me on the bed, unbuttoned my shirt and pulled it open. I watched the dancing shadows on the wall, cast by the flickering glow of the candles, as she began to gently rub my nipples with her finger tip. It was a sensual, pleasurable feeling. I couldn't remember anyone ever having done that to me before. Next, she kissed and gently sucked each nipple for several minutes. Then, for an instant, she held my right nipple between her teeth, working it in a soft biting motion, which made my body quiver.

She raised her head and smiled. "Unselfish love, Michael. Love given with nothing expected in return. Oh, its return is hoped for, certainly. But unselfish love is the giving of love not contingent on its being returned; love that is so abounding that it can't be locked in. When it is truly unselfish love, our actions are the result of this love: when we act and react with our hearts. Not with our logic.

"The love of parents for their children is unselfish, but we can also feel unselfish love in other ways, for other people--ways of which I am now going to tell you. These are two more stories of unselfish love. The story of Marisa and the story of Rachel."

She again took my face in her hands. "Look into my eyes, Michael; see the stories in my eyes."

I looked into their green depth: green like the sea--and felt myself falling into them. Sinking--as I heard her voice softly in the background....

THE GIFT

Marisa dropped the pencil, which had become almost impossible to hold, and began to massage her spasming hand. She slumped back in the chair, exhausted. Her symptoms were steadily becoming worse. She looked at the clock and saw to her surprise, that it was 3:00 A.M.

Her activities during day and night had become interchangeable the past few weeks. She would sleep awhile, then work as long as her stamina would hold out, and eat whenever she was hungry.

With a sigh, she painfully limped to the day bed and lay down. As she closed her eyes, she repositioned the ear phones on her Sony Walkman more comfortably against her head on the pillow, and let the music lull her as she drifted off to sleep.

When she awakened, it was 8:30 A.M. She felt somewhat rested and a little fresher. She got up, and leaned on the cane she had begun to use off and on recently. After snapping a new tape into her Walkman, she sat back down on the day bed and leaned back while she listened to the enchanting voice. This song was her favorite by him. It was the one he had been singing that day, sixteen years ago. That day! The first time she had ever heard his voice.

She had been in her senior year of college, with little time for listening to the radio, what with a double major in Fine Arts and Psychology, even though music was very important to her. When she was engrossed in her art projects, she would listen to one of her records for inspiration, rather than to the radio.

That day would be etched upon her mind and inside her heart forever. She had been coming back from the library on that beautiful spring day, and as she neared the dorm she had heard music coming from one of the open windows. When she drew nearer and could hear the music more clearly, she stopped. Spellbound! She had never heard anything like it. The voice seemed to penetrate into the core of her soul, with its intensity and total purity. And the words; they were poetry set to music.

When the song was over, she continued to listen. It was a local radio station. She flung open the door to the dorm and ran down the hallway to the bank of pay telephones. She looked up the number for the radio station and called the D.J., who told her the artist's name was Ian Davis. He was from England, and he had recently exploded onto the pop charts. She had left immediately for the music store to buy the album and he had remained her favorite throughout all of these years. His music deeply touched her heart and soul. She closed her eyes, savoring the nostalgia until the song was finished.

She gripped her cane as she stiffly rose from the day bed, and slowly made her way to the small kitchen. There was the wheelchair in the corner. She had decided it would be wise to go ahead and get it, so that it would be there when the time came that she would need it. She wondered how much longer it would be before she would be forced to use it.

She quickly looked away from it and carefully heated some water for hot chocolate. While she toasted two pieces of French bread, she took some margarine, and an orange which she had already divided into segments, out of her refrigerator. She tried to follow a low fat diet and to eat foods high in antioxidants. She felt her diet could play an important role in helping her go into a remission.

It had been two years now since she had been diagnosed with Multiple Sclerosis. Not pleasant news for anyone, but especially difficult for a graphic designer. Repeatedly more frequent headaches, muscle weakness, coordination problems, and finally the problems with her vision, had caused her to urgently seek out a thorough examination with her internist. She had feared a brain tumor, but after batteries of tests and several consultations with various other specialists, the result was M.S. She really hadn't known much about the disease, but since then she had studied everything she could find pertaining to it. Oddly, after all of the information she had tried to assimilate, she found she still didn't know a lot more of what to expect than she had when she had first received her diagnosis. It seemed to affect each person differently and at a different rate. At first she had been able to cope pretty well. But five months ago, she had become alarmed after suffering several falls caused by sudden, sporadic onsets of numbness in her hands and feet, accompanied by weakness in her arms and legs.

That was when she had sent her son, Stephen, to live with his father. Although Stephen had lived with her since her divorce six years ago, she felt he was now better off with her ex-husband. When her physical condition had begun to deteriorate, Stephen's life had also drastically changed. He had become very solicitous and protective of her until their roles had almost become reversed, with Stephen assuming the role of parent and she the child. When she became aware that this was happening, much against Stephen's wishes, she had sadly but firmly insisted that he live with his father. She wanted him to have the life of a normal twelve-year-old. He now came to visit with her every other weekend.

She reflected on this while she ate her breakfast in her newly remodeled kitchen. Her landlord, Gary, who owned the duplex and lived next door, had become her best friend and confidant. He had generously remodeled her kitchen to help accommodate her disabilities.

She had felt the duplex was ideal when she had first moved in. It had an open floor plan, patterned similarly to a loft, with one large room which contained a small kitchen area and a half bath at one end. At the other end it had a full bathroom and a small bedroom (which was Stephen's bedroom).

She used one corner as her studio, where she had her drafting table, and shelves in which she kept her art supplies, materials and files. She had several other columns of shelves to house the rest of her large collection of books, near a comfortable sitting area with the Victorian, pewter finish day bed (where she slept) and some cozy, high-backed wicker chairs. All three were mounded with cushions and pillows in various sizes. She had even wallpapered three lengths of fiberboard hinged together to make a folding screen, which she frequently used to separate her studio from the sitting area, especially when she had work in progress. She had been especially glad for the arrangement since the onset of her disease.

And Gary. She sometimes didn't know what she would do without him. She realized she had become far too dependent upon him, which wasn't fair to him, and frequently felt guilty because she suspected he had feelings for her that she would never be able to return. When she had tried to tell him of her feelings he had refused to listen, yet he was always cheerfully there when she needed him.

Thankfully, she was still able to support herself with her graphic designs. The advertising company for which she worked allowed her to do designs at home, and she was still covered by the company health insurance. She also had a steady clientele she had built up through the years, for which she did free-lance art work. However, she didn't know how much longer she would be able to keep up her rate of production now that her condition had taken such a downward turn.

Often her vision would become blurred and her fingers numb. But usually, if she rested for a while she would be able to continue whatever she had been working on. That's when her days and nights had blended together. They were now divided up into hours of sleeping and hours of working, regardless of the time--whether daylight or darkness.

She turned the tape over in her Walkman. She had all seventeen of Ian's albums. She had transferred his earlier vinyl records to cassette tapes. The clarity of his music was so much better through the earphones, and with the Walkman she could have his music with her always; whatever she was doing, wherever she was (except in the shower), his music could enrich and inspire her life.

She limped back to her drafting table and sat looking at what she had been working on before she had gone to sleep.

It was a montage of drawings of Ian, spanning his career from the beginning to the present. They were softly shaded lead pencil drawings, with a water colour backwash--ranging in hue and intensity.

She planned to give it to him at his concert in San Antonio tomorrow night. She felt it was the most precious gift that she had to give. A gift truly from her heart. A gift that was a part of her.

Each of her compositions was an individual expression of her innermost feelings and emotions. Something which was deep inside of her; something which she felt a need to get out. A private part of her soul. When such a work was completed, especially if she was pleased with the results, she felt such a feeling of exhilaration--almost as if she had just given birth--which in a way she guessed she had. She had created and brought forth something she had nurtured inside herself, something which hadn't previously existed. It was a beautiful feeling. One that was difficult to put into words. A feeling like no other.

She thought briefly of that other painting she had sent to Ian several years ago. An illustration of her interpretation of the mood and words of that first song she had heard by him. Since she had never received an acknowledgment, she didn't know whether or not he had even received it, or if he had received it, if it had pleased him. Maybe he hadn't liked it. She pushed the thought out of her mind.

She had never seen him in person and knew nothing about his personal life. But she did know that she had, at first, fallen in love with the timbre and intensity of his voice. Later, with the poetic beauty of his songs. And last, with his sensitivity and the caring nature of his soul, which she felt she had come to know from the small glimpses of his inner humanity he had given to the world through his music while maintaining his personal privacy. The love she felt for him was unselfish and pure--yet filled with deep passion.

She leaned back and critically eyed the drawing. She thought it was nearly finished. That was sometimes one of her biggest problems; the troublesome decision of when a work was finished. It was good. Probably the best she had ever done. She wanted it to be her best work, as it well could also be her last. At least for a while anyway.

She felt tears sting her eyes. She sometimes got tears in her eyes when she was finishing one of her compositions-- the emotion was so intense. But this time they were tears of grief. Grief for the life she used to know.

That was another day she would never forget. The day that had ended her life. At least, the independent and active life she had always known.

Dr. Lewis had greeted her with such a serious look on his face that day she had gone to his office for the results of her tests. She had been stunned! He had said her prognosis was guarded, whatever that was supposed to tell her. All she could do was to pray for a remission.

She changed the tape in her Walkman. Ian's music had helped her through so many crises and dark places in her life. At times, it made her heart soar. It was the well from which she drew comfort.

Though classified as rock, his guitar (which he seemed to make sing) was accompanied by the usual drums, as well as a flute, and a three-piece string ensemble. He was a true renaissance man, ahead of his time. As far as she knew, Buddy Holly was the first to use strings in rock music, and Ian had been the second, but on a broader scale. Now it had apparently become the hot thing, as several rock stars were doing concerts accompanied by symphony orchestras.

She eyed the drawing again. Yes, it was almost finished. And--by Heaven--it was good! She so very much wanted to give him something he would find to be truly beautiful, in return for the beauty his music had given to her. His music had always given her the courage to believe in herself. She may not even be alive much longer, yet a part of her would continue to live through her art. She felt the tears running down her cheeks and angrily wiped them away with her hands.

"Self pity sure isn't going to help," she scolded herself. She picked up the pencil and feverishly began to finish the drawing. As she grew deeper into her concentration, her fatigue was forgotten and she began to anticipate the concert tomorrow night.

When she had first found out about it, seven weeks ago, the time had seemed to drag by. Gary had gotten their tickets the very minute they had gone on sale--the best seats available, which were in the 6th row. She felt a surge of excitement. Tomorrow night! She could hardly believe she was finally going to get to see Ian in person--after all these years.

She put down the pencil and looked at the drawing. Was it finished now? She sat back again and peered at it with half-closed eyes. Yes, it was finished. And it was probably the best work she had ever done. She was ecstatic! But almost immediately her ecstasy was replaced by an almost overwhelming wave of fatigue. Her fingers and toes began to feel numb again. "Oh, God; please give me one more night to be ambulatory," she prayed.

She heard a knock at her door. "Who is it?"

"It's me. Your gallant knight," called Gary.

"Unlock the door and come on in. I'm decent."

"Oh heck. I thought I might catch you indecent," Gary said, as he unlocked and opened her front door.

She kept her door locked at all times, but since she trusted Gary completely, and he was her landlord, she had given him a key for emergencies.

"I just thought I'd come over and check to see how you were doing." He walked over to her drafting table. "Wow! That's really something!"

She grinned at him. "Thanks. I just hope Ian will think so."

"How could he not? It's beautiful."

She felt another surge of excitement overcome her fatigue for a second.

"I'll come over for you about noon tomorrow so we'll have plenty of time," Gary said. "The drive should take about two-and-a-half hours. Then we can get something to eat and rest before the concert."

"O.K." She smiled, and the fatigue again melted away. This time it didn't return. She began to feel refreshed and exhilarated again.

After Gary left, she thought she would take advantage of this newly found strength and write in the journal she had started keeping when her symptoms had begun to worsen. It was a good way to keep track of her disease. Someday she might write a book about this experience, if she was fortunate enough to go into a prolonged remission. Perhaps it might help someone else. She wrote for a while, then limped back to the day bed and slept. She slept for six hours. When she awoke, it was nighttime.

She sat up and looked at the clock. My goodness! She couldn't believe she had slept for so long. Usually she was only able to sleep three or four hours at a time. She felt rested again, now that the drawing was finished...or maybe it wasn't. She walked over to the drafting table with very little stiffness. "Oh, God; maybe I am going into a remission! Oh, please, let it be so," she prayed.

She critically eyed the drawing from various angles. Yes, it was finished. And it was still good! Often, when she thought she had finished one of her compositions, she would come back later to look at it and find flaws that needed correcting. But this time she was greatly pleased. She gently sheathed the drawing between two pieces of white poster board, enclosing one of her business cards containing her name, address and phone number, on which she had written a brief, personal note. She then wrapped it in brown paper and secured it with masking tape.

She felt better than she had in weeks. She walked to the kitchen area without limping and without the aid of her cane. She was hungry. In fact she was ravenous!

While she sauteed two skinned chicken breast tenders with onions and garlic, she prepared a small pan of brown rice, and heated a bowl of canned black beans to which she added a splash of red wine, several heaping spoonfuls of salsa verde, and some grated low-fat Monterey Jack cheese. To the rice she added ground cumin, chili powder, ground coriander and, finally, the cooked chicken cut into bite size pieces. After the cheese had melted into the bean mixture, she added some snipped chives and a few slices of avocado.

She dished up her food onto one of her good china plates and added a few blue-corn tortilla chips. She took the plate to the table, got out a silver fork and a cloth napkin, then filled one of her crystal goblets with red wine, adding an orange slice. This was the most cooking she had done, and the best meal she had eaten in a long time, and she relished every morsel and drop of it. She even put a scoop of non-fat chocolate frozen yogurt into a crystal sherbet dish, topped with a sprinkling of toasted almonds, which she ate for dessert with a silver spoon.

This was not only her reward for a work well-done (she always rewarded herself when she finished one of her art-works) but it was also a celebration; a celebration of life! She felt almost healthy again! She put a new tape into her Walkman and turned it on. The perfect ending to a perfect meal--listening to Ian's music.

She began thinking of the concert again, which caused her to feel a rush of excitement. Then she was struck with a horrifying thought. What if she did something dumb, like fainting. She had never been a fainter; then again she had never seen Ian in person. Abruptly she giggled as a ridiculous rhyme popped into her mind; a swooner for the crooner. Her heart felt light as she giggled again. Oh no, she thought; I don't want to be a swooner for the crooner. Then she laughed out loud, which momentarily startled her. She hadn't laughed out loud for a very long time.

After she rinsed her supper dishes and stacked them in the dishwasher, she felt so good she decided to reward her-self even more. She walked to the bookshelves and pulled out her new Sue Grafton novel. She loved Grafton's style of writing and her Kinsey Millhone character. She felt there was a little bit of Kinsey in many women, and probably in some men.

Marisa had always been a voracious reader until recently. Now she was usually too tired. Reading and books had always been one of her passions, along with music. She went to the day bed, settled herself comfortably among the pillows, turned the volume down a bit on her Walkman, and began to read--savoring the words.

She wasn't sure when she fell asleep. All she knew was that when she awakened she had a terrible headache. As she stood up, to her dismay, she realized much of the stiffness had returned. She looked at the clock. It was 9:30 A.M. She had probably slept for at least ten hours, but instead of feeling rested and refreshed, she felt terrible. Maybe she had slept too long, maybe that was why she felt so stiff and sluggish. She walked with difficulty to the kitchen, put some cereal into a bowl, poured on some skim milk, and began to eat. Her appetite was greatly diminished from what it had been last night. She turned on her Walkman and positioned the ear phones. There, that was better. Maybe that would help--hearing Ian's music.

When she had finished the cereal, she put the empty bowl into the sink and went into the bathroom. She turned on the water in the shower, laid her Walkman on the counter, and stiffly and painfully removed her clothes. She wanted to look her best at the concert.

Nearly two hours later, with difficulty, she finally finished lacing the front of her dress. She was wearing a white cotton sun dress, with cutwork lace inserts, and a lace up bustier style bodice. It was one of her favorites. She always felt romantic and beautiful when she wore it, like a character from a renaissance novel.

There was a knock at her door, followed by a voice which said, "Your carriage awaits my lady."

"Come in, Gary. I'm almost ready."

"Darn! Why is it you're always properly dressed when I come over?" He grinned as he came into the room.

"Thank you, Gary, for thinking of me as a woman, rather than as just some sick person."

"Of course I think of you as a woman. In fact, as a very beautiful, desirable woman." As he said it, he saw her wince in pain while she laced up her Grecian style sandals.

She took one last look in the mirror. A waif-like face stared back. A face that was a little thin, but not too bad, considering the toll her disease was taking on her body. Her hair had grown several inches past her shoulders, which was a little longer than the length she usually wore it, but she hadn't had the energy lately to get it trimmed.

She had taken some aspirin which had taken care of her headache. But her legs and arms felt weak, and her hands and feet were beginning to become numb, which made it difficult for her to walk because she was unable to adequately feel the floor under her feet. However, she refused to take her cane. Not tonight! Tonight she wanted to be a whole person again.

She picked up her purse and Gary picked up the brown paper wrapped package.

"I guess this is it, right? The moment of truth?" He said.

She smiled back at him, then briefly glanced at the wheel chair in the corner, which caused her to shudder as she limped stiffly out the door. Gary started to put his arm around her to help her, but she shook her head. He locked her front door for her while she looked up at the clear blue sky. What a beautiful day. She had always loved June. The beginning of summer. A rebirth. He opened the car door for her and saw the fleeting pain in her eyes as she lowered herself to the seat and swung her legs inside.

Oh, God; please let me have just this one more day, she silently prayed.

Gary had been right. Two-and-a-half hours later they were checking into the hotel they had booked for the night, with adjoining rooms. Since she was too tired to go out some place to eat, they had food sent up from room service. But she was only able to pick at her food; her appetite, by now, having completely deserted her. She desperately tried to summon up some of the excitement and energy she had felt yesterday.

* * * * * * * * *

Ian's plane had landed late. He was tired and in a depressed mood. He always got depressed, anymore, at the end of a concert tour. Ian Davis: rock star. For how much longer, he wondered? He had to come up with some material for a new album--and soon. He had been trying to work on it, but was just not very inspired lately. He had his own unique style of music, from which he had never deviated since the beginning, consisting of a lot of over dubbing (causing him to frequently think of his gratitude to Les Paul for developing it), and was thankful he had remained successful for so many years. Maybe he was beginning to feel his age.

He had a good solid fan base, but fans were fickle; if you didn't produce, they would find someone else to idolize. Some of the older fans would remain loyal, but the younger, newer ones wouldn't. Especially the groupies. They wanted to be where the action was. In fact, most of them were actually more interested in hunkage than in music.

He had enjoyed his share of them too. At first it had been exciting; a real high. But now he was always left with an empty feeling and some dislike for himself after one of the trysts. However, he was still flattered, as well as somewhat amazed, at the lengths to which some of them would go in order to meet him. Some were really great looking babes, too. Maybe he was becoming jaded. And now, of course, there was the threat of AIDS. He always practiced safe sex, but that was certainly not foolproof by any means.

After three failed marriages he had become somewhat disillusioned about women. In the beginning, with each of his wives, he had thought love would last forever. But all too soon, to his sadness, he would discover they weren't really interested in the inner man, but only in the superficial rock-star image and the perks that went along with the lifestyle. Often, deep inside, he suspected he was too much of a romantic at heart. Sometimes, he was even tempted to give it all up--all except his music. He could never give up creating music, for it was the driving force in his life; the food upon which his soul feasted. But he thought he could give up the rock-star part of it.

If only he could meet a woman who would truly love him for the man he was inside; not for his rock-star image. But then, unfortunately, he had also grown accustomed to the luxurious style in which he lived. He loved the comfort and security it provided financially, and he loved performing his music.

He sighed as he checked and tuned his guitars. The auditorium was beginning to fill with people. At least his concerts continued to be sold-out. Maybe he would be able to come up with some good new material when he got back to his home in England. He knew he'd better, if he wanted to continue his present way of life. Maybe that was part of the problem. Maybe he really was tired of this way of life. He shook his head. He was probably just tired from the tour.

* * * * * * * * *

Gary insisted on taking Marisa's hand as the usher escorted them to their seats. The walk from the parking lot had almost been too much for her. He had wanted to let her out at the auditorium door, and then go park the car, but she wouldn't hear of it. He wanted to pick her up in his arms and carry her, but he knew she would never allow that either--especially not tonight--at least not as long as she was still able to put one foot in front of the other. Their seats were on the aisle so it would be easier for them. He had made sure of that when he had gotten the tickets to get aisle seats. It made his heart ache to see how difficult it was for her to walk, and how brave she was.

Marisa's heart began to beat faster. She was finally here! She could hardly believe that after sixteen years she was finally going to get to see Ian in person. She carefully positioned the drawing on her lap and looked around. The auditorium appeared to be rapidly filling up, and she began to feel that rush of excitement again.

A few minutes later the houselights began to dim and an announcer said, "Ladies and gentlemen. Ian Davis."

It was almost too good to be true; she was actually, finally seeing him in person--and he was every bit as beautiful as she had imagined he would be! Like some god out of an ancient myth. She was awestruck. She began to smile when she heard his unparalleled voice begin singing his sensitive words of love and compassion--drawing her into the magic of his music--making her pain and discomfort melt away as she became totally entranced.

Gary looked at her and marveled at her beauty. He was so much in love with her, but was afraid to tell her how he felt. He was almost certain that she didn't return his love; oh, she was fond of him, but not in love with him. He couldn't risk scaring her, or ruining their friendship, especially not now--now when she needed him so much. He knew he would just have to content himself with the platonic relationship they had. He looked at the stage and felt a pang of jealousy.

The houselights came back up; it was intermission already. The first half of the concert seemed to have been over in a heartbeat. He was wonderful! Even better in person, which she never dreamed could have been possible. She looked around. Many members of the audience were going out to the lobby for refreshments and to tend to other necessities. When the aisle next to her had mostly emptied, she slowly stood up, putting one hand on the back of her chair to steady herself, while holding the package in her other hand.

Gary quickly stood up and held out his hand to her. "I'll take it for you."

"No, it's something I want to do myself." Stiffly, she began to walk down the aisle, carefully making her way towards the door at the side of the stage closest to them. When she reached the security guard standing in front of it, she said, timidly, "I have a gift for Mr. Davis. Could you please give it to him for me?"

"I can only give it to the tour promoter," he said, with a smirk as he looked her up and down. She felt her cheeks flush in embarrassment as she realized he thought she was a groupie.

"You don't understand," she said; "This is a very special gift I made for him."

"Yeah, I'll give it to the tour promoter in a minute. That's all I can do," he said, as he blatantly looked her up and down again.

She felt so ashamed, she hastily thrust it at him, then turned so fast that she stumbled and almost fell. He roughly grabbed her, and as he helped her regain her balance he said in disgust, "You probably shouldn't hit the booze so hard next time you come to a concert, lady. You're liable to hurt yourself."

She shook his hand off her arm and slowly limped back to her seat, feeling humiliated.

"Everything OK?" Gary asked, looking at her anxiously.

"Yes," she murmured, as she sank back into her chair. She clenched her fists in her lap and bent her head, unable to look at him, while biting her lip in an attempt to keep back the tears. After a time that seemed forever, the houselights finally dimmed and the second half of the concert began.

It was better than the first half and seemed to go even faster. By the end, people were standing and cheering. Marisa also stood up, even though her feet were now so numb she could barely feel the floor under them. Her hands were also stiff and numb, making it difficult for her to clap, and her vision was becoming very blurred.

Ian did one final song as an encore. It was the first song she had heard him sing that day at college--on the radio. She closed her eyes, then quickly opened them again. She didn't want to miss one second of looking at him, even if she couldn't see him clearly.

Then it was over. He left the stage and the houselights came up. The cheering and clapping and stomping continued, but he didn't return to the stage. People eventually began getting up and walking down the aisles to leave. She and Gary remained in their seats until most of the auditorium had emptied. It was difficult enough to walk, without having to fight through a crowd of people. When they too finally started to leave their seats, she put her hand on Gary's arm.

"Wait just a minute, please, I want to ask him something," she said, and she started walking towards the security guard who was still guarding the entrance to the stage wing. As she approached him, he recognized her and once again gave her his knowing smirk.

"I just wanted to know if he got my package," she stammered.

"Don't know. I gave it to the tour promoter," he said, as he continued to smirk.

"Could you please check?" she asked. "It's very important to me."

"Sorry. Can't leave my post."

Stiffly, she lurched away, and slowly walked along the space between the front row and the stage, looking up at the roadies dismantling the sound equipment.

"Show's over, Babe; time to go home now," one of them rudely yelled at her, while the others snickered.

She felt her cheeks flame and tears welling in her eyes, and again she felt humiliated. They think I'm a groupie. They don't understand, she thought. She looked towards the other stage door where there was a line of people who were apparently trying to get back stage to see Ian, some even holding gift-wrapped packages. Frustrated, she turned away and limped back to Gary.

"Did he get your drawing?" Gary asked, sensing her pain.

"I hope so; I don't really know. Maybe I'll hear from him: some kind of acknowledgment." Her legs now felt as if they were encased in concrete weights, making her unable to walk normally; all she could do was shuffle forward. Gary took her arm and guided her down the aisle, through the lobby, and out the front door to the warm, still night.

She looked up at the dark sky, which was so clear she could see what seemed like thousands of stars. Suddenly, they all seemed to become much brighter: like thousands of supernovas, and she began to feel as if she were soaring up towards them. Then they began to blur and she felt strong arms around her, holding her.

"Marisa, I'm going to carry you," Gary said. He picked her up as if she were a child, and carried her to the car. She was so exhausted, she didn't even care. He opened the door to the back seat and carefully positioned her inside. When they got back to their hotel he gently lifted her out and leaned her against him, holding her up with one arm while he locked the car door. Then he picked her up and carried her through the lobby, onto the elevator, and up to her room where he tenderly placed her on the bed, took off her shoes, and covered her with a blanket.

"Can I get anything for you?" he asked.

"Yes, I'd like some cold water, please," she said softly. "I don't feel very well."

He put some ice into a glass and filled it with cold tap water from the sink. She drank most of it and handed the glass back to him.

"Thanks, Gary. I think I need to sleep now." She put her head back on the pillow and was almost instantly asleep.

Gary went into his room, quickly yanked the blanket from the bed, and grabbed one of the pillows, which he brought back into her room. He sat down in the arm chair next to her bed, pulled the blanket over himself, and watched her while she slept, until he too finally dozed off.

Her sleep was filled with dreams; some good--some bad. In some, she was healthy and strong. In one of them, she was running on a tropical beach. First with Gary, then with Ian, and she was laughing. Then the sky grew dark and she was alone. She awoke crying. Her heart was so full of pain and disappointment she thought it would burst.

Maybe it was all a sham. Maybe Ian wasn't anything like his songs. Maybe he was a fake; maybe his music was a deliberately made-up facade. Maybe, in reality, he was a crude, callous, boorish man. In the back of her mind she again remembered that he had never acknowledged the other painting she had sent to him. Maybe the songs he wrote weren't from his heart and soul. Maybe, to him, they were all just meaningless words. No, she could never allow herself to believe that. She needed to believe in him--now more than ever. This time would be different. She would hear from him. Please, God: let it be so! But the tears wouldn't stop, and she eventually cried herself back to sleep.

* * * * * * * * *

In some ways, Ian was glad the concert tour was over, even though it also depressed him. It had been a grueling schedule and he needed to rest. He had given a good performance tonight, but then he always did. At least he tried to. He felt his fans deserved it. He was glad to get back to his hotel room. He couldn't wait to take a warm shower and go to sleep. That one babe in the front row had really been a good looker: the one dressed in shorts, boots, and a midriff top. During the concert she kept jumping up and "shaking it" in his face. She certainly made sure that he noticed her and he thought she would gladly be his for the night, if he so desired, but he just couldn't get enthused about the idea for some reason. He longed to meet a woman with wisdom and depth; a woman who could feel passion deep in her soul, not just with her hormones. A woman with a true inner beauty--as well as an outer attractiveness.

Right now, he was only looking forward to flying back to his home in England tomorrow morning--to some peace and quiet--where he could rest and concentrate on getting back to creating his music; the music he could lose himself in; the music that could wash away all the heartaches in his life.

* * * * * * * * *

The next day, after a late lunch, the local tour promoter returned to his office and picked up the large, brown paper wrapped package from his desk. "Oh hell," he muttered, "I was supposed to give this to Ian. I guess now I may as well go ahead and open it." He ripped the paper off the package, and as he pulled the pieces of the poster board apart the card inside fluttered unnoticed to the floor, landing under his desk.

"My God!" He sucked in his breath as he looked at the beautiful composite drawing of Ian at various ages. "This is really something!" he murmured to himself. "Too bad Ian's on his way back to England by now."

He looked around at the walls of his office. He had some pictures of a few of the artists he had promoted. Most were photographs, a few were caricature drawings, but, certainly, none were anything to compare with this. This would look really spectacular hanging on the wall behind his desk so people could see it as soon as they came in the door.

Maybe someday he would give it to Ian if their paths crossed again, but for now, anyway, it would really add some class to his office. Yes, indeed! It would really look impressive!

THE MUSICIAN

Long ago during tumultuous strife,
When all my yesterdays seemed like tomorrow,
There suddenly came into my life
A song that gently eased my sorrow.

A tender song from an enchanting voice,
A song of love and white satin nights;
A song which made me face my choice,
A song which banished my phantom frights.

That beautiful song, it gave me hope
Of a world that could be filled with light,
Rather than in darkness struggling to cope,
And made me wish with all my might--

That I could somehow find the way
To find a world in which to share
The words I'd softly wish to say--
To give of my depth of love and care.

As my life routine, year after year,
Flowed and eddied like a stream,
That haunting voice again I'd hear--
Awakening anew my hopeful dream.

A different song each time it'd be,
Though always with words of compassion and love,
With the same deep passion and sensitivity,
Surrounding and soaring to Heaven above.

And when, at last, I looked upon the face
Whence came that voice, so intense, so pure,
I knew why it haunted me, why time couldn't erase;
Reflections of your inner beauty will forever endure.

THE THINGS WE DO FOR LOVE

"You fucking whore!"

The words pierced Rachel's heart like an arrow. Even though what he said was true, that didn't make it hurt any less. In fact that was exactly what she was. A whore. A woman who did the seven letter word he had just said--for money. And since she allowed him to verbally defile her, he always gave her a generous tip.

She sometimes wondered if the extra money was worth it: the verbal abuse. But then she thought about the orthodontic braces that her thirteen-year-old daughter, Sara, had needed, and the $85 Nike running shoes that her ten-year-old son, Josh, wanted. And there were the doctor bills from her husband's mental breakdown that she'd had to pay. Oh, yes; unfortunately, it was worth it. Worth every penny. She tried to close her mind against the vile words and think about the money.

When her husband, Dan, a petroleum engineer, had been laid off from the company he had been with for the eighteen years since he had graduated from college, Rachel had been forced to join the work force, never dreaming it would end up being in the world's oldest profession.

Her client (some of the other girls referred to them as Johns, but she preferred to think of them as clients) began another spate of verbal abuse. He was getting close to his orgasm. She could always tell. The closer he got, the more invective his language became. His verbiage abruptly ceased and was replaced with a gasp, followed by a minute of heavy panting. When he was able to get his breath, he hugged her and said, "Thanks darlin'. You're always such a good sport. You know I don't mean nothin' personal."

"I know," she said softly, her mouth forming a smile, while her eyes remained cold and impersonal.

"Here darlin', a little somethin' extra for bein' such a damn good sport," he said, as he handed her some folded bills.

She took the money and stuffed it into the pocket of her white satin robe, which she then quickly wrapped around her naked body. A shiver unexpectedly ran down her spine and she suddenly felt very cold. After her client finished dressing, he said, "I'll see you same time next week darlin'," as he opened the door and walked out of the room. Actually, he was rather a nice man, and very generous. He had been one of her regulars for nearly two years.

The first time she had been with him, she had been in the business for less than six months and still somewhat desperate for money. He had told her, with embarrassment, that he couldn't reach a climax unless he could abuse her verbally--but only verbally--never physically, for which he promised to compensate her most generously. So she had reluctantly agreed. However, it had always made her feel uncomfortable and dirty and for the past few weeks, for some reason, it seemed to have become even more difficult for her to endure.

She took the bills out of her pocket. As she unfolded them she saw that he had given her three extra fifty-dollar bills, in addition to the usual fee of $200. He must have begun to sense her increasing discomfort, because he usually only tipped her $100.

Rachel sighed and walked into the bathroom, where she washed and prepared herself for her next client who would arrive in approximately twenty minutes. After she had freshened herself, she looked critically at her reflection in the full-length mirror. She had on a red silk and lace teddy which showed off her slim body, and probably looked "hot" to her clients. The closet in her room was filled with many articles of silky, lacy lingerie in different styles.

She decided she had time to make a quick telephone call home. Sara answered.

"Hi, Honey; how is everything at home?"

"Hi, Mom; everything's fine. Josh just went to bed and I'm finishing my homework. Dad's in the den watching TV. How much longer will you be?"

"Oh, I should be home in another hour or two. I may stop for some groceries, so don't worry. I love you." She heard the intercom in her room buzz, "Gotta go now, Hon; see you in a little while," and she hung up the phone. Her next client had arrived: the last one tonight. She suddenly realized she was very tired.

Her last client, who was new, seemed nice enough. He told her his name was Ted, that he was from Denver, and in town for a hardware sales convention. He said one of his colleagues had recommended her services. She was glad all he wanted was conventional intercourse--which didn't take long.

Afterwards, he proudly showed her pictures from his wallet of his wife and three children (a son and two daughters). He bragged about them for a few minutes, then abruptly paused as a look of embarrassment spread across his face. "I don't really cheat on my wife, you understand--I'd never do that. It's just when I go out of town to these conventions once or twice a year that I sort of kick up my heels a little bit. You know how men do? It doesn't really mean anything. I'd never consider having an affair, but this is different. This isn't like an affair. This isn't really cheating. You understand?" The guilt in his eyes pleaded with her to agree with him.

Rachel understood only too well. Many of her clients had that same attitude. She felt a little sick to her stomach. Some nights her job really got to her. Maybe it was just because she was tired. She nodded as she smiled at him, again only with her lips and not with her eyes, and said, "Yes, I understand. I understand perfectly."

That seemed to ease his conscience; he looked relieved, and smiled as he finished dressing. "Yep. Ol' Vern sure knew what he was talkin' about. You're one high class hooker. Yes-siree. If I ever get back, I'll sure give you a call."

He handed her the $200 fee (no tip this time) and walked out the door. Thank God! She was through with her shift! She quickly went into the bathroom and showered.

It was nearly 11:00 P.M. by the time she was in her car and on her way home. Since she needed groceries, she decided to go ahead and shop tonight rather than tomorrow. That way, maybe she would have time to go back to sleep for a while in the morning after she got the kids off to school.

The large supermarket was practically deserted at that time of night. She was engrossed in looking for a new kind of soup that Josh had requested, when she felt a hand upon her shoulder.

"Hey, Krystel, baby! I sure didn't expect to see you here."

In horror, she turned around. It was one of her clients. Krystel was the name she used when she was working. She felt the heat of embarrassment in her cheeks. She knew there was always a chance of running into one of them unexpectedly. It had happened a couple of other times. Luckily, she had always been alone, but it still upset her terribly. She had a secret fear that sometime it would happen when she was with one of her children, her husband, or one of her friends.

She looked quickly around in a panic, then began to calm down as she saw that no one else was near.

"I guess everyone has to buy groceries," he said, laughingly.

She felt her cheeks flush again. She tried to smile. "That's right." She hastily grabbed several cans of soup and put them into her basket. "Well, nice to see you. I need to go. Bye." And she turned and hurried to the check-out counter, paid for her items, and glanced quickly over her shoulder as she left. She practically ran to her car, threw the bag of groceries on the seat, got in and locked the door.

She looked warily around the parking lot. He hadn't followed her outside. But then why would he? Her hands were shaking as she fitted her key into the ignition. She knew she had overreacted but she couldn't help it, and she was disgusted with herself. She had only bought a few of the groceries she needed. Now she would have to come back tomorrow after all. She silently chastised herself for having allowed him to disrupt her plans.

When she arrived home, she unloaded her groceries and put them away. She was glad Sara and Josh were already in bed. She was too tired to play the charade tonight. Her family was so proud at how "successful" she had become at the public relations/promotional firm, which they thought was where she worked. Besides, she was still upset at running into one of her clients.

Rachel went to her husband's den and opened the door. "Hi, Honey."

He momentarily looked at her with a vague smile. "Hi, Rachel." Then he turned back to the program he was watching on television. "This is a really good movie. You want to watch it with me?"

She walked over and kissed him on the cheek. "No. I'm beat. I'm going on to bed."

"OK. I'll be up in a while."

Rachel wearily climbed the stairs. She was thankful her family didn't know what she really did to support them in the fine style they had grown accustomed to for so many years. As she put on her flowered cotton nightgown, she couldn't help smiling in irony at the thought of the lacy, sexy outfits she wore in that other bedroom across town. She turned off her bedside lamp and looked at the stars shining through the window. "Star light, star bright," she whispered, "Make this wish of mine come true tonight." She closed her eyes and wished that her family never find out about her job, and that she would be able to continue doing it for as long as necessary--with no problems. Then she went to sleep.

When she awoke the next morning, the house was quiet and Dan wasn't in bed beside her. She got up, put on her plaid flannel robe, and went downstairs. The kids had already left for school. She found a note that Sara had scribbled on a sheet of notebook paper and fastened to the front of the refrigerator with a magnet: Mom, we figured you were tired this morning, so we decided to let you sleep. Love, Sara.

Rachel could hear the TV on in the den, and when she looked in, Dan was softly snoring; asleep in his recliner. She quietly went back upstairs, took off her robe and got back into bed. She tried to go back to sleep but couldn't, even though she still felt very tired. She didn't have to be at work until 4:00 P.M. She thought about how she had panicked last night at the supermarket. She constantly worried about what would happen if her family found out what her job really was and she began thinking about how it had all started. That age-old question: What's a nice girl like you doing in a place like this?

* * * * * * * * * *

Dan had received a year's severance pay when he had been laid off. But after eight months had passed and he still hadn't found another job, he came home one afternoon from a job interview, put his face in his hands and began to cry. Rachel didn't know what to do. She had never once, in the fifteen years they had been married, seen Dan cry. She went to him, put her arms around him and just held him, not saying anything. He sobbed: deep racking sobs-- as if his heart was broken, and her heart ached for his pain; she loved him so much. He had always prided himself at being a good provider. He had also prided himself on how successful he had been in his career. It was almost as if he had suddenly lost his identity, along with his job, and she knew he was scared. So was she. She came dangerously close to crying along with him, but knew she had to be strong--this time for him.

Finally his sobs subsided--as if all the tears he had been capable of had been depleted. Then he abruptly stood, and without a word went upstairs. She knew he was embarrassed, although there was certainly no reason for him to be. Since that day he had been a different person. Almost like a child. He stopped going to job interviews, and the few times she had brought up the subject he had looked at her with such an agonized expression on his face that she could

almost physically feel his pain. So she stopped mentioning it.

He quit shaving and began wearing his robe around the
house all day rather than getting dressed. He also became
obsessed with watching television. He watched game shows,
soap operas, movies and, especially, all types of sports programs. There always seemed to be some program in which
he could become totally engrossed.

He eventually withdrew to the point where he stopped
eating. Rachel was beside herself with worry. She knew he
couldn't go on that way, and neither could she. When she
finally reached the point where she felt overwhelmed, she
had him hospitalized. He hadn't seemed to mind, as long
as he could continue to watch television. It was as if he had
completely separated himself from the real world.

The diagnosis was severe depression with functional
schizophrenia. He received three electroshock treatments
which seemed to help somewhat at the time. He was also
prescribed an antidepressant medication (which was very
expensive and, so far, had failed to noticeably improve his
condition). After a month of hospitalization their savings
were rapidly running out; they no longer had any medical
insurance, which had ceased with the termination of his
employment. So Rachel had no choice but to bring him back
home, and hope that somehow he would snap out of his
depression from continuation of the medication.

Rachel had a Bachelor of Arts degree with a major in
literature and a minor in French. Unfortunately, she didn't
have any of the education hours necessary for a teaching
certificate, and after six months of looking for a job the only
employment she could find was substitute teaching. But
even if she was able to work the full five days a week, she
only earned enough to buy food and pay part of the mortgage
payment. She was becoming desperate! Then after a particularly hectic day of substituting, on her way home she decided to try another employment agency: a new one which
had just opened.

The secretary took Rachel's name and while she waited
to be interviewed she began to balance her checkbook.

When she saw she wasn't going to have enough money to pay the house payment for the following month, she became angry and burst into tears. The secretary became concerned and told her boss, who quickly came out and escorted Rachel into her private office.

Rachel was unable to stop crying. Even though she was horrified and embarrassed by her inappropriate behavior, she couldn't seem to compose herself. The weight of all of the responsibility which had been unwelcomingly thrust upon her, along with the fear and resentment at a system that--with one quick blow--could destroy the life style of a family (which she had been bravely trying to hold together for the past few months), had all boiled to a head.

The owner of the employment agency, a very attractive middle-aged woman, kindly let her cry, handing her tissues as she needed them to wipe her eyes and blow her nose. Finally, after what seemed an eternity, Rachel felt herself regaining some of her composure and was able to stop crying. She was so humiliated, she stood up and began to hurriedly mumble an apology with the intention of leaving.

The owner stopped her, and with concern in her voice said, "Please don't go. At least give me a chance to help you."

Rachel stopped. "Do you mean you think you could find a job for me, especially after my disgusting display of lack of emotional control? You must think I'm terribly unstable and irresponsible."

"On the contrary; I think you are a woman in desperate need of help, which I hope I can give you. My name is Carol." She smiled as she held out her hand.

Rachel shook her hand and introduced herself. Carol asked her secretary to bring in two cups of tea, then smiled again at Rachel. "The tea always helps to calm me when I'm upset."

Rachel sat back down, and a few minutes later the secretary brought in two china cups on a small bamboo tray. Rachel sipped the tea. It tasted of oranges and cinnamon and was very good. She was even beginning to feel a little better. Maybe, just maybe, this woman, Carol, could help her. "Oh, please, God. Let her find me something; I don't care what it is, just so long as it pays well," she prayed in her mind.

After Carol finished interviewing Rachel as to her skills, education, and experience, she leaned back in her chair with a sigh. Rachel felt that familiar pang of hopelessness. She looked down at her hands clenched in her lap, waiting for the words, once again, that would tell her there were no job openings she was suited for.

"Rachel, have you ever given any thought to some public relations work?"

She couldn't believe what she was hearing. "Oh, yes; that would be very interesting. I think I'd really like public relations work. I like dealing with people."

Carol stared at her for several seconds, then smiled. "What I have in mind is a little different from what you are probably thinking of." Carol continued to stare at her. "You're a very attractive woman, Rachel. You're thirty-six and you look at least six or eight years younger." Rachel began to feel uncomfortable, which Carol seemed to sense.

"I'm sorry. I didn't mean to embarrass you, Rachel; it's just that a lot of women aren't suited for what I have in mind, and I'm not sure if you are. I want you to keep a positive and open attitude while I explain the position.

"You would be accompanying successful business men-- only men of the most impeccable manners--I assure you, to various social functions when they need an attractive escort. I have a lot of clients who often need this service. You would be paid from $150 to $200 each time, depending on the length of the function. You would be an escort only, and would never be expected to do anything you found distasteful."

Rachel was shocked. She wasn't sure how to react. She didn't know if she should be insulted or flattered. Now it was her turn to stare at Carol. Finally she cleared her throat and said, "I don't think that I'm suited for that type of thing. I've been a wife and a mother too long and I really don't think I'd be very good company for anyone as an escort." She stood up to leave. "I'm sorry I wasted so much of your time, and I do appreciate your kindness. I'll just keep looking for something else." She started to walk towards the door.

Carol stood, "I'm sorry too, Rachel; I wish you'd think it over. You could make a lot of money and would be working only as many nights as you wished. You'd still have your days free, so you could continue to do substitute teaching when you wanted." She leaned forward, her hand extended. "Please take one of my cards--just in case you decide to change your mind. I wish you'd give it a try, just once. Then if you don't like it, at least you wouldn't always wonder if you were too hasty. And who knows, you might even enjoy it. You'd be wined and dined in the finest surroundings, by very nice gentlemen."

Rachel took the card and walked out the door. She was still a bit in shock at the proposal. As she walked to her car she was even able to laugh about it. She couldn't imagine herself ever doing anything like that.

That evening at dinner, Sara, who was then eleven and in the sixth grade, enthusiastically announced that she had tried out for cheerleader at her middle school. That brightened Rachel's mood, and even Dan seemed to show a small spark of interest. Afterwards, as Rachel was putting away the leftover food and loading the dishwasher, she felt in her heart that everything would be all right. That some way she would be able to make ends meet on her meager earnings. If not, they would just have to sell their house, but she hated to even think of that; the real estate market was so depressed she knew they would never get anything close to what they had put into it.

Several days later, on the way to a school for a substitute assignment, Rachel's prestigious German car died on the crosstown freeway. Fortunately, she was able to nurse it onto the shoulder before it stopped completely. She got out, climbed over the small guard rail, and carefully made her way down the embankment. She felt a small stab of fear as she realized she was in not one of the safer neighborhoods. She had to walk for several blocks before she came to a small convenience store. First she called the auto club, then she called the school, explained her situation, and told them she would be there as soon as she could.

When the wrecker finally arrived, she told them to tow her car to the dealer. She wasn't sure where else to send it, although she knew the dealer would probably charge her more for repairs than anyplace else. She called a taxi, and after a forty minute wait she was finally, again, on her way to the school. She arrived an hour and a half late and the taxi fare was $4.65. The driver gave her a disgusted look when she only gave him a thirty-five cent tip, but five dollars was all she had in her purse other than some change. She didn't even know how she would get home.

When she reported to the office, the principal told her that he was sorry, but he had found it necessary to call another substitute when he was uncertain as to when, or even if, she would be able to make it to work. She felt tears of helplessness sting her eyes. She mumbled an apology and hurried out the door. That would look good on her record: having to hire a substitute for the substitute!

She continued to cry as she began to walk. Her feeling of helplessness suddenly turned to panic when she realized, with a shock, that her family was desperately close to becoming homeless unless she could find steady employment--and soon. She began to tremble. She was still in what she considered an unsafe neighborhood, and miles from home. After she had walked several blocks, she saw a bus stop bench, and although the pervading feelings of helplessness and panic remained with her, at least now her tears had dried.

As she sat on the bench waiting for a bus, she prayed that the driver wouldn't require exact change, and that the money she had left would be enough to get her home. After twenty-five minutes, a bus stopped and she got on. She told the driver where she lived and inquired how to get there. He scratched his head as he thought for a minute, then told her that the bus she was on would go to the downtown area. He told her on what street to get off, what the next bus was that she should take, and where to catch it. Then he gave her a transfer.

She followed his instructions, and two hours later she got off the bus six blocks from where she lived. Well, so much for mass transit--in the south side of town anyway, she thought. By the time she got home, her feelings of fear and helplessness had given way to exhaustion.

When she walked inside the front door, she was greeted by a blast of cool air. Dan had turned the air conditioner down again. She checked the temperature and saw that the thermostat was set on seventy-two. He knew, or at least he should, how high the electric bill would be, even when the thermostat was set at seventy-eight--where she kept it. She pushed it back up and angrily went into the den to give him a lecture on their dire state of economics. But when she looked at him, her anger vanished. He had the vacuum cleaner out and when he saw her, his face filled with such an eager, proud smile--one of his few smiles during the past year--that all she could do was go to him and put her arms around him.

"I know how tired you get, working every day, so I thought I'd help you with some of the housework," he said, still smiling. This was the first attempt he had made at doing anything useful since his breakdown.

Please, God, let him be getting well, she prayed in her mind.

"I didn't know you would be home so soon. I wanted to surprise you," he continued, his smile becoming tentative. "Maybe I took too long. I'm not very good at this." She watched as his smile disappeared and his happy mood quickly melted into depression again.

"Oh, no, Honey," she said hugging him; "There was a little mix-up and I don't work today." She couldn't bear to tell him about her car. "Thank you for cleaning up for me."

He gave her a plaintive look, then sat back down in his recliner and turned up the volume on the TV.

Rachel went to the kitchen, poured a decaffeinated cola into a large glass, added crushed ice, then looked up the car dealer's phone number. She inquired about her car and, after talking to several different people, the service manager came to the phone.

"Yes, Ma'am. We found the problem. You need a new fuel pump."

Rachel's heart sank. She knew it would be expensive.

He went on. "We have the total here. It'll cost $367.93. That includes parts and labor, plus tax of course. It'll take us three or four days. We have some work ahead of yours."

Rachel was stunned. She had figured $150; $175 tops. She told him to take his time. That she was in no hurry for it. She couldn't tell him she also didn't know how she would pay for it. She would use Dan's car until she could figure out something. He had quit driving when he'd suffered his breakdown, so she drove his car at least once a week anyway to keep the battery charged.

She spent most of the rest of the afternoon finishing the vacuuming that Dan had started--and worrying. As she rummaged around in the refrigerator looking for something to fix for supper, she came dangerously close to tears again when she realized that they were almost out of food, and that she didn't have any money. She went to the pantry and found a can of tuna fish, some rice, and a can of tomatoes.

She made a simple white sauce, added some cheese, the tuna, a chopped onion, oregano, the tomatoes (cut up) and some rice, then put it all into a casserole dish which she set in the oven to bake. She couldn't find any vegetables, but did find two apples which she cut up and mixed with vanilla yogurt. "Well," she thought, "so much for tonight's supper; I'll worry about tomorrow when it comes."

She was setting the table when Sara ran into the kitchen with a big grin on her face. "Mom, guess what?" She said breathlessly, "I made the cheerleader squad!"

"Oh, Honey. I'm so proud of you! That's wonderful!" Rachel hugged her. She had needed to hear some good news for a change.

Then Sara got an apprehensive look on her face. "There's just one thing, Mom; the outfits are going to cost $140. I know we don't have much money now--with Dad not working. If it's too expensive, I'll just tell them that I've decided I won't have enough time for my studies if I'm a cheerleader, because of all the practices."

$140! Rachel thought her heart would stop. She sat down. For a brief moment she felt that terrible feeling of panic again in the pit of her stomach. Oh, it was so unfair! She felt so inadequate. Why couldn't she find a decent job? She forced herself to look at Sara and smile. "That's OK, Honey. I have a little money saved back for just such an occasion," she lied. She silently vowed to herself that she would find the money somehow. That she would not let Sara be disappointed. Not when she had worked so hard. Sara was so sweet, and Rachel was very proud of her.

Later that night, Rachel lay in bed, awake and worrying, while Dan lay snoring softly beside her. He had never had any trouble sleeping since his hospitalization. She wanted to reach out to him. She wanted him to put his arms around her and tell her that everything would be all right. She wanted him to make love to her. But he seemed oblivious to their money problems. They also didn't make love anymore. She still loved him, but it was almost as if he had become her child, rather than her husband.

As the night wore on she began to develop a headache which steadily became worse. She finally decided to take some aspirin. After being unable to find any in the bathroom medicine cabinet she remembered that she had some in her purse. When she pulled the bottle out, something else fell to the floor. She picked it up and saw that it was Carol's business card.

She went back to bed and began to think about Carol's job offer. Maybe it wouldn't be so bad after all. She really wouldn't be doing anything "wrong," and she had to admit the pay was a heck of a lot better than what she was getting now. Then she thought about the $140 she needed for Sara's cheerleader outfit, and the money she needed to pay for the new fuel pump for her car, and the groceries she urgently needed so that she could feed her family. Then there was the house payment that was due in another week, and Dan's medical bills. She didn't have a teaching assignment for tomorrow, so she decided to call Carol first thing in the morning and see how quickly she could start. Once she had made her decision, she realized her headache was gone and she was able to go to sleep.

After Rachel got Sara and Josh off to school, and Dan was in his den watching *Family Feud*, she called Carol, who seemed delighted to hear from her. She told Rachel she had a job for her that evening if she was available, and that the pay would be $200. Rachel couldn't believe it. She told her she was definitely available and Carol gave her the details.

Rachel was to be an escort for a man who was in town for business, planning to entertain several clients and their wives. Since she and Dan had enjoyed an active social life before he had been laid off, she already had a lot of nice clothes. She wouldn't have to worry about buying something new to wear.

She was able to find a carton of Egg Beaters and a jar of pimentos, so she made a Spanish omelet for supper for Dan and the kids. Tomorrow she would be able to buy some groceries. While her family ate supper she sat with them, although she didn't eat, and told them that she had found a job in public relations which would require her to attend various dinners and social engagements at night. They all seemed to accept her explanation and were happily congratulatory.

She drove Dan's car to the hotel where she would meet her client; she didn't know what else to call him--certainly not a date. When she went into the hotel bar she gave the waiter her first name, as she had been instructed to do, and was seated at a small table.

She had spent a considerable amount of time and care on her make-up, her hair, and in choosing what she would wear, and felt that her extra effort had paid off.

In a few minutes she was joined by a well-dressed, prosperous looking middle-aged man who introduced himself. He was very polite. Soon they were joined by three other couples and her client introduced her to them as an old friend of his.

They adjourned to the hotel dining room where they had a sumptuous dinner, and afterwards they danced. Rachel actually surprised herself by having a good time. She enjoyed the conversation and social interaction--something she hadn't experienced in a long time.

When the evening drew to an end at 1:00 P.M. and the other couples left, her client handed her an envelope (which she put into her purse), thanked her, and walked with her to her car. She drove home, and not until she had pulled the car into the garage did she open the envelope. Inside were two one-hundred dollar bills. Now she was glad she had decided to take this job. It really was fun mixing with people and being treated like she was something special.

The next morning she called Carol, thanked her profusely, and asked when she would get another assignment.

"As a matter of fact, I have a job for you tonight if you want it. The same type of thing, only this time it's at a private residence."

Rachel told her she would be happy to do it. Again, she enjoyed herself. The client was very polite, and at the end of the evening she was given an envelope which, this time, contained $150. Rachel couldn't believe her good fortune. "Wow," she thought; "if I can work four nights a week, I'll be making at least $30,000 a year, and if I can continue to substitute teach, and if we're careful, we should be able to make it. It was too good to be true!"

She was able to work eight nights during the next two weeks, and earned $1,450. She was elated. Not only was the money terrific, but she enjoyed the people and the social life. She also enjoyed her nights off at home with her family. On Friday night, Dan went to his den right after supper, and she, Sara and Josh watched a television movie together while they lay on her king-size bed. They even had popcorn. Sara told her how much she enjoyed being on the cheerleader squad and Josh told her how he was going to try out for his school soccer team. Rachel hugged them both and was thankful she was going to be able to provide for them financially.

The following Monday morning, Carol phoned her and asked if she could come to the office for a chat. With a sinking feeling in her stomach, Rachel told her that she would be there in an hour. What if one of her clients had complained? But she couldn't imagine why one of them would do that. She was always very careful how she acted. She was a perfect lady, never drank more than one or two drinks, and that was usually only wine.

By the time she arrived at Carol's office, her palms were sweaty and she had a knot in her stomach. Carol must have noticed her uneasiness. "Relax, Rachel. I have had some very favorable feedback about you. All of my clients were quite impressed with both your looks and your demeanor." She paused. "I just don't know quite how to say this." She paused again.

Rachel felt her heart beat faster. She must be going to tell me something bad, she thought.

Carol cleared her throat. "Rachel, not only were my clients impressed with you, they were also very attracted to you. Several of them have asked me if you would perform extra services--for which you would be generously paid, of course." She abruptly stopped.

Rachel gave her a bewildered look.

"What I'm trying to say, Rachel, is that they want to sleep with you. Make love with you."

Rachel was shocked. She couldn't believe what she was hearing. "Oh, no! I could never do that!"

"That's what I was afraid of," Carol said with a sigh. "You see...most of these clients...they want more than just an escort--eventually. Most of them want a relationship of a closer nature with their escorts, and if you don't wish to provide that extra service...well...most of them will find another escort who will. I hope you understand. If you don't want that type of arrangement, I probably won't be able to get as many jobs for you. As a matter of fact, there will probably be only one job a week, or maybe even only one every two weeks. I'm really sorry. That's just the way it is. The world is a tough place sometimes, and I'll certainly respect any decision you make."

Rachel was still in shock. But as the full realization of what Carol was telling her began to sink in, she felt that all too familiar panicky feeling begin to invade her body. What would she do for money? She would be back to square one again. Finally, she asked meekly, "There's nothing else you can do for me?"

Carol slowly shook her head.

Then Rachel felt the tears start. Oh, God! Why did she always have to cry? She thought, as she dabbed angrily at her eyes. After a few minutes, partly out of fear, and partly out of desperation, she said quietly, "OK, I'll do it. I don't have any choice. But what about...you know," she could feel herself blushing as she paused, "AIDS?"

Carol smiled. "Don't worry, Rachel. You'll be given a training session by one of my other girls. She'll answer all of your questions and give you lots of tips. All of my girls practice safe sex and I only have the highest type of clientele, as you have seen." She laughed. "It's not like you'll be standing out on a street corner and having to worry about some pimp beating you up, or getting arrested by some vice cop posing as a John. Who knows? You may even like it."

Rachel doubted if that would ever happen. She couldn't believe what she had just agreed to do. But she had grown so weary of worrying about money that she couldn't stand to go through it again. And she couldn't bear to let her family down. She vowed she would keep looking for some other employment. That this would just be temporary until something else came along where she could earn enough to cover their living expenses.

Carol's voice interrupted her thoughts. "Go to this address this afternoon at 1:30 and meet, Denice, who will give you your orientation," she said, as she handed Rachel another one of her cards with an address she had written on the back.

Rachel went home and fixed a sandwich for Dan. She was too nervous to eat. If he knew what she was about to do, he would be horrified. She had always been somewhat conservative, sometimes even a little shy in their lovemaking. Never in her wildest dreams had she ever thought she would be a call girl. A Call Girl! She still couldn't believe it. My, God; what had she committed herself to?

She found the address with no problem. It was an impressive eight-story condominium on Ocean Drive. The woman who opened the door was beautiful. She had shoulder length auburn hair, perfect make up, and was dressed in a long, silky hostess gown. She gave Rachel a friendly smile as she invited her in. The apartment was beautifully furnished, with elegant tapestry love seats, satin finished cherry wood tables, and soft lighting. The woman introduced herself merely as Denice (no last name). She motioned for Rachel to sit down and asked if she would like something to drink.

"Yes, that would be nice," Rachel said, as she realized her mouth was dry and her stomach was full of butterflies.

"White wine OK?"

"Fine," Rachel said, settling back on one of the love seats. This wasn't anything like what she had expected, but then she wasn't really sure just what she had expected. Denice brought two crystal goblets filled with white wine, handed one to Rachel, and sat down across from her on the other love seat.

"Carol told me you're new at this, so I'll go over some of the details with you."

Two hours later, Rachel thought she pretty well understood how it all worked--what would be expected of her, and how much she would be paid: she would continue to go out on the escort duty, but rather than going home after the party, or dinner, or whatever the function, she would stay and avail her services to her client. She would be paid an additional $150--for the extra service. $75 would go to Carol, and $75 she would keep. Also, any extra tips she received were hers. If the client didn't have an appropriate place (hotel room, etc.) for the extra services, Rachel was to bring him to this address, which surprised her. She had thought that this was Denice's home.

She was also told to always make sure she had on sexy, lacy underwear, as scanty as possible, because most of the clients enjoyed watching their "ladies" undress, which was to be done in a slow, provocative way. The more Rachel was told, the more she was sure she wouldn't be able to go through with it.

Denice seemed to read her mind. "Don't worry, Rachel; it's not as bad as you think. You'll soon get the hang of it--

no pun intended," she said, laughing. "Carol wanted me to give you this," and she handed Rachel the address and name of her next client. It was a dinner party scheduled for that evening.

Rachel stopped on the way home at Victoria's Secret, and bought some new bras and panties. She dressed carefully that evening, spending even more time than usual on her grooming. Denice had also explained, in detail, the ways of protecting herself against AIDS, so Rachel was armed with a variety of different styles of condoms, as well as a spermicide containing Nonoxynol-9. (Nonoxynol was supposed to kill the AIDS virus.) Rachel found it wryly amusing having to use a condom and a spermicide, when she'd had a tubal ligation shortly after Josh was born. She put the spermicide into her purse along with some of the condoms.

She didn't enjoy the dinner party. She was too nervous to eat and only picked at her food. What if when the time came she couldn't do it? She drank several glasses of wine so that she would be more relaxed. Her client was actually very nice, and not a bad looking man. But she had been a virgin when she had met Dan, and he had been the only man in her life--until tonight. She would just have to keep in mind, as Denice had told her, that this had nothing to do with love or emotions or even her own personal enjoyment. (Although, according to Denice, some of the girls did enjoy the sex they had with their clients, in a purely physical way.) That this was strictly business, and the cardinal rule was to never become emotionally involved with a client.

Since her client had his own hotel suite, she didn't have to take him to the apartment. After his other guests had left, he sat down next to her on the sofa, kissing her softly on her temple as he put his arm around her and pulled her close to him. They sat that way for several minutes, then he cupped his hand under her chin, gently tilted her face, and kissed her softly on her mouth. After several minutes of kissing, he stood, took her hand--helping her to her feet, and guided her into the bedroom. He lay down on the bed and asked if he could watch her undress.

Rachel was now so nervous that her legs were trembling. She reached around to unzip the back of her dress in the same slow, provocative way Denice had shown her, but her palms were sweaty and her fingers felt clumsy. When she got the zipper about halfway down it stopped, refusing to go any farther, and she realized it was stuck. By now she was shaking all over. She tugged and tugged, but it wouldn't budge. She was mortified! She must look like a complete fool. She should have known she wouldn't be able to do this--not even when she had no other hope of supporting her family. In desperation, she burst into tears.

Her client immediately stood up and put his arms around her. "What's wrong sweet lady?"

She couldn't even look at him. "This is my first time and my zipper's stuck," she managed to gasp out between sobs. Then to her horror, she got the hiccups. If she would have been able to have yanked her zipper back up, she would have run from the room, but she couldn't go out into the hall half-dressed. Her client led her to the bed, held her, and began to stroke her hair.

"Don't worry. I'll help you." He worked with her zipper and quickly got it unstuck, then slid her dress off. He looked at her for a minute. "You're so beautiful," he said softly. He put his arms around her again, but this time pulled her down to the bed on top of him. He unfastened her bra and began to caress her nipples. Her body felt numb, but at least she had stopped crying and shaking, and her hiccups had subsided. He gently eased off her bra. Then her panties. She tried not to think about what was happening. Thankful, her body remained numb. She really didn't feel anything, and soon it was over. He held her for a minute, then sat up and lit a cigarette.

He grinned at her as he asked, "It wasn't so bad now was it?"

Rachel smiled meekly back. "No," she said in all honesty. "You've been very nice; thank you for being so patient and understanding."

"My pleasure," he said. "You were worth it. You're beautiful."

Rachel had never thought of herself as being beautiful, and it made her feel good to hear him say it. That was what she needed right now. Carol had been right about one thing. Her clients were gentlemen. Then she panicked! She had forgotten to use a condom and the spermicide. What if she had been exposed to the AIDS virus? He didn't look like the type of man who would be HIV positive, but then how did someone look who was HIV positive? She would have to be more careful next time, and now she would have to get an AIDS test.

He thanked her and gave her the customary envelope, which she put into her purse. She went into the bathroom and quickly dressed. She felt dirty, but not as badly as she had thought she would feel. She guessed if something was important enough, no matter how distasteful it was, there was a way to get through it. It was called SURVIVAL! When she came out of the bathroom, her client lay on the bed-- asleep. She quietly let herself out of the room, making sure the spring lock was on before she closed the door.

When she got home, she took a quick shower. Dan was asleep and didn't even stir when she got into bed beside him. She looked at his face, which was so peaceful and innocent that it brought tears to her eyes. For the first time, she had cheated on him. But she couldn't think like that, she told herself. She had gotten no enjoyment from it. It was merely business. In her heart she was still true to Dan and that was what really mattered. Finally she was able to go to sleep.

The next morning she called Carol who told her to drop by later so they could settle-up, and she could give Rachel her next assignment for that night.

At the second encounter Rachel was more relaxed. Carol had told her to practice putting condoms on a peeled banana so that she would be more adept at it the next time. "Make it part of the foreplay," she had told her. When the time came, Rachel still felt like she was all thumbs, even practicing all afternoon. But she certainly wasn't going to forget to use one from now on. Her family was too important to allow herself to take such a risk ever again. She also remembered to use the spermicide.

Each time it got a little easier. Although she still didn't enjoy it, neither did she find it detestable. She eventually learned to distance herself: to make it almost seem as if it was happening to someone else. The physical motions also became routine. Almost like brushing her teeth or tying her shoes. Two weeks after her first encounter, she went to the health department for an AIDS test which was, thankfully, negative.

About three months after she had begun the extra services, Carol again requested her to come into the office, and, once more, Rachel was apprehensive. Maybe one of her clients had been displeased, although they had all seemed complimentary. She knew she didn't pretend to be as passionate as she should be, but by now she had acquired a certain amount of technical skill, which seemed to be what most of her clients desired.

When Rachel arrived at the office, Carol told her what good reports she had been receiving. Then laughed as she said, "See? I told you it would be more pleasant than you thought." She then began to explain how Rachel could make even more money. She told her that most of the girls who worked the way Rachel did were her newer girls, and that after awhile they progressed to working only from the apartment. "You would work a six-hour shift, during which you would have three to five clients," she said.

Rachel had thought that by now she was beyond shock, but she had been wrong. Somehow, this would put it all on a different level. She would no longer be able to fool herself into thinking that she was merely providing extra escort services. To put it bluntly, she would be, simply, a prostitute. A hooker! Before she could think of a response, Carol went on.

"I'm sorry, Rachel, but I have to start my new girls in as escorts; I can't let you stay in that position. I have other girls to work in. If you want to stay with me, you'll have to begin working out of the apartment. Try to think of it as a promotion. You'll be making a lot more money, and you'll develop your own clientele.

"You'll have your own room at the apartment, with a private bathroom and telephone. My girls each work a six-hour shift. You'll have two other girls working when you do, in addition to Denice, who acts as a hostess, makes the appointments, and generally manages everything.

"What I need to know is what shift you want. They run 4:00 P.M. to 10:00 P.M., and 10:00 P.M. to 4:00 A.M. I leave the mornings and early afternoons open for special bookings. Most of the girls on the late shift, the 10:00 P.M. shift, sleep at the apartment rather than leaving so early in the morning. That way, they can sleep as late as they want. There's usually not much activity after 2:00 A.M. anyway.

"Some of my girls are college students. One is even in her second year of medical school. So far, she's been able to pay her way through college by working for me. She works the late shift, which is perfect for her. I imagine you'll want the early shift though--more plausible working hours to explain your job to your family--right?"

Rachel didn't know what to say. Again, she really had no choice. Unable to find words, she tried to swallow the uncomfortable lump that had formed in her throat as she nodded at Carol.

"Don't worry, Rachel, you'll get used to it. It really won't be that different. The fee will be $200, which you'll get half of. You'll also make more in tips; I guarantee. You'll probably pull in at least $75,000 this year. Maybe even closer to $100,000, with tips. You'll only be working four nights a week. Tuesday, Wednesday and Thursday every week, and alternating Friday and Saturday for the fourth night. If you need a night off because one of your children is sick, or for a school or social function, I'm very understanding and flexible about that. Just so long as it doesn't happen too often. You'll also need to buy some sexy lingerie, since that is all you will need to wear while you're working."

Rachel nodded again. Now she had a knot in her stomach along with the lump that was still in her throat.

"Do you have any questions?"

Rachel shook her head.

"Good!" Carol came around the desk and Rachel stood up. Carol hugged her. "I'm so glad that you're going to stay with me. I've had a lot of compliments on you."

Rather than returning Carol's hug, Rachel kept her arms stiffly at her sides. She was still in a state of shock. How naive she still was. And she had thought she had become so worldly during this past year. It was really almost amusing in a sick way.

Rachel walked out of Carol's office and slowly made her way to her car, her feet feeling like they were encased in lead. She got into her car and just sat there--thinking. Maybe it wouldn't be that bad. After all, she had thought she could never do what she had been doing, and she had learned to adapt. She guessed she would learn to adapt to this too. She would have to.

Then she thought about the money. She would be making a lot more, probably at least $25,000 a year more. She didn't think Dan's condition would ever get any better. To her, he seemed to be just the same as he had been when he was first released from the psychiatric hospital. In fact, he seemed content in his present role.

She started her car and drove to Victoria's Secret, where she frequently shopped now, and bought several sexy outfits. When she got home, she also placed some orders with catalogs specializing in provocative lingerie. (She had been receiving them the past few months and suspected Carol had put her name on the mailing lists.)

Since this was a Monday, she didn't start her new hours until tomorrow night, so she prepared one of her family's favorite dinners: lasagne. She enjoyed spending the evening with them. Even Dan seemed to be more animated.

She was nervous the following night, but not nearly as nervous as she had been that very first time when her zipper had gotten stuck. It really wasn't all that different, other than getting used to being with more than one man during the evening. The bedroom was simply, but tastefully furnished, with its own private bath, and it was nice to be able to shower before going home. Eventually, it all became routine, and she was able to think of herself as someone who was merely providing a necessary service.

Some of the clients weren't as well mannered or sophisticated as the ones with whom she had come into contact when she had been working as an escort. A few times, several of them had even become somewhat demanding and rude when she refused to comply with requests which she felt to be beyond the limits of what she was willing to do. But mostly, the clients were nice, and she had encountered no problems that she hadn't been able to handle.

She only had three clients whom she considered to be mildly kinky (besides the one who verbally abused her). One needed to be scolded and spanked, one requested her to wear a black hooded cape along with a Lone Ranger type mask, and the other always asked her to put small chips of ice inside her vagina before they had intercourse. The rest of her steady clients only requested conventional intercourse or fellatio, and she always insisted they wear a condom for both.

Several of her colleagues told her she would make a lot more in tips if she provided some of the more exotic requests.

"You can fake some of it," said Lou Ann. "They can't tell the difference." Lou Ann delighted in telling the other girls how she faked "Around the World" with a small plastic tubular container topped with a wedge shaped sponge (bought in an office supply store), normally used for moistening envelope flaps and sticking on stamps. She would fill the little plastic tube with warm water, then turn it upside down and squeeze to moisten the sponge. It was small enough so that she could keep in wedged between the mattress and box springs, and bring it out only when she needed it. She swore that not one of her clients had ever dreamed they weren't getting the real thing, which was worth at least a $200 tip.

Amy, the medical student, had spent some time in Bangkok where she had picked up some exotic tricks. Several of her clients preferred the oriental pleasure of the string of beads, which she had introduced them to. She also had a ring, similar to the one Marilyn Chambers had, which she said some her Johns found to be extremely exciting. And she was skilled at some very unusual positions, some of which Rachel considered to be nearly contortionistic.

Rachel had come to enjoy exchanging confidences with the other girls. After all, they were the only ones with whom she could discuss anything about her job or ask questions-- other than Carol of course. Even though they each had different personalities, they were all fun to be around, and if met in any other setting, no one would ever dream of the way in which they earned their livings.

There were just two things that Rachel lived in fear of, and as time passed, the fear became worse. She was afraid of contracting the AIDS virus, and she was afraid her family would find out what she was doing. She didn't know how she could ever make them understand why. God knows, she had never intended to earn her living this way, but when she thought back on it, she had really never had any other choice. And, unfortunately, still didn't.

There was no way she could ever come close to earning the kind of money she was making doing anything else. Dan had never questioned, in depth, what she did to earn such a lucrative salary. Maybe deep down he didn't want to know. As far as her family knew, she worked for a very successful public relations and promotional agency which had many clients.

* * * * * * * * *

So that was what a nice girl like her, was doing in a place like this. Supporting her family in the only--and most profitable--way she knew how.

She finally did go back to sleep for several hours. When she awoke, she quickly dressed and went to the grocery store, finishing the shopping that had been interrupted last night. After she had put away the groceries and dusted the downstairs furniture, she made some sandwiches for herself and Dan, which she took into the den. Dan was watching *Geraldo.* Ironically, the subject of the show that day was housewives who earned extra money as prostitutes. Rachel almost choked on her sandwich. The women all wore disguises.

Finally, when the show was over, Rachel quickly prepared a casserole for Sara to heat up for supper. By the time she had finished writing a note of heating instructions, which also included what vegetables to serve, it was time for her to shower, change her clothes, and leave. On her way to work she made a quick stop at the health department for the result of her latest AIDS test. Thank God; it was negative again. She had herself tested every six months and always worried until she got the result, praying each time that it would continue to be negative.

When she got to work she changed into a black silk camisole and a matching butterfly thong bikini. She looked at her clock, seeing that it was almost time for her first client. With a small sigh of resignation, she slowly walked to the kitchen to get a small container of ice chips.

THE EVE OF THE BEGINNING (CONTINUED)

I felt myself swimming up from that green depth, only now Schere's eyes were dark again: this time, a deep purple color. I realized that I was getting used to the strange sensation and enjoying myself. This was better than any movie, but it certainly wasn't what I had expected when I had followed her home.

I knew I was free to leave anytime I wanted. The scarves which held me were merely tokens of bondage. I had only to sharply jerk my arms and my hands would be immediately freed. But, curiously, I had no desire to leave. I felt a warmth and a peacefulness. I was, also, still absolutely captivated by her.

And her stories...they were magic. I could actually see the characters so vividly, it was as if they were real. I thought for an instant that maybe she had slipped me a hallucinogenic drug like LSD or Peyote, but I had neither eaten nor drunk anything, other than that one beer at Anytime.

Schere leaned over me again as she said, "Now we come to the opposite of unselfish love, Michael. This time I will tell you of the unpleasantness of love gone awry; of selfish, possessive love; of twisted love; of love turned to hate. I will tell you the story of Lora and the story of Diana," she said, as she took my face in her hands.

I looked into her eyes and immediately felt myself spinning into their deep purple, seething maelstrom, as I heard her voice softly begin...

WRATH OF THE GRAPES

I can still hear that sound of the explosions--echoing in my mind--as I pulled the trigger...over and over. It had almost deafened me as it reverberated inside my skull. I didn't count them. I just kept pulling the trigger until the explosions were replaced by clicks which I was barely able to hear because of the ringing in my ears.

I shot him! I killed him! I looked in horror at all the blood and closed my eyes, but I still seemed to be able to see the red through my eyelids.

My lips were peeled back from my teeth in what probably looked like a wild grimace, making my teeth feel dry. I ran my tongue around them, which didn't help much; my mouth was dry. I gasped, sucking in a huge whoosh of air as I dropped the pistol, then ran into the kitchen. I grabbed a glass, filled it with cold tap water and quickly gulped most of it down--causing me to retch--and the water came pouring back out of my mouth as I vomited into the kitchen sink. I vomited for what seemed like hours--until my sides hurt and nothing was coming up but air and yellow bile.

I sank to my knees and lay on the floor in a foetal position, the ceramic tile feeling cold and smooth against my skin. My eyes were tearing. I wasn't crying: it was from the force of the vomiting. I don't know how long I lay there waiting for the police to come. After a while, when I didn't hear any sirens and no one banged on the door, I thought maybe it hadn't really happened.

I raised my head and the stench of the vomit made me start to retch again. I pulled myself back up and turned on the water faucet and the garbage disposal--in some strange way finding it symbolic to watch in horrified fascination the last remains of my dinner swirling down the drain--and I giggled--on the verge of hysteria.

I looked at the floor of the doorway which led from the kitchen to the dining room. There was the gun. It had happened. My eyes began to tear again, only this time I was crying. Crying for all of my lost dreams. Crying in horror at what I had done. And crying for the three lost lives: mine, my baby's, and Roger's. Roger, my husband: my now-deceased husband. My murdered husband! I shuddered. I couldn't bare to look at him again. I'd probably faint, at best, and at worst go stark raving mad. Either way, the choices weren't good.

I went to the kitchen wall phone and dialed 911. I calmly gave my name and address, and told the operator that I had just killed my husband. Then I sat on the floor with my arms around my knees, hugging them to my chest with my hands clasped tightly together, the phone dangling by its cord next to me...and waited.

Soon I began to hear the sirens in the distance, growing steadily louder and louder, until they finally ceased in front of my house. Someone rapped sharply on the door.

"Open up! Police!"

I continued to sit--unable to move. "Come in," I yelled in a raspy voice that didn't sound like mine. It sounded as if it had come from a very old person. But then...that's how I felt.

A uniformed police officer kicked the door open and came in at a crouch with his gun drawn. Another followed closely behind in the same procedure--while I just sat there--blinking at them.

"I shot him," I said. Only this time in a high squeaky voice, which sounded almost like one of the Munchkins from *The Wizard of Oz*--and then I heard myself giggle again. I didn't know why; it just seemed to burble out of my mouth on its own.

The officers gave me a strange look, then looked at each other. One nodded and started towards me, while his partner walked over to the doorway where he could see the gun lying on the floor. The one officer knelt in front of me and the other recoiled in horror when he reached the doorway.

"My, God!" he said, as he turned toward his partner. "She really did shoot him. Or at least someone did." He bent down as he took a ball point pen from his shirt pocket, which he carefully put through the trigger guard and lifted the gun. He looked at it for a few seconds. "Smith and Wesson .38 Police Special," he said, as he put it into a plastic bag for evidence. "He's a real mess!" Then the one kneeling in front of me started reading me my rights...and that's when I fainted.

The next few months I can't remember very well. I know I saw doctors: some were psychiatrists and some were psychologists. I remember a lie detector test, or rather, I remember being hooked up with the wires leading from me to the machine. They had also done a similar test with wires on my head hooked to a machine. I think it had been called an EEG. I can't remember the results of either. Maybe they said the lie detector test was inconclusive, but I'm not sure. I felt like it was happening in a dream; as if all of my movements had become slow and heavy--like I was under water.

I barely remember the trial. Considering my lethargic, disinterested condition, my lawyers felt it would not have been in my best interest for me to take the stand in my own defense. Instead, they decided they'd rather force the prosecutor to prove his case against me, which--to their stunned surprise--he did. Because the jury found me guilty of murder.

I was given a fifteen-year sentence, and it was only after I had been incarcerated for two months and witnessed the brutal beating of one of the other inmates that I felt myself finally emerge from underneath the water. That beating brought back all of the painful, bitter memories which had led up to the murder.

It had all begun only six months after Roger and I were married. In fact, the first time occurred on our six-months' anniversary. I knew Roger frequently drank too much, but always only wine, never hard liquor. It had never really been a problem to me before. It was a Friday night and I had made a special dinner. I had even set the table with fresh flowers and some of the china and crystal that we had received as wedding gifts.

I had prepared linguine with white clam sauce (which was one of Roger's favorites), a crisp green salad, and hot garlic bread. I had even made Zabiogne for dessert.

When it became late and he hadn't come home or phoned, I began to worry. But as the time passed, I became angry. Then I alternated between worry and anger for nearly three hours. Finally, he called and said he had gone to happy hour with some of the guys and would be home in a little while. I was really angry by then and hung up on him. I was no longer hungry, so I put the food away and went to bed.

Because of my anger I was unable to sleep, so I decided to read and had become engrossed in a John D. MacDonald, Travis Mcgee mystery when Roger eventually made it home at 2:30 in the morning.

He staggered around the bedroom and I could see that he was in a defiant mood, wanting to pick a fight with me. I tried to ignore him but he kept belittling me and telling me what a worthless wife I was because I wouldn't get up and fix him some dinner. I became hurt and upset. And he had such a wild look, I also became a little frightened of him. I had never seen him act this way. He had been argumentative before, when he'd been drinking, but never to this extent.

He leaned over me, abruptly grabbed my book and threw it across the room, then began to shake me. I started to cry, and that's when he hit me--right in the mouth with the palm of his hand. Luckily my teeth were okay, but my lip started to bleed, and that made me cry even more. Then he stormed out of the bedroom while yelling a string of curses at me.

Horrified, I ran into the bathroom to rinse my mouth, locking the door behind me, and anxiously spent the rest of the night on the bathroom floor, where I lay crying and shivering from fear and cold, until I finally fell asleep.

I awakened early the next morning to loud snoring coming from the bedroom. I cautiously opened the door and saw Roger asleep on the bed with his shirt unbuttoned and his pants pulled down to his ankles, with his shoes still on. I wasn't sure whether he just hadn't bothered to take his pants off over his shoes because it was too much trouble, or when in his drunken state he couldn't figure out how to take off his shoes so he could remove his pants he had just finally given up and gone to sleep. Whatever the reason, he looked ridiculous.

I grabbed my jeans, a denim shirt, my Reeboks, and some clean undies, then tiptoed to the other bathroom where I locked the door, took a quick shower, and hurriedly dressed. My lip didn't look too bad, just a small cut with a little puffiness. I quietly let myself out of the front door, and went for a walk for several hours around the neighborhood while I did a lot of thinking.

When I finally returned home I had decided to move in with Meg, my best friend (since I had no family to turn to), at least temporarily...until I could come to some kind of more permanent decision. When I reluctantly opened the front door, Roger rushed to me. He had showered, shaved, and made scrambled eggs, bacon and coffee. He hugged me and started apologizing. He then began to cry, and when I looked into his eyes I felt so sorry for him; he looked just like a scared little boy. So, of course, I forgave him.

We ate breakfast and then made love. Roger was so sweet and gentle--so loving--and kept apologizing over and over; he said he couldn't believe he had hit me, and vowed on his life that he would never--ever--hurt me again.

Everything was fine for almost nine months. Roger couldn't have been a sweeter husband. He still drank too much at times, but during those times I would try to maintain a low profile, as they say. If I just stayed out of his way, he would ignore me.

The next time it happened on Super Bowl Sunday. I don't even remember what teams were playing; I'm not a big football fan. Apparently, the wrong team won.

Again, I was in the bedroom reading when Roger came to the doorway and just stood there, with a strange look on his face--staring at me. I looked up and smiled. But when he didn't return my smile I began to feel uneasy. I said, "Hi Hon." But he just continued to stare at me. I got an icy feeling in my stomach and the hairs on the back of my neck began to stand up as I said, "Can I do something for you?"

He laughed--a dry chuckle. "You? Do you really think you could do something that would please me, you pathetic piece of garbage?" he sneered.

The icy feeling in my stomach turned into a big cold ball. I knew I should try to get away from him but he was blocking the doorway. If I could make it to the bathroom I could lock the door and climb out the window, but to get to the bathroom I would have to go past the bedroom doorway.

He began to walk towards me, with a drunken swagger. "What's wrong? Are you too stupid to think of something to say?"

With a sinking feeling, I realized I had waited too long. When he reached the bed he bent his upper body over me and I was able to smell his sour breath and see how glassy his eyes were, as well as the difficulty he was having in focusing them.

He grabbed me by my hair and shook my head back and forth. I let out a cry and tried to put my hands up to my face to protect myself, but then he grabbed my arms, pinning them behind me, holding them with one of his hands while he slapped my face--hard--the force causing my head to jerk back. I saw stars. He hit me again, only this time in my nose with his fist. I heard, as well as felt, the crunch of bone, which was immediately followed by a hot gush of blood.

With a mixture of tears and blood running down my face I started to shriek. "Stop! Oh, please, Roger! I beg you! Please don't hurt me anymore!"

And he did stop, but just stood there glaring at me for several seconds...then he began to rape me! He grabbed at my jeans and ripped open the snap, breaking the zipper as he yanked them down. By this time he had the upper half of his body on top of me, pinning me down against the bed. He grasped my panties--ripping them down the side--roughly entered me, and immediately lost his erection.

I was still crying, and blood was still running out of my nose--all over the sheets, as well as onto the duvet cover which I had proudly sewn. I thought maybe he would stop then, but he became even more abusive.

"You worthless, shit-for-brains, bitch! You can't even keep a man excited long enough to satisfy him. What good are you?"

He slapped my face several more times, which apparently did something for his hormones because he was able to penetrate me again and brutally force me to have inter-course while holding me down by my arms. When he fin-ished he stood up, zipped his pants, and staggered out of the bedroom without saying another word. Then I heard the front door slam and his car start.

By then I was crying so hard that my body shuddered with each sob. For a while I just lay there, bleeding and sobbing, unable to move. Finally, as my tears subsided and my nose began to stop bleeding, I got up and painfully walked to the bathroom. I was stiff and sore all over.

When I saw my reflection in the mirror, I shuddered in dismay at the face that looked back at me. I couldn't believe it was my face. The bottom part was red with smeared blood, my eyes were puffy, my cheeks were covered with blue and purple bruises, and my hair was wild and matted. But the worst was my nose. It was pushed over to one side and swollen to at least twice its normal size, which made me start to cry all over again. I knew I needed to see a doctor.

I got out a fresh wash cloth and cleaned the blood from my face as gently as I could, then it suddenly dawned on me that I'd better get out of there fast--in case he came back. I hastily brushed my hair and hurried back into the bedroom. I grabbed my jeans, quickly pulled them on, not even bothering with underwear, and found some safety pins to hold them together at the waist. I got out an old college sweat shirt that was long enough to hide the broken zipper of my jeans, and shoved my feet into my Reeboks, leaving them untied. I grabbed my purse, ran to the garage and got into my car. I hit the garage door opener button and as soon as the door was up far enough to clear the top of my car, I burned rubber all the way down the driveway and into the street, not bothering to close the garage door.

Luckily, there was a new hospital about half a mile away. I peeled into the emergency room parking lot, got out of my car and ran inside. By this time I was in a lot of pain and my nose had started to bleed again, probably from all the rushing around. One of the nurses saw me and hurried over. "What happened?" She asked.

"I was in an auto accident," I lied. "I accidentally ran into a post with my car and hit my face on the steering wheel."

She gave me a doubtful look.

"My gas pedal stuck," I said lamely.

She gave me a quick preliminary exam (I think they call it triage), handed me an ice bag for my nose, and told me to take a seat in the waiting room. I did as I was told, and in a few minutes the admitting clerk called me to her desk. I gave her the information she needed and showed her my insurance card. She told me to again take a seat in the waiting room, and that they would call me in a few minutes.

After about thirty minutes I was able to see a doctor, who also asked what had happened and I told him the same story about the gas pedal.

He peered at me and said, "Looks more like a fist to me."

I began to cry again. He gave me a phone number for the Battered Women's Shelter and told me I really needed to talk to them. I nodded. I needed to do something, that was for sure. I was afraid to go home.

After they took a set of facial X-rays, the doctor set and taped my nose, examined the rest of my face, gave me some samples of pain medication, along with a prescription, and again told me that I should call the Women's Shelter.

I went back to the waiting room to the pay phone and dialed the number. As soon as it started to ring, my heart began to beat faster. If Roger found out that I had told someone what he'd done, I didn't know what else he would do to me. I almost hung up, but then a pleasant voice answered and I told her my story; she gave me the address and I drove to the shelter.

I spent the night there, and talked a lot with a counselor and some of the other women victims. I talked to Roger on the phone the next day. He was angry at first, then contrite. He began begging me to come home. He cried and said he would never do it again, and to prove it, he would do whatever I wanted--if I would just come back home.

I took five days of sick leave away from my job and ended up staying at the Women's Shelter for two weeks. During those two weeks Roger and I talked many more times on the phone. He also talked on the phone with the counselor, who recommended that he find a good therapist. Which he did.

When I was finally convinced that he was really serious about getting help, I returned to our home. It was like being on a second honeymoon. Roger was wonderful! He went to therapy once a week, and after a few months (on the advice of his therapist), he also began to attend Alcoholics Anonymous meetings. I had never been happier.

This time it lasted almost fifteen months. Roger changed jobs, receiving a more prestigious position with a much larger salary, only now he had to travel about one week out of the month. That's when he began to miss some of his therapy sessions and he also quit going to the AA meetings. When I mentioned it to him, he kissed me and said, "Don't worry, I'm cured. I know how to handle myself now when I'm stressed."

Like the fool that I am, I believed him.

Mostly, I wanted to believe him because I suspected that I was pregnant. I took a home pregnancy test and it showed positive. I was elated, but I didn't want to say anything to Roger until it was confirmed by my doctor. I made an appointment with my gynecologist, who confirmed that I was, indeed, pregnant. Probably about eight weeks. That was what I had been praying for: a baby.

Roger was away on one of his business trips when I found out, but I didn't want to tell him on the telephone; I wanted to tell him during a romantic dinner at home. I wasn't really sure how he would take the news. I hoped he would be as happy about it as I was, even though he'd been under a lot of stress lately with his new job. I also had a nagging suspicion--deep inside--that maybe he had started to drink again when he was out of town. But I had no proof, and pretty much tried to push it out of my mind. He was due home the next day.

I had prepared another special dinner: curried chicken with rice pilaf, homemade yeast rolls, green beans almondine, and for dessert a rich chocolate meringue pie. (Roger loved chocolate.) I couldn't wait for him to get home so I could tell him my wonderful news.

I had lighted white candles all over the living room and dining room: small ones, fat ones, tall ones. It looked so romantic. I had also arranged a centerpiece bouquet of fresh flowers; lilies, gardenias, and baby's breath in a tall crystal vase. I put on what I thought was a romantic dress; a dark flowered print in a translucent, soft gauzy material, with a black body suit and black leggings underneath. On my feet, I wore black lace-up boots. I had even put one of the gardenias in my hair.

When I heard his car drive up, I met him at the door with a crystal flute glass in each hand, filled with sparkling grape juice. (I didn't drink wine anymore either, because of his problem. Anyway, now that I was pregnant, I especially wouldn't drink any alcohol.)

When he opened the door, I said, "Welcome home, my love," and held out one of the glasses to him. To my astonishment, he knocked the glass out of my hand, and it shattered against the tile floor. I felt like my heart followed it and also shattered...when I saw the look in his eyes.

He had obviously been drinking again. To my dismay, he just stood there glaring at me--like that other time. But I still didn't realize how much danger I was in. I really believed in my heart that he would never hurt me again. What a fool I was! He grabbed my wrist and started dragging me into the living room. I dropped the other glass and it shattered on the floor.

He threw me down on the couch and said, "I suppose you want me to think you missed me while I was gone."

I couldn't speak. I guess I was in shock. I gulped, in a desperate attempt to say something, and he hit me across the mouth with the palm of his hand. I started to cry. I knew I had to get away from him, or this time he would hurt me very badly--or maybe even worse. Now, I not only had my life to think of, but also my baby's life.

I jumped up, and as I tried to run to the front door he grabbed me by the back of my dress. He threw me to the floor and I hit my head on the hard tile, which stunned me long enough for him to kick me in my side. I tried to draw myself up into a ball to protect my abdomen.

"What a liar you are," he sneered at me. "You want me to think that you're playing the good, devoted little wife while I'm out of town, when actually you're out whoring around, having a good time at my expense."

My mouth flew open. "No," I wailed; "I don't know why you would ever think that. I love you. I would never cheat on you. Oh, please, Roger; just listen to me. I have something so wonderful to tell you!"

"Nothing you would ever tell me could be wonderful--you conniving, little bitch!"

With that he kicked me again--and again--and again... until I blacked out. When I regained consciousness, the smoke detector was going off from the ruined dinner burning on the stove. I tried to drag myself to a sitting position; my insides felt like they were on fire. Then I realized I was lying in a pool of blood. Oh, my God! My baby!

I half crawled--half staggered--to the wall phone in the kitchen, and dialed 911. I grabbed a dish towel and stuffed it between my legs to try to stop the bleeding. I also thought some of my ribs might be broken because it hurt terribly to breathe. I didn't see Roger, but I took a large carving knife from one of the drawers--just in case--and held it in front of me as I sat on the hard, cold tile floor, waiting for the ambulance to come.

"Oh please, God! Please don't let me lose my baby!" I prayed, over and over, until the paramedics finally arrived.

At first, they started to check my vital signs, but when I told them I was pregnant and that I thought I was losing my baby, one of them muttered, "Load and go!" Then they quickly lifted me onto the stretcher and loaded me into the ambulance. A few minutes later when we arrived at the hospital, I was briefly checked in the emergency room where they started an IV in my arm, then immediately sent to an operating room. That was the last thing I remembered for a while.

When I finally woke up, I hurt all over. At first, I didn't know where I was, then suddenly I remembered, and started yelling for a nurse; almost immediately one appeared at the door.

"Sh, Mrs. Dugan! You'll alarm the other patients, and you're not doing yourself any good to get so upset."

"Please tell me if my baby's all right," I pleaded.

"Just a minute; I'll get the doctor. He's the one who needs to talk to you."

"No! Just please tell me," I yelled, as she hurried out of the room.

I guess I knew the answer. I had such an empty, aching feeling in my heart.

A doctor who was unfamiliar to me walked into the room. I looked searchingly at his face as he came over to my bed. He took both my hands in his and said, "Mrs. Dugan...Lora; I'm so sorry. We did everything we could. Unfortunately, you hemorrhaged, and we couldn't save your baby."

I closed my eyes and started to cry. Feeling the pain of the loss was nearly unbearable.

He went on talking, but I wasn't really listening--I was so swallowed up in my grief--until I heard him say hysterectomy. Then, startled, I looked at him and said, "What did you say?"

"I said, there wasn't any other choice. We couldn't stop the hemorrhaging; in order to save your life, we had to do a hysterectomy."

"No! Oh, no!" I began to wail. "No! Tell me it isn't so; it's a mistake; you have me mixed up with someone else. Please!

Please!" Then I felt the stick of a needle in my arm and everything turned black.

I don't know how long I slept. It seemed like days. When I would awaken, I would start crying, then soon a nurse would come in, and mercifully, give me another shot. One day, when I woke up and became aware of my surroundings, a nice, gray-haired, grandmotherly nurse was anxiously standing beside my bed.

"You have a visitor," she said. "Your friend Meg is here."

I nodded, the nurse went to the door, and Meg walked into the room carrying my weekend suitcase with her. She came over to the bed and kissed me and the tears started running from her eyes. Then I started to cry and we just held each other...crying...until our tears finally stopped.

"Roger is in jail for assault," she said. "He tried to hang himself with his bed sheet, but the guard got him down in time."

I hadn't really thought about Roger. I guess I had just tried to block him completely out of my mind. I felt such a rage; it made me feel drained. I wished he had hanged himself. "How long are they going to keep him there?" I asked.

"I'm not sure," she said. "He says he doesn't want to live anymore, after what he did to you. They can't charge him with murder because he says he had no idea that you were pregnant. They've moved him to the psychiatric section."

I turned my head away from her. I was crying again, but this time it was from the anger and rage I felt toward Roger.

Meg took my hand and told me I'd been in the hospital for five days, and that I could probably go home in a few more. She insisted that I come to stay with her when I was released. I thanked her and told her I would think about it. We kissed each other and she turned to leave.

"Oh," she turned back towards me; "I brought some of your makeup, a book, and a couple of your nightgowns," she said, as she motioned toward my suitcase, which she had set in the corner.

I nodded. "Thanks. I don't know what I'd do without you."

She waved and went out the door.

I had a lot of thinking to do. I had to plan a new life for myself, for when I was released from the hospital. Then I fell asleep again.

I did do a lot of thinking over the next few days, and had pretty much decided what I would have to do to restore my life to any type of order for the future. I took an indefinite leave of absence from my job (I was too embarrassed and too depressed to return yet) and stayed with Meg for a month. I knew Roger wanted to see me. He even wrote me a letter, begging me to forgive him, telling me that he would gladly give his life if it could change what had happened.

After several weeks I went to see him. He was still in the psych. ward and looked terrible. He had lost weight, and his eyes were haunted and sad looking. I sat down and took his hand. Then he got down on his knees, hugged me around my waist, laid his head on my lap and began to cry. He told me again, over and over, how sorry he was. I didn't say anything; I just patted his head--as if he were a child--while he cried.

When I moved back into my own house, I found that Meg had thoughtfully cleaned up all remains of the fight and the burned dinner. By the time Roger was able to get out on bail, which the police were kind enough to inform me of in case he tried to hurt me again, I had decided what I was going to do. I wasn't afraid of him anymore and I knew he would never hurt me again.

I called directory assistance and got Roger's new phone number. He was living in a little apartment hotel in the North Beach area. We were still legally married, and, since Texas is a community property state, if we divorced everything would be split down the middle. I had already gone through a good part of the money in our savings account, what with the necessary expenses of monthly bills; house payment, car payment, utilities, etc. I telephoned Roger and told him we needed to talk about our future and, to his surprise, invited him to dinner the following evening; he eagerly accepted.

I wanted everything to be perfect, so I spent the following morning running errands and making some extra special last minute purchases. I marinated flounder filets, which I grilled, and I roasted sliced new potatoes with their skins on, brushed with olive oil and seasoned with thyme. I baked corn muffins, and tossed a fresh spinach salad to which I added sliced avocado, tomatoes, Greek olives, and a tiny bit of crumbled bleu cheese. Dessert was going to be extra special.

When Roger rang the doorbell, I had everything ready. I had on black jeans (I had been wearing a lot of black lately), an ivory satin blouse, and a tapestry vest. Roger meekly came inside when I opened the door. He seemed like a different person. I almost felt sorry for him...for a second.

"Come in," I said, as I led him into the dining room. "Sit down; dinner's almost ready."

I had put a cluster of white candles, of various sizes, in the center of the table, and had twined English ivy around some of the taller candle sticks. It was really quite a beautiful effect, especially with the Battenburg Lace place mats and napkins. I was again, using our good china and crystal.

I put the food on two plates and carried them to the dining room table. Then I brought in a wine carafe filled with Chardonnay. "Don't worry," I said, as Roger gave me a startled look, "It's nonalcoholic."

I watched him while he ate. He seemed to be enjoying the food. I hoped he was; I wanted it to be very special for him. He didn't say much. He really looked awful--as if the spark of life had gone out of him; like he was just an empty shell of the man he used to be. Well...maybe I could remedy that.

After we had finished our meal, when I picked up our empty plates to take them back into the kitchen, Roger started to get up too.

"Can I help," he asked?

"No, no. Sit," I said. "I have a very special dessert for us."

I had made a beautiful, strawberry, four-layer cake, with whipped strawberry frosting, garnished with fresh strawberries. I brought it in on a crystal pedestal cake stand, along with two dessert plates. I cut a large piece of cake for each of us, while Roger watched me with a bewildered look on his face.

"I don't understand why you're being so nice to me," he said.

"You think I'm being nice to you?" I asked. "Why shouldn't I be nice to you; you're still my husband aren't you?"

He continued to look bewildered, then gave a little shrug and smiled meekly at me. We finished our cake in silence.

"Would you like some more?" I asked him, with a smile.

"No, I'm stuffed. Thanks. That was the best meal I've had in a long time."

"Good," I said, as I picked up the empty plates. "I was hoping you would enjoy it; in fact, it was very important to me that you would."

I took the plates back to the kitchen, and that's when I opened the cabinet and got out the gun. I walked back to the doorway between the dining room and the kitchen and said, "Roger?"

He looked up, and the smile that he had begun, froze on his face. He looked bewildered again. "Lora, what are you doing?"

"I'm going to see that justice is done, Roger. I'm going to kill you. You murdered my baby; our baby. I know you'll probably only get six months in jail--at the most. Maybe even a suspended sentence. That's just not fair. So I'm going to make sure that justice is done. A life for a life. Don't you think that's fair, Roger? I even allowed the condemned man to eat a hearty last meal. In fact, I made sure of it. Isn't that more than fair, Roger? You weren't fair to our baby."

"But that's different," he stammered. "I didn't know you were pregnant. Please! Give me another chance!"

"I already gave you several chances, Roger. One too many. Like the old saying goes, Roger: fool me once, shame on you; fool me twice, shame on me. Well, I'm making sure you're not going to fool me for a third time."

Then he jumped up from the table so fast that he knocked his chair over backwards, and I shot him. He turned and started to run, and I just kept pulling the trigger, over and over. Hearing those explosions, over and over, until they eventually became clicks.

Since I hadn't killed him when he was in the act of beating me, the district attorney indicted me for murder. (Which it certainly was! I admit that.) But my lawyers decided that a jury would be too sympathetic to convict me on a murder charge: what with the prior two beatings on record, along with the facts that I had stayed in the Battered Women's Shelter for two weeks, and that I had lost my baby and was unable to have any more because of the brutal beatings.

However, they were wrong. I guess in a way I'm lucky that I wasn't given the death penalty or life in prison, because it had been premeditated; I had carefully planned it down to the last detail.

I come up for parole in three months. I don't care whether it's granted or not. I really don't have much to live for. It doesn't matter to me where I spend the rest of my life: whether it's behind bars or out in society.

I've begun to write poetry the past year. I think some of it might be pretty good. I haven't shown it to anyone yet, but I may decide to in the future. I might show some of it to Meg. She comes to visit me fairly often. But for now, it's about the only way I can express some of the feelings inside of me. So it's still pretty private.

I saw the prison shrink for a while, but didn't feel like he was very interested in me as a person, so when I refused to say anything during the therapy sessions, they were discontinued. I didn't really care one way or the other. I only care about being able to write my poetry...because that's the only time I can get that sound out of my head...when I'm writing my poetry: that sound of the explosions--echoing in my mind--as I pulled the trigger...over and over.

WHEN?

Vengeance, is it ever justified?
When can violence be excused?
Perhaps when deepest love has been denied,
Causing sensitive thoughts to become confused?

When fever pitch of wrath and rage
Of raw emotions reach their peak?
When tormenting wars within us wage?
When peace is all we desperately seek?

When embers that once burst into flame
Fade to death mournfully slow,
From coals to ashes--who can we blame
When winds inside the heart coldly blow?

When through despair we reach insanity
Of jumbled emotions, fear and pain;
When violence becomes our final destiny
What can we possibly hope to gain?

I, DIANA: THE HUNTRESS

The insistent ringing abruptly exploded her peaceful sleep. She sat up, instantly awake. "Not again," she groaned, her heart beginning to beat faster as she picked up the phone. "Hello?" she said tentatively.

A whispery male voice said, "Diana, are you wearing something sexy?"

Shaking in a mixture of fear and anger, she slammed down the phone. It was 1:30 A.M. and this was the third night in a row that he had called her. The scary part was that he knew her name, which meant he wasn't just some random dialer. She turned off the ringer on her bedroom phone, deciding to let her answering machine in the living room pick up any more calls; she had to get some sleep. But sleep was a long time in returning. The last time she remembered looking at the clock it was 3:00 A.M.

She awoke at 6:30 A.M., feeling tired and jittery. She showered, and as she blow-dried her hair she knew she couldn't go through another night like the past two. She would go to the telephone company on her lunch break and change to an unlisted number. But that still wouldn't do anything to help assuage her uneasy feeling about him knowing where she lived from her address listing in the directory.

After she had finished applying her makeup and gotten dressed, she went into the kitchen, poured a large glass of cold orange juice and heated a blueberry bran muffin. She began to drink her juice while she checked her answering machine. She had four messages. The first one was that same voice.

"Diana, Diana! You're making a mistake. You shouldn't ever refuse my calls. I love you, Diana." Then a pause. "Sweet dreams, Diana."

The second contained no voice message, but she felt sure it was him. The line had been kept open during the allotted message time on the machine and she was able to hear a faint rustling sound, as well as someone breathing.

As she listened to the third message, she gave a startled gasp of dismay.

A deep male voice said, "Miss Koenig, this is the Texas Highway Patrol. We're sorry to inform you that your parents have been in a serious accident. Please call as soon as possible and ask for Trooper Doug Wills." He had left a phone number which she immediately called before listening to the fourth message.

Diana's heart was hammering so loudly in her ears that when a female voice answered she was barely able to gasp out her request to speak to Trooper Wills.

"I'm sorry, ma'am; we don't have anyone here by that name. Are you sure it's the Texas Highway Patrol you want?"

"Yes! Yes!" Diana yelled. "He left this number and said to call him. His name is Doug Wills. Are you positive he doesn't work there?"

"Yes, ma'am, I'm positive. Can I, perhaps, assist you in some way?"

Diana repeated what Trooper Wills had said, then gave the woman her parents' name and address in Dallas.

"Hold on a minute please, ma'am, while I check." After a few, seemingly endless minutes, the woman was back on the phone. "We have no record of anyone with that name being in an accident."

Diana mumbled a thank you and hung up the phone. In a frenzy, she dialed her parents' phone number, which her mother answered on the second ring.

"Mom, are you all right?" she burst out.

"Why yes, Honey, why do you ask? You sound upset."

"Is Dad OK?"

"He's fine; he's sitting right here at the kitchen table, drinking coffee and reading his newspaper. Diana, what's wrong?"

"Thank God!" Diana sucked in a deep breath of air. "Someone called and left a message that you and Dad had been in an accident. I was nearly frantic."

"Oh, Honey; I'm so sorry. What a terrible thing to do! We're both just fine. Who would do such a cruel thing?"

"I don't know, Mom. I'm just relieved that you and Dad are all right. I'm OK--now that I know. You have a nice day; I'll call you again soon. Love you. Bye."

"Love you too, Honey. Bye-bye."

Diana's hands were still shaking as she gulped some of the orange juice, and her stomach was in such a knot that she was unable to eat her muffin. She played back the fourth message.

"Well, well, Diana; by now you must realize how important it is to take your calls, rather than letting your answering machine take them for you," the whispery voice said. "Next time, you'd better talk to me. Trooper Wills sends his love."

The cold glass of orange juice slipped from her hand and crashed to the floor.

"Damn!" She said. "What a way to start off the day!" She already felt exhausted as she got some paper towels and cleaned up the mess. By then it was 7:45 and she was supposed to be at work by 8:00.

She grabbed her purse, locked the apartment door, and ran outside to her car. As she unlocked her car door, she noticed a wad of paper stuck underneath the windshield wiper on the driver's side. She reached around and picked it up. It was a Hershey's chocolate kiss wrapped in a piece of white tissue paper, tied with a piece of thin gold cord. She flung it away as if it burned her hand. She was almost certain she knew who had put it there. She gave an involuntary shudder as she climbed into her car. Now she had no doubt that he knew where she lived.

Diana grimaced as she remembered her full schedule of clients; she just hoped she could get through the day. She felt as if she were standing on the edge of a deep pit. When she arrived she looked cautiously around while she locked her car door, but noticed no one peculiar.

Great! Now I'm becoming paranoid, she thought.

When she got to her office she locked her purse in a desk drawer, then went to the employees' lounge and poured herself a cup of coffee. Caffeine usually made her jumpy, but today she felt she needed something to pep her up. Two nights in a row with very little sleep were taking their toll.

Back in her office she picked up a printout of the case load schedule for the day. She was a counselor in a family planning clinic and, although the salary wasn't the greatest, she felt that her job was very important. Most often it was unwanted children who were the ones abused and/or neglected. She counseled clients in all areas of reproductive measures: birth control methods, pregnancy termination, sterilization, and so forth. Although fulfilling, it was also sometimes exhausting.

When she was finally able to take her lunch break, she hurried to her car and made her first stop at the telephone company. She had her phone number changed--the new one unlisted--which made her angry because of the inconvenience it would cause, and also ordered Call Return. At least with that service she would be able to call him back after he called her--giving him a taste of his own harassment. Maybe that would show him that two could play this vicious game.

They also advised her of Caller ID, Call Blocker, and Call Trace, but she decided not to add the extra expense of any of those services yet. Hopefully, changing her number would take care of the problem.

She bought a salad to take back to her office, and while she ate she called the police to report the calls. They weren't even as helpful as the telephone company had been. They, too, advised her to change her phone number. When she told them she had already had it changed, they then suggested the same various telephone options. However, they also pointed out that he could very possibly be calling from a pay phone or some other public telephone, and that even if they were able to catch him there really wasn't much they could do--unless he directly threatened her life or she wanted to press charges against him for harassment.

Exasperation and helplessness caused her to become even more angry. Her hands were shaking as she called a locksmith and arranged to have him come to her apartment after she got home from work. Rationally, she realized that this was probably an overreaction, but she just couldn't push the fear out of her mind of him knowing where she lived. Somehow she was able to make it through the afternoon.

That evening the locksmith put a second deadbolt lock on her apartment door, and keyed locks on her windows. Of course, someone could always break a window, but that would make a loud noise and probably alert one of the other tenants in the apartment complex. The cost of all the added security was nearly two hundred dollars, quite a bite out of her meager savings, which angered her still further. She hated the feeling of being victimized--of her life being invaded.

The rest of the week progressed uneventfully, then another, and eventually she had nearly put the phone calls out of her mind. But on the third week, one night when she returned home from working out at her health club, she had another message on her answering machine which was just dead air, with no voice message, but with the same rustling noise and breathing in the background--like that other time. Somehow she was sure it was him. But how could he have gotten her new number? It was unlisted. When she tried to use her Call Return, she was answered by a recorded message informing her that the number couldn't be reached by that method, which meant that it could either be long distance or made from a cellular phone. It was probably a wrong number, she chided herself, she was probably just being paranoid again.

Unfortunately, she wasn't just being paranoid. At 1:00 A.M. when her phone rang, she drowsily began to reach for it. Then, with a dreadful premonition, she felt the hairs prickle on the back of her neck as well as a tingling sensation running along both of her arms. She was instantly, fully awake. No! It can't be! She thought, as she continued to let it ring. After she had counted thirty rings, she reluctantly picked it up, not saying anything.

As she held the receiver against her ear, she heard the whispery voice say, "Diana, it took me a while to get your new number, but you should have known that you can't get away from me. True love will always find a way, Diana. Don't try to hide from me again. You don't want me to get angry with you, do you? Now, I'll let you get your beauty sleep; you're so beautiful, Diana. I'll be calling you again soon. Sweet Dreams." The line went dead.

Horrified, Diana continued to hold the phone to her ear... listening to the dial tone...unable to move, the icy fingers of fear running up and down her spine to the accompaniment of her pounding heart. Not until the mechanical recorded voice, advising her to try her call again, had changed to an insistent unpleasant beeping was she able to put the phone down--at last severing the connection. When she tried Call Return again, and received the same message that the number couldn't be reached by that method, she let out a sob. "Oh, God! What should I do?"

With shaking hands, she dialed 911 and told the operator what had happened, but when the operator asked if she had been threatened, Diana knew, with a sinking feeling, that the police wouldn't be able to do anything to help her-- even before she replied that she hadn't. However, the operator told her that they would send a patrol car to check the area. So Diana sat--shivering--by her living room window, anxiously peering out through the blinds into the parking lot until, twenty minutes later, she saw a police car drive slowly by, shining its spotlight around. It made several sweeps, then was gone. She felt so helpless she began to cry.

How ironic, she thought, I was named for Diana, the Roman goddess of the hunt, and I am the one being hunted. She eventually summoned the courage to return to her bed where she lay awake for hours...afraid that as soon as she fell asleep he would call again. Eventually, though, she did go to sleep; but he didn't call again.

When her alarm clock went off the next morning at 6:30, she slowly emerged from her deep dreamless sleep, at first thinking that it was her telephone ringing. When she realized it was her alarm clock, she shut it off with a feeling of relief. At least he hadn't called back. Maybe if she just answered her phone whenever he called, and let him talk, he would get tired of it and find someone else to victimize. She showered, dressed, hurriedly ate some black cherry yogurt, and left for work. This time there were no surprises on her car.

When she arrived at the clinic she again looked cautiously around as she locked her car, but, thankfully, didn't see anyone suspicious. Maybe he was just some nut who got off calling women at night. Maybe she was just one of several he called; perhaps fear was causing her to overreact.

She put in another busy day at the clinic and decided to stop at her health club for a workout on her way home. She usually tried to work out at least three times a week, and always felt better when she did. She kept her workout clothes and swim suit packed in a canvas bag in her car, so that whenever she chose to stop at her club she wouldn't have to go home first.

She was just getting ready to leave her office when the receptionist beeped her intercom and told her she had a phone call. When she answered it and no one responded, at first she thought she had picked up the wrong line, but when she said, "Hello," a second time, the whispery voice answered, "Hello, Diana. I just wanted to hear your voice. Soon we will be together so that I can hear you and see you whenever I want."

Diana was shaking so hard that she dropped the phone. "No! No!" She moaned. Then she snatched it back up again, holding it in both hands as she angrily shouted: "You son of a bitch! I'm not going to let you victimize me anymore. You're a sick bastard and I'm not going to allow you to continue to disrupt my life! Do you hear me?"

"Oh, Diana," he sighed; "Please don't call me those terrible names. That really hurts my feelings. I love you, Diana. I only want us to be together. It's our destiny. You can't fight it. It's going to happen no matter what you think. It will happen, Diana! We will be together!" The line went dead.

"You bastard!" She yelled again, before slamming down the phone. There was only one thing left for her to do--she had no other choice. She had to protect herself. She took out her phone book, looked in the Yellow Pages for the listing and called the number.

"Yes, ma'am, we're open until six," the man who answered the phone said in response to her question. She wrote down the address, grabbed her purse and hurriedly left.

The salesman was very helpful; he showed her several different types and she finally decided on a Smith & Wesson .38 pistol. It felt more comfortable in her hand than some of the other models, and it packed enough punch to do what she needed. She refused to play the victim any longer. She was going to be strong and be worthy of her name.

The salesman showed her how to hold it with both hands so that her aim would be more accurate, and to enable her to more easily control the kick--if she had to use it. She also bought ammunition and he showed her how to load the gun, as well as how to clean and oil it.

She had never fired a pistol before; she had done some target shooting while in college with a .22 rifle, and had always enjoyed it. But she knew that shooting at cans and bottles with a rifle and shooting at another human being with a pistol, were incomparable. She wasn't even sure if she could shoot another human being, but was reasonably certain that she would be able to if she was threatened. She had a sudden shiver at the thought and planned to go to a shooting range for instruction as soon as she could.

When she arrived at her health club, Diana felt more confident than she had in weeks. Even though she wouldn't be in actual possession of the gun until after the five-day waiting period, she felt as if she had, at last, regained control of her life.

She quickly changed into her workout clothes and headed for the weights. She didn't try to build bulk with the weights, just some minor sculpting--fat burning, and some added strength--and was proud of her slender, yet muscular body.

As she went through her repetitions she looked around the club at some of the other members.

It had occurred to her that the whispery voice might belong to someone with whom she had had some minor contact in the past. She had only moved to the area eight months ago and hadn't had time yet to form any close friendships. However she had so many acquaintances from various facets of her life that the possibilities were endless: one of her clients, or someone connected to her job in some other way; someone at her bank, grocery store, or other places with which she did business. It could even be someone from here, although she didn't know any of the other members.

She studied some of the other people in the weight room. There was a tall, attractive blond man, probably in his early thirties, at one of the other weight machines working his pectorals. He looked like he was really into body building. In fact, he was a hunk! She hoped he wasn't the whispery voice.

Another man, probably in his late forties and balding, who looked like a professional type, was working on the stair-stepper. He was about six feet tall, with a very muscular build. Neither of them seemed to be paying any attention to her.

When she had finished her repetitions, she went to the juice bar and bought a large pineapple slush. While she sat at a small table drinking it, she again looked around at the other members. None of them seemed to be paying any attention to her. They all seemed to be intent on their own workouts.

For several minutes she watched a tall man with reddish, thinning hair, who looked as if he had just joined; he didn't look to be in very good shape. Although slender, he was flabby. When he noticed her looking at him he began to stare back, and she quickly looked away in embarrassment. She was certain she hadn't seen him here before. Maybe he was the whispery voice and had joined the club just to watch her! *There I go being paranoid again,* she thought. *It won't be long before I start looking under my bed and in the closets every time I go home.*

After finishing her juice, she went into the locker room and changed into her swim suit. She found it refreshing to end her workout with a swim. She started out with laps, then slowed to a relaxing float. As she drifted around the pool her mind returned to checking out the other members. She had never really paid much attention to any of them before.

There were three other people in the Olympic sized pool; two women and a man. The man had gray hair, a carefully trimmed mustache, and was probably nearing sixty although he appeared to be in very good shape for his age and looked like he was also quite a ladies' man. The two women were probably in their late forties or early fifties, and they all seemed to know each other.

Diana finished her swim, took a quick shower, dried her hair, and dressed. By then it was nearly 10:00 P.M. When she was leaving, the muscular man who had been on the stair-stepper was also leaving. As he politely held the door open for her, she looked at his face and said, "Thanks," but he merely nodded and went the opposite way to his car without giving her a second look.

For a minute Diana stood just outside the door looking warily around the parking lot. When she didn't see anyone, she quickly ran to her car, unlocked the door, got in and hastily relocked it. She looked around again and still didn't see anyone.

She went through the drive-through at a Wendy's on her way home and ordered a grilled chicken salad and, as an after thought, some French fries. She didn't usually eat French fries, but tonight she seemed to have a craving for them. She took her food home and, again, looked warily around before getting out of her car. When she didn't see anyone, she quickly gathered her canvas bag, her purse and her food, locked her car and hurried inside, then locked both deadbolts on her apartment door. She checked her answering machine but there were no messages.

She poured herself a large glass of soda and ate her food. Then she hung up her wet bathing suit in the bathroom, threw her workout clothes into the round, Mexican willow basket she used as a laundry hamper, and went to bed. She began to read Stephen King's, *Gerald's Game*, as she waited for the phone to ring. She finally dozed off around midnight, sleeping peacefully until her alarm went off the next morning at 6:30.

Between the workout and the uninterrupted night's sleep, she felt more like her old self again. And the knowledge that she would soon be in possession of a gun added even more to her peace of mind and courage.

After repacking her canvas bag for the health club and putting it by the door so she would remember to take it to her car, she ate a toasted frozen waffle topped with sliced apples and vanilla yogurt, then quickly finished getting dressed for work. Just as she was ready to walk out the door her telephone rang. She almost let her machine pick it up, but was afraid it might be her parents.

"Hello," she said.

The whispery voice answered, "Good morning, Diana; I hope you slept well. I want you healthy and well-rested when we finally get to be together. It will be soon now, Diana. Very soon. I can hardly wait! Oh, I love you so much, Diana!"

"Not till Hell freezes over you son of a bitch!" She yelled. "Do you hear me, you bastard? Not until Hell freezes over!" She slammed down the phone. Her heart was pounding and she began to tremble. She clenched her fists, tears of anger springing to her eyes, then tried Call Return again, even though she was certain she would receive the same recorded message--and she was right!

"I won't let him victimize me. I won't! I am Diana, the huntress, not the hunted, and I'm not going to forget that!" She sat, repeating it over and over until the trembling finally stopped and her heart resumed its normal rhythm.

She gathered up her canvas bag along with her purse, and cautiously opened her front door. She looked warily around the parking lot, and when she didn't see anyone, she locked her apartment door, ran to her car, quickly un-locked it, got in and relocked it, then looked around once more before driving to work.

Luckily, there was a small case load today. She counseled only two clients in the afternoon, and after writing up her counseling notes she began to go through her files to see if perhaps any of her former clients could be the whispery voice. She found a few possibilities: one in particular. When she called the police and updated them on her harassing calls, the officer advised her to either get Caller ID or Call Trace. She felt that Caller ID would be a waste of money, more than likely proving useless for identification purposes since her caller was sure to have his number blocked or, more probably, was using a cellular phone. She decided that Call Trace would be more efficient.

Diana immediately called the telephone company and requested Call Trace be added to her service, then listened carefully as the service representative explained how it worked: After hanging up from a call she wanted traced, she was to wait ten seconds, pick up her phone, then when she heard a dial tone she had to press a specific code. If the trace was successful, an announcement would give her further instructions if she wanted to take legal action. If the number couldn't be traced, she would also be advised. On a successful trace the phone number, time and date of the call would be automatically recorded on telephone company equipment. However, the information would be provided only to telephone company security and, if she decided to file a complaint, to the proper law enforcement agency.

Diana was elated. Now she felt certain that soon she would be able to find out who the bastard was and put him away so that he wouldn't be able to bother her, or anybody else for that matter, ever again.

She quickly dialed the police again and was put through to an officer. She excitedly explained her situation, and that she had just subscribed to Call Trace. But, unfortunately, her elation was short-lived. He was polite, but slightly apologetic as he explained to her that even if they did find the identity of her caller, they couldn't charge him with anything more than harassment unless she was threatened with extortion, bodily harm, or death.

"Didn't Texas pass an anti-stalking law?" she asked.

"That's right, but what is happening to you doesn't come under the definition of stalking--according to the law. You've received no threats and you've never seen him watching you--that you're aware of. He's never tried to see you, as far as you know, and has never made an attempt to enter your home either with or without your permission, or tried to harm you. Should he ever make any type of physical contact with you, then maybe we could put him under a restraining order. But restraining orders don't always work the way they are supposed to either. Possibly though, with Call Trace, we can at least find out his identity so we can keep an eye on him."

She sighed. "Well, I guess you're doing what you can, even if it doesn't make me feel any safer." She didn't mention the gun to him. Somehow, she didn't think he would approve, and she wasn't in any mood for an anti-gun lecture. She thanked him and hung up.

That evening she didn't go to her club; her depression had returned. She only ate half of a tuna fish sandwich and a nectarine for supper. She really wasn't very hungry. Then she watched television for awhile; a movie on HBO that she found difficult to concentrate on. She took a shower, washed and blow-dried her hair, then went to bed at 10:00 P.M. and resumed reading *Gerald's Game*. Although it was entertaining, as King's books usually were, she found it too scary to be enjoyable in her present frame of mind; she kept identifying a little too closely with the female victim.

Instead, she decided to read an issue of Vogue magazine she had recently bought. It made her drowsy, and she finally dozed off. This time he called at 2:00 A.M. Again, she was abruptly awakened by the ringing of the phone. She lay in the dark, unnerved and trembling. Dear God! How much longer must she endure this torture? Then she remembered the option of having the call traced, and quickly picked up the phone. "Hello."

"Diana, why did you call the police? I know you did. Do you really think they can prevent us from being together? You foolish girl. We are destined to be together. I wish you would hurry up and accept that what I'm telling you is the truth. There's nothing you can to do prevent it. You're just wasting your energy. Oh, Diana; I love you so much. It won't be long now, my darling. Sweet Dreams, Diana."

For a few seconds she just sat there...listening to the dial tone. How did he know she had contacted the police? Was he just guessing or did he actually know? That was what really scared her. He seemed to know so much about her. Then she remembered to hang up, count to ten, then pick up the phone and press the code, immediately after which she called the police and gave them the information.

Now she was excited as she hastily got dressed and sat in her living room to wait for the results. She was going to press charges! You bet! She was going to let him know he couldn't disrupt her life and get away with it! She was even afraid to accept a date with anyone, afraid he would turn out to be the whispery voice. Her life was on hold until she could get him out of it--one way or another.

Finally, after waiting nearly an hour, there was a knock at her door. "It's sergeant McKenna, Ma'am, Corpus Christi Police Department."

She looked through the peephole in her door. There stood a man in uniform with a police car parked in the lot behind him.

"I need to see your identification, please," she said.

When she could see him holding up his wallet with his badge and ID, she unlocked both of her deadbolt door locks and let him into her apartment.

"Ma'am. I'm afraid I have some bad news. We traced the number to the Denny's Restaurant about a mile from here on the Expressway. When we went in and looked around, no one was near the phone. We questioned everyone in there and no one remembers seeing anyone use the phone. We also asked for a description of anyone who was in there late at night on a regular basis and came up empty. I'm really sorry, but we'll keep trying. Sooner or later we'll catch him."

Diana felt like someone had hit her in the stomach. She had been so sure they would catch him and that this nightmare would come to an end. She was so disappointed she wanted to cry, but refused to let herself do that in front of the officer. She sat down and stared at him, trying to compose herself.

"I guess what you're saying then...is that I'm pretty much on my own...is that right? Until he hurts me in some way--or kills me--you can't do anything? That you can't even do anything to help me to prevent it?"

The officer shuffled his feet and looked uncomfortable. "I guess that's about it, ma'am. I'm sorry. I wish there was something I could do to help you--believe me; but according to the law, there isn't. Just be very careful, and maybe he'll get tired of harassing you. Maybe, eventually, he'll find another person to try to victimize." With that he left.

Diana was weak with rage, mainly because she felt so helpless. She would just make sure that she had her gun with her at all times--as soon as she got it--and made up her mind that she wasn't going to let him disrupt her life anymore.

She had just finally gotten back to sleep when she was abruptly awakened once more by the ringing telephone. Thinking it might be the police, she hurriedly answered it.

The whispery voice said, "Diana, you called the police again. I really wish you hadn't done that. It would be so much easier if you would just accept my love for you. It won't be much longer now my darling, I promise. We'll be together forever--very, very soon. Sweet dreams my beautiful Diana."

Without much hope Diana again went through the Call Trace procedure, then called the police. And, again, it turned out to be the same number: Denny's! Out of despair she began to cry. It made her angry that he had such power over her behavior; such control over her life--which in turn made her cry even harder. "Damn you, damn you, damn you!" she screamed, as she began beating her fists against the pillows, until finally, out of exhaustion, she fell asleep.

When her alarm woke her the next morning, it all seemed to have been a terrible nightmare. But no! That was only wishful thinking. She still felt such fatigue she knew she would be unable to function at work today, so she called in sick--something she rarely did. She went to the kitchen and made a cup of coffee. She had to make some kind of plan to regain control of her life.

While sitting at her table drinking the coffee, she felt some of the tiredness leaving, but it was replaced by a jittery nervousness. She thought, with a wry amusement, that soon she would probably begin to develop facial tics and agoraphobia. She tried to think of ways to regain control of her life. She got a pen and a piece of paper and made a list.

First, she called her parents and told them she was still receiving crank calls, and had decided to unplug her phones for awhile; she would call them every morning to make sure they were all right. She didn't tell them how scared she had become or how victimized she felt, because she didn't want them to worry. She just told them she was doing it so that she could get uninterrupted sleep. Then she unplugged her phones. The last, and most important item on her list was to always have her gun with her! Three more days to go; she would just have to stay at home until then.

She felt a little better--not quite as helpless. She took a long, warm, herb-scented bath, then went back to bed and slept blissfully for six uninterrupted hours. When she woke, she felt much better. She ate some soup and a sandwich, watched some TV, read some magazines (she still didn't feel up to resuming reading *Gerald's Game*), and finally dozed off again while watching more TV.

She pretty much followed that same routine for the next three days, which seemed to drag by. On the third morning she called to check on the status of her gun, and was told that she would be able to pick it up the following afternoon.

When she awoke the next morning, she already felt more in control again. She showered, blow-dried her hair, and dressed for work. She plugged in one of her phones, made a quick call to her parents--assured them that she was fine--then quickly unplugged her phone again.

After she had eaten some yogurt for breakfast, she looked at her reflection in the mirror and told herself sternly. "I must remember that I am Diana, the huntress--not the hunted," and began to feel almost brave.

As before, she opened her front door and looked cautiously around. When she didn't see anyone, she hurriedly locked her apartment door, ran to her car, unlocked it, and immediately relocked it as soon as she got in. When she got to work, she hastily locked her car and entered the building after, again, first looking cautiously around. She was certain that she now had good reason to feel she was being watched all of the time. That it wasn't just paranoia.

Work was routine and her coworkers were glad that she was back. She assured them that she must have just had a virus, and that she now felt fine. Even though she did feel better, she still dreaded answering the phone. Each time she received a call, she was afraid she would hear that whispery voice...especially now that he was unable to reach her at home because of her unplugged phones. In fact, she fully expected him to call. By the end of the day when he hadn't called, she felt so confident that she decided to work out at her health club. Maybe he had given up. Maybe she should have unplugged her phones in the beginning.

As soon as she left work she stopped and picked up her gun, putting it carefully inside her purse. Back in her car, she placed her open purse on the seat next to her, with the opening facing towards her. She couldn't believe how much courage the gun gave her even though she knew it was against the law to carry a concealed weapon without a permit. But what was she supposed to do? The police could offer her no help or protection, and she was tired of being victimized. What choice did she have? She couldn't just helplessly allow some "nut" to hurt her--or worse.

She stopped on the way and ate a grilled chicken sandwich. At the club she glanced around the parking lot, and when she didn't see anyone, she opened her purse, took out the gun, held it in both of her hands the way the salesman had showed her, aimed it, then put it back into her purse. Yes, the gun really made her feel in control again.

She went inside, changed into her bike shorts and leotard, then began to survey the other members. There were more women here this time, and she didn't see any of the men whom she had noticed the last time. There was a sandy haired man with lots of freckles, probably in his middle thirties, running around the indoor track. Two men who looked really into body building were working out with weights together. In fact they looked almost as if they were in love with each other. She smiled to herself as she began her workout routine with the weights. Next, she took a turn on the stair-stepper, and by then it was time for a break.

She got a large orange juice at the juice bar and sat drinking it while she watched some of the other members. There were a man and a woman, probably in their late fifties, who appeared to be novices at working out. One of the trainers was helping them. After she finished her juice, she changed into her swim suit and dove into the pool.

There were a half dozen other people in the pool; four women and two men, all swimming laps. One of the men had on goggles and was really pushing it. He looked like the same man who had held the door for her when she had been leaving the last time she was here. It was hard to tell with the goggles. She didn't know whether to speak to him or not. She didn't want to be rude, but when he didn't acknowledge her she just decided to ignore him. She swam laps at first, then finished with some easy breast strokes and floating. She stayed in the pool for nearly an hour.

As she was getting out she heard someone call her name. She turned and saw it was another woman also getting out of the pool. She looked vaguely familiar; then Diana realized it was one of her clients whom she had counseled about six months ago. The woman and her husband had come in for joint birth control information. They were in their early forties and had finally decided on vasectomy. The woman asked if Diana would join her for a drink, and since her swim had worked up a thirst, she agreed.

While they drank their juice, the woman told Diana how grateful she was for her counseling information, and how pleased she and her husband were with the decision they had made. The praise was a real boost for Diana's self esteem, which she realized she had needed. She was beginning to feel more and more in control of her life again.

After she had showered and dried her hair with one of the club hair dryers, she ran into the woman again as they were both leaving. The woman explained that her husband was picking her up in a few minutes and asked Diana if she would wait so he could say "hello" to her. By this time it was almost 11:00 P.M. and Diana was a little fearful of leaving by herself, so she agreed.

They were waiting by the door together when the woman's husband drove up. Diana went to the car, shook hands with the husband and exchanged the usual polite amenities, then looked warily around the parking lot as the woman and her husband drove off, but she didn't see anyone. There weren't many cars left either. One was parked directly in front of hers, with half a dozen others scattered around the lot. Then she remembered the gun in her purse and gave a sigh of relief, feeling a little safer as she ran to her car.

It was while she was unlocking her car door that she suddenly felt something tight gripping both of her ankles. She let out a startled cry as a quick, strong tug pull her viciously to the ground, causing her to hit her buttocks hard against the asphalt--momentarily knocking the wind out of her. She realized there were two strong arms reaching out from underneath her car, the hands grasping her ankles. Then a man hastily crawled out from under her car where he had been hiding...waiting for her. She was temporarily immobilized by the surprise of the attack, and before she was able to get back her breath, she felt a rag being stuffed into her mouth. He pulled out a wicked looking hunting knife and held it to her throat.

"I told you we would be together soon, Diana." His voice was husky, but even without the whispery telephone disguise she was able to recognize it. "I won't hesitate to kill you if I must! If I can't have you, I'll make sure nobody else will either. I'm prepared to die if necessary; at least then we can be together in the after life--if we can't be together here on Earth."

With the knife still held against her throat, he dragged her to the car parked directly in front of hers, opened the unlocked trunk lid and roughly shoved her inside. He quickly tied her wrists together in front as well as tying her ankles together.

She was too shocked and scared to try to resist him! Then she realized in further panic that she had dropped her purse. She fought back the tears of helplessness as she looked up into the face of her attacker. It was the muscular, balding man who had been in the pool tonight: the one who had held the door for her when she was leaving the club the last time she was here.

He held the knife to her throat again. "I'm going to take the gag out now, Diana. I hope I can trust you not to scream, because I meant what I said."

Diana knew she must stay cool if she was to have any chance at all of escaping. Somehow she knew he meant every word he said, that he was capable of killing them both. He was obsessed!

"Please," she begged softly, "Would you get my purse for me? It has my makeup and other personal items I need so that I can look pretty for you."

"You won't need it, Diana. I have everything you will ever need. Besides, I like you better without makeup; I like you to look natural."

"It also has pictures of my parents in it. Oh please, you can't deny me those--not if you really love me as much as you say you do."

"Don't ever doubt my love for you, Diana!" He paused for a minute, as if thinking over her request. "OK. I'll get it for you. It probably wouldn't be a good idea to leave it laying in the parking lot anyway."

She heard him walk away. Half a minute later her canvas bag and purse were dumped into the trunk on top of her before the lid was slammed down. It was so dark and cramped inside the trunk that she felt a claustrophobic moment of horror, and for a few seconds she had to bite her tongue to keep from screaming.

She heard his car door shut, then the sound of the engine. As the car started to move, he began to talk to her. "You know, Diana, the first time I saw you was at the club, and I knew then that we were destined to be together. It wasn't hard to get information from the club about you. I have my own CPA firm and am very respected in the community, so I could get information about you from many different sources. It's a small world, Diana. It's amazing who knows who in this town, and how easy it is to find out almost anything you want to know about someone--if you have the right contacts. There isn't much I don't know about you.

"I have a lovely home, which will now be your home, too. I had the master bedroom suite on the second floor enlarged and redecorated--just for you, Diana. It's all done in your favorite colors, with a large walk-in closet full of clothes in your size. But they're much sexier clothes than what you're used to wearing.

"I have hurricane shutters on the windows--which have been locked shut--so please don't think about trying to escape. It's quite impossible. I've thought of everything. You will be mine from now on, my lovely Diana!

"I have such exciting plans for us! I also had the master bathroom enlarged, and mirrored all of the walls and the ceiling. I even had a whirlpool bathtub, large enough for two people, installed. Oh...the things we will do in that tub, Diana. Oh, the things we will do!"

His voice had grown even huskier and he stopped talking for a few seconds. "I have some wonderful movies for us to watch and act out together. Movies some people might consider pornographic or perverted, but I consider them erotic and stimulating. You have such a beautiful body, Diana. I can hardly wait. We are going to have such a wonderful life together, at last, my lovely Diana!"

He then proceeded to describe various sexual acts which he was anticipating sharing with her--some of them so twisted and perverted that she almost vomited. He was one sick bastard! She had been scared before, but now she was terrified! He intended her to be his sex-slave for the rest of their lives.

As he continued to talk, she was able to move around enough in the cramped trunk to grasp the strap of her purse and pull it up towards her. Lying on her right side, in a curled up position, she was able to unzip it by holding it between her knees and chest, even with her wrists tied together.

Now, the combination of the stench of the exhaust fumes coming into the trunk, fear, and the filth he was telling her he expected them to do together, did cause her to vomit. And afterwards, she started to shake, but a few minutes later she was able to regain some of her strength and some of her composure.

Remember, you are Diana (she thought) goddess of the hunt--not the hunted! She kept thinking this over and over, trying to block out the words he was saying to her as she carefully worked the gun out of her purse. She continued to maneuver it until she was able to grip her right hand around the handle with her right index finger on the trigger, while steadying it with her left hand, similar to the way the salesman had shown her. She was ready for him! "Now, I'm Diana, the huntress; no longer the hunted, you bastard," she whispered softly to herself.

She tried to relax as much as possible, so that her arms wouldn't cramp, and a few minutes later she felt the car slow down and turn sharply, as if into a driveway. She heard a garage door open, then a few seconds later the car stopped and the engine was turned off.

"Well, here we are, Diana. We're home now--forever to be together," he said, as she heard the automatic garage door closing.

"Now, please, Diana; make it easy on yourself and don't try to get away. It's impossible anyway. You would just be wasting your precious energy. Besides, I have much better ways to put it to use," she heard him saying as he walked around to the trunk and fitted the key into the lock.

Diana tensed her muscles, ready for what she had to do. She heard him saying, as he unlocked and began raising the trunk lid, "At last, Diana! You're finally mi..."

And she was even able to smile in smug satisfaction, as she glimpsed the fleeting, startled look of horrified disbelief on his face--just before she pulled the trigger and silenced him...PERMANENTLY.

He pulled out a wicked looking hunting knife and held it to her throat.

THE EVE OF THE BEGINNING (CONTINUED)

As I emerged, this time, from the magic of the stories, I was touched by the anger and desperation that Lora and Diana had felt. My eyes were wet as if I had been crying, and I quickly closed them again for a few minutes. I wondered if I had cried, and, in a flash of macho pride, felt my face grow hot with embarrassment.

When I did eventually open my eyes, for a moment I panicked. Schere was gone. However, after testing the strength of my bonds I was somewhat reassured. They were still loose: merely tokens of bondage. That strange, exotic music was still playing softly in the background, and as I watched the dancing shadows I noticed that she had been replacing the candles as they burned down with new ones.

Then she walked into the room, carrying a silver tray which she set on the bombe chest next to the bed. It held a clear glass bucket containing chipped ice and a bottle, two crystal flute glasses, and a plate with some type of food. She poured a glass of what looked like champagne for each of us. Rather than untying my hands, she held the glass gently to my lips. I drank thirstily; it was champagne and tasted mellow and cold as I swallowed. I looked at the label on the bottle. The brand was Cristal.

"I thought perhaps you could use some refreshment," she said, as she held out something for me to eat.

I took a bite. It was a tiny pecan tart with a flaky crust, and it was delicious! Next she fed me sliced kiwi fruit, chocolate-dipped strawberries, and pieces of smoked Edam cheese, followed by more sips of the champagne. I hadn't realized how hungry and thirsty I was. She continued to feed me and, as my appetite became satisfied, I was eager for more stories. Suddenly I became fearful that the evening was over: that she would untie me and send me home. I didn't want the night to end.

"I hope you haven't run out of stories," I said.

She shook her head and smiled. "Oh, no, Michael; we still have more stories. Some very important ones yet to come."

"Good," I sighed, as I settled back and got comfortable.

She took my face in her hands and smiled. "These are the stories of love between humans and animals, Michael. Don't ever forget our very special furred, finned, and feathered friends: the ones God put here to fill a very special place in our lives. We must recognize the essential importance of respecting the habitat of our fellow Earth dwellers: the animals. These are the stories of Marian and of Janna."

Once again, this time before she had to tell me, I looked into her eyes--now golden-brown, warm and soft like velvet--eagerly anticipating the next stories in her eyes.

THE BOND

Marian was so cold she was shivering, yet her face felt hot and feverish as she walked to her car in the parking lot. Her muscles ached from the effort. By the time she reached her car, which couldn't have taken more than thirty seconds, she was exhausted--nearly drained of energy. She wasn't surprised. "It must be my turn for the flu," she thought, and was glad it was Friday. She just wanted to go home, take a hot bath, and sleep.

In her car she closed her eyes and lay her head back against the seat to rest for a few minutes before driving home. She hadn't felt very well this morning when she had gone to work, and by the afternoon her muscles had begun to ache and she had become weak and feverish. Practically all of her coworkers had already had it, and all had said that it had really made them feel miserable, but that the worst part only lasted for twenty-four hours. When she finally felt a little stronger she started her car and drove home, grateful that she only lived a few minutes from where she worked.

At home she was immediately greeted by her four housemates, Chester, Big Foot, Trois and Scotty: her cats. Three were neutered males, and Trois was a spayed female (also her third cat, which was the reason for her name). They not only allowed her to share their house with them, they were also her best friends and companions.

After they had each taken turns rubbing against her ankles, Chester stood on his hind feet with his front paws stretched upwards towards her. He always wanted a hug when she came home.

"Mea'am," he said.

She bent down and hugged his soft, yet firm little body, and in return, he gave her his little love nip on her chin. When she stood up, she had to steady herself with her hand against the door frame. She was beginning to feel woozy.

After putting some dry food into their dishes, refilling their water bowls with fresh water, and scooping out their litter boxes, her energy was nearly depleted.

She carefully washed her hands in the bathroom, then took her temperature. To her astonishment, it read 103.4 degrees. Wow! That was high--especially for an adult! No wonder she felt so rotten.

She turned on the hot water tap--all the way--and as the water sluiced into the tub, quickly filling it, she took off her clothes; by the time she climbed in, she was shivering. She slowly sank into the hot water which nearly scalded her before she turned on the cold water tap and adjusted the temperature. She lay her head back and closed her eyes, the warm water comforting as it swirled higher around her body.

Suddenly the bathroom door was pushed open as Chester stuck his head in and made his peculiar little cooing sound. She opened her eyes and looked at him--his emerald eyes peering back at her as if he knew something was wrong. She had read that cats had psychic abilities; however, she didn't know if she believed it. But then, Chester was a very special cat.

She loved all of her cats, and they were each unique in their own individual ways, but she and Chester had a special relationship: an extraordinary bond. When he had been a very young kitten he had become severely ill, apparently with distemper. She had nursed him through a number of crises, and in each he had come perilously close to dying. During those times she had prepared baby rice cereal, with a tiny bit of strained chicken added, which she had put on her finger tip and placed on the roof of his mouth so he wouldn't starve. It had been necessary to do this about six times a day, along with shooting water into his mouth with a small syringe (the needle removed) so that he wouldn't dehydrate.

Being too weak to eat or drink on his own, he had just lain limply on her bed, like a lifeless, stuffed toy animal. Occasionally, when he would cry out in pain, she would pick him up and hold him against her chest, patting his little bottom as if he were a human baby.

The episodes occurred frequently for about six weeks. He would get better, then worse. When he had been at his worst, she had looked into his sick little eyes and pleaded with him not to die. She had told him about the fun he would have as a full-grown cat--frolicking and playing; about all of the good food he would enjoy; of how much she loved him, and how much she would miss him if he died.

She didn't know exactly what had kept him from dying, but eventually he had begun to get stronger and to grow, with the terrible sick episodes finally ending. He never did quite catch up to his brother in size, but he had grown to be a very handsome, healthy cat. He loved to hunt and often brought her rubber bands, pieces of string, toy mice-- whatever he could find--as if to show her what a mighty, fearless hunter he had become. He also seemed especially sensitive to her moods.

Sometimes, she thought he actually thought of her as his mother. In her mind, she saw him as a valiant little cat: a fighter, and the mighty hunter she thought he fancied him- self to be. That's why she also called him her Cheetah.

She felt that God had put animals on Earth to coexist with man, not for man to exploit or use for his own means. She felt cats and dogs, as well as many of the other higher orders of mammals, were here to be our special friends and companions and, at times, our mentors. Her cats had such deep faith and trust in her, she knew she could never do anything to betray it.

As she reflected on her love for animals her shivering finally subsided, but was replaced by greater fatigue and weakness. She reached forward and unstopped the drain, but when she stood she once again felt so wobbly that she had to put out a hand against the wall to steady herself. And as soon as she emerged from the warmth of the bath water she began to shiver again.

She grabbed her towel and quickly rubbed herself dry before slipping on a warm fleece sweat suit, followed by some heavy cotton socks. She walked weakly to the kitchen where she swallowed two aspirin tablets with half a glass of water. Then, thinking she might feel stronger if she ate something, she opened a can of tomato soup, dumped it into a bowl, added a bit of water, and put it into the microwave to heat. While it was heating, she went back to the bedroom and put on her old, comfortable, cotton terry robe. But she still continued to shiver.

After the soup had heated for a few minutes, she took the bowl to the table. Since she was too tired and weak to eat it with a spoon, she just lifted the bowl with both hands and drank it; the soup felt pleasant and soothing going down her throat--warming her body. But it also seemed to heighten her feeling of almost overwhelming fatigue. She put her head down on the table for a few minutes, and that's when the nausea hit.

She hurried to the bathroom--just barely making it there in time before the soup came back up. Afterwards, while washing her face, she was hit with such a wave of weakness she was afraid she would pass out. That was one of the disadvantages of living alone--rather--of not sharing a house with another human being; there was no one to take care of you when you were sick. Her parents lived more than two hundred miles away in Houston.

She staggered to the bed, half crawling the last few feet. Even with the down-filled comforter pulled tight around her she was still cold. As she lay curled up on her side, she began to shiver--so hard this time that her teeth began to chatter. Chester jumped up onto the bed and nestled his little body into the curl of her abdomen, sharing his warmth, and gradually her shivering and tooth chattering subsided.

She didn't remember falling asleep, but when she awoke it was dark and she was very hot. Her mouth was dry and her throat felt scratchy. She turned her head towards her night table to see what time it was and spotted a cup of crushed ice, much of which had already melted into cold water. She grabbed it and drank thirstily. Then she looked at the plastic cup in puzzlement. She didn't remember getting it. She must have gotten up while she was half asleep and, in her feverish state, not remember having walked to the kitchen. Luckily, her refrigerator dispensed ice by merely pushing a container against a lever on the outside of the door. She finished the water, leaving about an inch of crushed ice in the bottom of the cup, and as she replaced it on her night table she noticed it was 1:00 A.M.

By the time she lay back down in the bed, she had already begun to feel cold, and soon the shivering began again. Chester had been lying on the foot of her bed--watching, and he moved back to her, this time nestling his warm little body against the small of her back. He was soon joined by the other three cats who also snuggled their soft warmth against her body. After a few minutes passed, she stopped shivering, then lapsed into a restless sleep which remained dreamless...until the bird appeared.

It was a large black bird; a bird of prey, possibly a falcon, and it was stalking her. She tried to run, but it was one of those dreams where no matter how fast or hard she tried, she was never able to move forward. The large bird was gaining on her--closer and closer--until she could feel the air currents from its mighty beating wings as its dark shadow fell upon her. When she looked up, she was able to see its glaring red eyes, and could feel the heat of--as well as smell--its pervading fetid breath.

Her heart was hammering in her chest and she was gasping for breath, her body drenched in sweat. Twisting and turning--desperately trying to escape from the bird's exuding, overpowering evil--she was suddenly filled with terror that she was going to die.

Now the huge bird was reaching for her with its sharp talons. She could hear her heart pounding in her ears as she put her hands above her head to try to fend it off. She knew that it had come for her; that it intended to carry her back to its nest, where it would rip her flesh into bite sized pieces with its notched bill, and greedily devour her.

As she began to thrash her arms in a frantic attempt to beat it away, she heard a menacing hiss--followed by a loud screaming yowl, and the bird veered away from her. She heard wild flapping, accompanied by loud rustling, hissing, piercing screams, and yowls, which lasted for several minutes. Finally, she heard a crash--followed by silence, and the nightmare suddenly ended. She fell back against the pillows in exhaustion, and was immediately swallowed back into dark, dreamless sleep.

She was very hot when she was awakened by the feeling of something wet and rough moving against her cheek. When she opened her eyes, Chester was licking her face with his sandpapery little tongue. When she turned on her bedside lamp, she noticed scratches all over the backs of her hands, and that the bed was a twisted, jumbled mass of sheets and blankets. She must have done a lot of thrashing during that terrible dream. She shuddered as she remembered how real it had seemed.

She turned her head to see what time it was, and saw that her alarm clock and book had been knocked to the floor. Luckily, the cup full of partly thawed ice had remained untouched. Except...she was certain that it had been nearly empty after the last time she had drunk from it. She must have been so delirious with fever that she didn't remember getting up and refilling it.

Chester was again watching her intently. He made his cooing sound and lay down on her chest. He rubbed his little nose against hers and that was when she noticed that his right ear was torn, a tuft of hair had been pulled out of his forehead, and there was a scratch on his nose where a drop of blood had dried. "I wonder which of the other cats did that to him," she thought, as she took a long drink of water from the glass. Then she put her head back down on the pillows and drifted back to sleep, with Chester still lying on her chest--as if keeping guard over her while she slept.

This time her sleep was dreamless, peaceful and restful. When she awoke it was 10:00 A.M. and she felt as if her fever had broken. Chester was still perched on her chest--keeping guard--and looked at her warily. She pulled his head forward and nuzzled his nose against the side of her face. "You're such a good little friend," she told him. When she sat up she noticed that the other three cats were sitting in a row at the foot of her bed, also watching her.

"You guys must be hungry," she said as they just sat there, continuing to stare at her...unblinking.

She felt much stronger and shifted Chester from her chest to her shoulder, then carefully sat on the edge of the bed and put her feet on the floor. She still felt a little woozy, but not nearly as much as she had yesterday.

She got up and carried Chester into the kitchen, with the other three cats following close behind. She put some food into their dishes, then patted each one separately on its head, and each, in turn, stopped eating, nuzzling the side of its face against her hand as she did so. She discovered that the others also had some tufts of hair torn from various parts of their bodies, and Scotty also had a torn ear.

That's strange, she thought; they've never fought with each other before. They must have really gotten into a brawl about something. She hoped it wouldn't become a common occurrence.

She made some hot chocolate and fixed a piece of toast which she carried back to her bedroom on a tray. She was beginning to feel tired again, but the bed was such a mess she decided to straighten it before getting back in to eat her breakfast. She set the tray on her dressing table and began to tidy the sheets and blankets.

That was when she noticed the feathers scattered among the bedding. At least half a dozen of them: long, black feathers. Where could they have come from? She seldom allowed her cats to go outside, so there was little chance that one of them could have caught a bird. Besides, these feathers would have had to have come from a very large bird.

As she gathered the feathers together into a bundle, she heard the familiar cooing sound. She turned around to see Chester sitting in the doorway of her bedroom--watching her. He cooed again, as if he could read her mind and was answering her question. When she looked into his slanted emerald eyes, he peered knowingly back. Suddenly the terrible nightmare came crashing vividly back into her mind. As she remembered the huge black bird trying to attack her, she began to shiver again--violently. Only this time it wasn't from the fever!

YOU

Into my heart you silently crept,
On your tiny velvet feet;
You nestled against my side while I slept,
Your cuddly body warm and sweet.

Such prideful stature in your walk,
Valiant hunter that you are,
Rivaling Orion when prey you stalk--
Diligently searching near and far.

Though some say you look with arrogance
Upon your world--that you're distant and aloof,
It's merely your discerning intelligence;
Deciding what is worthy of your time, needs proof.

I wonder at your funny mercurial moods:
From a softly purring ball of fur,
To teasing playfulness, which often preludes
A rapid, sinewy, whirlwind blur--

Metamorphosing abruptly to elegant dignity,
When you gently jump into my lap,
And gaze at me in affectionate serenity,
Before you snuggle for your nap.

SWIMMER

The tepid water felt sensuous against Janna's skin as she watched yellow pinwheels spinning against the red-orange insides of her closed eyelids. She was lying on her back...relaxed...drifting, under the bright afternoon sunshine. She loved the feeling of buoyancy she had while floating in the water: a feeling of freedom; a feeling of being suspended in time.

As she arched her back even further, she felt the water playfully seep over the top of her hair, touching her forehead. She spread her arms wide to the side. Now she was in the shape of a cross, legs together, toes pointed. She felt beautiful and graceful--almost as if she and the water had become one.

Today the water was smooth: like molten glass. She moved her arms, changing from a horizontal to a vertical position as she opened her eyes, then swam to the edge of her pool. As she climbed out her legs felt heavy from the abruptness of leaving the water.

She had gotten a good workout today and her stamina was steadily increasing; she was able to swim underwater for almost a minute and-a-half without coming up for air. Tomorrow she would go to the Padre Island beach for her workout. It was time to test her endurance in the ocean.

She looked at the clock as she dried her arms and shoulders with a large beach towel. Wow! It was four o'clock already! She had been in the pool for nearly two hours; it hadn't seemed like it could have been more than an hour. "I'd better hurry," she thought, as she opened the French door into her bedroom; Richard, her husband, would be upset if dinner was late.

She quickly turned on the hot water in the shower, letting it run full blast while she peeled off her wet bikini and threw it into the bathroom sink. She then adjusted the water to a pleasantly warm temperature before stepping under the spray.

Ten minutes later, while blow-drying her hair, she thought about her workout with a rush of pleasure. She had only been working out in the pool for six weeks and was pleased with the progress she had made so far. Yes, tomorrow she would do her swimming workout in the ocean. She could hardly wait!

During dinner Janna was in a happy mood as she enthusiastically told Richard about how her swimming prowess was improving. She had been a competition swimmer while in college, even winning several state contests, but had practically given it up for the past eight years since her graduation. When one of her favorite aunts had recently died and left her some money, without hesitating she had spent it all on putting a swimming pool in her back yard. Richard had considered it to be a foolish and wasteful use of her inheritance. He had wanted her to invest it.

But Janna hadn't cared; South Texas, with its mild climate, was ideal for a pool. Swimming was possible for at least six months out of the year. More, if you didn't mind the cooler water temperature. She was even considering buying a wet suit so she could continue to swim on the warmer days during the winter months.

She thought Richard would be proud of her renewed accomplishment. Instead, he gave her a look of disgust and said, "That's all you talk about anymore! Swimming! To me, it's totally boring and I'm sick of hearing about it. I wish you'd never had that pool put in. Let's change the subject!"

Tears stung her eyes and she felt almost as if he had slapped her. She looked down at her food and mumbled an apology--although she didn't feel like one should have been necessary. Then Richard began telling her about his day, which he did every evening at dinner. He was a CPA and she thought HIS job was boring, but she would never hurt his feelings the way he had just hurt hers by telling him she found his conversation boring. She only halfway listened to him as she finished her dinner--the other half of her mind preoccupied with planning her outing tomorrow.

The next morning, after she and Richard had eaten their breakfast and he had left for work, Janna quickly did her routine household chores. Then she made a black bean, tomato, and avocado pita sandwich, which she put into a small plastic cooler she had already partially filled with ice. She added several bottles of water, a kiwi fruit, and an orange. She also filled a large thermos with ice.

By 11:00 A.M., she was on her way to Padre Island. It was such a beautiful sunny day, she could hardly wait to feel the warm gulf water around her body. She loved being in water more than anything she could think of.

After she had parked on a secluded area of the beach and unloaded her towels, blanket and cooler, she waded into the surf until it reached her waist, then swam hard against the tide until she was well past the third sandbar. As soon as she began to tire she swam back to shore at a restful pace, allowing the tide to help carry her. When she stepped out of the surf, the warm sea breeze, along with the brilliant sun, began to immediately dry her wet body. She sat on the blanket and basked in the delicious warmth while she ate her sandwich and drank some of the chilled water.

Afterwards, she walked along the beach, picked up a few shells, and watched the amusing antics of the sand crabs as they warily scurried in their mad, sideways dashes from hole to hole. What cute little creatures they were, with their strange protruding eyes. She rested a few more minutes, then went back into the water for another workout to test her endurance. She knew it was dangerous to swim alone, but she felt so at home in the ocean that she had absolutely no doubts that she wouldn't be safe. She felt the sea to be purifying and cleansing, and believed that all life on Earth had surely been born of the sea.

This time, shortly after she had passed the third sandbar, she saw a dorsal fin slicing through the water. She felt a stab of fear as she stopped swimming and began to tread water. Maybe she should swim back to shore. There were sand sharks in the water which were seldom aggressive to people; however, there had been a few isolated instances of shark attacks. Her heart began to beat faster as she remembered one from several years ago; a teen-age girl had miraculously survived a completely severed arm from a shark bite.

She began to swim back to shore as rapidly as she could, while trying to fight back a steadily increasing feeling of panic. Suddenly, right in front of her, the creature jumped in a wide arc through the air. It was a dolphin. A beautiful, bottle-nosed dolphin!

She began to swim towards the place where the dolphin had been and experienced a brief pang of alarm when she felt something bump against her leg. Then, only a few feet away, the dolphin surfaced again. It faced her and let out a spate of its peculiar rapid chatter. Janna was convinced that Dolphins had their own language and communicated with each other much the same way humans did.

When she saw a second dorsal fin, just before another dolphin surfaced, she stopped swimming again and began to tread water--entranced. The first dolphin swam close enough to her so that she could have reached out and touched it. But she didn't want to do anything that might frighten it away.

Janna and the dolphin eyed each other for a few seconds. Then, as the second dolphin swam closer, she noticed it was accompanied by a small calf. Both of the adult dolphins began to chatter--almost as if they were trying to tell her something. When the second dolphin gently bumped the calf towards her, she noticed the set of plastic rings, one of which was tightly stuck, encircling the front part of the calf's little snout--binding its mouth closed. With dismay, Janna realized the calf would soon starve unless the rings were removed. While the two adult dolphins continued their rapid chatter, she cautiously approached the calf. Then, she reached out her hand and gently stroked its forehead for a few seconds before carefully removing the obstructing rings--the type commonly used to hold a six-pack of cans together.

Janna was so angry she wanted to cry. This poor baby dolphin would have died if the rings hadn't been removed. She was always careful to cut all of her plastic rings open and the middle section in half, before discarding them, so that something like this wouldn't happen.

The two adult dolphins ceased their chatter and turned away from her--followed by the calf--gracefully arced through the air and dove underneath the water. She felt as if she had been touched by magic.

She swam ashore, dried herself with her towel, packed her things into her car, and drove home with mixed emotions. The feeling of magic was still there, but it was marred by a deep feeling of anger that more people weren't environmentally minded. Human beings were often so self-centered. They forgot they weren't alone on this earth: that they inhabited the planet along with other animals, many of which had existed long before man had come along.

That evening, during dinner, she didn't tell Richard that she had gone to the island, or about the dolphins. She merely listened as he told her about his day.

She stayed home the next two days, which were Saturday and Sunday. She and Richard went to a movie Saturday night, and Sunday, she read while he watched golf on television. She was anxious for tomorrow.

The next morning, after Richard had gone to work and she had done her daily chores, she again packed a lunch, something to drink, and headed to the island. However, much to her disappointment, this time she didn't see the dolphins. It had probably just been one of those special occurrences that happens only once in a lifetime, she thought.

The following day, she again went to the island and swam hard, working on her endurance, but before she realized it she had swum farther past the third sandbar than she had intended. Since she was beginning to get tired and winded, she decided she had better swim back to shore.

Suddenly, she felt herself being pulled violently under the water and knew immediately that she had been caught in a riptide! For a few seconds she panicked, swallowing water. She sputtered as she briefly returned to the surface, the salt water stinging her eyes and burning her throat; but as she desperately tried to get her breath she was rapidly pulled back under the water.

She had always heard that when caught in a riptide it was best to go with it, rather than trying to fight against it. However, she was choking and swallowing water, and as she neared the point of exhaustion she became terrified that she was going to drown. Then, abruptly, she felt herself being bumped by something under the water. She was lifted to the surface and bumped again, and the lifting and bumping continued until she was out of danger. When she was finally able to get her wits about her, she realized the bumping and lifting were being done by a dolphin. She wasn't sure if it was one of the same ones she had seen several days ago; but, for some reason, her intuition told her that it was.

The dolphin stayed close by her side until the water was shallow enough for her to be able to stand. She tentatively reached out her hand. The dolphin began to chatter but it made no attempt to leave her. She gently and carefully touched its nose, then slowly stroked its head as she began to talk to it, telling it how grateful she was that it had saved her life. The dolphin stopped its chattering while she was speaking, and when she stopped, it began its chattering again--almost as if it knew what she was saying--as if they were carrying on a conversation. Again, she had that feeling that she was experiencing something truly magical.

Finally, the dolphin swam to deeper water, gave a mighty thrust, arced through the air, then dove underneath the surface. In fascination, she continued to watch the dorsal fin swim rapidly away, until she could no longer see it. She reluctantly turned, walked to her car, dried herself and drove home. Again, she didn't tell Richard about her trip to the island, or about the dolphins--and especially--not about being caught in a riptide.

The next day she could hardly wait to get to the island, to see if she would see her dolphin friends. As soon as she arrived, she hurriedly swam out to the third sandbar and, after a few minutes, she saw a dorsal fin. One dolphin surfaced, then a second, then a third: she saw the calf was also along. They swam around her and chattered, and as she began to swim, they swam along with her. One of the adults gently bumped her several times, as if wanting to play. Impulsively, she reached out and took hold of its fin. As the dolphin began to swim faster, she hung on tight, letting it pull her rapidly through the water. It was exhilarating!

When the dolphin finally stopped, it nuzzled its head affectionately against her side. Soon the other two were beside her and they began to chatter. She took hold of the other adult's fin, and, again, she was rapidly pulled through the water. It was better then jet skiing. The dolphins eventually pulled her into more shallow water and stopped, and she reluctantly let go of the fin. They briefly chattered at her, then abruptly turned and swam away. She walked through the shallow water and onto the beach. What an enchanting experience!

The following day, after she had swum out to the third sandbar she was soon joined by the dolphin family (that was the way she now thought of them); only this time they had additional dolphins along. She counted nine of them. She was enthralled as they swam around her, chattering. Then one of them bumped against her side and she took hold of the dorsal fin--just before it took off. Once again, she was taken on a magical, rapid swim. Woman and dolphin: swimming together as if they had become one. They swam for hours--until Janna was physically exhausted, although mentally exhilarated.

She realized she and the dolphins had been swimming under water a good part of the time, and it seemed she was now able to hold her breath for a much longer period than she had been able to in her pool. But then she brushed away the thought as probably being only wishful thinking.

The next day was Friday and she hurried to the island as soon as she could; she had become obsessed with spending as much time there as possible. As soon as she reached the third sandbar the dolphins appeared. She swam with them for hours and when she realized it was time for her to go home, she left with great reluctance.

That evening at dinner Richard began to talk about her swimming, only what he was really saying--Janna sadly realized--was that he was glad she had ceased being so preoccupied with it. Richard was extremely controlling of her. During most of their married life, in order to keep peace, she had usually deferred to his wishes and wants by putting hers second; it had just always seemed easier that way. Being an Aquarian, she found any type of discord in her personal life to be extremely upsetting. Since she hadn't mentioned her swimming lately, he mistakenly thought she had given it up.

She felt a flash of anger. She shouldn't have to hide something she loved so much. It wasn't fair. Then she felt guilty for the deception, which in turn made her angry again at him for causing her to feel guilty. After all, it was only swimming. It wasn't like she was having an affair. But this thought caused her to feel even deeper guilt because, to her, the sea was every bit as seductive as any lover could ever be.

The weekend seemed to drag by--endlessly. On Saturday, she did some house cleaning, and in the evening she and Richard attended a business dinner given by the company he worked for.

On Sunday she went for a swim in her pool. She asked Richard to join her, but he was trying to catch up on some work he had brought home from the office. Since she was curious about the length of time she was now able to hold her breath during underwater swimming, she decided to wear her diving watch. She swam a couple of laps on the surface, then took several deep breaths and dove under the water, keeping a close eye on her watch as she swam. After two minutes had elapsed she was just beginning to feel as if her air was running out. She continue to swim, watching the time, and felt no urgency to take a breath until she had neared two-and-a-half minutes. She could hardly believe it. As far as she had been able to research, the underwater record was two minutes and forty seconds.

When Monday morning finally arrived, she awoke with a tingling excitement of anticipation in her stomach. After hurriedly completing a minimum of her routine chores, she headed to the island. Upon arrival she quickly swam out to the third sandbar. When no dolphins appeared, she was filled with an almost overwhelming sense of disappointment. She continued to swim, still able to enjoy the senuous feeling of her body gracefully moving through the water, but she had gotten so used to the magic of swimming with the dolphins that, after such a wondrous experience, she didn't think swimming by herself would ever be quite the same again.

She rolled over, closed her eyes, and began to float on her back, resting in the water. Suddenly she was startled by a familiar nudge against her buttocks. She opened her eyes, saw a dolphin, then another, and soon was surrounded by them. Without hesitation she grabbed hold of the nearest fin. The dolphin immediately took off, pulling her through the water with the others following, and she felt as if she had returned home from a long journey.

For the rest of the week she went to the island every day. And each day she was promptly greeted by the dolphins as soon as she reached the third sandbar, where they would joyfully set forth on their communal swim. She dreaded the weekend, and when it arrived she busied herself by thoroughly cleaning everything in her house. She did yard work with a vengeance: pulling weeds, and trimming shrubbery which had grown ragged and uneven during the past several weeks of neglect.

Finally, Monday arrived, and as soon as she could gather up the necessary items she needed to take, she hurried to the island. As usual, she feared that this time the dolphins wouldn't be there. But once again, shortly after she reached the third sandbar, they appeared. And, once again, she enjoyed a magical afternoon of swimming and playing with the dolphins. They chattered at her and she seemed to sense what they were trying to say. When she spoke to them, she had a strong feeling that they were able to sense what she was saying. It was if they were able to communicate with one another, but each in their own separate language.

Every day that week she went to the island and swam with the dolphins. By now they were swimming a great distance past the third sandbar: much farther than she ever would have dared to venture on her own. But she felt perfectly safe, because when they were a long way from shore the dolphins were always able to know when she was becoming tired, and would lift her above the surface-- buoying her until she rested. Then they would allow her to soar off with them again, taking turns escorting her--a fin clasped firmly in her hand.

She was able to tell them apart now; she still wasn't sure which were male and which were female, but was able to distinguish their small individualized characteristics.

At the end of the week she became depressed. She dreaded weekends: each had become more difficult to endure. Friday night, shortly after dinner, Richard went to play softball with some of his friends from work. They were trying to get a league team together. She was tempted to go to the island for a night swim, but lost her nerve. She was afraid she wouldn't have enough time before Richard returned home, and she would never hear the end of it if he thought she had gone there swimming at night by herself.

On Saturday, after swimming in her pool, when she began to shave her legs in the shower she noticed there was no stubble. She usually shaved her underarms and legs every day because she liked for her skin to feel smooth--and there was always stubble. But this time, strangely, she could find no signs of any. Furthermore, when she looked at her arms, the soft downy hair which had always been present, was now gone. Her arms were completely smooth! She looked closely at her pubic hair, and to her astonishment, it, too, had thinned dramatically!

When she finished her shower, she peered intently at her eyelashes and eyebrows in the mirror, but they appeared to be the same as they always had. Also, the hair on her head appeared to be unchanged. However, when she began to comb her wet hair, she felt her comb skip lightly over the top of her head--as if it had gone over a small ridge of some type. She hadn't experienced any pain, just an unusual sensation.

She gingerly touched the top of her head with her fingertips and felt a strange, raised circle. She had never noticed anything like it before. She got out her hand mirror and tried to see the top of her head. As near as she could tell, it looked like a slightly swollen circle with a small indentation in the center, similar to an inverted nipple. She hoped she wasn't getting ringworm or some kind of scalp disease.

When Monday finally arrived, she hurried to the island. Each Monday she still had a nagging feeling of uneasiness that the dolphins wouldn't be there. But they were there-- waiting for her as always--just past the third sandbar. She spent a delightful afternoon frolicking and swimming, hating it when the time came for her to go home, wishing she could just remain with the dolphins--indefinitely. She was developing such a closeness with them: a binding kinship. She had always been somewhat introverted, and she realized she had come to feel more comfortable being with the dolphins than she did being with people. It was almost as if they had become her family, and the sea her home.

That evening after her shower, when she dried between her toes she noticed a thickening of the skin--almost as if her toes were beginning to grow together. Maybe she should se a dermatologist. The indentation was still on the top of her head and appeared to be getting deeper. It wasn't painful or sensitive in any way, and her hair covered it so it wasn't noticeable, but it bothered her because she knew it shouldn't be there. And because of that, along with the disappearance of her body hair--and now the skin deposits between her toes--she became alarmed that she was developing some terrible and rare dermatological malady.

Early the next morning she called her dermatologist's office, but the earliest appointment she was able to get was in three weeks. "Well," she hoped, "maybe by then, whatever it was it would be gone." She almost decided not to go to the island, but seemed unable to keep herself from going. Swimming with the dolphins had become the most important thing in her life, and there wasn't anything she could do to change that.

The rest of the week passed in her regular routine of spending her days on the island and dreading the weekend. Richard was now on a softball league, and was often not at home. He asked her to come along with him to some of his games, which she did--and enjoyed. But in the back of her mind now, when she wasn't swimming with her beloved dolphins, was the nagging worry that there was something terribly wrong with her.

She frequently found herself fingering the indentation on her head. Richard had observed her doing it so many times that he had questioned her about it. And she had guiltily lied, telling him that she had bumped it when she had raised up suddenly and hit it on the bottom edge of one of the kitchen cabinet doors which she had forgotten to close. Luckily, he had accepted her explanation.

She wasn't sure why she hadn't told him the truth. She supposed in some deep inner part of herself lay the tormented, secret belief that her medical maladies had something to do with the dolphins. But intellectually, she told herself that that was absurd.

The weekend passed slowly. She swam in her pool, but it just wasn't the same; she missed her dolphins. When she swam with them she felt almost as if she was one of them, and they seemed to accept her as such.

She also had added another worry. Recently her skin had begun to feel painfully dry and leathery whenever she was out of the water. When her skin was wet, it felt sleek and smooth. But when she wasn't in the water, she had to continually apply lotion to her skin to feel even a little bit comfortable. She would be glad when she could see her dermatologist; yet on the other hand, dreaded the diagnosis. She was now convinced that there was something terribly wrong with her.

Finally it was Monday again. This time, she didn't even bother with any household chores. As soon as Richard left for work she put on her bikini, made some tuna fish sandwiches (she seemed to have developed a recent craving for fish), grabbed a thermos of water and a towel, then headed for the island. She was filled with a consuming need to be with her dolphins.

She quickly swam to the third sandbar and a few minutes later she saw the first dorsal fin. A graceful dolphin arced through the air, then back into the water before surfacing just a few feet away from her. It began the usual spate of chatter and she felt as if it was greeting her and telling her that she had been missed. She told it that she had missed it and was glad to be back, while experiencing a certainty that it understood what she was saying. Soon they were surrounded by the other dolphins, and she noticed that the little calf had grown considerably since she had removed the plastic rings.

All of the dolphins, except the one who had greeted her, rapidly took off swimming. The one who had greeted her seemed to be waiting for her, so she grasped its fin, and then it followed rapidly after the others. They swam under water for several minutes.

As they surfaced for air, she had a strange sensation on the top of her head: as if she had blown air out of it. But that's impossible, she thought, as she put her hand on top of her head. With a shock, she realized that the indentation she had been worrying about was apparently some type of blow hole, similar to that of the dolphins. But that was ridiculous! It couldn't be!

For a few seconds, she experienced a panicky, horrified fear, and prayed that she was asleep--in the midst some surrealistic nightmare. The dolphin bumped playfully against her side but she was too upset to play. "I don't feel well. I have to go home," she stammered as she began swimming towards the shore, the dolphin accompanying her until she reached water too shallow to swim in. She ran hurriedly across the beach to her car.

As soon as she arrived home she took a shower and, before drying her hair, once again examined the indentation on the top of her head in the mirror. It appeared to be a well-formed, round indentation, slightly larger than it had been before, but still not tender or sore. Just there! And her skin felt extremely uncomfortable, dry and itchy, until she smeared lotion all over her body.

She felt sick with fear, and began to cry as she put on a pair of panties and a long T-shirt. Richard had left a note saying that he was at one of his softball games, inviting her to meet him there. But she didn't feel like she was up to seeing anyone right now.

She lay down on her bed and curled into a ball--hugging herself--then began to cry. Even though she had a desperate need to tell someone of her fear, she felt she had no one in whom she could confide. Especially not Richard! She knew he would find a way to blame her for her malady, being certain that in some way it was her fault. That she had done something to have caused it (which she probably had, she thought guiltily). But that was impossible. She couldn't have caused this to happen to herself. She continued to cry until she fell asleep.

She dreamed she was a dolphin, spending her days swimming and playing in joyful abandon with other dolphins: other dolphins who never judged her or criticized her but who accepted her for herself; who loved her for herself. And she had the freedom of the sea. The endless, beautiful sea. If she swam forever, she would never be able to find an end to the sea. She could feel the waves caressing her: the soothing water like cool wet silk against her irritated skin.

Abruptly she woke up. Her skin was dry and itching again, making her miserable! It was nighttime and Richard still wasn't home. A feeling of overwhelming loneliness washed over her as she thought about her dream, while fingering the indentation on her head--which she was now convinced to be a blow hole.

She thought of the peaceful contentedness and jubilation she always experienced when she was swimming with the dolphins--which was the only time she was happy now. She thought about how pleasant the water felt against her body; about how graceful and beautiful and serene she felt when she was in the water; and--most of all--about how beloved she felt when she was with her dolphins. She listened, and thought she could hear their distinctive chatter...calling to her.

Suddenly, she knew what she had to do. Actually, she really had no other choice. She yanked off her panties and shirt, then quickly pulled on her bikini and grabbed her car keys. She didn't bother with a towel--she wouldn't need one. This was the last time she would be going to the island. This time she wasn't coming back.

...to her, the sea was every bit as seductive as any lover could ever be.

THE EVE OF THE BEGINNING (CONTINUED)

I was touched by the beauty of the relationships between the two women and the animals. I fondly remembered my boyhood dog, a female Irish Setter I had named Flame because of her beautiful color. We were best buddies! She would meet me at the door when I came home from school; she would sit at my feet during meals (while I slipped bits of food to her under the table--unnoticed); and she would sleep with me. That dog adored me, and I her. She had been fourteen-years-old, often in pain from arthritis, hard of hearing, and probably nearly blind--but still loving--when she had died peacefully in her sleep. I cried for days afterwards but had never gotten another dog, although I had often thought about it. Or maybe a cat. A cat would be more practical as a pet, since I was gone from home most of the time. Cats didn't have to be taken outside to go to the bathroom, or for exercise.

Once more I felt the wetness in my eyes. Schere must have seen it too, for she took my face in her hands again, only this time she kissed my eyes. Then she knelt beside me and held me, my face pressed tenderly against her breasts as she said softly: "It's good to cry, Michael. Most women have the wisdom to realize this. In fact, it has been written that God counts the tears of women. Men should allow themselves to cry when they feel the need."

I felt the tears come readily--unable to stop them--and felt her kissing them away as they slid down my face. Oddly, I wasn't embarrassed. It was as if a secret door hidden deep within my heart, which I hadn't even been aware existed, had been opened--allowing a torrent of sadness welled inside of me to burst forth. After several minutes my tears began to subside.

She continued to hold me...caressing my neck...my shoulders; I could feel the softness of her hair brushing delicately against my skin. I was beginning to recognize the difference between sensuousness and sensuality. (She was an excellent teacher.) She kissed my eyes again, then gently traced the outline of my lips with her finger tip.

"Michael, next I will tell you of the stories of Mitty and of Charlene: of love unfulfilled."

She took my face in her hands and I looked into her eyes, smiling through the last vestige of my tears, as I anticipated the next stories in her eyes.

THE SECRET LIFE OF MITTY WALTERS

A hot dry breeze blew across her face causing her to stir. Her limbs felt languid. She didn't want to open her eyes yet; the sheik would return to her soon. He had been so passionate, yet tender, through the long blissful hours they had spent together during the night. She turned her head and lifted her damp hair off the back of her neck, then snuggled deeper into the soft sheets.

As she heard the delicate tinkling of a water fountain in the distance, her pulse began to quicken, and a feeling of warmth enveloped her which had nothing to do with the arid heat of the room. She didn't know how long she would stay here. He had told her that she was by far the most beautiful, fascinating woman he had ever seen, and that he was captivated by her lovely eyes.

"Mitty, are you awake?" he asked softly.

"Yes, my dashing ravisher," she murmured.

"Mitty, wake up. It's nearly seven fifteen; the kids will be up any minute and I have to leave soon.

She reluctantly opened her eyes just as her husband Larry finished tying his necktie.

"Don't forget, I'll be several hours late tonight," he said.

Mitty got out of bed, put on her faded blue cotton robe and went into the kitchen. She plugged in the coffee pot, put some bread into the toaster, and had just finished putting a pitcher of orange juice on the table when her husband walked in with the morning newspaper, reading the front page headlines as he sat down.

"Well, I see the price of gasoline is going up again. I guess we'll just have to buy you a bicycle to get around on," he said jokingly.

"I suppose so," she said absently, while buttering the toast.

As she set two cups of coffee on the table, he looked at her curiously and said, "Are you all right? You look a little flushed."

"Yes, I'm fine, just not awake yet; you know how I am in the morning, especially when the weather's so hot."

He was back to reading the paper before she had even finished answering his question.

Thirty minutes later she stepped out of the shower, and as she wrapped the towel around her torso she looked at her reflection in the full-length mirror...

"Ladies and gentlemen, now the moment you have been waiting for! Ms. Constellation of 1995: Mitty Walters."

She smiled radiantly and let her eyes barely mist with tears as she stepped up to the microphone. In a husky, sensuous voice she said, "I've dreamed of this moment many times, but never thought it would come true."

She began her walk along the runway amid cheers and wild whistles while a tenor voice began singing, "The Most Beautiful Girl in the World."

As she passed the judges' section she heard one of them say, "By far the loveliest winner we've had since the pageant began seven years ago."

She lifted her chin high and felt as if she were floating. She WAS the most beautiful girl in the world!

As she stood at the end of the runway, one of the most talented, successful Hollywood movie producers stood up and said, "Ms. Walters, don't sign any contracts until you've had a chance to hear my offer. I'll give you twice as much as any other studio, and a lifetime contract."

She blew him a kiss. Then the music changed to a rock version of "Counting to Ten," accompanied by a loud knocking sound.

"Mommy! Mommy! Mikey got peanut butter all over the couch!"

Mitty hurriedly hung up the towel and put the faded robe back on. When she opened the bathroom door her six-year-old daughter, Eryne, grabbed her hand and exclaimed,

"Mommy, Mikey fixed himself a peanut butter and jelly sandwich and was sitting on the couch eating it while we were watching TV and a man on *Sesame Street* was carrying a bunch of cakes and fell down the steps and spilled them all and Mikey started jumping up and down on the couch with his sandwich and fell on it and got peanut butter and jelly all over everything!"

It still amazed Mitty that her daughter could talk so long without stopping for a breath, especially when she was tattling on her four-year-old brother. She hurried into the family room to find Mikey sitting calmly, staring at the television in angelic innocence.

"Did you drop your peanut butter sandwich?"

"Mommy, I ate my samwich and it's all down there now," he said, rubbing his tummy.

She looked questioningly at Eryne who promptly said, "It's under him; he's trying to hide it from you."

Mitty lifted Mikey up, and sure enough there was a gob of smashed bread, peanut butter, and grape jelly smeared not only all over the couch, but also on Mikey's round little bottom. She couldn't even spank him without getting it all over herself too.

"Go to your room and take those pajamas off!"

Mikey began to whine. "Don't spank me! Don't spank me!" as he backed out of the room while Eryne smugly watched.

"Mikey's really going to get it, isn't he Mommy?"

"Yes, Eryne, Mickey's really going to get it," she sighed.

By two o'clock she had finally gotten the house straightened, the beds made, herself dressed, the children fed their lunch and in their rooms for some quiet time; plus, she had gotten the peanut butter and jelly washed out of the couch which had taken more than an hour.

She sat down in a big comfortable chair to relax for a minute and thought: "I'm twenty-nine-years-old, still reasonably attractive, and spent my morning in a faded robe scrubbing out peanut butter and jelly. Sometimes I think I'm going crazy. And it's still only June. School won't start again for two more months."

She picked up a week-old magazine she hadn't had a chance to read yet. She opened it to a bright, double-page advertisement depicting an immaculately groomed, smartly-dressed, youngish woman who was asking the reader if she would like to earn big money working in her own decorating business...

"Yes, Ms. Walters, your call to London is ready now."

Mitty picked up the phone. "I want the Etruscan tapestry and the ebony tables here by Monday, and not a day later!"

"Yes, Ms. Walters. Please be assured that you will receive them before then. If we lost your business our importing firm would go bankrupt."

As she put down the phone, her number one assistant rushed in.

"Ms. Walters, do you think the peach and ivory damask draperies will be ready this afternoon? Mr. Triumph plans to entertain tomorrow night and wants them hung with your personal supervision; after all, you are the most sought-after interior designer in the world."

Mitty stood up. "Yes, I'll see to it personally. Tell Mr. Triumph I'll be available tomorrow morning at ten o'clock. Today, I have to meet with the president aboard his plane for lunch; he wants me to redecorate his private living quarters at the White House."

She was contemplating various furniture arrangements when the phone began to ring. After it had rung six times she started, and picked it up.

"Hello?"

"Mitty, where were you? It took you so long to answer the phone," her husband said.

"I was outside," she lied.

"Well, I just wanted to tell you I'll be even later than I thought tonight, so don't wait dinner for me; I'll eat a sandwich or something and probably won't be home until after you're asleep. The district manager is coming in tomorrow and we want everything to be perfect."

"OK, Larry, thanks for letting me know. Goodbye." It seemed Larry was hardly ever home anymore.

The washing machine had just gone into the spin cycle when she put down the phone. I guess I'll wait for it to stop so I can put the clothes in the dryer, she thought, as she sat down on the kitchen stool.

Vroom, Vroom, Vroom; the steady, pulsating sound was comforting...

"All systems go: three--two--one! We have lift off!"

Her heart was beating rapidly as the rocket lifted off the launch pad, heading for the moon. She could imagine the headlines. "FIRST MOON WALK BY FEMALE ASTRONAUT!" She was very lucky to have been chosen for the mission. NASA wasn't sure how well a mission would work with two men and one woman on the moon for a week, but decided that with all the pressure from various women's and other equal rights groups that they would send her. Of course, she was also the most highly qualified of the astronauts for this particular mission. She was the world's most brilliant geologist. She relaxed as she heard the voice from mission control advise them that they were progressing on schedule.

Burt, the mission commander smiled at her and asked, "Feeling okay?"

"Just fine; in fact, exuberant!" she answered.

Kit, the other crew member looked at her and winked. "Just think, Dr. Walters, how are you going to fight off two virile men for week? You're one of the most beautiful women I've ever seen, and we're going to be way up there on the moon with the nearest other human beings thousands of miles away."

She smiled to herself and wondered what NASA would say if they could have heard this conversation. She knew the mission would be highly successful. Not only was she brilliant and beautiful, but she also had an abounding energy. She closed her eyes. Vroom, Vroom, Vroom...then silence.

The engines have quit! She thought in wild panic. She opened her eyes and stared at the quiet washing machine, realizing that the clothes were ready to be put into the dryer.

As she poured a glass of soda, she giggled and said to herself; "I must be really losing it."

Then the phone rang again. This time it was her friend, Sue.

"Mitty, how about going to a movie with me tonight?"

Sue was divorced, and when she felt like going out at night and didn't have plans with a man, she usually called Mitty. Mitty seldom went with her on those occasions, but from the way she had been feeling the past few days, she thought it might do her some good to get out.

"I'd love to go, Sue. About eight? I have to get a sitter. And I like to get the kids fed and ready for bed before leaving them with a sitter."

"Eight'll be fine; see you then."

* * * * * * * * *

Mitty had on her new flowered sundress that showed off her slender body. She had washed her hair after Sue had called and it was sleek and silky. She felt almost beautiful. The sitter was watching television with the children, who were ready for bed. She realized how much she was looking forward to tonight when the doorbell rang. Sue was here.

"Goodbye, Mrs. Chadwick. I should be home early," she called gaily as she went out the door.

After the movie, when she and Sue had reached their car in the parking lot, Sue looked at her watch. "Gee, it's so early yet. I don't feel like going home; how about a drink at that new club that just opened?" Mitty didn't particularly want to go home yet either, so she readily agreed.

As they stepped inside they could see the club was crowded; however, the waitress managed to squeeze them in at a small table in the back. The lights were muted pastels with a haze of smoke spiraling around them which made Mitty feel as if she were in a dream. After they had ordered their drinks, she giggled and said, "I feel like a different person. This night out has really done me some good. You wouldn't believe what an awful rut I was getting into."

"Oh, yes I would. I've been there; remember? But I was able to get out of mine before it swallowed me completely."

Mitty didn't think Sue really had "been there," because she had no children and had always done pretty much as she pleased while she had been married. Sue's husband, rather than Sue, was the one who had wanted the divorce. But Mitty didn't argue the point. She just smiled and said, "Yes, you did; didn't you?"

The music was nice: mellow blues. Mitty sipped her red wine and began to relax as the effects of the alcohol slowly seeped through her body creating a heady warmth. A bland looking man asked Sue to dance. Mitty didn't mind sitting alone. From the combination of the music and the wine, she was beginning to feel dreamy and uninhibited...

The smoky haze spiraling around the pastel lights seemed to grow thicker, and the music softer. When she took another sip of her wine, she saw the man standing at the bar-- watching her.

He must be her connection, but she must be very careful not to make a mistake; this was a very important assignment for the I.I.B. She was one of their top agents. In fact, she was already practically a legend; nearly in a class with Mata Hari. The man she was supposed to contact was known to her only by reputation. He was supposed to be extremely handsome and a master of the "bedroom arts," which no doubt contributed to his success in getting vital, secret information. The microdot, which contained names of the top leaders of a major Middle Eastern terrorist organization, was safely glued to her inner left thigh.

She looked seductively at the man over the rim of her glass. He returned her look, and their eyes locked for a longer time than a mere casual glance. He raised his eyebrows as if in a pleasurable appraisal of what he saw. She dropped her lashes, then coyly looked again briefly over her glass before looking down into her wine. Yes; he must be the one. He was certainly handsome enough. He had a definite charisma about him; a rugged, yet tender quality. In fact, he was one of the most appealing men she had ever seen.

A shadow fell across the table. She looked up and there he was. He smiled in a self-assured way and said, "Pardon me, but I couldn't help noticing you from across the room. Do you mind if I join you?"

He had the slight trace of an accent, but she wasn't sure what kind. She looked into his eyes and smiled demurely as she said, "If you wish."

He sat down and offered her a cigarette which she declined. He lit one for himself and as he exhaled the smoke she noticed it had an aromatic smell, almost like a rich, exotic pipe tobacco. She realized it must be one of the foreign blends. It had to be him. That was the clincher; her connection had his cigarettes specially blended from the finest Turkish tobaccos.

"Let's find a quieter place where we can be alone," he said softly. He took her hand and she felt as if she had been caressed. He stood and gently pulled her to her feet, then carefully guided her out through the pastel haze which, by now, had become a thick fog.

She looked up into his eyes and said, "You know you have to find what you want without my help, so I can be sure that you're the right one."

He looked at her in a puzzled way, then smiled in amusement. "Ah! A lady with a sense of humor; what a perfect touch."

She smiled back at him as he guided her to a beautifully restored Jaguar XKE roadster. "Yes," she thought, "that's the kind of car he would drive." The breeze felt good blowing through her hair as they drove through the warm night with the top down. The I.I.B. would be proud of her. She would certainly make this assignment a success. But then, she had never yet let them down.

Soon they pulled into the parking lot of a luxurious high-rise apartment building on Ocean Drive. As they rode up in the elevator, he put his arm protectively around her waist.

His apartment was decorated in impeccably good taste, with several large leather sofas and arm chairs, and European antiques. He poured her a glass of red wine while she sat on one of the oversized sofas. He turned on his CD player; the music was exotic--like East Indian music--with flutes and sitars. She found it exciting and erotic. He sat down next to her and put his hand on her left knee.

She wondered how long he would wait to take the microdot. Naturally, he wanted to be sure he had the right contact, too. Well, she certainly wasn't in any hurry. He was so attractive, she hoped he would take his time. After all, she had understood when she had signed on with the I.I.B. that it would be part of her job as an agent to be a seductress; to make love with different men if it proved necessary to serve the purpose of duty to her country.

He softly brushed her ear with his lips as he put his arms around her and skillfully pulled down the zipper on her dress. With his upper body he gently pushed her down; at the same time he lifted her legs up onto the sofa. As he slid her dress off, she could tell he was also highly proficient at his job. He kissed her throat and whispered, "My little treasure; you are truly a serendipity." Then his mouth covered hers and she felt as if she were drifting in space...

Abruptly, she stiffened, waiting for the telephone to ring, or for the alarm clock to go off, but nothing happened. He began to caress her all over her body, while murmuring romantic endearments.

"Why doesn't Eryne or Mikey or Larry come in and stop this," she thought frantically? "It's never gotten to this point before. It's always been interrupted." But he kept on kissing her: her eyes, her neck, her shoulders. She felt a moment of panic as she thought: "Eryne, Mikey, Larry! Where are you? Save me!"

He continued to caress her and kiss her, and when she felt the weight of his body fully upon her, she suddenly realized that this was real; her children or her husband couldn't stop what was happening to her. This wasn't a fantasy. This was reality: a reality which now could not end until the fulfillment was reached, and her brief moment of panic was replaced by a consuming passion.

She chuckled softly. He stopped kissing her and looked at her quizzically. She looked back, deeply into his eyes, and smiled, "If you're going to make love to me, at least tell me what your name is. Or shall I just make one up for you?"

JUST FOR THE MOMENT

When we met
You said it was just for the moment,
But I thought you would forget
That it was just for the moment.

You said you would tell me no lies,
That it was just for the moment,
When I looked into your eyes
And agreed, that it was just for the moment.

You said, together we would have fun,
But that it was just for the moment,
Though for me the agony had begun,
Because it was just for the moment.

Forever alone, now, I guess I'll be,
Because it was just for the moment.
Unfortunately, I had fallen in love, you see,
Even though I had said, that it was just for the moment.

As I lift my face upward--I feel such pain,
Because it was just for the moment.
I can't tell my tears from the rain;
I wanted forever . . . not just for the moment.

1-900-4-U-VENUS

"He's tied me to the bed and taken away my clothes! All I'm wearing are my black lace panties. I need someone to rescue me." She purred in a silky, sultry voice. "He said he was going to have his way with me when he comes back," she continued.

"Tell me exactly what he's going to do to you," the man said, breathing heavily.

She paused briefly to pick up a large Styrofoam cup containing a milk shake, and took a sip through the straw. Then, in the same sultry voice, she began to tell the man on the other end of the phone line of explicitly erotic acts. She glanced at the clock. He had been on the line for more than ten minutes now, and she felt pleased with herself.

After the call ended, she opened a package of Twinkies she had stashed inside the drawer in her small desk, and quickly stuffed half of one of them into her mouth, savoring the taste of the sweet gooey mixture of cake and creamy filling. After she had finished the second half, she went into the bathroom and washed the sticky crumbs from her mouth and fingers.

When she returned to her cubicle she saw that the phone light was blinking. the charges wouldn't begin until she was actually on the line. She picked up the combination earphone/speaker/headset, and positioned it on her head.

"Hello. This is Venus."

"Hi, Venus; this is Adonis. Tell me what you're wearing tonight?"

It was one of her regulars. She was amazed at how many horny, lonely men there were out there. "I've been waiting for your call, Adonis. Tonight I'm wearing a filmy white chiffon gown--that's so sheer, you can see my body through it. It's cut very low in the front, showing most of my ripe, ample breasts. The hem just barely covers the top of my smooth, slender thighs. And special, just for you--because I was dreaming about you and hoping that you'd call--I didn't put on any panties. Oooh! And when the chiffon brushes softly against the tops of my inner thighs, I imagine that it's your fingers there-caressing me." As she talked, her voice became softer and huskier.

"Oh, Venus! Oh, Venus!" Was all he managed to gasp.

She continued talking, telling him more things that she pictured him doing to her. After the call was completed, she signaled to her supervisor that it was time for her thirty-minute supper break. She could hardly wait to eat. She felt like she was practically starving. She was also tired. It took a lot of energy to come up with the (in her opinion) positively brilliant, imaginative, and often kinky responses. Some-times she even astounded herself.

She put her hands against the top of the small desk and wearily pulled herself from the comfortable chair, then walked down the narrow hallway to the little kitchen area at the back. The main room was large, divided into ten, small partitioned cubicles, each containing a small desk, a telephone, a large, plush, comfortable chair, and most important (next to the phone), a clock. She had been work-ing here as an operator for more than two years. The com-pany's name was Fone Fantasy Friends.

Of course, her name wasn't really Venus: her real name was Charlene. But Venus was the name she used with her clients. She opened the small refrigerator, took out the large Ruben sandwich in a cardboard container, and put it into the microwave to heat. As it was heating she pulled out a pint container of German potato salad. When the sandwich had heated sufficiently, so that the thick slices of imported baby Swiss cheese had melted into the multiple layers of ultra thin sliced pastrami, she carried it to the small table, along with the potato salad and a plastic fork.

She took a large bite of the sandwich. Ah! It was perfect. She hungrily devoured the food, alternating bites of sand-wich with forkfuls of potato salad, and washed it all down with a can of diet cola. She felt a lot better. Now she would be able to maintain the energy it took to finish out the second half of her eight-hour shift as the number one requested "fone friend."

She returned to her cubicle, sat down, and for desert ate a Snicker's candy bar and the other Twinkie before signaling to her supervisor that she was ready for another call.

It was 2:30 A.M. She worked the 10:00 P.M. to 6:00 A.M. shift and liked working nights. She wasn't a very social person, except when she was on the phone with a client. Suffering from low self-esteem, she was extremely shy around other people. So by working nights and sleeping days she seldom had to be around strangers.

After attending college for two years, majoring in library science, she had been so shy and insecure she couldn't face the thought of continuing the other two years to obtain her bachelor's degree. She had chosen library science as her major, because, for as long as she could remember, she had been in love with books and stories. Especially fantasy. And it was now mostly due to her vast reading that she was so successful in her present career. At times, she was still amazed that she was actually a phone-sex operator.

Shortly after college she had taken a job at the public library, but had never really felt comfortable working there. She had liked working back in the stacks--she liked being with the books--it was the people who bothered her, and it had steadily become increasingly more difficult for her to have to work at the front desk. She always felt like people were talking about her and making fun of her behind her back.

Quite by accident, she had run across the advertisement for her present job in a local magazine. However, the ad had merely described the position as an "imaginative telephone operator in a unique setting." At the time she had had no idea that the position was for a phone sex operator. (If she would have had the smallest inkling, she never would have even considered applying for it.) The "imaginative" part was what had attracted her attention.

She had always been blessed (or cursed) with an extremely active imagination. Since childhood, she had constructed minor fantasies about nearly everything in her life. She had even once briefly tried her hand at writing fiction, but when she had tried to put all of those wondrous, imaginative thoughts (which had always seemed to be overflowing from her mind) down on paper, she had frozen--the thoughts all suddenly disappeared. Vanished, like magic! Poof! Gone!

She hadn't thought she would really have a chance at getting the job (even not knowing what it was), but had become so miserable working at the library that she was near desperation. She had thought that if she was working as a telephone operator, she wouldn't have to be around strange people. Not face to face. Oddly, she had never had any problem talking to people on the telephone. It was just when they could see her that she would become insecure, confused, and panicky.

It had taken just about every ounce of courage she had been able to summon to force herself to go for the interview. The woman who had interviewed her had been very nice, but when Charlene had found out exactly what kind of operator they were hiring, she was even more convinced that she wouldn't be hired. However, when she had done the phone test with the interviewer posing as a client, Charlene's imagination had come alive. The interviewer had been very impressed and, as if she could read Charlene's thoughts, had told her: "Honey, all we care about is whether you can deliver for the clients. If you can convince them that you're beautiful and sexy, then that's all that counts."

Charlene had been hired on the spot. That was probably another reason she liked the job so much. Not only did she not have to face her clients, but when she described herself to them she became confident and felt sexy. She became like her descriptions.

Each time a client called, she skillfully used open-ended questions until she was able to find out what type of look each of them preferred, and whether conventional erotica or kinky erotica turned them on. Then she played on those preferences and desires. She even kept a diary so that in case they called back again she could refer to it. That was probably the reason she had developed such a large number of regular clientele.

And the money was great! She was paid very well for what she did. She had even recently been toying with the idea of taking a few correspondence courses in management and maybe someday starting her own business. Why not! Then she would really make big money. It wouldn't take a great deal of money to set it up, and she had been regularly saving a large part of her salary. Her needs were simple. She lived in a small apartment and her clothes were plain. She mostly wore jeans, with a tank top in hot weather, and a sweater in cold weather.

Her phone light was flashing again. "Hello," she answered in her silky phone voice. "This is Venus."

"Hello, Venus; this is Superman."

She smiled. Superman was one of her regular clients...and one of her favorites. He was highly imaginative himself and always challenged and pushed her to new heights in her fantasies. She felt her heart rate quicken in anticipation of the game.

"Oh, Superman," she said in a low, husky voice, "I dream about having your strong arms around me and I start to melt. I wish you could take me away with you right now. I'd let you do anything to me that you wanted. My body is yours, to fulfill your wildest, craziest desires."

"Venus, I'd sweep you up into my arms as if you were a feather. And we'd fly to the far side of the sun--to planets of such beauty you could never imagine--where we'd be totally alone among the stars. I'd do things to your body, the likes of which no mortal man has ever done before." And he proceeded to tell her, in great erotic detail, exactly what he desired to do to her, with her responding in similar erotic fantasism.

That phone conversation lasted nearly thirty minutes. He only called once every two weeks (probably when he got paid, she thought). He must have a good job, because he invariably ran up quite a substantial bill when he called.

His calls always turned her on. (And his were the only calls that did.) She often found herself thinking about him, and wondering what he looked like. Maybe he was like her. But she couldn't picture him being like her. He was so forceful, so erotic, so confident...on the phone. But then...so was she on the phone.

It was now going on 3:30 A.M. This was the time of night when the calls reached a lull. She was thirsty again, so she quickly walked to the kitchen area and took out another diet soda which she took back to her desk and drank while eating a bag of cheese puffs. Her next call didn't come until after four o'clock. This time it was someone she was unfamiliar with. Someone who, she was reasonably sure, was calling for the first time. She could usually tell. They sounded timid and hesitant their first time, and were inhibited until she was able to draw them out. Until she was able to teach them to tap into their inner fantasies.

At 5:00 A.M. she ate another candy bar. She always seemed to get so hungry at work. This time it was a Hershey's with almonds. She only had two more calls before her shift ended. There wouldn't be many now until after 7:00 A.M., when the graveyard shift workers got home from their jobs.

When she saw Judy walk out of the elevator (the girl who took her place on the next shift), Charlene threw away her candy wrappers, empty cheese puff bag, empty milk shake cup and soda cans, picked up her purse and nodded at Judy as she handed her the headset.

Charlene wasn't particularly friendly with any of the other girls. She just did her job, then quickly left when her shift was over. She rode down in the elevator, and while walking to her car she decided to stop at Denny's to eat breakfast. That way she would be able to go to bed as soon as she got home, and sleep interrupted until midafternoon.

The hostess seated her in a small booth in the nonsmoking section and gave her a menu. By this time she was very hungry again, and the food smells wafting from the kitchen caused her stomach to begin to rumble. She ordered waffles, an omelet (with an order of salsa on the side), hash browns, bacon, and a large glass of orange juice. She never drank coffee in the morning; the caffeine kept her awake.

She pulled a paperback novel out of her purse (a steamy, Gothic romance) and began to read. Some of her best sources of inspiration came from these books. When the waitress brought her food, she continued to read as she ate.

At first, she thought she had imagined the voice: it was so familiar. She froze, a forkful of waffle--oozing maple syrup--halfway to her mouth. It wasn't possible, she thought, as the syrup dripped unnoticed onto her lap. She put the bite of waffle into her mouth, then laid the fork on her plate. She raised her open book higher so that it was in front of her face, pretending to read, her eyes mechanically moving across the words, which failed to register in her mind.

She heard the voice again. Yes, now she was certain. It was Superman! He was sitting in a booth behind her. She jammed the paperback inside her purse and hurriedly finished what was left of her breakfast--not tasting the food--just chewing and swallowing as fast as she could. Then she suddenly relaxed when she realized he couldn't possibly recognize her--as long as she didn't talk.

When the waitress came by and asked if everything was all right and if she needed anything else, she merely nodded her head and whispered, "Just bring my check, please."

The waitress gave her an odd look, and in a few minutes brought her check. Embarrassed by her behavior to the waitress, Charlene left an overly generous tip. She was dying to turn around and look at Superman, but didn't feel she could do so without drawing attention to herself. She quietly eased herself out of the booth and walked to the cashier. Only then did she feel it safe to turn around.

There were two men sitting across from each other in the booth behind the one where she had been sitting. One was balding and obese, while the other was tall, slender, and handsome. Both were well groomed and nicely dressed in business suits. They were talking in low tones and she was unable to hear them clearly from where she was. She couldn't tell which one was Superman. Was it the tall, handsome, slender man...or the obese, balding man?

After she paid the cashier, she pretended to look at the headlines of the morning newspapers in the display case while she tried to listen. But she still couldn't hear them. She still couldn't tell which was Superman.

She stood there for such a long time, reading the headlines over and over, that the counter personnel finally began to give her strange looks. So, in embarrassed disappointment, she reluctantly turned towards the door to leave. When she reached to open the door, she was momentarily startled as she saw her reflection in the plate glass door, and quickly averted her eyes. As she walked across the parking lot to her car, she continued to wonder in tormenting frustration, which of the two men was Superman: the one who was like her...or the other one?

THE EVE OF THE BEGINNING (CONTINUED)

I emerged from the stories with feelings of anticipation and amusement. I had experienced so many different emotions this night.

Schere was smiling. "You see, Michael, we all need love, and if we don't find it in one place, we will search for it in another. You have tried to find a substitute for love in your profession, but it hasn't worked. You must be honest with yourself. Please be aware that we are all human beings first, and male and female second; maybe what each of us feels deep inside our hearts isn't really all that different because of our genders. Maybe we're a lot more alike in what we want and need than what we've come to believe.

"Unfortunately, all too frequently our love is not returned, which is sad and deeply painful. But we must always continue on, no matter what. Sometimes, if we are very lucky, and keep our faith, we are given a second chance: we are blessed with a new and even more pervading love which, this time, is returned.

"Next, I will tell you of this deep pain of unrequited love. The story of Bob and the story of Leatrice. Look into my eyes Michael. Look and learn from the stories in my eyes!

VOYEUR

Startled, I quickly moved my head away when her eyes seemed to stare directly into mine--then laughed as I realized how absurd my fear was that she would actually be able to see me watching her. Her window was at least sixty feet away across a courtyard. Besides, I didn't have any lights turned on, and my telescope was behind the sheer curtain covering my glass patio door. No. There was no way she could see me, I thought, as I readjusted the focus.

I had first begun watching her while she was moving into her apartment, instantly becoming infatuated with her. And as I continued to watch her over the following weeks, I began to fall in love with her, even though we had never met. That's when I deliberately struck up a friendship with Mrs. Hardy who lived next door to her, and found out that her name was Pam.

Oh, I knew that the situation was probably hopeless, but I still couldn't help my feelings. I couldn't just turn them off although, God knew, I often wished I could.

She was tall and slender, with shoulder-length, dark auburn hair. She moved with the easy grace of the professional dancer which, in fact, I soon learned she was. Not one of those topless dancers in a bar, but an Isadora Duncan style, modern dancer, and she had recently opened her own studio.

I felt myself blushing when I thought about them--the topless dancers. I used to go to the topless bars; titty bars, as some of the other guys at work called them. I had always been painfully shy around women, but at the titty bars, in my deluded naivete, the women had made me feel special and almost worldly, especially when they had smiled at me and danced up close to me. Then when I eventually realized (with embarrassment) that they were only hustling for a tip, I had stopped going.

Pam was dancing now. Oh, how I wished I could hear the music she was dancing to, but even without being able to hear it I still found myself entranced. She danced with such passion that her body seemed to exude a radiance of ener-gy--which I often imagined I could feel flowing across the courtyard to me--filling my heart and body. Sometimes the feeling was so real--so intense--I would feel compelled to look at myself, convinced that I would see my body glowing.

But I knew that was ridiculous. I frequently fantasized about how I would meet her, and how she would fall in love with me at first sight. I knew that I had to choose the right time very carefully. Everything had to be perfect, and I felt certain I would know in my heart when that right time would be.

It was after Pam had lived there for two months, and after I had fallen hopelessly in love with her, that I saw him come to her apartment for the first time. He was tall and, I suppose, handsome: the kind of guy to whom women are attracted. That first time when he came to her apartment, she had been dressed up and they had gone out, probably to dinner, and I had restlessly watched and waited until she returned home at a very late hour. He hadn't stayed, but she had kissed him good night, and while I watched that kiss I had felt a rage of jealousy seethe through my body, the depth of which amazed me. I hadn't even realized I was capable of such an emotion.

Pam went out with him again two days later, and when they returned from their date she invited him into her apart-ment, causing me to suffer the agony of watching them making out her living room sofa. Even though I again seethed with jealousy, I became very excited while watch ing--which caused me to feel guilty later. However, I still didn't feel that the time was right yet for me to meet her.

I thought maybe she would get tired of him and stop seeing him, and actually convinced myself that she would. That's when the time would be right for me to meet her; I'd just have to wait for that time.

But he and Pam continued to date, while I patiently waited for her to get tired of him. Then after five months, to my horror, he spent the night with her. I became so upset I started shaking. The combination of the physical pain of my longing for her, with the deep hurt of her being with another man, was almost more than I could bear. As usual, I watched the two of them making out on her living room sofa, but when they reached the point where always before she had made him stop, that night he picked her up in his arms and carried her into her bedroom.

I was so shocked I became nauseated. But to my shame, as if in some masochistic compulsion, I refocused my telescope until I had a clear view of her bed, and continued to watch. I became so excited watching them make love, mingled with my nearly unbearable desire for her, that I came close to fainting.

I had never made love to a woman...not really. I was thirty-four-years-old, and thought of myself as still being an almost virgin. Oh, sure, I had gone through several fumbling, unsatisfactory sexual encounters with various girls, but being the shy man that I am, I had never known the fulfillment and joy of making love to a woman: a passionate woman who would return my ardour.

The experience of watching Pam making love both excited and upset me to such a great extent that I was unable to get out of bed the following morning, which, thankfully, was a Saturday. When I thought about it, I was filled with such an overwhelming sense of loss that it caused a tight, sinking feeling in my stomach; I became weak--and so dizzy when I tried to stand that I feared I would pass out.

By the middle of the afternoon, when my physical symptoms began to ease somewhat, I knew I had allowed myself to become involved in a serious situation: that I had become obsessed with my love for Pam. I now felt an extreme urgency to find out not only my rival's name, but as much as I could about him...and to finally meet her. I roused myself from my bed and looked through my telescope. However, Pam and her lover had apparently left her apartment earlier.

I trained my telescope on the apartment next door to Pam's and watched Mrs. Hardy pick up a basket filled with dirty laundry topped with a box of detergent, and head out of her apartment, most likely to the laundry room on the first floor.

I hastily stripped the sheets off my bed, grabbed some towels from my bathroom along with a box of detergent, threw them all into my laundry basket, then rushed down to the laundry room. I got there just as Mrs. Hardy was adding detergent to two of the washing machines.

I had continued to cultivate the friendship with Mrs. Hardy so I would have access to information whenever I needed it, which I did now--desperately! I struck up a conversation with her, and casually worked my way around to Pam. I hadn't tried to find out the guy's name earlier; I hadn't wanted to seem too nosey, possibly making Mrs. Hardy suspicious. But, as luck would have it, Mrs. Hardy was somewhat of a busybody, and was only too happy to share her information. She had no idea that I even knew Pam (which, in reality, I didn't). I knew her only vicariously-- through my telescope...and in my dreams.

Mrs. Hardy told me that the guy Pam had been dating was an intern at the medical center and that his name was Dash Justin. Dash! That's just great! I might have known the guy would have a name like Dash! Mrs. Hardy even proudly volunteered the information that she had good reason to believe Dash had spent the past night with Pam, shaking her head in disapproval, while I once again felt that sick, woozy feeling at hearing her words, making it necessary for me to have to lean against the washing machine for support.

I felt sweat breaking out my forehead, and began to take slow, even breaths. Mrs. Hardy noticed my discomfort and abruptly stopped her monologue. "Are you all right?" She asked with concern.

"Yes," I answered weakly. "I was sick all night--with a flu bug I guess. That's why I'm washing my sheets. I was running a fever and perspired all night. I thought the worst had passed, but I guess it hasn't."

"You poor dear," she cooed. "Why don't you come home with me and I'll make you a nice hot bowl of chicken soup while we wait until it's time to put our laundry into the dryers?"

I raised my head, the woozy feeling having passed. I thought I would be all right if only she wouldn't mention Pam's romantic liaison. "Yes, that would be nice. Thank you." I finished putting my dirty laundry into the washer, added detergent, and followed Mrs. Hardy out of the laundry room to the elevator.

Inside her apartment I wondered if I was making a mistake, but now I didn't know how I could gracefully refuse her offer of the soup. She seated me comfortably in a rust-colored velvet recliner before going into her kitchen.

She began to rummage in the freezer compartment of her refrigerator while she talked. "I keep the chicken soup on hand all the time. I make up a big batch, then freeze it in smaller containers so that whenever I need it, all I have to do is heat up a container in the microwave."

I reclined in the chair with my feet up and closed my eyes. "What am I doing here?" I thought, as I heard her clanking around in the kitchen. When I heard the hum of the microwave, I decided I'd eat the soup, then go home as soon as I could without hurting her feelings.

I was feeling almost breathless again at being so close to Pam's apartment...her bedroom, in fact, just behind the wall beside the recliner. I opened my eyes and reached out, my fingers spread, and touched the wall which felt cool and smooth. I began to move my hand up and down the wall, as if caressing it, and imagined I could feel the warmth of Pam's presence emanating through it--through my hand and into my heart.

I stopped abruptly, feeling foolish, when Mrs. Hardy said, "Here we are; all ready. Do you feel up to sitting at the table, or would you rather I brought it to you on a tray?"

I quickly stood, thankful for an excuse to get farther away from that wall which shared Pam's apartment. I was afraid if I continued to sit there, I'd get that woozy feeling again, or even worse, pass out. I would be totally mortified if that happened. I was already breathing faster and my pulse had stepped up its speed a few notches. "No, I'm fine. I'll come to the table," I said, as I walked through the doorway into her small dining area.

I sat down at her table and she brought me a bowl of soup in a rimmed china soup bowl setting on a matching dinner plate. I hadn't seen a rimmed soup bowl since long ago dinners at my grandmother's house and, for a brief instant, was overwhelmed with poignant memories of myself as a young boy, sitting safe and snug on my grandmother's lap.

I need to get a grip on myself, I thought, as I eyed the centerpiece bouquet of artificial flowers. I deliberately studied the bright colors of the mixture of silk lilies, mums, and other flowers I didn't know the names of to divert my mind from my frustrated, melancholy mood. I realized Mrs. Hardy had said something, and looked at her as she set another plate of soup on the table across from me before sitting down.

"I'm sorry. I didn't hear what you said."

"I said, go ahead. Don't wait for me." Then she quickly got up again. "Oh, I forgot the cheese and crackers. We need some cheese and crackers."

I tasted the soup which, to my surprise, was very good. I didn't know exactly why, but for some reason I had thought it probably wouldn't taste very good. As I continued to eat, I actually did begin to feel stronger and more in control, and surprised myself even further by accepting a second bowl. Mrs. Hardy apparently didn't feel that dinner conversation was required, so we ate in silence--she with gusto. I declined a third bowl, but with genuine praise for the soup, which caused Mrs. Hardy to blush.

Even though I did feel somewhat better, I was anxious to get out of her apartment. I still felt intensely uncomfortable at being so close to where Pam had made love to another man last night. And, once again, just thinking about it made that woozy feeling return.

"I guess it's time to get back to the laundry room. The clothes are probably ready for the dryer." I said. "I really enjoyed the soup, Mrs. Hardy. Thank you. Can I save you a trip and put your things into the dryer for you? I'd be happy to."

"Oh, no, Dear; thank you, but I like to get out of my apartment as much as possible, even if it's only to the laundry room. I don't have many friends or much of a social life anymore, so any excuse I have to get out, I do." She looked at me with an embarrassed smile. "I'll bet it's hard for someone young and handsome like you to imagine anyone actually looking forward to doing laundry."

I smiled back at her, knowing exactly how she felt, but refusing to admit it to her.

We walked out of her apartment together, and while she locked her door, I walked to the elevator and pushed the down button. She had just joined me when the elevator doors opened.

I felt my legs go weak as Pam stepped off. This was the closest I had ever been to her, and she was even more beautiful in person: positively radiant! To make matters worse, Dash was with her.

"Oh, Mrs. Hardy. I'm so glad to see you! I want to share my wonderful news! I'm engaged!" she gushed, as she held up her left hand, a beautiful diamond ring on the third finger.

As the light caught the sparkle from the diamond, it seemed to intensify and focus directly into my eyes in a blinding glare. I suddenly became violently ill again, feeling as if the two bowls of soup I had just eaten were sloshing in tidal wave madness inside my stomach. I realized I was panting and began to take slow even breaths, along with rapidly swallowing in a desperate attempt to keep the soup down.

The hallway started to spin and I sank to the floor in a kneeling position, bending my head forward towards the floor as I broke out in a drenching sweat. Along with the dizziness and nausea, my insides were also screaming in an agonizing mixture of embarrassment and frustration. I couldn't believe what a spectacle I was making of myself, but felt powerless to stop. I fervently wished that the floor would just open up and I could disappear--forever!

To my further shame, which I hadn't thought possible, Dash rushed over to me, bent down, grabbed my wrist, and began to take my pulse as he yelled over his shoulder, "Pam, call 911 for an ambulance!"

"No! I don't need an ambulance. I'll be all right," I managed to gasp. "It's merely a little touch of the flu. It'll pass in a minute. I just need to get back to my own apartment," which, I thought, might as well have been on the moon, because I didn't think there was any way I could make it there by myself.

"We'll help you," Dash said. Then all of them helped me up and into the elevator, where we rode to the ground floor. They helped me cross the corridor joining the two wings of the building (which seemed about equal to a walk across the Sahara) and into the other elevator.

After what seemed to have taken hours (but was really only minutes), we finally reached my apartment. I fumbled shakily with my key, unable to fit it into the lock. Then Pam took it, and while I stood meekly propped between Mrs. Hardy and Dash (with my hand tingling from when Pam's hand had briefly touched it), she unlocked my door.

They helped me inside where I weakly thanked them and tried to send them on their way so I could, at last, be alone in my humiliation. But they wouldn't hear of leaving me until I was securely ensconced in my bed, which, to my increased dismay, was bare of sheets.

Pam was the one who found the linen closet and made up my bed. By then I was so miserable I was past humiliation. I was just waiting to die, which seemed a very real possibility at any moment. After I lay down on the fresh sheets (which seemed charged with electricity every time I thought about Pam's having touched them) Mrs. Hardy and Pam walked out of the bedroom, leaving me alone with Dash.

He held out his hand saying, "We haven't been introduced, but my name is Dash. Dash Justin. And I'm a doctor."

I limply shook Dash's hand and said, "My name is Bob." It was all I could manage.

"Actually, my name's Dashiell," he said with a mock grimace, followed by a wide grin. "My mother is a Dashiell Hammet fan, so consequently that's how I got tagged with the name. I learned early on that Dash was much more acceptable to my peers, especially after several bloody noses and black eyes while I was in grade school." He laughed. And even though I tried not to, I couldn't help but like the guy.

"Lie down and I'll give you a quick exam--free of charge, of course," he said, laughing again. "Make sure that's it's only flu and not something more serious."

He asked if I had a thermometer, which I did, and told him where it was. He called for Pam, told her where it was, and she brought it to him. Every time I looked at her I thought my heart would beat out of my chest, and was afraid Dash would see how she affected me. How would I explain that? I thought desperately.

But Dash was concentrating on the examination. "I don't have my stethoscope or blood pressure cuff with me, but your pulse seems steady and strong, although a little fast." He looked in my eyes and ears, at my throat, and probed, poked, and percussed various parts of the rest of my body. I had no tenderness in my abdomen, and only a slight fever: 99.2 degrees. I was amazed that it wasn't higher. I felt so hot, I was afraid my body would spontaneously combust.

"I think you're probably right, Bob. That it's nothing more serious than the flu, but I'd feel better if you have your own doctor check you as soon as possible, just to make sure."

"Yes, I will," I agreed. I just wanted them all to leave so that I could be alone in my anguish--so that I could die in peace.

Dash started to walk out of the bedroom, then turned. "Is there anything we can get for you before we leave?"

"No, I'm just exhausted. I think I need to sleep now, but thanks for all you've done."

Mrs. Hardy and Pam, with anxious expressions on their faces, joined Dash at the bedroom doorway. "How's the patient?" Pam asked, looking at Dash with unabashed admiration.

"I think he'll be all right. It probably is only the flu. With rest and lots of fluids, I'm sure he'll be OK." He turned back towards me. "Bob, you have Mrs. Hardy's phone number don't you? In case you start feeling worse?"

"Yes," I answered, then closed my eyes. I heard them walk to the front door, heard it open, then close. At last! Now I could wallow in my self pity and misery in privacy--before I died. Only after a few minutes, when I realized that I wasn't going to die of humiliation, I suddenly had another terrible thought. My God! What if Pam had looked through my telescope? She would have seen that it was focused directly on her bedroom window. I lurched off the bed and stumbled in a wild panic into the bathroom where I promptly lost the two bowls of Mrs. Hardy's chicken soup; grateful in the back of my mind that I had at least waited until I was alone, so as to be able to preserve whatever small shred of my personal dignity I might have managed to retain.

Surprisingly, I felt somewhat better after getting rid of the soup. But when I looked at my ashen face, glassy eyes, and wildly messy hair in the bathroom mirror, I looked such an apparition I almost laughed. That's when I realized that I was close to hysteria. "Only women get hysterical, not men!" I thought. Hysteria. It even came from the word hyster: Greek for uterus. And since I didn't have a uterus, I couldn't become hysterical, I thought, in a desperate attempt at logic. Then I turned on the cold water and stuck my head underneath the faucet.

After a few seconds, with help from the shock of the cold water, I felt myself regaining a semblance of self-control. I stumbled back to my bed, lay down on my back and pulled the coverlet up to my chin, my wet hair soaking through the clean pillow case, causing a soggy spot on my pillow, and felt myself drifting off into the blessed escape of sleep.

When I awoke it was dark. At first I felt disoriented, but as the previous events of the most humiliating day of my life came flooding back, I remembered the added worry of the possibility of Pam having looked through my telescope at her apartment, and knew I could never face her again.

The next few days I spent in bed, calling in sick at work, and mostly slept. When my mind was able to comprehend that I couldn't lie in my bed and vegetate for the rest of my life, I got up, took a shower, shaved, and decided to once again rejoin the world of the living. But I couldn't bare to look at my telescope, let alone look through it.

The next few months were a jumble of monotonous routine. I would get up in the morning, eat breakfast, go to work, come home, fix supper, then go to bed and read until I was able to fall asleep. I didn't answer my phone, I just let my machine pick up the messages, none of which were really important. My parents called several times, also Mrs. Hardy. Periodically I returned the calls to my parents, telling them how busy I was at work with a new project, but not to Mrs. Hardy.

Then one Monday evening, as I began the mundane chore of cooking my supper while listening to my phone messages, I heard Mrs. Hardy's excited voice.

"Bob! Pam and Dash were married yesterday on a small yacht out on the bay, and they invited me! Oh, it was such a beautiful wedding, and Pam was the loveliest bride I think I've ever seen. The movers came today and moved her things out of her apartment. She and Dash are in Greece now, on their honeymoon, and when they return he starts his surgical residency in Houston. I just thought you might want to know. I hope my new neighbor will be as nice as Pam. She was the sweetest..." and the machine beeped as the allotted time on the tape came to an end.

I sank into a chair. She was gone! Pam was gone for good! Even though I had known it was coming, the finality of it was still very difficult for me to accept. I continued to just sit, I guess in a stupor, because the next thing I knew I could see the sun beginning to peak its head above the trees. I felt like I had lost a part of myself. I went to the bathroom, took a shower, dressed, and left for work.

That evening when I came home, as soon as I walked in the door, for some reason my eyes were drawn to my telescope. I had been too embarrassed to even think of looking through it after imagining the horror of Pam discovering that I had been watching her--believing that I was some kind of pervert or something. But then maybe she hadn't. Maybe it was only in my guilt induced paranoiac imagination. I guessed I'd never know for sure. I had thought about asking Mrs. Hardy if Pam had looked through my telescope, but finally decided I didn't really want to know.

However, as if being pulled by some magnetic force, I was drawn across the room and compelled to look through it. To my astonishment, it was focussed on the sky above the roof of the building wing across the courtyard, rather than on Pam's apartment. I had been so intent on not looking at it since my day of almost terminal humiliation, I hadn't noticed that it was pitched at a higher angle. Now I was sure that Pam had looked through it, and probably out of outrage had angrily repositioned it. I was relieved that I would never see her again; although I was still convinced I'd always be in love with her.

I angled the telescope back down to focus on Pam's vacant apartment and felt a deep, empty longing as tears stung my eyes. It was my own fault, I thought in disgust. I should have forced myself to overcome my shyness and meet her sooner. Maybe if I had, things would have turned out differently. Maybe it would have been me, rather than Dash, honeymooning with Pam in the Greek Islands.

I looked at Mrs. Hardy's apartment. She was sitting in that rust-colored, velvet recliner, watching *Hard Copy* while she ate a frozen dinner from a TV tray, which made me realize that I also needed to eat something, even though I wasn't hungry.

I turned on my own TV, then fixed a pimento cheese sandwich which I ate while watching Monday Night Football. But, to my chagrin, I fell asleep somewhere during the third quarter.

I spent the next few days in the same monotonous routine I had been following since Pam's engagement--with one exception. I was once again looking through my telescope. Being an astronomy buff, I had originally gotten it to study the stars. But when the stars had been so difficult to see well, with the city lights reflected against the sky, out of the boredom I had begun to aimlessly focus it on the building across the courtyard.

In the beginning, I had felt somewhat like Jimmy Stewart in *Rear Window* (one of my favorite movies). However, rather than witnessing a murder like Jimmy had (which I think probably would have been much easier on me in the long run), I had found Pam. Only I had never really had her. I had only had her image in the refraction of a lens. And that was when I began to feel like Dudly Moore in *Ten*.

Now, foolishly, I again began to watch the tenants in other apartments across the courtyard, ending each session with self punishment by looking at Pam's empty apartment-- rubbing salt in my wounds. Maybe I really was becoming masochistic.

A week to the day following Mrs. Hardy's message on my answering machine about Pam's wedding, after I had eaten supper I focused my telescope on the apartments across the courtyard in my usual nightly routine. Only this time I was drawn to Pam's apartment first. There were lights on. Maybe she was back, I thought with a manic feeling of exhilaration. Maybe her marriage hadn't worked out. But when I focused on her living room I could see that it was filled with someone else's furniture. Not hers. A large easel had been set up with its back facing the window. The window faced north. Of course, I thought. The north light is what artists always want--at least they did in stories and movies.

As I watched, a small girl, actually she was a petite woman--but young looking--walked to the easel and set a canvas on it. She was dressed in jeans and an unbuttoned denim shirt with the tail out, over a black tank top. Her hair was long and dark, nearly to her waist, loosely fastened at the nape by a barrette which allowed wispy strands to escape around her face.

I stopped breathing for a second. She was the most enchanting creature I had ever seen. I immediately forgot about Pam--as my heart felt like it was flying out of my chest on a magic journey, all on its own, to join the full moon hanging low over the roof of the building. I was in love again!

I watched her while she painted, fascinated by her intense concentration. Finally, when she turned off the living room light and went into her bedroom, I continued to watch while she undressed. She was dainty and slender, with a waif-like body, reminding me of a wood nymph or a water sprite. She went into the bathroom, and I studied the room while I waited for her to return. She had a black metal bed which looked like it might be an antique, or at least a collectable, swagged with gauzy material hanging from the ceiling, giving it a romantic, whimsical look. I was intrigued by her imagination. Pam had slept in a bed with an ordinary wooden headboard.

Then the girl returned and took off a white terry cloth robe, under which she was wearing only a blue cotton tank top with a matching cotton string bikini. Apparently that was what she wore to sleep in. She got into bed and read for a while, and I continued to watch her until she turned off her light.

The next day, as soon as I got home from work I called Mrs. Hardy. "Bob," she said. "I had just about given up on ever hearing from you again. I still have your sheets and towels you were washing that day when you got sick."

I apologized for not calling sooner, feeling guilty for ignoring her the past several months. I was dying to ask her about her new next door neighbor, but before I could bring up the subject she invited me to her apartment for dinner, saying she had some leftover lasagne in her freezer; I eagerly accepted.

When I arrived at her apartment she already had her table set, with china in the same attractive pattern in which she had served me the chicken soup, and I could smell the inviting aroma of lasagne heating in her microwave. "Sit!" She said, motioning towards the table. I tried to think of ways in which I could bring up the subject--without looking too eager--of her new neighbor, while she bustled around transferring the lasagne to a serving dish, which she set on the table, followed by a basket of warm garlic bread and a bowl of green salad.

"Well, Bob," she said, sitting down, "I have a lovely new neighbor. Her name is Lisa Kullen, and she seems to be every bit as nice as Pam. She's an artist; she works as a commercial artist for an advertising company during the day, and paints what she calls "legitimate art" at night and on weekends, which she's trying to get some galleries to show."

"That's nice," was all I could say. She had caught me completely off guard by her candor. I began to eat the lasagne, which was really very tasty; in fact, the first food that had tasted good to me since Pam had gotten married.

"By the way, Bob, do you still have your telescope? I looked through it that day you were sick," she said, giving me a knowing look. "Then Pam wanted to look, too, but before she did I angled it up towards the sky. Might be a good idea in the future if you remembered to do that when you're through looking through it--just in case."

I could feel my face burning in embarrassment as I hastily looked down at my plate while chewing the huge forkful of lasagne I had nervously stuffed into my mouth, but deeply grateful that she had saved my dignity. And thankful that Pam hadn't looked through my telescope to find it focused on her apartment.

Mrs. Hardy continued, changing the subject. "Lisa just moved here from out of town and doesn't know anyone. You ought to try to get acquainted with her. I'd be happy to introduce you."

I felt my stomach go into a knot. No, I thought frantically! I'm not ready to meet her yet. I'm too shy. I need to get more courage first. I'll know when the time is right, I thought, with a foreboding feeling of *deja vu.*

I swallowed the last of the lasagne in my mouth, and raised my eyes to Mrs. Hardy's face. "Yes, I would like to meet her, but not tonight. Soon, though. I promise," I said, my heart beating faster. We chatted about other trivial things while I stayed and helped her with the dishes--although I could hardly wait to get home to watch Lisa. LISA!

Such a musical name. When I was ready to leave, Mrs. Hardy gave me my neatly folded clean sheets and towels she had been saving.

My heart was singing as I rode the elevator down from her apartment, crossed the corridor and rode up to my apartment. I spent the rest of the evening in giddy euphoria, watching Lisa paint. Then I watched her undress and get ready for bed again, but this time, when I was finished watching, I remembered to angle the telescope up towards the sky before I went to bed. As soon as the time is right, I'll meet her, I thought, just before I drifted off into blissful sleep.

However, for some reason, once again I was unable to summon the courage to meet her; soon I began to get that familiar panicky feeling. Afraid I would blow it again by waiting too long. It almost made my physically ill thinking about it. I knew I couldn't go through another experience with Lisa like I had with Pam. But the more panicky I became at the thought of waiting too long, the more scared I got when I thought about trying to meet her.

I began to scrutinize my face in the mirror for hours, combing my hair different ways with gel or mousse, practicing different facial expressions, and saying phrases. I bought several different kinds of cologne, trying to decide which one she would like best.

I decided I had a reasonably nice face, and my body was OK. I was just a hair over six feet tall, and had always been lucky with never having had a weight problem; I could eat anything I wanted without gaining. I didn't really work out, but did swim laps in the apartment pool on a fairly regular basis. I had one of those lean, stringy muscular builds.

I dressed nicely and tried to keep up with current fashion trends. I had been somewhat nerdy in high school and college, and made up my mind after I had earned my master's degree in marine biology that I would concentrate on changing that image, which I had--on the outside. Unfortunately, I guess I was still a nerd on the inside. I wasn't sure how I could change that, or even *if* I could. And, in the meantime, my panic continued to grow.

I began to practice introducing myself to her in front of the mirror. "Hi, my name is Bob." Or, "Hello there. We haven't met, but my name is Bob. What's yours?" Or, "Where have you been all my life you gorgeous creature?" But somehow, nothing seemed to sound right.

Then one Saturday morning, after Lisa had been living there nearly five weeks, I realized I desperately needed to do my laundry. I had been so engrossed in watching her that I had not only run out of clean clothes to wear, but my entire apartment had become a disorganized mess, as well! I had always been fastidiously neat and had never let it get like that before, not even when Pam had gotten married. Dirty dishes were piled up in the sink, newspapers and books scattered around the living room. I really needed to tidy things up. OK, I resolved, but first I'll gather up my laundry, and while it's in the washer I'll come back and tidy up before I watch Lisa paint.

I wouldn't even take a quick peak at her because I knew that if I did, I would be unable to tear myself away and nothing would get done. So I didn't even touch my telescope. I threw on an old college sweat shirt and the only pair of clean jeans I had left, with holes worn in both knees (which, for some reason I was unable to fathon, was now fashionable). I didn't even take time to comb my hair with gel, I just ran my fingers through it, leaving it kind of halfway neat--but fluffy.

I jammed my feet into my Reeboks, without socks, because all my socks were also dirty. But then, going sockless was also now fashionable--at least among some circles. Next, I thought with irony, the trend will be to go without underwear. Or maybe it already was, for all I knew.

I grabbed some dirty pillow cases and jammed them full of dirty laundry. After I had filled three, I bundled them under my arms and rode down on the elevator, hurried to the laundry room and dumped them on the floor in front of the washers. "Damn, I forgot the detergent," I muttered in disgust. Now I'd have to waste time going all the way back up to my apartment for some.

As I barged out of the laundry room, I almost ran into someone. It was Lisa! I had almost charged into her like the proverbial bull in the china shop.

I just stood there staring at her, as my heart began to pound and the little voice inside my head screamed, "No! I'm not ready yet. I need to practice some more in front of the mirror."

She smiled a dazzling smile and I could feel its warmth surround my heart, which by now was beating as fast as it did while I was swimming laps.

She held out her hand as she said, "Hi. My name is Lisa Kullen," her smile becoming (if possible) even more radiant.

I felt paralyzed and became terrified that I would make a fool of myself by being unable to speak or move. Then, to my amazement, I watched my arm reach out and grasp her hand firmly in mine, and heard my voice say confidently, "It's a pleasure to meet you, Lisa. My name is Bob, and by the way, you wouldn't happen to have any detergent I could borrow, would you? I seem to have forgotten to bring mine. Then maybe we could go to my apartment and get better acquainted over a cup of cappuccino while we wait for our laundry." And I heard that other little voice singing inside my heart, telling me the right time had, indeed, finally come!

YOUR FACE

Whenever I close my eyes, I see your face
Etched on hidden tableaus inside my heart;
Enchanting outlines I can lovingly trace . . .
In secret; privately savoring its beautiful art.

While in my bed I restlessly lie
Awake--late into darkest night--
Aching with loneliness and longing; I sigh.
How will I survive this hopeless plight?

Wildly delicious thoughts of you
Possess my soul--invade my brain;
Erotic dreams I can't subdue
Penetrate my heart; bittersweet pain.

In mystical warmth of moonlight's glow
Your eyes now appear, darkly shining--
Beauty emanating--starting to flow;
Spreading; surrounding; love redefining.

This wondrous silken illusion, I bless;
Your innate goodness transcending space--
Denying reality of love's delusion. Oh yes!
Whenever I close my eyes, I see your face.

THE SURPRISE

Leatrice was so excited she could hardly wait. Graeme had a surprise for her, and she was positive she knew what it was: a diamond ring. He was going to ask her to marry him!

When he called last night he had told her that he hoped to arrive in town between 6:00 and 6:30 this evening, and for her to be dressed up. He had said he was looking forward to taking her out to dinner to celebrate a very special surprise.

Following his phone call, she had spent the rest of the night filled with romantic dreams, both while she was sleeping and awake, and this morning she had hurried out to buy a new dress and have her hair done. She bought champagne, and even caviar for hors d'oeuvres. She had also tried on her dark blue negligee--again; the one she had never worn--yet--the one she had been saving.

She blushed whenever she thought about the negligee. It was soft and silky, with the bodice made of lace. She had never worn anything even remotely like it. But tonight she planned to wear it for Graeme when they made love for the first time--to celebrate their engagement.

Leatrice was forty-eight-years-old and had never been married. In fact, she was still a virgin, and often thought she was probably the only female over the age of fourteen who *was* still a virgin. But she was proud of the fact that she had saved herself for her husband. Although, for the past few years she had all but given up hope of ever finding a husband. That is until she had met Graeme.

She considered herself to be a handsome, attractive woman for her age. Oh, maybe her figure was a little plump, and she had a few gray streaks in her short, neatly styled hair, but Graeme had never seemed to mind.

She and Graeme had been seeing each other for a little more than eight months now. They had met, in all places, at the drug store. Leatrice was a registered nurse and was the Director of Nurses in a local nursing home. She had stopped at the drug store on her way home from work to pick up her prescription for estrogen. (She certainly was not about to allow herself to be miserable with hot flashes and mood swings, and possibly even osteoporosis. Not when she could prevent them with estrogen replacement therapy.)

As the clerk handed her the prescription, a man standing next to her asked the clerk whether it was better to take an antihistamine or a decongestant for a cold. Leatrice glanced at the man out of curiosity and saw that he was quite handsome, approximately her age, and appeared to be in great discomfort, for which he was desperately seeking some kind of relief. His eyes and nose were red, and he sounded very congested when he spoke.

When the clerk gave him a blank look, Leatrice jumped in with, "Oh, it's better to take just a decongestant for a cold; you only take antihistamines for allergies. You poor dear, you look miserable." She proceeded to explain to him that she was a nurse and gave him several suggestions for treating his cold. He was genuinely grateful and invited her to join him for a cup of coffee, saying it was the least he could do to thank her.

So that was how it had begun. They had gone to a nearby coffee shop, where they had talked and laughed over the coffee, and enjoyed each other's company so much that they had ended up having dinner together. By the time they had finally parted it had grown very late, and when he invited her to join him for dinner again the following night she had readily accepted.

She had learned that he was a technician for a national office equipment company, that he lived in Dallas, that he had to travel a lot in his work, and that he came to town on a regular bi-monthly schedule. He had been widowed five years ago and had a twenty-three-year-old daughter named Mary Ann, to whom he was very close.

Leatrice felt like she was on cloud nine. She had only had two serious relationships with men in her past: one when she had been in her early twenties, and the other when she had been in her late thirties. Unfortunately, neither had worked out. Leatrice had steadfastly refrained from engaging in sexual intercourse in both relationships, and both had primarily ended because of that refusal to participate in the intimacy of making love. She'd had very little experience with men otherwise.

But she did have a secret addiction to romance novels which she avidly read in her spare time. She had always felt that, some day, she would meet a man who would arouse the flames of passion within her to such an extent that she would be swept away and lose her virginity. The same kind of passion the heroines experienced in the novels. And the more she read the romance fiction, the more convinced she became of it happening. She also felt that she had gained a certain amount of technical knowledge about sex from the stories, so she would know what actions would be expected from her--when that time came.

Every two weeks when Graeme came to town (he always called her the night before), they spent as much time together as each of their respective work schedules allowed. They frequently ate dinner together, and on the occasions when she cooked for him he always told her that she prepared the best food he had ever eaten. They went bowling, dancing, to movies and plays, and walked along the beach on the warm sunny days. They talked endlessly about anything and everything, and had a great many things in common.

One of the things Leatrice most admired about Graeme was his total respect for her. He had always been a perfect gentleman, and had never once made a pass at her or suggested behavior she deemed improper. He had held her hand while they walked along the beach, had kissed her good night on the cheek, and had hugged her, but that had been the extent of their physical contact.

After only several months of being with Graeme, Leatrice knew that she had fallen hopelessly in love with him, and was reasonably sure that he was falling in love with her. They always had such fun together. Sometimes they would laugh so hard that their eyes would run with tears and their sides would hurt. He would hug her on those occasions and tell her that she was his best buddy, and that he didn't know what he would do without her.

After they had dated for six months, Leatrice was certain that it was now only a matter of time before Graeme would ask her to marry him. She felt, deep in her heart, that they were meant to be together: that they were true soul mates. And that was when she had shopped for the special negligee.

She had spent weeks searching for just the right one: not too provocative, but not too prudish. Something dignified and elegant--yet feminine--and not so revealing that it wouldn't still be flattering to her plumpish figure. When she had finally spotted the blue one, as soon as she had tried it on, she had known it was perfect. And blue was his favorite color. Tonight, at last, she would finally get to wear it! Her heart began to beat faster and she felt a tingle of excitement in her abdomen at the anticipation. Oh, they would be so happy together! They were so right for each other!

After she returned home from her shopping, she hurried around tidying up her small house. She always kept it immaculate anyway, but did a few last minute things, including placing a vase of fresh flowers on the living room coffee table, and one on the dresser in her bedroom. She also placed a few spice scented candles in the living room and in her bedroom. Tonight was going to be so perfect. Whenever she thought about it, she would feel that tingle of excitement, and warmth would flow through her body. Then she would feel herself blushing.

She took a bath, soaking in a fragrant bath oil, then perfumed her body. She had never done that before and it made her feel sexy. It was almost as if all of the erotic feelings that she had held carefully in check for so many years in a kind of suspended animation--waiting for just the right time--were now ready to burst forth.

Following her bath, she carefully applied makeup to her face, then put on her new dress (also blue). Even with the few pounds of extra weight, she thought she looked quite attractive when she looked at her reflection in the mirror.

She went into the kitchen, got out two of her crystal wine goblets, and a small crystal bowl into which she emptied the caviar and added a small silver spoon. She put crackers on a small crystal plate, then got out two small china plates and two linen napkins. She put it all on a tray which she carried to the living room, then set it out on her coffee table in what she thought was an artistic arrangement (after several different tries).

She put some CDs (Tschaikovsky and Dvorak) on to play. Now she was ready. It was past six o'clock and Graeme should be here any time. She sat on the couch to wait. After what seemed like hours, during which she got up several times to look out the window, then at her reflection in the mirror for another recheck of her hair and makeup, she heard his car out front.

She watched from her window as he got out of his car, walked around it and opened the door on the passenger's side. A lovely young woman got out. "Oh, he's brought his daughter, Mary Ann," she thought. Yes, that would be just like him to want her and Mary Ann to meet, now that she was going to be Mary Ann's stepmother. That must be part of his surprise.

With a big smile on her face, Leatrice flung open her front door. Graeme was beaming as he and the young woman walked up the steps to join her. Leatrice again felt like she was on cloud nine. She held out her hand and Graeme clasped it tightly in his. Then he grabbed her to him and hugged her while the young woman stood behind, smiling shyly.

"Oh, Leatrice," Graeme said, still beaming. "I have such a wonderful surprise. I could hardly keep from telling you last night on the phone, but I wanted to tell you in person. I know you're going to be so happy for me. I want you to meet Kristy, my new bride. I've told her all about you, about how you're my best buddy. I just know you're going to love her as much as I do!"

THE EVE OF THE BEGINNING (CONTINUED)

As the stories ended, and I was again cognizant of my surroundings, I thought about the only deep love I had ever felt--which was for Joy. Although that love had been returned, until I had decided that it was no longer important to me, I could imagine how I would have felt if my love hadn't been returned; I felt a twinge of pain, so deeply inside my heart, it caused a sudden, involuntary shudder.

I tried to block the pain from my mind as I looked into Schere's knowing eyes. She had that secret little smile on her face again, and I suddenly felt naked--as if she was able to look inside my soul--but I was unable to look away from her.

She leaned over me again, and put the open palm of her right hand against my left cheek as she continued to look into my eyes. "Oh, Michael; sometimes life gives us more pain than we think we can bear. One of the saddest things is to find love, only to lose it. Sometimes it is taken from us against our will. Other times we willingly throw it away, which can then cause us to be unable to love ourselves."

She began to tenderly stroke my face as she talked. "To lose love can be truly devastating. Often, when we lose love, we also lose ourselves. But we must never lose our dreams, Michael, for dreams are what keep us believing in ourselves."

Then she gently took my face in both of her hands again. "I am going to tell you of the sorrow of love lost: the story of Cindy and the story of Victoria."

I looked avidly into her eyes, now dark cobalt blue--with golden reflections from the candle flames--and felt myself being pulled into their mystical depth as her voice began to softly speak the words...

LEGACY

I didn't know why Billy Joe had to go and die, leaving me with our six kids to raise all by myself. At first, I couldn't believe it was possible to feel so much anguish and still go on living. Sometimes I felt like just giving up. Like maybe jumping off the Harbor Bridge, or out in front of a truck on the freeway or something. But I didn't--mainly because of the kids. Now I feel so guilty from having had those feelings, and wish with all my heart that I could take them back. The thought of the kids being without me makes me cry. It's hard enough for them being without their dad.

It's just that I missed him so much! At times, I could actually feel physical pain--deep down inside my heart. And during those times I thought my heart might even burst, the pain would get so bad. But it never did. Or, at least, it hasn't yet.

I'm only thirty-years-old; much too young to be a widow. Billy Joe and I became lovers when I was only two weeks into being fourteen. I had been thirteen (but looked every bit of eighteen) and he had been sixteen when I had first seen him, and I thought he was just about the sexiest guy alive. I'd usually see him when I'd be walking to school. He would drive by in his truck, with some of his friends, and they would always whistle and wave. Finally, one day when he had driven past me without any of his friends with him, to my surprise, he suddenly stopped, backed over to the curb, and asked if I wanted a ride to school.

Without a second's hesitation, I had eagerly run to the passenger side. He leaned over, opened the door, and I climbed in. We never made it to school that day. And I didn't find out until after I got home that one of the vice principals had called my house to see why I wasn't in school. Boy! Did my dad ever give me a whippin' with the belt that night for skipping school. But my folks didn't know I had been with Billy Joe; they were mad enough without knowing that. I had lied and told them I'd been with some of my girlfriends. That we had hung out at a movie. But that day had been worth the whippin'.

It had happened in the month of April, in the middle of spring. Billy Joe and I had driven out to the beach on Padre Island where we had played in the sand and waded in the surf. Just like two little kids. We had also made love--the first time for me--on a blanket back in the dunes. Even though it had hurt a lot at first, it had been wonderful! I knew that day that I had fallen in love with him, and that it would be that way for the rest of my life.

Billy Joe had been surprised to find he had made it with a virgin. I think it kind of shook him up at first. He was real apologetic. Said I should have told him, and that if he'd known he never would have done it. He told me, later, that he'd never made it with a virgin before--that I was his first-- which just made it all the more special for me. That made it seem almost like he was a virgin too, and like it was the first sexual experience for both of us.

My folks thought I was too young to date, so I had to sneak to be with Billy Joe. I'd tell them that I was going to one of my girl friend's house and then meet Billy Joe. But I never skipped school again. I learned my lesson about that the first time. I had always been a good student and was careful to continue to keep my grades up, so my folks wouldn't get suspicious. They had always hoped I'd go on to college after I graduated from high school. I had always pretty much thought I'd win a scholarship, and so had my folks, because we didn't have any extra money for college. I had a pretty good shot at it too, until I got pregnant.

Of course when I started to show, my folks found out and I had to quit school. The school might have let me continue in some kind of special classes, but my folks were too embarrassed for people to see me that way and forced me to drop out. Billy Joe was upset about my pregnancy, too, at first. I was fifteen by then, and he was eighteen.

To my parent's relief, Billy Joe decided he wanted to marry me. So on my sixteenth birthday, when I was seven months pregnant, Billy Joe and I exchanged wedding vows in a small ceremony in my parent's living room with just my parents, grandparents, my brother and sister, and Billy Joe's parents, grandparents, and his brother and sister-in-law present. My sister was my maid of honor and Billy Joe's brother was his best man.

After the ceremony, Billy Joe told me that he was actually secretly pleased at the thought of becoming a daddy. He also told me that he had been planning to marry me anyway, after he had graduated and gotten a decent paying job. (At that time, he was working in a local supermarket as a stocker for several hours after school and on weekends.) And even though he was a terrible student, he did manage to graduate with the rest of his class.

I didn't think there had ever been a love as deep and true as the love between Billy Joe and me. I didn't see how there could be. When we made love…it was like something magic. All he had to do was touch my hand, or even if I only just looked into his eyes, I would be practically on fire with wanting him. It's no wonder I got pregnant. We never used any protection. I think maybe I secretly wanted his baby inside of me; oh, not to try to trap him into marrying me, or anything like that, but because I wanted to give him something that was a part of both of us. Something that was a part of our love.

And I had never had any doubts that we would be married. I trusted in his love completely. He was always doing special things for me. Not just when we were dating, but even after the kids came, in fact, right up until that night he died. While he was alive, he always made me feel special; like I was the most beautiful and desirable woman on the face of the Earth, even after having six kids.

Our first baby, our love child, was a girl. We named her April, because that was the month when we'd had our first time together. She's thirteen now. God! The same age I was when I first laid eyes on her daddy. I sometimes wonder if she has some boy she secretly feels the same way about that I felt for her daddy back when I was her age.

I remember when I was her age--how I used to dream about her daddy, and about what it would be like for him to hold me and kiss me--long before he ever noticed me. I get scared when I think about her feeling that way about some boy, because I need her strength now. Especially with the other kids. April's always been such a good, responsible girl. Even when she was a baby she was always good.

It had been necessary for us to live with my folks until April was six-months-old. Then, Billy Joe got a good job as a roughneck with an oil well drilling company and we were able to move into our own apartment. I had never been happier in my life. I felt like I had truly been blessed by having Billy Joe and April. I didn't miss going to college one bit.

Lord knows, we never planned to have six kids. But after April was born I nursed her, and everyone told me that as long as I continued to breast feed I couldn't get pregnant. I was naive and believed them, so it was a shock when after I started throwing up several mornings in a row, I finally went to the doctor for some stomach medicine and he told me that I was pregnant again. April was only four-months-old.

This time it was twins. Girls again. We named them Molly and Melinda, and they were really a handful. April was only thirteen-months-old, but had already been walking for two months so she could now get around and into things pretty fast. Billy Joe and I talked about maybe one of us getting fixed so we wouldn't have any more kids, but that's all we did was talk. We never did come to any kind of a decision, so I started using foam to keep from getting pregnant again. It seemed to work pretty well because four years later, I still hadn't gotten pregnant.

By now, Billy Joe had become a driller and was making a lot of money--at least to us it was a lot of money. A lot more than either of our families had ever had while we were growing up. The only bad thing was that Billy Joe had to be gone away from home a lot. Now that he was a driller, he had a lot more responsibility and had to stay out on the drilling locations for longer periods at a time. I always missed him so much when he was gone. It seemed almost like a part of me was lost. I guess it was the piece of my heart that he took along with him.

But we were able to buy a nice little house. It had three bedrooms and two bathrooms, which was luxurious compared to what we had grown up with. Neither of us had expensive tastes and Billy Joe never wanted me to work. He thought it was more important for him to earn the living and for me to stay at home with our babies, and since he was now making so much money, I was glad that he felt that way.

Maybe it was because his own mamma had always had to work in a factory to help make ends meet. He used to tell me how lonely it had been when he would come home from school and she wouldn't be there. I thought I was surely the luckiest woman in the world.

Billy Joe bought me a sewing machine, so I taught myself how to sew and made all the curtains for our house. Then, as I got better at it, I started sewing clothes for the kids and for myself. It made me real proud, especially when people complimented us on how nice we looked. It made Billy Joe proud too. He used to brag about it to all the guys on his crew.

We bought some of our furniture new, and some I found in secondhand shops: Old wooden pieces that I would refinish or paint. I used to study pictures in some of the women's magazines and sort of developed a knack for decorating. I was proud of the way our house looked, and thought if I had gone on to college, maybe that's what I would have become; an interior decorator.

Billy Joe was proud of our house too, and we'd often invite his crew and some of the other drillers and their families over for barbecues or to play cards. Some of the single guys would sometimes bring their girl friends. But most of those single guys were pretty wild, and after only one thing. So some of the girls they brought to our house embarrassed me, and I didn't want my kids being around them. They were just as wild as the guys. I know it must have bothered Billy Joe, too, because he finally talked to them, and after that they started bringing nicer girls around.

We enjoyed our life together and playing with our kids. I thought Billy Joe was about the best father in the world, besides being the most loving and attentive husband. And that wonderful magic was still there when we made love, just like it had been in the beginning. I could never picture myself being loved by any man other than Billy Joe. I know when we got married, with me being pregnant at the time, and with both of us being so young, that most people only gave us chances of "between slim and none" of making a go of it. I guess we proved to everyone we were the exception to the statistics.

Billy Joe adored his three daughters. He used to refer to us as his four beautiful ladies. But I knew, deep down inside his heart, that he was a little bit disappointed because he didn't have a son. His brother had two boys now, and whenever our families got together I would see how Billy Joe sometimes looked at his brother with envy when he was "roughhousing" with his boys. you just couldn't play that way with little girls, even if they were tomboys. And our girls certainly weren't tomboys. They were all little ladies, and only liked to play with girl things.

So I stopped using the foam. We had good health insurance, and I just knew if I prayed real hard every time we made love (which was most every night when he was home) that when I got pregnant again, this time, for sure, it would be a boy. And I was right, at least partly. Three months after I stopped using the foam, one morning when I woke up I had that old familiar queasiness in my stomach and barely made it to the bathroom in time before I threw up.

When I told Billy Joe, he was really surprised that I was pregnant again. Then I confessed and told him what I had done, and he hugged me and said, "If that's what you want, then that's what I want too, even if it turns out to be another girl." But this time I seemed to be gaining an awfully lot of weight really fast, and realized at this rate I'd be a whale by the time I would be ready to deliver.

The doctor did an ultrasound and told me it was twins again. That idea had briefly crossed my mind, but I had thought the odds of two pregnancies in a row being twins would be next to impossible. Shows you how much I knew. But when the doctor also told me that one was a boy, I didn't care how many babies I was carrying.

When I told Billy Joe I was carrying twins again, but that one was a boy and one was another girl, he hugged me-- then picked me up and spun around while holding me, even with me already being so big and heavy. He sat me down on the couch and kissed me, then put my feet up and told me he was going to order pizza to celebrate. I told him that was fine with me, but to get a giant size because I was eating for three now, and if our boy expected to grow up to be as big and strong as his daddy was, I needed to feed him a lot.

When we told the girls that they were going to have a little brother, as well as a little sister, they started dancing around and jumping up and down. It was one of the happiest nights of my life. One of those times you know you'll remember as long as you live, no matter however long that may be.

Billy Joe found some old party hats left over from one of the kid's birthday parties and we each wore one while we ate the pizza. He even found two birthday candles which he put on the pizza and lighted, then he had us all sing happy birthday to be, to the two new babies who were still inside my womb. I wondered if they could hear it, and if they could, if they thought they were going to be born into a family of crazy people. But we were only crazy with love, I thought happily.

After the girls were asleep and Billy Joe and I were in bed, we made passionate, tender love. And, once again, I knew I would never forget this special night. The joy and happiness just seemed to overflow from my heart, and I wondered how I had ever been so lucky as to have been blessed with such a devoted husband and wonderful children.

When I was getting close to my due date, I had gotten so big that my doctor thought it would be best for me to go ahead into the hospital so they could induce my labor. He didn't want to take any chances, especially since Billy Joe was away from home so much. So that's what we did. They put me in this beautiful hospital room--they called it a birthing room--that looked almost like a regular bedroom (only the bed was different) and Billy Joe got to stay with me.

They began the IV drip to induce my labor and, since it was my third pregnancy, in no time at all we had another beautiful daughter and a handsome son. They each weighed in at almost six pounds, which is really big for twins. Billy Joe was about the happiest man alive, and I was about the happiest woman. He looked at me with such a depth of love shining in his eyes, for giving him a son, that it brought tears to my eyes. It was the most wonderful, beautiful look I had ever seen.

When we took the babies home, the girls were so excited that they couldn't keep from dancing around, and they all wanted to hold the babies, especially their brother. We named the twins Nathan and Nicole. They were healthy and not a bit fussy. I thanked God that he had answered my prayers and given us such wonderful babies, and, especially, for at last letting me give Billy Joe a son.

Well, that was it for us, as far as kids were concerned. Five was more than we had ever planned to have--not that we had actually planned any of them...except maybe for these last two. And Billy Joe hadn't even had a part in planning them. They had been pretty much a private plan just between me and God.

Billy Joe and I discussed what we should do about birth control. It wasn't that we really didn't want any more kids, it was just that we didn't feel we could afford any more. We were starting to feel a little crimp in our budget, even with the good money that Billy Joe was making. Billy Joe decided that it would be easier for him to get fixed, rather than for me to. We were afraid to rely on birth control. Besides, I was nursing and couldn't take the pill. So he said on his next vacation that he'd go get fixed.

And he did, but the doctor forgot to tell him that he had to have a zero sperm count before it was safe not to use any other kind of protection. So you can imagine our amazement (the twins were nine-months-old), when I awoke one morning with that same, unmistakable queasy feeling in my stomach, and barely made it to the bathroom in time. As I leaned over the commode, throwing up, I thought, NO! It can't be. Billy Joe was out on the rig working, and I didn't know how I would tell him I was pregnant again.

At first, I thought maybe the doctor had made a mistake and had done the procedure wrong, or maybe it had grown back together. All I knew was that I was pregnant, and the only man I had ever been with in my entire life was Billy Joe. Then I became fearful. Maybe Billy Joe would think I had been with someone else. In tears, I called my doctor who explained to me how it had probably happened.

When Billy Joe came home, I waited until we were in bed that night to tell him I was pregnant again, and what my doctor had told me. At first, he looked at me with suspicion. Then when I got tears in my eyes, his face softened. He told me he believed me, and that he didn't really think I'd ever been with anyone else.

I started to cry harder and said, "What if it's twins again?"

Billy Joe looked at me in shock, like that idea hadn't occurred to him yet. Then we both started laughing. We laughed until our sides hurt. Finally, he said, "If it is, then we'll just have seven kids instead of six. And when people see us out with them all, they'll just say, 'There goes two passionate people who are very much in love!'" Then we started laughing all over again.

We went to the urologist who had fixed him, and he told us what had happened. He did another sperm count, but this time it was zero. The doctor said sometimes it takes several weeks before there's no more sperm left. I guess we had just assumed everything was OK too soon.

Even though we really hadn't planned to have another baby, deep down inside Billy Joe and I were both happy about it, once we got used to the idea. It's just that our house was beginning to get a little cramped. The three older girls were in one bedroom and the twins were in the other. We really needed another bedroom. We didn't think we could afford to move to a larger house, but Billy Joe thought that we could afford to add on to our house, especially if we did a lot of the work ourselves.

Even though I hadn't gained weight fast this time, and was pretty sure it wasn't twins, I was still apprehensive when I went for an ultrasound. However, after the doctor had assured me that there was only one baby, and that it was another boy, I was ecstatic! I could hardly wait to tell Billy Joe the good news. He was elated, and told me that it was truly a miracle.

We named him Matthew, and by the time he was born we had already started building the addition to our house of another bedroom and bathroom. It had been exciting and fun, designing how we would build it and drawing up the plans. Billy Joe had decided he could do most of the work himself, other than pouring the concrete slab foundation and some of the plumbing and electricity.

We decided that since we were adding another bedroom and bath, we would make it a large master suite and give April the bedroom we now had. When we had finally gotten the plans the way we wanted them, we shopped around until we were able to find a building contractor who was willing to work with us on the things we couldn't do by ourselves. It took us almost two years to get the addition completed, but it really turned out beautiful, and April was delighted to have her very own bedroom and bath. We put Nicole in the room with Molly and Melinda, and Matthew in the same bedroom with Nathan. The kids all seemed to be happy with the new arrangements.

I sewed new curtains and bed spreads for all of them, and we repainted some of their old furniture, as well as buying a few new pieces, so all six of them would feel special. By now April was ten, and my three older kids were in school. Only the three younger ones were still at home. Every time Billy Joe was home, we did special things together as a family. Mostly, we went to the beach. The kids especially loved going to Padre Island. Billy Joe and I loved it there, too. It was still our special place and, besides, we were still practically kids yet, ourselves.

I often thought that my getting pregnant at such a young age had been a blessing in disguise. Billy Joe's and my life together had worked out better than I ever could have hoped or dreamed. Sometimes I almost felt like a character out of a romance novel. But not really. In the romance novels they were always beautiful career women. The only career I had ever had was being a full-time wife and mother. Also, I knew I wasn't beautiful. Although, even after having six kids, I had kept my figure, and Billy Joe thought I was beautiful. That was the only thing that really mattered.

Then one rainy Friday night in August when April was eleven, we were all eagerly awaiting Billy Joe's return from the rig where he had spent the past six days. He was supposed to have four days off, and we were looking forward to camping on the beach at Padre Island. When it got to be several hours later than when he said he'd probably be home, I began to get a little worried and sent the kids on to bed. The rig was nearly a hundred miles away, so a lot of things could have happened, especially since he was riding with one of the other guys. (The crew nearly always rode together in the same car and took turns driving.)

When he didn't call, I started pacing the floor. He usually always called if he was going to be delayed. Maybe the relief driller had been late in getting to the rig, or maybe the car had broken down. If the car had broken down somewhere out on a lonely stretch of the highway, he might not have been near a phone. (None of the guys had car phones, except the toolpusher.)

I finally went to bed, but was unable to sleep. I kept looking at the clock. The time seemed to drag by. I guess I eventually dozed off because the next thing I knew, the door bell was ringing. I got up and threw on a robe. I was pretty sure Billy Joe had taken his house key, but maybe not. Or maybe he had lost it. I was just so relieved that he was finally home. I glanced at the clock as I ran out of the bedroom. It was 3:30 A.M.

I threw back the deadbolt and opened the door. But it wasn't Billy Joe. It was a State Trooper. I felt a lump in my throat and a knot in my stomach.

"Are you Mrs. Cynthia Thompson?" he asked.

The lump in my throat grew bigger as I tried to swallow it. "Yes," I answered weakly.

I shivered, even though it was hot and sultry after the rain.

"Is your husband's name William Joseph?"

I nodded, my heart beginning to beat hard against my chest, and I could feel the hairs on the back of my neck standing up.

"Ma'am, I'm afraid I have some bad news for you. Your husband's been in a serious accident."

I clenched my fists as my heartbeat increased its speed. "You've got to take me to him," I begged. "Please! I need to be with him. He needs me. Please!" I grabbed hold of his arm. I couldn't help myself. I had to hold on to something.

"I'm sorry, Ma'am," the trooper said, guiding me into the living room. He gently sat me down in one of the big comfortable wing chairs (which happened to be the one where Billy Joe always sat). "You can't do anything to help him now. He didn't survive."

I just sat there. Numb. Then I began to sob. "No! It's a mistake! It wasn't him! It couldn't be him. You see, he's the only man I've ever loved. The only man I'll ever love. He can't be dead. He's only thirty." I choked out. Then I couldn't talk any more. The lump got too big. All I could do was sob.

The trooper asked me if I had any family or friends to call. I motioned to the telephone stand. He went to it, saw the small book beside the phone and brought it to me. After I had opened it and pointed to my parent's name, he called them. I continued to sob, and in a little while my parents walked in the front door. My mom came over and put her arms around me while my dad and the trooper walked back to the entrance hall to talk.

I later learned that the car had skidded into the path of an eighteen wheeler. Billy Joe had been in the front seat, and he and the driver had both been killed instantly. The other two men, who had been riding in the back seat, were in critical condition. One of them later died and the other is still paralyzed from the waist down.

Fortunately, we had mortgage insurance, so the house was paid off. And Billy Joe had a $30,000 life insurance policy with the company. Since the accident had happened while he was on the way home from work, my dad told me I was probably entitled to some type of compensation. But I couldn't think about any of that right then. All could think about was that I had lost the love of my life. The kids were what saved my sanity. I was so thankful for them: I could see a different part of Billy Joe in each of them, which gave me great comfort. In that way, at least, I would always have him with me.

Several months after I had buried Billy Joe, my dad took me to a lawyer who told me he would sue the drilling company (which still hasn't been settled), so the kids and I wouldn't have to worry about money. Since the house was paid for, if I was really careful, I was able to make ends meet from the social security benefits--without having to dip into the insurance money. But after ten months of mourning, I finally faced the fact that Billy Joe was never coming back, and that I had six kids to support, who I hoped would some day go to college. So I decided to get my GED and try college myself.

I had no trouble passing the GED and, after talking to the counselor at the local junior college, I decided to try to get my degree in social work. I had always liked helping people and had made good grades in the social sciences when I was in high school, so I enrolled for the fall semester. I knew I would have to spend some of Billy Joe's insurance money, but after I graduated, I'd be able to provide a good living for my kids. Besides, going to school might help fill the terrible empty place in my soul that Billy Joe had left when he died. I knew I would never be able to love again, or give myself to another man. Not as long as I lived.

School was hard at first, and my grades were just barely passing. But by the second semester, I had gotten into the swing of the new routine and had developed better study habits. My kids all helped me, too. I still marveled at how I had been blessed with such sweet children, but then (I realized) they were just like their daddy in that respect.

And they were all really proud of me when I made the honor roll. We even ordered a pizza and celebrated. I remembered that other special night when we had celebrated with pizza; the night I had told Billy Joe that we were going to have a son. I knew he would have been proud of me too, and suddenly I felt such a wave of grief! Sometimes I still missed him almost more than what I thought I could bear.

At the beginning of my second year of college one of my sociology professors suggested that we go as a class to the blood bank and donate a pint of blood. When she stressed how important it was that the community be involved, we decided that it was a good idea. The next afternoon all of us who had decided to donate met in the parking lot and we all drove there together. I felt good in my heart that I was going to do something to help others. And I could almost feel Billy Joe there beside me--telling me how proud he was of me too.

When we got to the blood bank, I was a little scared at first. I had never donated blood before. We filled out the forms and some of the others went on ahead. Finally, it was my turn. I felt a little light headed at first, but I realized I was hyperventilating and slowed my breathing, and then I felt better. Afterwards, we all went for coffee and doughnuts and I was glad that I had done something that might save someone's life. Maybe even some other woman's husband who had been injured in an accident, but who would now be given the chance to live because of the blood I had just donated.

Two days later was when my bubble burst. I was just about to leave for school when I got a phone call from the director of the blood bank. He asked me to come in; He said he needed to talk to me as soon as possible. They had told us when we had donated that they would be screening our blood for all kinds of abnormalities. I became afraid that I might have leukemia or some kind of anemia.

I had classes all morning, so I told him I wouldn't be able to come until the early afternoon. But I had such a feeling of dread, I couldn't concentrate on my classes anyway, and thought it would have probably been better if I had gone on in to talk with him that morning; the waiting just made my fears worse.

When I got to the blood bank, I had to wait about fifteen minutes before I was able to see him. I asked one of the technicians if she could tell me anything and she told me she was sorry, but that the director was the only one who had the information.

Finally, he came out and asked me to come into his office. He had such a serious look on his face, I knew it must be something pretty bad. My heart started to beat faster and my mouth got dry. He asked me to sit down, which I did. Then he sat down behind his desk and cleared his throat.

"Mrs. Thompson, there's no easy way to tell you this." He paused a few seconds. "I'm very sorry, but your HIV test was positive. When it came up on the general panel, which sometimes shows false positives, we did further, more specific testing. But, unfortunately, it definitely came up as positive."

I couldn't believe what I was hearing! He was telling me I had AIDS! It had to be some kind of mistake. There was no way possible that I could have AIDS. I had never had a blood transfusion, and certainly had never used any kind of illegal drugs. I would barely even take an aspirin for a headache. "No," I said. "There has to be a mistake. There's no way I could have AIDS! Or ever have come into contact with AIDS."

"I'm so sorry, Mrs. Thompson. And you don't have AIDS: you're HIV positive. There's always the possibility that a cure, or at least a viable treatment will be found before you start showing any symptoms of AIDS. Of course, I advise you to see your doctor as soon as possible. And please! Don't ever give up hope!"

I just sat there for a while with my eyes closed, my fists clenched in my lap. Then the tears came. The director continued to sit at his desk, but remained silent. Finally, when I was able to stop crying, he asked if there was anything he could do to help.

I told him no, not unless he could find a cure. Then I got up and managed to stumble out of his office, down the short hall, and outside to my car. I just sat in my car for a while--thinking. Thinking about what I would do. Wondering what would happen to my kids, and how in the world I could have possibly gotten this cursed disease. I wondered about my dentist, but thought that was a very unlikely possibility. I had never had any medical procedures that I thought could have made me HIV positive. About the only thing I had ever received medical care for was giving birth to my kids.

I drove straight to my doctor's office and told the receptionist it was an emergency. Since by now it late afternoon there were just a few other patients left in the waiting room. After about forty-five minutes, but what seemed like forty-five hours, I was finally led into an examination room. When my doctor walked in I burst into tears again.

"Oh, Doctor Hayward," I blurted out. "I have AIDS!" Then I began to sob hysterically.

He looked at me in alarm, called for his nurse, and asked her to draw up something, I don't remember what, but it was probably Valium, or something similar. The next thing I knew he was giving me a shot in my arm, and a few minutes later I felt calmer.

"Now, Cindy," he said kindly, "Tell me why you think you have AIDS."

I told him about the blood bank, and he immediately suggested that we do another test to make sure. He examined me, then had his nurse take some of my blood, and said he'd have the results in about two weeks. He told me not to worry, because he saw no evidence of any symptoms of AIDS, and when we got the test results, then we would deal with whatever it showed.

I picked up hamburgers for the kid's supper--but I couldn't eat; I had no appetite. I told the kids I wasn't feeling well and went on to bed. The days seemed to drag by, but, on the other hand, I dreaded what my doctor would tell me. I still couldn't get it out of my mind that there had been some kind of terrible mistake, because I couldn't imagine where I ever could have possibly come into contact with the AIDS virus. It just wasn't possible.

Towards the end of the two weeks, the nurse phoned and told me to come in. I went that next morning rather than going to my classes. I hadn't been able to concentrate anyway, and had even briefly considered dropping out of school.

Dr. Hayward sat me down in a chair in his office and, rather than sitting behind his desk, he sat in a chair next to mine and took both of my hands in his. "Cindy, I'm very sorry; but the second test confirmed that you are, indeed, HIV positive. I wish there was something I could do to change it, but there isn't. However, you're in good health otherwise, and you never know when a cure or an effective long term treatment might be developed."

I guess I was past the crying by then. But I felt such anger! More than anger--a deep, inner-seething rage! Why me? And I was still bewildered about where and how I had become infected. When I told this to Dr. Hayward, he looked at me with deep sympathy, and then told me the most probable possibility was that Billy Joe had been infected. That Billy Joe was the one who had given it to me. At first I thought I had heard wrong.

"Billy Joe?" I said incredulously. That idea had never entered my mind. "Oh, no, Doctor. That couldn't be true. It's just not possible. Where would he have gotten it?"

Then I realized how stupid and naive I was, and had been. "You mean Billy Joe was with another woman sometime? It would have had to have been another woman, because I'm sure he wouldn't have been with a man." The thought of that made me giggle; then I realized that I was coming dangerously close to losing it. Dr. Hayward realized it too.

"Cindy, I know that Billy Joe loved you. You could see it in his eyes every time he looked at you. After all, I delivered all of your babies and saw how he was whenever he was around you. Don't ever doubt that Billy Joe loved you. But sometimes men do strange things, especially when they're away from home. Whatever he did, it had nothing to do with you, or his feelings for you."

I shivered. My heart felt cold. My body felt cold--in fact-- so cold that I didn't think I'd ever be able to feel warm again. How could Dr. Hayward tell me not to doubt Billy Joe's love for me when I apparently hadn't been enough for him? That he'd also had to have other women, or at least one other woman.

Dr. Hayward paused and held my hands tighter before continuing. "Cindy, this is one of the hardest things about being a doctor, telling patients and their loved ones that they've been diagnosed with a serious--potentially terminal illness. I can feel your pain and fear, and I hate to compound those feelings....But it's imperative that we have your children tested--as soon as possible. We have no way of knowing when you contracted the virus...if it was before or during any of your pregnancies.

I heard what he was saying but my mind and body had gone numb. My heart felt like it had turned into a cold stone inside my chest and I began to cry. "Oh God--not my babies too!" I thought. Dr. Hayward continued to hold my hands until I was able to stop crying. Then he gave me some tranquilizers and told me to come back in a week. That by then he would have been able to have done some research and decide what our best course of treatment was. And, he also told me not to ever give up hope.

Well, that was four months ago. Thank God, the kids all tested negative. Dr. Hayward started me on AZT and told me to come in for a routine physical examination every three months, and other than taking good care of myself that's the only treatment for now, anyway. So far I'm healthy, and haven't noticed any unusual symptoms. I haven't told the kids about me being HIV. I don't see any reason to worry them. Besides, they're too young to understand anyway.

I pray every night that I'll get to live long enough to see them all grow up, and that a cure will be found before I develop any symptoms. That's about all I have to hang on to. I also decided to stay in school. I still need to support my kids, as long as I'm around.

It's even harder now, because the deep aching pain of losing Billy Joe has now been replaced with a seething burning wound--which will never heal--deep in my soul, because I wasn't woman enough for him. Because he had to have some other woman or women besides me. I wonder how many there were and how many times he was with someone else, and if they were prettier than me, and if they were better lovers? I wonder if he did things with those other women that he didn't do with me? Wild, kinky things.

I remember some of those wild women his crew used to bring to our house and I wonder if it was one of them. I wonder how he could ever have done something to risk putting me through this torture. Even worse, to put our kids at risk of getting the virus, or being without both of their parents. How he could have been so thoughtless? So cruel? So stupid?

But worst of all, I'm constantly tortured by the agony of losing Billy Joe twice. Once when he died in the automobile accident, and the second time...when he died in my heart.

GOODBYE!

As I say goodbye to you
I'm bidding farewell to love untrue.
To parched tears shed in silent cries--
Caught in maelstrom of deceit and lies.

I think of fervent hours we spent,
The words of love I thought you meant
When joined together--our bodies wrapped
In passionate surrender--I was trapped

Within your web of dark conspiracy,
Deliberately woven from my fantasy,
Charmed by your cunning duplicity--
Deluded, in my naive simplicity.

When, suddenly, illusions cruelly shattered
Into pieces, like delicate crystal battered
Against a floor of cold hard stone;
You left me: lost--frightened--all alone.

You betrayed my love; you played a game!
And though the answer's still the same,
Over and over my heart asks why?
As I try to say . . . my last Goodbye!

SCREAMS!

It was the first mansion I had ever seen--up close--just like something right out of a movie. I had never been inside a mansion before, and as I rang the doorbell, for a brief moment I was intimidated by all the grandeur. I also had some misgivings about being here at 7:30 in the morning; but that was the time she had insisted on for the interview.

The door was opened by an elderly woman in a uniform, who looked at me with a hint of distrust; I assumed her to be the housekeeper or a maid. From the size of the house I was sure there had to be a staff of domestic help, including several gardeners.

"Hello," I said, still somewhat in awe of my surroundings. "I'm Abigail Adams; I have an appointment to see a nurse named Janet Oakley--about a private duty nursing position."

She nodded in return, invited me inside, and ushered me through an opulent foyer into a large, elegant sitting room. A middle-aged woman wearing a blue suit was sitting on a damask camelback sofa, drinking something out of a cup which I assumed to be either coffee or tea. "Mrs. Adams is here, Ma'am," the uniformed woman told her.

The seated woman smiled as she stood and introduced herself, holding out her hand. "Hello. I'm Janet Oakley. I'm the one who spoke with you on the phone." Then she looked past me. "That will be all, Gerda, and please close the doors behind you." I glanced back over my shoulder in time to see the woman in the maid's uniform closing the double doors to the sitting room.

"Well, Mrs Adams, please sit down. You need to fully understand the situation here before you make your decision as to whether or not you'll want the position. Actually, it's a very unusual case. Would you care for coffee?"

"Yes, thank you; that would be nice--and please call me Abby." I sat down opposite her on a wingback chair positioned on the other side of a carved wooden coffee table. She smiled as she lifted a silver server from the table and poured coffee into a china cup which she then handed to me. "Cream? Sugar?" she asked as she indicated the silver creamer and sugar bowl. I helped myself to both, then leaned back in my chair and took a sip.

She put her cup down on the table and folded her hands in her lap. "First, Abby, I'd like for you to tell me a little about yourself."

I, too, set my cup down. "Well, I'm married. My children are grown; my son graduated from college a year ago, and my daughter is in her second year at Baylor University. My husband travels a lot in his work, and I've been rather bored lately with so much extra time on my hands. I worked for several months in the OB/Gyn department at the new hospital, but decided I'd rather do private duty. I've always been especially interested in psychiatric nursing, and I like the one-to-one, provided the patient isn't violent, of course." I paused. "I have a Bachelor of Science degree in nursing... but I guess you already know about my work experience and my education from the resume I sent. I'm not sure what else you want to know," I said, as I thought: "or have the right to know." I was beginning to wonder if perhaps I had made a mistake in applying for this job.

Janet smiled again. "I'm sorry if I seem overly curious. It's just that it will take a special kind of person for the nursing duties here." She stopped for a moment, lost in her thoughts, then sighed. "Maybe it'd be best if I just explained the circumstances to you. Then we can decide, together, if it's the right situation for you."

She picked up her cup, drained the coffee remaining in it, then thoughtfully replaced it in its saucer before beginning. "There are only four people living on this estate--which covers five acres: Mr. Lodge and his daughter, Victoria, and two servants; Gerda, the housekeeper--whom you met when you arrived--and her husband Karl, who is in charge of the grounds. They've been with Mr Lodge since before Victoria was born. There are three other daily servants and two land-scapers.

"Mr. Lodge is seventy-eight-years-old and his daughter is forty-one." When she saw the look on my face, she shook her head. "It's not what you think. It's not a geriatric case. My advertisement was the truth. The job is of a Psychiatric nature, but not in the usual sense. The patient isn't violent--and it's not Mr. Lodge. He's a healthy, vibrant man, espe-cially for his age. When you meet him, you will be quite surprised. He is an avid exerciser, eats only healthy food, and is very active. When he's here, he swims daily, and has his own gym on the premises where he works out with his personal trainer--who comes four days a week. He even still rides whenever he visits his friends in England who have horses.

"He's also much in demand with the ladies--a number of whom he seems to keep quite happy, in spite of his age. He travels a lot. Spends a lot of his time in Europe. He seems to be uncomfortable living here....I often wonder if it's be-cause of guilt.

"It's his daughter Victoria," Janet continued. She paused and shook her head. "She's the patient. She's still a beautiful woman and could travel to any part of the world if she wished, but she never leaves this house, even seldom goes out onto the grounds. She has her own suite of rooms on the third floor where she spends most of her time painting." Janet stopped talking and looked at me, her eyes shiny with unshed tears.

I felt a little uncomfortable, and said, "But I imagine Mr. Lodge is a very wealthy man. Hasn't Victoria received treat-ment? I'd think she would have been treated by the best doctors possible and be on some kind of medication. Does she suffer from agoraphobia? From what I've read, it can respond very successfully to treatment in the majority of cases."

Janet had by now regained her composure. "Yes, what you are saying is true. The best doctors have examined her.

Frankly, I don't think Victoria wants to be helped. I think she wants to remain in her delusion, for that's what it is, you see. I've been her nurse now for nearly eleven years and have become emotionally attached to her; I feel almost as if she were my sister." She held up her hand as she sensed I was about to interrupt her.

"I know, I know! Nurses aren't supposed to become emotionally involved with their patients. And this is the first time it's ever happened to me, to this extent anyway. But you know as well as I do that for any nurse, who continues in the profession for any length of time, that there are going to be cases where we will become emotionally attached to a patient, especially in a situation such as this."

She was right, I thought, as I remembered one of my first patients from many years ago: the handsome young man with the broken leg suffered in an automobile accident, who had become my husband barely a year later.

"I've met a wonderful man and we're going to be married in two months," Janet continued. "Unfortunately, I will be moving to London where he resides. He's a photo journalist, whom I met last year while on my vacation. Victoria will have to have adequate time to get to know and become comfortable with whoever takes my place, so she'll be able to adjust as well as possible to my absence. She's a lovely woman: gentle, soft-spoken, and very talented, as well as still being beautiful. Oh, it's all so sad."

She stopped as her eyes grew shiny again, and a tear slid down her cheek. She took a handkerchief from her pocket and wiped the tear away, but another quickly followed in its wake. She sat for several minutes, quietly crying, waiting for the tears to stop. I was still having second thoughts, but I was also intrigued. It certainly sounded like a case out of the ordinary--which I'd always been attracted to.

Janet wiped away the last of her tears. "I'm sorry, Abby; I'm embarrassed. I really didn't think I would break down. It's just that leaving is going to be hard on me, too, and I know I'll worry about her. I need to find just the right person to take my place. Someone who has a heart full of compassion and empathy. That's what Victoria needs. When she was in her second year of high school, her mother died of cancer. She had a succession of three or four stepmothers after that, none of whom she was close to. And I'm the only close friend she's had--since her illness.

"You would be more of a companion to her, rather than a nurse. In fact, you won't even wear a uniform. It's better if you just wear your regular street clothes. She only needs the medical nursing care in the morning, shortly after she wakes up. For the rest of the day, all is required is that you be a friend to her. The only friend she'll have.

"I'm sorry, Abby; I know you're confused. I need to tell you Victoria's story. She was a lovely young debutante, as well as a very promising artist. She studied for two years at the Chicago Art Institute, then decided that she would learn more if she studied in Paris. So she went to Paris and studied for three more years. And I hear she was quite the belle over there. She had men literally falling at her feet, begging her to marry them. Wealthy men, titled men, famous men. Even several actors and rock stars, it's rumored.

When she returned to the "States," she had her first exhibit at a small, but prestigious gallery in New York. That's when she fell in love with another up-and-coming young artist. It was love at first sight, from what I've been told. He was quite an intense young man, with the dark brooding good looks one might associate with the concept of what an artist is supposed to look like. And, from what I understand, he had rather a Bohemian lifestyle, including numerous love affairs with his models and other women--even after he and Victoria began to date.

His name was Vincent: like Van Gogh. Only his last name was Roden. I often wondered if Vincent was his real name, or one that he had pretentiously assumed because he thought it would enhance his image." She waved her hand, "but that's neither here nor there. The important thing is that Victoria had fallen very much in love with him. She and Vincent lived together for nearly a year, then decided to get married. So she returned here, without him, to make the preparations. I still wonder if he really loved her, or planned to marry her merely for her money.

"Anyway, Victoria made her wedding plans. She mailed out the engraved invitations and had a beautiful bridal dress and veil especially designed and made just for her. The wedding was to take place at four o'clock on a Saturday afternoon in May, at the Church of the Good Shepherd. Oh, it was to be the society event of the year. People from all over the state had been invited. The reception was to be held here, in the garden, with an orchestra and everything. Only, that day, Vincent never made it to the ceremony."

I drew in a breath. "You don't mean he left her waiting at the altar, do you?" I asked incredulously.

"Yes. I'm afraid that's almost exactly what he did do. So the story goes, when she talked to him two nights before the wedding he told her he wouldn't be able to arrive here until late on the night before the wedding was to take place, and that he would check into a hotel and call her. And he did call, around midnight I understand. One of his artist friends from New York was to be his best man and had come with him. Vincent apparently told Victoria that he and his friend were going to go out for a few drinks--sort of a little bachelor bash. So she didn't call him the morning of the wedding. She didn't want to wake him. And she hadn't suspected anything might be wrong when he didn't call her. She just thought he was sleeping late and probably hung over.

"Victoria arrived at the church, along with her flock of bridesmaids who were all old school friends. They were in the bride's dressing room, excitedly helping each other dress, and had even opened a bottle of champagne. The church began to fill with guests, and Victoria had no idea that Vincent hadn't arrived yet. When four o'clock came, her father knocked at the door of the bride's room, and when she opened it, she was able to hear the organist playing the list of songs she had selected to be played prior to the wedding march.

"She expected her father to tell her that he was ready to escort her to the church sanctuary: that the ceremony was about to begin. But instead, he told her that Vincent wasn't at the church yet. Victoria couldn't believe it. She telephoned Vicent's hotel, but the desk clerk told her that he had already checked out. She assumed that he was on his way to the church and had just been delayed--certain that he would be there any minute.

"They waited until 4:30. By then the guests had become restless, and the organist had played the list of selections several times, even adding a few songs of her own; her fingers were beginning to get tired, and I guess Mr. Lodge finally had someone tell her to stop. The pastor had also announced, several times, that there would be a short delay.

"By 5:00 P.M., after the third delay announcement, everyone had become very uncomfortable; many of the guests started to leave. By 5:30, most of them had left. But Victoria remained steadfast in her faith that Vincent would eventually show up. She continued to believe that he had somehow been unavoidably delayed, and that someday the two of them would look back at the experience and laugh.

"However, her friends were becoming embarrassed for her. For they were just as convinced, by now, that Vincent was never coming. Eventually, they each quietly changed out of their bridesmaid's dresses and slipped out of the church, at a loss for words. Most of them were stunned beyond belief that something this terrible had happened to someone as beautiful and desirable as Victoria.

"Victoria remained in her bridal gown, refusing to leave the church. Her father tried to get her to leave with him, but she lashed out at him: told him that he had always wanted to believe the worst of Vincent, and that she knew he had secretly never been happy about her marrying him. She was right, too. There were lots of rumors, at the time, that Mr. Lodge had paid Vincent off--not to marry Victoria, that he had given Vincent a handsome sum to go far away and never see her again.

"Victoria sat in that room all night. Alone! The Pastor also tried to get her to go home. But she became upset, almost to the point of hysteria, refusing to budge from the room.

"The next morning Mr. Lodge brought their family doctor to the church, who injected Victoria with a sedative--one strong enough to knock her out--then he and Mr. Lodge took her home. When she woke up, she became so distressed and hyperactive that they were forced to have her hospitalized. After several weeks, when she hadn't improved, Mr. Lodge had her moved to an exclusive private clinic where she stayed for six months. When she returned home, she appeared to be normal for several weeks.

"Then one morning when she woke up, she thought it was her wedding day and began to get ready to go to the church. But as soon as she sat at her dressing table and looked at her reflection in the mirror, she began to scream. Terrible, bloodcurdling screams of anguish. Heartbreaking screams of total despair. No one was able to get her to stop. After her screaming had gone on for fifteen minutes, Mr. Lodge telephoned the doctor who came to the house as fast as he could and gave her another injection. A private-duty nurse was hired to stay with her. Several hours later, when Victoria woke up from the sedative, she appeared to be calm, but was delusional. She now believed that it was the day before her wedding and spent the rest of the day doing precisely the same things she had done on the actual day before her wedding.

"Wanting to do anything they could to avert another outbreak of the hysteria, and those piercing, heart-wrenching screams, her father, the nurse, and the rest of the household staff went along with her delusion. However, the following day was an exact repeat of the day before. When she awoke in the morning, she again thought it was the morning of her wedding day. She began to get ready to go to the church and, once again, it was when she looked into the mirror that the screams began. The nurse gave her another injection, which knocked her out for several hours, then when she woke up, she again thought it was the day before her wedding and did the same things she had done on that day.

"One of those things she had done, was add some finishing touches to a portrait of herself and Vincent embracing, which she had painted for him as a surprise wedding gift. She had planned to give it to him when they returned from their Hawaiian honeymoon. And that's what she now always does in the afternoons. She'll paint on a new composition for a while, then finish that painting of herself and Vincent.

She's been finishing that same painting for seventeen years. Maybe just one stroke, maybe not any; sometimes she'll just look at it. Then she'll ask me if I think he'll like it--her eyes shining with such deep love."

Janet shrugged, her eyes brimming with tears again. "That's the way it always is. She relives those same two days, combined into one, over and over--exactly the same. Victoria certainly isn't a difficult patient, and the only actual nursing is the sedative injection every day. The many doctors who have treated her all agreed that they don't want it given until after she starts to scream. They always have hope that each new day will be the day when she'll be able to cope with what happened: to adjust to her life, and awaken free of the delusion. It's been almost eighteen years now since that day...since the day Vincent left her waiting at the church.

"In the beginning, Mr. Lodge went through many nurses until he was finally able to find one who would stay. That one was here for six-and-a-half years, but was older, and when her health began to deteriorate she had to move to Florida to be near her children and grandchildren. It was as hard for her to leave as it is for me. I'm the one who took her place. And I almost didn't. That's why I wanted you here so early in the morning: to see how you will react.

If you decide to take the job, you would need to be here by 7:30 every morning. But you would be able to leave at 3:30 in the afternoon--so you would have the rest of the day to yourself. I think this is the only fair way to do it. For you to see for yourself what it's like. It's the screams that they can't stand. It's like someone's soul is dying. Such terrible screams of agony!" She shivered. "Screams like you've never heard before. Screams as if someone is ripping her heart out of her chest." She looked at her watch. "She'll be waking up very soon now; A few minutes later she'll look into the mirror--and that's when she'll need me."

She stood and motioned towards the coffee pot. "I'll have Gerda bring you some fresh coffee. And please! Don't leave until I get back! I have a feeling about you. That you might be the one who will be able to take my place. But you need to see what it's like. Just make yourself at home. I need to go to her now. I need to be there when she wakes up. I'll be back soon. It never takes long." And she quickly left the room.

I thought she had probably greatly overdramatized the situation. It was a very sad story--true; but surely it couldn't be as bad as she had said. Gerda brought in a glass coffee carafe and refilled my cup. Afterwards, she peered at me intently for a few seconds, as if trying to read my mind, then quickly hurried from the room. I added cream and sugar to my coffee, picked up the cup and took a sip. I knew one thing, someone sure did make good coffee.

After a few more minutes I began to get restless. I stood, then started walking around the room, carrying my cup and enjoying the coffee while looking at the beautiful paintings on the walls. There were several Renoirs, and a Matisse (which I was pretty sure were the real thing). It might not be so bad to work here, I thought. The job certainly seemed easy enough, and the salary was excellent. The screams couldn't be all that bad. Yes, I had pretty much made up my mind to take the job.

On the far wall, there were some particularly lovely paintings hanging together in their own grouping. When I looked at the signature, I saw that they were signed with only the initials, V.L. They must be some of Victoria's paintings, I thought. They were exquisite. The dramatic lighting effect, from very light to very dark, was what made them so special. Yes! She was very talented. I enjoyed another sip of coffee while I examined the paintings more closely.

Suddenly, the silence was shattered by the most gut-wrenching scream--the likes of which I had never in my life heard before--followed immediately by another and another. The china cup slipped from my fingers and smashed against the marble floor as I frantically clamped my hands over my ears to shut out those agonizing screams. Piercing screams of such bone-chilling anguish--they penetrated my soul; I felt that if I couldn't shut them out, they would most certainly, literally, break my heart!

THE EVE OF THE BEGINNING (CONTINUED)

This time I emerged from the trance--dream--spell--whatever the stories were, swimming up through the blue depth of her eyes with mixed emotions: with both sorrow and hope. Schere was still holding my face in her hands. She smiled, not the Mona Lisa smile this time, but a warm, playful smile. The smile of a lover.

"True fulfillment of love is not only a deep, passionate physical desire, but also a passion for the union of the mind and of the soul, which can sometimes be even greater than the physical desire. Only when this passion for the mind and soul of another is also a burning desire to be consummated, can love be forever enduring. Otherwise, it is merely lust. Most women realize this, but men can also feel this same way.

"Michael, remember to look into the eyes of your beloved while you are making love, so that your souls can join together along with your bodies: for the eyes are the windows into our souls."

She continued to smile. "Michael, I will now tell you of romantic love: that overpowering, unexplainable chemical attraction that happens spontaneously between two people, which is truly magical, yet often turbulent. Many consider romantic love to be the most important and the most exciting. These are the stories of romantic love: the story of Myra, and the story of Glenda."

And I looked hungrily into her eyes with a feeling of excitement.

DANCER OF THE SCIMITAR

He was here again. She always knew when he was here. She could feel the warmth of his eyes watching her...even before she would see them. His wonderful, gentle, wistful eyes. The first time she had seen him, she had thought his eyes were brown, but later realized they were dark blue. They made her think of the old Gypsy song, "Dark Eyes." She wondered if he wore tinted contact lenses or if that was their natural color.

Her thoughts abruptly shifted back to her dance. Her professional name was "Maia" (Bona Dea). The second Pliad; daughter of Atlas; mother of Hermes. When she danced, she would tend to lose herself in the intensity of the music, and became "Maia".

In a gliding motion, she swept up her sword from one corner of the dance floor, carefully balanced it on her head and did a series of forward camel walks--followed by several hip thrusts, before sinuously undulating to her knees. She shifted her weight to her left hip, and with the sword still carefully balanced on her head, began a slow, sensuous body roll. This was the part of her dance which demanded her full concentration. After four of the rolls, she ended in a kneeling position and lowered her upper body straight back to the floor in a serpentine roll.

She took the sword from her head, placed it on her abdomen, and did four stomach flutters, then lifted the sword and held it high above her head as she quickly rose to her feet in one fluid motion. She again balanced the sword on the top of her head, during several minutes of hip shimmies, which became faster and faster--her hips synchronized with the beat of the drum--then three quick turns, which made her chiffon skirt swirl and float gracefully about her. When the music stopped, she grasped her sword in both hands, executed a low bow, and ran off the stage and up the stairs to the dressing room.

When she was four-years-old she had heard the "Sabre Dance" for the first time, which had immediately become her favorite music, and from that time she had known that someday she would dance with a sword.

As she changed into a denim shirt and jeans, her thoughts again turned to the man with the wistful blue eyes. This was the sixth week since she had first noticed him sitting alone in the back. The sixth week since she had first noticed his wonderful eyes. He was always in that same place, but only for her dance. When she arrived at the small Greek restaurant to get ready for her dance, she was never able to find him, and by the time she had changed out of her costume and come back downstairs, he was always gone.

Several times she had asked some of the waiters about him, but none seemed to remember him. But she couldn't forget his wonderful eyes, which seemed to penetrate to the core of her soul.

After she had finished changing into her clothes, she went back downstairs to the small table near the kitchen where she always sat to enjoy eating the marvelous Greek dinner she looked forward to, following her dance.

As she ate, she glanced around the restaurant--looking for him while savoring the flavor of the dolmathes--but, as usual, he wasn't there. After she finished her meal, she continued to think about the man with the wonderful, dark blue eyes, and wonder what he was like.

She sighed. She was tired, and tomorrow she had a new patient who would be exceptionally challenging. The belly dancing was something she did for fun. Even though she got paid for it, she would have done it for free; in fact, she often did free performances at charitable functions and various types of benefits. Her day job, the one she actually supported herself with, was physical therapy.

She had worked very hard at building herself a respected reputation among the medical community, and had been able to open her own clinic a year ago. It was doing well and she was pleased with herself, but her dedication to her career and to her dancing had left her with precious little time for any kind of social life.

She began to think about a tentative treatment plan for her new patient tomorrow. His name was Ray Sandifer and his physician had given her his history. Actually, he appeared to be quite a remarkable man. He was a few years older than she, and in spite of inheriting millions from his family (making it unnecessary for him to have work), he had still managed to become one of the most successful and sought after architects in the area.

Several months ago, he had suffered a severely fractured leg in a skiing accident, involving crushed bone and other complications which had required several surgeries. He was now ready for physical therapy. According to his orthopedist, although the odds were against it, Mr. Sandifer was determined to regain full use of his leg, and she was just as determined to make sure he achieved his goal.

* * * * * * * * * *

Sandi watched intently as Maia carefully positioned the sword on her head. (The sword: ancient symbol of phallikos--"embodiment of generative power.") He was enchanted by her dance and he was fascinated by her. She was graceful and ethereal. He had discovered her weeks ago, quite by accident, when he had come to the small Greek restaurant to eat dinner. It had been his first outing on his own since his injury--after he had learned to manage his cast and crutches.

He enjoyed Greek food, but had never dreamed that he would become so captivated by a belly dancer, of all things. He was fascinated by her snake-like movements, reminding him of "Stop, Stop, Stop," a song by The Hollies popular in the late sixties, and smiled as he recalled some of the words.

He had always considered himself to be sophisticated and worldly, and had done extensive international traveling. He had seen a number of belly dancers and, although he had always enjoyed the sensuous, seductive dance, Maia was different! He had also had a number of relationships with highly educated and beautiful women, and although Maia wasn't beautiful in the classical sense, she had a magical quality of vitality, combined with an exquisite delicateness. When she danced, she was radiant. She put such deep feeling into her dance, she was dramatic and mystical.

Her looks were also totally opposite to those of the women he had found attractive in the past. She was a fair, petite woman, with small high breasts and a narrow waist (which also made him think of Elton John's song, "Tiny Dancer"). She had a slender, yet muscular build: lithe and limber. In the past, he had always preferred tall, dark, voluptuous women, and Maia was certainly in no way voluptuous.

Since that first night, he had come back each week to watch her dance: it was the one thing in his life he looked forward to the most. He had even begun to fantasize about her--erotically--although, realistically, he feared they would have little or nothing in common. Although he wasn't a snob, he was wise enough to realize that similar interests and education were just as important as physical attraction in sustaining a fulfilling, long-term relationship. But he also realized, with embarrassment, that he was a romantic.

He wanted to meet her, but not until he was again what he considered to be a whole man. He was afraid she would reject him outright, or, even worse, that she would feel pity for him in his present condition. He couldn't dare to take a chance on either, so had decided he wouldn't attempt to approach her yet. She was obviously a very physical person, and he wanted to be physically equal to her when they finally met.

He had worked very hard to become one of the most successful architects in the area, and he knew he could work just as hard to become well again.

Since that first time he no longer dined at the restaurant; he didn't want her to see him the way he was. He would call ahead and order his dinner to be packed for take-out, then arrive just in time watch her dance. He always sat in the back making sure that his crutches were carefully concealed. As soon as she finished her dance, he would have one of the bus boys carry his dinner to his car for him. Tonight was no exception.

At home his live-in housekeeper transferred the dinner to fine china dishes before serving it. He always ate it in his dining room with candlelight and wine. It had almost become a ritual, and he fantasized about the time, he hoped in the not too distant future, when Maia would be sitting across from him, sharing the delicious food.

It was late after he had finished his meal and he was tired. He wanted to get a good night's sleep so he could make the most of his first physical therapy session in the morning.

His doctor had made the appointment for him. The therapist, who was supposed to be the best and the most knowledgeable of the newest treatments, was a woman, which had surprised him. Her name was Myra Middaugh. He pictured a large, gray-haired, masculine woman. But if she was as good as his doctor said she was, he didn't care what she looked like--just as long as she could help him to get well. When he went to sleep, he was looking forward to his therapy the next morning, determined to work hard so that he could fulfill his fantasy of finally introducing himself to Maia.

* * * * * * * * *

She was in one of the treatment rooms, making sure all of the equipment was ready for Mr. Sandifer's therapy as the time drew near for his appointment. While she was once again looking over the information his doctor had given her so that she would be completely familiar with his medical history, she noted that although his first name was Ray, he preferred to use his nickname: Sandi. She was acquainted with his work because she had always had an interest in architecture, and had been impressed by the buildings he had designed, with their unique blend of function and style. Her thoughts were interrupted as her receptionist walked into the treatment room.

"Mr. Sandifer is here, Myra."

She turned around and let out a small gasp as her heart skipped a beat, when she looked into that familiar pair of gentle, wistful--and now, also, totally startled--dark blue eyes.

The sword: ancient symbol of phallikos...

BISHERT/BISHERTA

John couldn't believe it; right before his eyes Debbie's face suddenly changed to someone else's--while he was talking to her! Someone he didn't even recognize. His heart began to beat faster as he blinked his eyes. Was he losing his mind! Then, just as suddenly, her face changed back again. It was probably from fatigue. He shook his head. He had been stuck with another stressful twelve-hour emergency room duty. Although he was glad that he had become a doctor, he sometimes wondered why he had chosen emergency medicine as his specialty. He looked around the room, then back at Debbie, one of the ER nurses, and, thank God, she still looked like Debbie.

Just then, two paramedics brought in a gunshot victim with femoral artery bleeding, and he temporarily forgot the bizarre occurrence of the changing face. Six hours later when he walked to his car, he was too exhausted to remember it.

* * * * * * * * *

While she was singing, Glenda scanned the sea of faces in the audience at the small country western bar. It was one of her songs: the one she had just written. She couldn't tell for sure, but judging by the applause when she finished, they liked it. She felt a warm glow of pride. It was the first one of her songs that she had performed in public. The band had backed her one hundred per cent, and it was mainly from their encouragement that she had summoned the courage to sing it tonight. She took several bows as the applause continued, then walked off the stage for a brief intermission.

"Wow, Glenda," Travis, her lead guitarist and good friend said as he put his arm around her shoulders. "I told you they'd like it. It's a good song."

"Now, Trav," she said, as she smiled at him. "You know you're prejudiced. You're such a good friend, you'd like anything I wrote."

"No, Glenda, that's not true. Hey, let's grab a quick beer before the next set."

"You have the beer, I'm just going to have a soda for now," she said. She sat down at one of the back booths, while Travis went to the bar and got their drinks. Glenda looked around, noting the wide differences in the ages of the patrons. They ranged from young twenties to the middle seventies. Maybe the song *was* good. Maybe she *would* get that recording contract she had been praying for.

After Travis returned, she was in the midst of telling him about the other two songs she had almost completed writing--when suddenly his face changed! She was sitting there--looking at him--and his face became someone else's. Someone she didn't even know. At first she thought she must be hallucinating. That someone had put something into her soda, or maybe she was having a stroke. Then, just as suddenly, his face changed back. She blinked her eyes. What was happening to her?

She looked around the room, first at the patrons dancing to the juke box, then at the bartender. They all looked normal, the way they were supposed to look. Her heart was pounding as she stared into her glass; she was afraid to look at Travis again.

When it was time for the next set, as they took their places on the small stage Travis leaned over and asked, "What's wrong Glenda? Are you feeling ill? You look as if something's spooked you."

She finally forced herself to look at him. "No, Trav, I'm fine. Probably just a little tired," she said, while thinking: "thank God, he still looked like Travis!" The rest of the evening was uneventful, and by the time she went home she was so tired that she had forgotten about the bizarre face changing.

When she went to sleep she began to dream that she was in Nashville, appearing at the Grand Old Opry. Then the dream changed, and she was a passenger, riding in some type of small sports car. When she looked at the driver, she awoke with a start. It was a man with the same face that had been on Travis earlier in the evening. Her heart began to beat faster, as she wondered: "what is happening to me?"

She got out of bed and went into the kitchen for some water. After a few sips she began to calm down. I must remain calm and rational, she thought. She went into the living room and sat on the couch. Honey, her golden retriever, came over and put her head on Glenda's lap. "What's going on, girl? Am I losing it?" she asked as she patted Honey's head.

She thought about the face. It was still crystal clear in her mind. Actually, it was a very nice face. Dark hair and intelligent brown eyes. A sensitive, earnestly intent face. She probed her memory but couldn't recall anyone she had ever seen who looked like that, nor anyone who drove that kind of car. "Strange," she mused. Finally, she went back to bed and was able to sleep peacefully for the rest of the night.

For her day job, she was a hostess at one of the nicer seafood restaurants downtown. She worked the lunch crowd, usually just four or five hours a day, which gave her time for songwriting and rehearsing. With her day job, and the four nights a week singing at the county western bar, she was able to support herself and Honey, not in a grand style, but well enough, barring any emergencies.

She had written several songs which she had recently recorded onto a demo tape and sent to some of the major record companies. She was hoping and praying for a recording contract. She felt in her heart that her songs were special, and she knew her voice was not only good, but unusual. Not everyone lived in Nashville who made it in C/W music. Willie Nelson, George Strait, and Freddy Fender were fellow Texans.

She was working every spare minute on trying to write enough songs for an album, in case a contract would come through. She had worked very hard the past several years, practicing and perfecting her voice as well as her guitar and songwriting skills--all of which had left her little time for other areas of her life.

The next few days were uneventful, filled with work and practice. On Saturday night, when she was particularly tired after performing, she arrived home at 2:00 A.M. and fell asleep as soon as her head hit the pillow. She began to dream that she was sitting on a sandy beach in the moonlight. It was so real, she could hear the gentle lapping of the surf against the shore. She looked up, and there he was--standing in front of her. The man with that face; again!

He took her hand and gently pulled her to her feet. Then they started dancing to beautiful music--enchanting music--played by an unseen symphony orchestra. They stopped moving, still holding each other, and looked into each other's eyes. She felt breathless. He took her face in his hands, tilted it upward, and tenderly kissed her mouth. As she felt his taut, muscular body pressed tightly against her, an intoxicating warmth began to spread through her body. Then, abruptly, she woke up.

Perspiring profusely, she felt disoriented, and for a minute she wasn't sure where she was. The dream had been so real that for an instant she thought she was still on the beach. Her heart was beating fast and her mouth was dry as she sat up in alarm. Then, when she was able to see the familiar surroundings of her bedroom take shape from the moonlight shining through the window, she began to calm down. But she continued to feel the warm glow his closeness had aroused in her, and her heart was still beating faster than usual.

* * * * * * * * *

John looked at his watch as he pulled into a burger joint, fast food drive-through; it was 1:30 A.M. He had just finished a twelve-hour Saturday night shift in the ER and was almost too tired to eat, but knew he needed to. He couldn't go without food. He ordered a grilled chicken sandwich and a Sprite. He took his food home, ate, took a quick shower, and thirty-five minutes later he was in bed.

He began to dream that he was sitting on a warm sandy beach. The full moon bathed everything in a silvery glow, giving an almost surreal effect. He could hear the sighing of the surf as he turned his head, and there she was. The girl with that face! The face he had seen on Debbie several days ago. It was an interesting face. In fact, a beautiful face: beautiful in its sincerity and warmth. It was a face that touched his heart and caused it to beat faster.

He got to his feet and stood in front of her, then took her hand in his and gently pulled her to her feet. He took her in his arms and they began to dance to beautiful music which came from an unknown source. She felt so light that he tightened his arms around her, afraid she would float away. They stopped dancing and looked deeply into each other's eyes. He put his hands on each side of her face, gently tilted it, and tenderly kissed her mouth, then held her even more tightly. He could feel her soft, yielding warmth pressed against him. Then, abruptly, she was gone--like a puff of smoke.

He woke up. His heart was pounding, and for a few seconds he felt breathless. He thought he was still on the beach and felt confused before he began to recognize the familiar shapes of his bedroom. His sexual excitement was still very much in evidence, and when after a few minutes it showed no signs of going away, he frustratedly went into the bathroom and took another shower. He hadn't had an experience like this since his high school days.

* * * * * * * * *

Glenda was trying to concentrate on writing her song: the one she had started early this morning when she had been unable to sleep. It had been inspired by last night's very realistic and provocative dream. Her working title was "Mystery," but her mind kept wandering back to the dream. She couldn't get the man out of her mind. He had such a nice face: ruggedly handsome, with the most beautiful eyes. Eyes that expressed a strong, caring sincerity--such an innate goodness, which she had never seen in anyone else. And she knew that this would be the best song she had ever written.

* * * * * * * * *

John was eventually able to go back to sleep and didn't wake up again until shortly before noon. When he did awaken, he was ravenous. He ate a large bowl of cereal, followed by several pieces of toast which were washed down by a tall glass of orange juice. He tried to read some of his new medical journals, but found he was having difficulty concentrating. He couldn't get the woman out of his mind. What was happening to him? He had always been so rational and scientific.

Finally, he reached such a point of restlessness, and since he didn't have to go back to work until 11:00 P.M., he decided to go for a drive. He was proud of the restoration he had done on his 1956 MG roadster and enjoyed driving it, but after he had driven aimlessly around for an hour he decided to see a movie. He went to the closest mall where there was a theater, but once inside he had difficulty concentrating on the story. He kept seeing her face in his mind and almost felt as if she were sitting beside him. Several times he even looked at the vacant seat next to him, almost certain, each time, that he would see her quietly sitting there.

Luckily, John didn't have any trouble concentrating at work that night. They were so busy with two auto accidents, an abused child, a drunk who had fallen off the roof of his house, and a female gunshot victim (who had been shot by her boyfriend's wife) that he didn't have time to think of anything other than saving lives. Five hours later, he finally had time to get a cup of coffee and a sandwich at the cafeteria. But as soon as he sat down, there she was again in his mind, but so real, it seemed more nearly like a hallucination than a daydream.

"Hey, John, how's it goin'?"

He turned around to see his best friend Dave, a Psychiatric resident, walking towards him carrying a tray. They were seldom able to spend much time together, what with their current, usually conflicting schedules, and John was glad for the diversion.

"Hey, Buddy, you look tired," Dave said, as he put his food on the table. "They got you on one of those resident burnout schedules that makes you wonder why you ever wanted to become a doctor?"

John smiled. "That's about it, my friend." Then, before he could stop himself, he began to tell Dave about his dream, trying to make a joke out of it. He also told him about the alarming experience of Debbie's face changing. "It's probably from fatigue and stress--right, Dave? Or am I losing it?" He tried to make his voice sound light.

Dave grinned. "Yeah, good buddy; they're probably working you to the point where you can't tell reality from fantasy." As Dave studied him more closely, he could see that John was worried in spite of his attempt at levity. Dave thought for a few minutes while he ate his sandwich. Then he smiled at John and said,"I'll bet it's your Bisherta. Yeah. That's probably who it is. She's trying to find you before you work yourself to death."

John gave him a puzzled look. "My Bisherta? What's that?"

"She's the woman who was created just for you. She's like your soul mate. The one you're fated to be with. It's one of my beliefs."

Dave was of the Jewish faith, and when John had accompanied him to his nephew's Bar Mitzvah, last year, he had been impressed with the beauty and solemnity of the ceremony.

"You don't have to be Jewish to have a Bisherta--or Bishert, which is the masculine version--although, unfortunately, we don't always end up with our Bisherta or Bishert. Since we have the freedom of choice, being the lowly human beings that we are, we often end up--due to our own fault--with the wrong person."

"You're serious about this aren't you Dave? Do you really think that's who this woman is?"

Dave gave him a sheepish grin and shrugged. "Can you think of a better explanation? You're one of the sanest persons I know; I really don't think you're hallucinating, and I don't think you do either. There are lots of things that can't be explained. You know that. You've seen patients everyone thought didn't stand a chance of surviving, end up making a complete recovery. Sure, it's not often, but it does happen. Who knows? Maybe THE BOSS MAN is trying to tell you something. Give it some thought."

John didn't know what to think...other than that Dave believed what he was saying to him. He knew Dave had an uncanny perception about people's innermost feelings, which was one of the things that made him such a damn good shrink. He grinned, feeling better, and said, "A man of science! Yes, sir, Dave, that's what you are!"

As Dave stood up to leave, he said, "Medicine is also an art. Remember?" He clapped John on the shoulder and strode off.

John went back to the ER, where the rest of the evening's emergencies slacked off to a more reasonable pace. Now, when he saw her face in his mind, he had a different perspective. He began to study her features and still liked what he saw. He even looked forward to the image. He realized, with somewhat of a shock, that he was probably falling in love with her. His problem now was to try to discover if she really existed, and--if so--who she was and where he would be able to find her. But, for some reason, he had a gut feeling that in due time--a very short due time--that they would meet. He was certain of it!

* * * * * * * * * *

Glenda worked on her song for the rest of the morning. Since it was Sunday, it was her day off from both of her jobs, so she decided to go to a mall to do some shopping in the afternoon. At the last minute, she almost changed her mind and went to see one of the movies, but decided she wouldn't be able to concentrate and just browsed in some of the stores instead. She found a pair of sandals like she had been looking for, which she was able to buy at a reasonable price. Maybe finding them was an omen of good luck. When she got home, she took Honey for a walk around her apartment complex grounds.

That night she worked on her song some more and was pleased with the way it was progressing. Although his face still kept popping into her mind, it was beginning to give her inspiration, rather than distracting her. When she went to sleep he was again in her dreams. This time they made love--with such a deepness of cojoinment that they reached simultaneous, fiercely intense orgasms, and when she awoke the next morning she felt serene and fulfilled.

In the following weeks, Glenda became accustomed to the new man in her life, even if he was a mysterious phantom. He no longer alarmed her; she now welcomed and looked forward to seeing his face suddenly appear in front of her eyes. She knew that she was falling in love with him, and the only frustration she felt was in not knowing who he was, or if he was even a real person, one that she could hope to meet. But, for some reason she had a deep feeling that they would meet, and that it would be soon. Mostly, she felt light and happy and seemed to have an unending supply of energy, no matter how little sleep she got.

Approximately a month after that first panicky moment when she had first seen his face superimposed on Travis, she finished her song, "Mystery." She decided she would sing it at the bar the following night, which was a Saturday. She rehearsed it with the band several times; they were reassuring and enthusiastic. She felt like it would be a special night. A magical night. Who knows, maybe he'll even be in the audience, she thought, with a thrill of anticipation.

She dressed carefully for the performance that night. She had butterflies in her stomach, almost as much as that night two years ago when she had given her first performance. She wasn't scared, just full of adrenaline-induced excitement.

The small C/W bar was packed. She kept searching the faces, but didn't see anyone who resembled him. The last song they performed was "Mystery." She was still excited, but felt a strong disappointment because he wasn't in the audience. She realized she had written the song for him. She had been so certain that he would be there. However, even though disappointed, she still had enough excitement within her to sing her song with such a depth of feeling that she got a standing ovation. The audience loved it.

Afterwards, Travis hugged her and guided her to a table in the back where they had a cake with "MYSTERY: NO. 1" written on it. The band members all hugged her and assured her that it was only a matter of time before she would have a recording contract. They even toasted her with champagne.

By the time the party was over it was after 2:00 A.M. It had been a long, but exhilarating night, and would have been perfect if only *he* had been there.

* * * * * * * * *

John was working another twelve-hour shift in the ER, even though he had tentatively made plans to go with Dave to some little C/W bar. He wasn't wild about that type of music; he was more into jazz, blues, and classic rock. However, he always enjoyed Dave's company, and the bar was supposed to have a hot band with a dynamite singer. Unfortunately, he had been on call tonight, and just as he was about ready to walk out his door his beeper had gone off. Poor old Dave had had to go by himself.

He was finally able to grab a quick cup of coffee during a short lull around 11:30 P.M. and was still disappointed that he wasn't out with Dave. So far, the ER had really kept him busy. Saturday night was always that way. And he knew that after midnight it would get wild again, becoming even worse after the bars closed--till about 3:00 A.M.--before it would slack off again.

* * * * * * * * *

Glenda got into her car and began to drive home. She was still vacillating between disappointment and the exhilarating remnants of an adrenalin high. Maybe she would never meet him. Maybe she would end up in Nashville, or even Branson, Missouri. But, then again, maybe not. As she started to turn the corner a block away from her apartment building, a pickup truck suddenly appeared out of nowhere. She swerved to try to miss it, but reacted too late. She could see the truck looming ominously in front of her--then heard loud crashing and crunching--just before everything went black.

* * * * * * * * *

It was nearly 2:30 in the morning, and since midnight the ER had been a cross between a zoo and a circus of horrors. John had just stabilized a patient with a stab wound dangerously near the aorta who was now on his way to the OR, when two paramedics rushed in with an unconscious victim from an automobile accident.

"Female--probably in her middle twenties," yelled one of the paramedics as he and his partner hurriedly wheeled the stretcher into the ER. "Her vitals are okay, but she's still unconscious."

"She was broadsided by a drunk driver who apparently only received minor injuries," the other paramedic said disgustedly. "It's a good thing she was wearing her seat belt."

They had already started an IV and had her lying on a backboard with her neck in a cervical collar. John rushed over to check her pupillary response. When he bent over the unconscious woman he let out his breath in a gasp. One of the paramedics looked at him in alarm. "You okay, Doc?"

"Yeah," he managed to say, "Just tired."

It was *her*! It was the girl in his dreams: the one Dave had said was probably his Bisherta. "Oh, please, God! Please don't let her to be seriously injured," he silently prayed! When he started to check her eyes, his hands were shaking so badly he could barely hold his penlight. He knew he had to calm himself. Her life might depend on it. Their whole future happiness might depend on it.

He tried again. Her pupils were equal and reactive. That was good. And her vital signs were still normal. Maybe it was just a simple concussion. He began to gently examine her head. She had a large bruise on the left side of her forehead, but he couldn't see any depressions or other obvious signs of a skull fracture. He checked her reflexes, which appeared to be normal. Good!

He called for the portable X-ray to do a skull series; the wet reading showed no obvious fractures. He was bending over--anxiously looking into her face--thinking how beautiful she was, even with her hair mussed and the bruise, when she opened her eyes and looked directly into his.

She let out a little gasp. His pulse quickened and he smiled in relief as he took hold of her hand to give her his strength and comfort. He already knew he wanted to be with her for the rest of his life. He had, at last, found his Bisherta!

* * * * * * * * *

Glenda was dreaming that she was at the bottom of a black lake. She was swimming, trying to find the surface, but it was so dark she couldn't tell whether she was swimming towards the bottom or the top. As she swam, she began to hear noises. Voices: people talking. She heard someone say, "Good. Her vital signs are normal."

She caught a glimmer of light and began to swim towards it. Her head hurt. Then she felt the presence of someone beside her. She wanted to move but she felt too sluggish. Her eyelids were heavy but she struggled until she was able to open them.

She let out a little gasp. She couldn't believe it. She was looking into that face from her dreams! It was really him. She wasn't dreaming this time. She was finally, actually looking into the endearingly earnest face that she had come to know and love so much. He smiled at her as he took her hand in his, and she could feel his strength flowing to her. As she smiled back, she already knew she didn't want him to ever leave her. And, somehow, she knew that he wouldn't.

YOUR SONG

Your song: it made me fall in love;
My heart into the words it drew.
It tamed the falcon into a dove,
And turned black skies to rainbow hue.

A shadowy figure, tall and fair,
Lithe of limb, gentle, yet strong,
I'd see him standing beneath the stair
When'er I'd here your song.

I knew someday he'd take my hand
And that the words I longed to hear,
While dancing in moonlight on the sand,
He'd softly whisper in my ear.

Like the surf, our hearts would pound--
Increasing in intensity,
While cries of passion's sweet, sad sound
Would join the crashing of the sea.

Our bodies entwined, desire temporarily sated,
I'd close my eyes and sleep awhile;
Drifting through ecstasy of two souls consummated,
I'd hear your song. My heart would smile.

THE EVE OF THE BEGINNING (CONTINUED)

This time, I emerged from the stories still in a half-arousal state of excitement, which I'm sure Schere was well aware of. She smiled, only it was no longer the smile of a lover, but the smile of a friend: a friend who loves and accepts us, in spite of our frailties.

She took both of my hands in hers and looked searchingly into my eyes. "Yes, Michael. Romantic love is what gives life special meaning, as long as it is faithful and true. But in order to find true romantic love, we must first find the beauty within ourselves--to love ourselves. And that love will shine outward, surrounding us with its radiance.

"But sometimes this is not an easy thing--to love ourselves. It is essential for us to learn that we are each unique and special in our own individual way. Only when we can recognize and accept our most intimate truths, are we then able to be the best that we can be. Only then will our spirits be set free and be able to remain truly free. That is when we will be able to love others; to find that all-important romantic love we all crave to make life more meaningful and complete.

"Michael, I am now going to tell you of this most important of all loves; the love which makes all other loves possible: the love of self. This will be the last story: the story of Justine."

And I looked hungrily into her eyes with a feeling of great sadness; as this unforgettable night was drawing to a close, I looked at the last story in her eyes.

FLIGHTS OF FANTASY

Justine Johnson felt a drop of sweat slide down the valley between her breasts--into the well of her navel, while the stocky, balding man peered intently at her over the top of his bifocals. They had been haggling over the price for several minutes now, and she was hot and tired and wanted something cold to drink. She was almost ready to turn around and leave when he suddenly smiled and said, "OK; you can have it for ninety-five dollars."

Maybe he had sensed she wouldn't go any higher. "It's a good TV and hasn't been used that much. I'm sure you'll get many hours of enjoyment from it," he said, as she handed him the cash. She carried it to her car and set it on the back seat as he followed her down his driveway. "Here's the remote," he said, holding it out to her. "You don't want to forget that." She took it and hastily jammed it into her purse. Thank God! This was her last garage sale stop of the day.

Garage sales were Justine's hobby. Every Saturday she woke early, went through the paper, then spent the day making the rounds of the most likely sounding sales. She usually looked for old jewelry or glassware, but for some reason the small color television set had caught her eye. She seldom watched television, but maybe now she would more often. Most of the few shows she had watched in the past (shows her mother enjoyed watching) she had found to be inane and boring.

When she drove away she was already having misgivings. Ninety-five dollars! She hardly ever spent that much money at one time. "Oh, well," she thought, "if mom's TV conks out, at least we'll have another one she can watch."

When she got home, her mother was sitting in the living room with her best friend, Mrs. Wilkinson. They were engrossed in a deep discussion about one of the editorials that had been in the morning paper. Justine carried the television set to her bedroom, set it on her dresser, then called the cable company and made arrangements to have it hooked up on Monday.

When she went back into the living room to tell her mother (who wouldn't open the door to strangers) about the cable company, her mother was surprised that Justine had bought a television set. "Why do you want to go and squander your good money on something like that when you can watch this one here in the living room with me, anytime?"

Although Justine was thirty-four-years-old, her mother often made her feel as if she were still a small child. And she hated that feeling! She sighed; "Mamma, you know I don't care for the programs you watch. I just thought it would be nice to watch some of the shows on the educational channels in the evening. Some might be helpful for my class."

Disgusted with herself for feeling guilty, Justine walked back to her bedroom and pulled off her shirt and slacks, which were damp with perspiration; late August was a hot month for garage sales. She looked at herself in the mirror, while pulling on a pair of shorts and a tank top and winced at the reflection of the plain, plump woman, with long hair unflatteringly pulled straight back from her face into a ponytail. Sometimes she detested the way she looked almost as much as she detested her life.

When Justine had turned thirty she had abruptly realized, with a sense of anguish, that her boring life would probably never change. She had always been shy, and had always done whatever her mother had asked of her--without question. She had also always considered herself to be unattractive, which she had compensated for by being a straight-A student. She could count on one hand the dates she'd had in high school and college...combined.

There were only two things in her life which she found ironically amusing: one was her name. Her mother, who had always been devoutly religious (becoming even more so after Justine's father, a Marine officer, had been killed by sniper fire in Viet Nam), had named her only daughter after (the feminine version) a first-century Christian martyr. In her mother's mind, the name stood for justice and honesty.

While Justine had been in college the writings of the Marquis de Sade had made the rounds through her dormitory; although Justine certainly hadn't been one of the "in crowd," she had been able to borrow them to read out of curiosity. She had been shocked and revolted, yet, in some perverse way, also strangely titillated (although she never would have admitted it, even to herself).

But now, she found it humorous that one of his title characters shared her name and always had a private laugh when she thought of how horrified her mother would be if she ever discovered the content of "Sade's" writings about her namesake character.

The other thing that amused Justine about her life was that, contrary to probably everyone's impression who knew her, she was not a virgin. By some fluke, she had been invited to her high school senior prom by a pimply-faced boy (whom she hadn't even liked) who had brought along a pint bottle of vodka and a six-pack of orange soda.

They had left the dance early and gone to the local make-out parking place, where he had mixed her a drink so strong that it had at first burned her throat and made her gag. It was her first experience with alcohol, but since she hadn't wanted her date to think she was unsophisticated, she had forced herself to drink it. Then, as she began to enjoy the giddy, reckless, alcohol induced feeling, it had become easier to drink.

When her date began to kiss her, she pretended to respond. As his ardor increased she became more curious, and before she realized it they were having sex. (She never thought of it as making love, as that had been the least of any of her emotions during the act.) She hadn't been repulsed by the event, but neither had she been impressed. In fact, she was surprised that it hadn't been a particularly earthshaking occurrence, one way or the other. But she was wise enough and sensitive enough to realize that with the right person, and with love and passion, that it could be earth-shaking.

She had suffered a short period of panic afterwards, worrying that she might have become pregnant since they hadn't used any protection, but she had started her next period right on schedule; after that she had always thought of it as a learning experience. She was even secretly glad that, at least, she wouldn't die a virgin. And she was also very amused at the thought of how shocked her mother would be at the knowledge that she was no longer a virgin.

Other than that, Justin's life had been uneventful. After she had graduated from college she had gotten a job teaching Kindergarten at one of the local public schools, and moved back in with her mother. Due to her mother becoming widowed (when Justine was only seven-years-old), her mother had been overly protective throughout Justine's childhood. But as soon as Justine had reached adulthood, her mother had become clingy and dependent upon her.

By the time Justine reached adolescence, she had already begun to feel stifled and trapped in a lifestyle not of her own choosing, but didn't know how to change it. She often thought that she must have been born with a "guilt gene." She was convinced (though it was not born out by science) that a "guilt gene" surely did exist which was often inherent to the female of the human species. So, not knowing what else she could do, she had continued to try to please her mother by allowing her mother to dictate her life.

After they had eaten the Sunday dinner (which Justine had prepared while her mother had been attending church) her mother went next door to play Canasta, and Justine turned on her new television set. Even though she was only able to get five local channels, which included the PBS station, she watched several shows, which she enjoyed, and began looking forward to the wide selection she would have with the cable.

On Monday afternoon when Justine returned home from school, she was given the full details about how her mother had been forced to miss out on a shopping expedition with her friends, just so the cable TV man could hook up Justine's new television set. So, in order to make it up to her, Justine prepared one of her mother's favorite dinners: batter-dipped fried chicken, with milk gravy and mashed potatoes. She even baked home-made biscuits and told her mother to invite her friend, Mrs. Wilkinson.

The dinner conversation mainly consisted of her mother and Mrs. Wilkinson discussing the merits and plaudits of the TV/radio commentator, Rush Limbaugh. They were two of his most adoring admirers. Personally, Justine found him to be a blatant misogynist, and thought he subconsciously substituted the microphone for his male member. It amazed her that so many women were so enamoured of him. She felt he inflamed hate and discord among the more unstable, as well as attacking and degrading the most defenseless and vulnerable segments of society: women, the homeless, victims of AIDS, environmentalists, and animals--to name a few; the ones who had the least power with which to fight back. The people for whom he seemed to have the greatest approval were: white, Anglo, affluent Republicans--preferably male.

But he apparently had some type of charisma, because he did have a very large following, so it was possible she could be misjudging him. She always tried to keep an open mind when making judgments. Maybe that was one of the things that bothered her the most about him: he didn't.

After Justine had finished washing, drying and putting away the supper dishes, she went to her bedroom to try out some of the cable programs on her new TV. She fervently hoped she wouldn't be disappointed. She lay down on her bed, turned the TV on, and enjoyed an Agatha Christie mystery on the A & E network. Then, after watching the local news, she began to channel surf.

"Welcome to the Fantasy Channel," said a remarkably handsome man with a distinguished British accent. She had never heard of the Fantasy Channel.

"Tonight, our movie is *Island of Paradise*, starring Royce Harrison and Tina St. John." Justine had never heard of

Tina St. John, but she was familiar with the handsome Royce Harrison. If she were ever to have a romantic fantasy involving a movie star, he would, without a doubt, be the one.

Even though it was past her usual weeknight bedtime, she was so fascinated that she began to watch. She soon became so enmeshed in the plot, it was almost as if she had become a part of it. Tina St. John (who Justine kept thinking looked vaguely familiar, but was unable to place where she had seen her before) was striking attractive.

As soon as the movie was over, the handsome announcer was back on the screen saying, "And your special number tonight is 'four'." Justine wasn't sure what that was all about, but for some reason felt compelled to write it down. She grabbed her checkbook out of her purse and wrote it on the back of her check register.

For the rest of the night she was unable to get the movie out of her thoughts. It had been a swashbuckler, the plot centering around Tina being kidnapped by a highwayman (Royce), whom she had fallen in love with and accompanied on his escapades. Much of it had Tina and Royce riding on a horse together--galloping like the wind--in a wild attempt at fleeing their potential captors. At times it had seemed so real--almost as if she were Tina St. John. When she went to sleep she continued to dream about the movie, and that she had become Tina St. John.

The next morning when Justine awoke, she felt more rested than she had in weeks. She had an enthusiasm and an energy that she hadn't felt for a very long time. While she was at school, the day seemed to fly by, and when she got home she hurriedly fixed supper. It was her mother's bingo night, so Justine would be home alone, and she could hardly wait to turn on her television set!

Finally, her mother left and she quickly cleaned up the kitchen. After she took her shower, she turned on her television set to watch while she dried her hair. She began to channel surf again, found a program selling makeup, and soon became engrossed in watching how plain looking women, chosen from the audience, were glamorously made over. Some of the results were astounding.

Justine looked into the mirror and began to scrutinize her reflection, surprising herself when she decided that she actually did have nice features. Nothing on her face was either overtly too large or too small. When instructions for ordering the makeup were shown on the screen, Justine wrote down the toll-free number which she immediately called, placed an order and charged it on her Visa card. In the four years since she had gotten the card, she had only used it once before, and that was when she had ordered a birthday gift for her mother.

Afterwards, she eagerly searched for the Fantasy Channel, but was unable to find it--which she found odd. Unfortunately, she couldn't remember what the channel number was, but when she went to sleep she again dreamed of Royce Harrison.

The next night when Justine was ready for bed, she turned on her television and began to carefully run the numbers of the channels, looking for the Fantasy channel. When that didn't work, she tried to remember how she had found it the other time and began to push random combinations of numbers. Just when she was about to give up, the handsome announcer appeared on the screen and she heard that delightfully accented voice saying, "Welcome to the Fantasy Channel. Tonight, our movie is *Flashing Swords*, starring Royce Harrison and Tina St. John."

Justine was delighted! She had finally found it. Then she remembered that she had actually pushed a series of four numbers, rather than two. When the first two hadn't resulted in any type of broadcast, she had rapidly pushed two more. Yes, that was it! It had been 19 and 61. The year she had been born. Well that was easy enough to remember.

She quickly became entranced in the movie. However, shortly after it began, she apparently fell asleep; in her dreams she became Tina St. John as the drama vividly unfolded. When it was over, she awoke and could remember every detail. She thought about it for a while, and when she went back to sleep she again dreamed about it. A dream so real--it was as if it were actually happening all over again.

The next night, Justine was in such a hurry to watch the little TV set that she stopped on her way home from school and bought a frozen, family-sized entree. She hurriedly heated it in the microwave, then emptied it into a serving dish, rather than putting it on the table in its own plastic container, and her mother never knew that it was something Justine hadn't prepared. She was able to get into her bedroom earlier that way.

She quickly showered, dried her hair, and was at last ready to watch her television. When she turned it on, she immediately pushed 1961. But there was just dead air and static--as if the station was off the air. She continued to push numbers at random, then tried channel surfing, but was never able to find the Fantasy Channel.

In fact, there seemed to be something wrong with the cable: most of the stations were off the air. Well, maybe they were working on it. Disappointed, she was about to turn it off when the screen suddenly came alive with three gorgeous people in exercise outfits: a man and two women. They were working out with small dumbbells and talking about burning fat and body sculpting by exercising with free weights.

Justine got up from her bed and began going through some of the motions along with them. It really wasn't that difficult, but she could see it would be better with the weights. She felt energized and compelled to follow their routines, and before she realized it the program was over. She was amazed when she realized that she had been working out for forty-five minutes, and even though she was out of breath, dripping with perspiration, and nearly exhausted, she felt invigorated. This must be what they mean by endorphins, she thought.

The program immediately following was about being fit by cutting fat from your diet. Justine had always pretty much taken food for granted, but as the show progressed she realized that she mostly ate foods which were very high in fat. The show gave instructions on how to identify and figure daily fat gram consumption, plus tips and recipes for following a low fat diet.

After the program, Justine took another quick shower, then slept restfully and peacefully. The next day at school, in the teachers' lounge at lunch time, she began to notice what some of her colleagues were eating. Several of the younger, thinner women were eating yogurt and fruit. Some of the others were eating sandwiches of various types, and some were eating the food from the cafeteria. Justine looked at her two salami with mayonnaise sandwiches and bag of corn chips, and ended up eating only half of one of the sandwiches and none of the corn chips. However, by the time school was out she felt like she was starving.

On the way home from school she stopped and bought some scales for her bedroom, a set of two five-pound hand weights, and some ankle weights. Next, she stopped at a grocery store and bought some small containers of nonfat fruit-flavored yogurt, turkey breast, pita bread, fruit, and some low fat, individual frozen entrees. She realized it would also be good for her mother (who was overweight to the point of being morbidly obese) to begin eating more healthfully.

That night, although Justine tried, she was unable to find the exercise program. She had enjoyed it the night before so much that she began to do as much as she could remember on her own. After forty-five minutes, she showered and went to bed. She tried the Fantasy Channel, but after several minutes of being unable to find it she decided to just go on to sleep.

When she dreamed, she again became Tina St. John and was in a movie with Royce Harrison. It was so vivid that she could feel her heart pound in fear of the villain, and the thrill of sexual excitement when she was in Royce's arms.

The next night, after supper, she was able to find the workout show and did the routines along with the instructors. Afterwards, she found a channel advertising "oldies" in classic rock-and-roll. Justine had never been allowed to listen to rock-and-roll while she was growing up. Her mother had told her that it was the devil's music.

Justine found herself intrigued by the energy and freedom which seemed to emanate from even the tiny bits of songs the commercial featured. Then, once again, she called an 800 number, this time ordering cassette tapes, even though she had nothing to play them on.

The next day, on her way home from school, she stopped and bought a Sony Walkman and, to her delight, when she arrived home she found a large package waiting for her. It was the makeup she had ordered. That evening, by coincidence (or was it...she wondered) she was able to find the channel featuring the makeup show.

She applied the makeup to her face along with the experts as they did their make-overs, and when she studied the finished product in her mirror she was astounded. She looked remarkably like Tina St. John. Only a heavier, less glamourous version. She was so pleased that she went to sleep with the makeup still on her face, and dreamed the wonderful dreams that she had become Tina St. John.

Several weeks later, after much practice, she finally found the courage to wear the makeup to school. On that morning she arose half an hour earlier than usual, and before dressing for school she washed her face and slowly applied the makeup, carefully remembering the instructions from the television program.

At lunchtime, in the teachers' lounge while she was eating her vegetable pita sandwich and fruit, several of her female colleagues commented on how attractive she looked wearing makeup. She also noticed several of the male teachers staring at her, and felt herself blushing. She wasn't used to being noticed. Although she was somewhat embarrassed, she was also secretly pleased. As long as she could remember (anyway since her father had died) she had always been in the background. Nondescript. Unnoticeable.

When school was out, she was in a rush to get home. Her mother was watching an old movie on AMC so Justine hurried to her room and looked at herself in the mirror. She was again startled yet pleased at the difference in her appearance. But then, as she examined her reflection more critically, she realized she drastically needed to do something about her hair, as well as her weight. The weight she had already started to work on. But her hair! That was another problem.

She had worn it long since junior high school. In a way, it was her security blanket--sometimes almost making her feel as if she were a female version of Sampson. Also, her hair was thick but baby fine, which she felt would cause difficulty in achieving an attractive cut. Even if it could be decently styled, she thought she probably wouldn't be able to maintain it--especially with the sea breeze and humidity. Besides; the length, which was nearly to her waist, was the one (and only) thing about her that made her feel feminine. As she continued to study her reflection, she decided she couldn't cut it...not yet anyway. For now she would just have to let it stay the way it was. She had already wasted too much time worrying about it; it was time for her to prepare supper.

Justine had recently bought a small grill that fit over the large stove element on which she cooked fish and vegetables skewered together on short bamboo picks. She also prepared rice pilaf and warmed some French bread. Her mother often complained now about their meals; she missed the fried and fatty foods, but Justine noticed that her mother was also losing weight. Justine had lost eight pounds and, to her delight, some of her clothes had become loose.

After dinner, she hurriedly cleaned up the kitchen, rushed into her bedroom, turned on her TV, found the exercise show, and went through the forty-five minute free weight exercise routine before taking her shower. After she had towel-dried herself, she began to apply body lotion and noticed she could already see the difference in her muscle tone. She was becoming firmer. She couldn't notice any other great difference in her overall appearance yet, but she certainly felt better.

In her bedroom she began to channel surf. Tonight she was having difficulty finding something interesting to watch. First, she tried a sampling of the big three networks, and was disappointed each time. Next she tried the PBS channel, where she found a man giving instructions on how to paint a landscape. She watched in fascination as he took a bare canvas and transformed it into a lovely water and mountain landscape in only thirty minutes.

Justine had majored in fine arts, as well as elementary education, and at one time had indulged herself in fantasies of studying art in France. For a while, she had even fooled herself into believing that she would actually be able to do it someday...before she had been abruptly jolted back into the real world shortly after her graduation from college. She continued to paint for several years after she started teaching, but then lost interest and put away her sketchbooks, pencils and paints. The paints had eventually dried up and she had thrown them away.

But the PBS show had piqued her interest--to such an extent that she opened the antique trunk in which she stored her keepsakes and found some of her old sketchbooks from college. She had always been very critical of her artwork (as she was with everything she did) and looking at them after all these years, with a different perspective, she realized that she probably did have talent--if it could ever have the chance to be developed. That night her dreams were filled with ideas of compositions for paintings.

The next day after work, she went to one of the local arts/crafts stores and bought several sketchbooks, soft lead pencils, kneaded rubber erasures, twelve small tubes of water colors, and six various sizes of water color brushes. She was suddenly filled with such great enthusiasm, she could hardly wait to begin sketching again!

When she got home, to add to her good spirits, her music cassette tapes had arrived. She had ordered from every advertisement she had seen which featured rock-and-roll. She now had music beginning with the '50s: Buddy Holly, Duane Eddy, Eddie Cochran, Gene Vincent, Chuck Berry, Little Richard and others. And the '60s and the '70s, which consisted of mostly British rock groups; The Beatles, Led Zeppelin, The Moody Blues, The Rolling Stones, Foreigner, Pink Floyd, Bad Company, The Eagles, the inimitable Jethro Tull, and many more. So many--it was hard to know where to begin.

She arranged them in chronological order and began at the beginning: with the fifties. The first tape she popped into her Walkman was a composite of the early greats. The true pioneers of Rock-and-Roll. That early Rockabilly sound of rhythm and blues, where it had all begun--with a mixture of blues, soul, jazz, and country-western music (then primarily referred to as hillbilly or cowboy music).

She was immediately in love with the sound. The primitive, wildly free, booming pulsating bass; the twangy rhythm of the guitars (oh, how she especially loved the guitars), and the simple honesty of the lyrics, all of which made her pulse quicken. She had never danced. She didn't even know the first thing about it (other than the clutching and wrestling movements of the two slow dances she had attempted with her date at the prom).

This was also the night that she found MTV!

For the next five days after school, Justine began driving to some of the more interesting areas of town, where she would sketch before going home. She also started going to the library on weekends and doing research on some of her favorite music groups. Although she liked all of the music, she soon developed special favorites. She had bought some new tapes by those groups, which she now often played in her Walkman. One of the groups which intrigued her the most was The Moody Blues. They had pioneered symphonic rock, and had successfully endured for more than twenty-five years. She loved their versatility: sometimes their music was hauntingly sensitive, sometimes bordering on the esoteric, while other times excitingly vibrant, but always with their unmistakably, unique sound. She was also fond of Foreigner, Led Zeppelin and Bad Company.

She had also tried to do research on Tina St. John, along with the music groups, but, strangely, she was unable to find anything about her.

As the weeks turned into months, Justine's life became full. She was on a regular exercise program, had begun to draw and paint again, had been turned-on to the wonderful world of classic-rock music, and was slowly, but steadily, losing weight. She also enjoyed her nights of watching programs on her little television set. She was now only able to find the Fantasy Channel on weekends, but her weeknights were always filled with fanciful dreams. Many, to her surprise, of a very erotic (if not explicitly sexual) nature.

At first she had been disturbed and felt guilty about the sexual realism, but the dreams fed the hunger that had recently been awakened inside of her. A hunger she would never have dreamed existed, but nonetheless, a hunger which demanded to be fed. So the dreams became a delicious secret, one in which she could think about and relish whenever she wished.

She had made the mistake, early on, in casually mentioning the Fantasy Channel to some of the other female teachers, which had elicited blank stares from all of them. A few had told her that they seldom had time to watch TV-- with the necessary duties to both a career and family--and the others had told her that she must be mistaken, because on the local cable system no such channel existed.

At first, Justine had been very distressed by this, and had even thought for a brief time that maybe she was losing her mind; that perhaps she had drifted into a world of unreality. But when she finally convinced herself that she was mentally stable and wasn't escaping into a world of unreality, she decided not to question where The Fantasy Channel came from, but rather to just enjoy it.

Every weekend, she lived in a secret dread that this would be the time when she would eagerly turn to The Fantasy Channel, only to find that it had disappeared. Justine realized that she was deriving much of the pleasure and fulfillment in her life from her fantasies, but she couldn't bear to give them up. They had become part of her world. Part of her day-to-day existence, and, if she had nothing else, she would always have her fantasies.

Sometimes when she heard the phrase, "Get a life," she thought the saying fit her perfectly. But in her own way that was what she was desperately trying to do. Not only did she now have her wonderful, romantic, passionate dreams at night, she also had wonderful daydreams. Fantasies that she would some day go to France and devote time to the art she had always loved. To be able to study the great masters in depth. To randomly sketch as much and as often as she wished--then to commit those favored sketches into painted compositions.

She didn't even care if she received critical acclaim or recognition. It would be enough of a reward just to be able to create and to be able to express the emotions and great depth of passion inside of her; the passion which she had been keeping bottled up for so many years. It needed to be free--much as an effervescent wine gleefully bubbled forth from the bottle in which it had been kept imprisoned, when the cork was removed.

And she still yearned for love. To meet that special some-one to whom she could give her abounding love. The one who would not only gladly receive it, but who would joyfully give it back to her in return. She now had a strong feeling that someday it would happen. It had to! But until that time she would have to be content with her fantasies.

The movies on the Fantasy Channel now not only starred Royce Harrison, but also other unknown men--each special in his own way. And each made love in his own way--which always stopped before intercourse. Most of the movies cen-tered around dramas featuring either horses or the sea; often both. Through these movies, she felt she was strangely becoming experienced and worldly in the ways of love, re-gardless of having had only that one miserable experience with sex.

In the fantasy movies, when she seemed to become Tina St. John, she was able to give of some of the deep passion within her. And on those mornings after, when she awoke and looked at her reflection in the mirror, she appeared to glow with an aliveness that she could actually see. It was as if she had a golden aura surrounding her. A halo that encircled her whole body. She never felt any fear of it, only a slight feeling of awe mixed with a strange serenity.

About every six weeks, at the end of one of those special movies, the handsome announcer would again say, "Your lucky number this week is..." and when he would give the number, she would always write it down. She had them all written in her checkbook on the back of her check register. She didn't know why, but she had a compulsion to keep track of them. She didn't think she could have kept herself from writing them down even if she had tried. It was almost as if she became possessed when the numbers were given. By Christmas, she had four of the numbers, and felt that in some strange way they would eventually be vitally important to her life. She never told anyone about them.

Two days before New Years when Justine weighed herself, she was delighted to see that since the beginning of her fitness program, which she had rigorously followed, even with all of the Christmas baking her mother had done-- along with the baked goodies friends of her mother had given to them, she had now lost thirty-two pounds. Recently some of the male teachers at her school had been striking up conversations with her. One had even asked to take her to dinner, but she had declined. She considered him boring, pompous and arrogant, and after being with the beautiful, sensitive men in her fantasy movies she wasn't about to lower her standards.

January was a dreary month, even in South Texas. January was usually the month of winter "blue northers," and this year was no exception. Although she was in a comfortable routine now, with her exercise program, her art, her music, and her wonderful little enchanted television set, she decided it was time she did some reading. Books had always been Justine's best friends. However, in the past she had mostly read mystery stories; she was a devoted fan of Agatha Christie, Dick Francis and Sue Grafton. Now she thought maybe it was time she broadened her horizons.

She began to scan the *New York Times* best seller list in the Sunday newspaper every week, and found several titles which intrigued her so much that she decided to buy the books and read them. She had even begun to read poetry again, something she hadn't done since college.

Justine remembered one particular time while she had been in college, when a young man had written a romantic poem for one of the girls who lived in her dormitory. Rather than being touched and flattered by the poem, the girl had thought it amusing--ridiculing the young man behind his back. Justine's heart had ached for him, and oh, how she had envied that girl!

Unfortunately, Justine knew she was not the type men wrote romantic poems about. But that didn't stop her from wondering what it must feel like to have a man love her so much that the passion would drive him to write a poem, or, better yet, a song--just for her. How lucky those women were! She often wondered if they realized how much. And doubted if many of them truly did.

Months ago she had come to the conclusion that she was a hopelessly incurable romantic. But along with it she had also become a Romanticist, and considered herself to be a Renaissance Woman.

Spring rapidly began to burst forth, and with it--even with her dreams and fantasies--Justine began to feel a newfound restlessness. She had lost another seven pounds, with only six more to lose to reach her goal. She had bought a few new outfits, quite different from the old knit trousers and tunics she used to wear, and had even read several issues of Vogue magazine. She had taken Home Economics in high school where she had learned to sew, and one Saturday on an impulse she bought a sewing machine, even though she hadn't sewn for many years. She also bought several patterns and some fabric and decided to see if she could sew some new clothes: ones of her own design. She had thought maybe she could alter some of her old clothes to make them fit better, but then decided against it. They looked so dowdy and dull they didn't seem to suit her now.

And her hair still didn't suit her. Maybe it was finally time to do something about it. She carefully studied the hair styles on the models in the fashion layouts. She knew she didn't want it cut drastically short, but maybe some cut just from the ends would be OK. It was also such a drab, mousy color. Not dark enough to be brown and not light enough to be blond.

Then she saw an advertisement for brush-on highlights. "Why not?" she thought. Although she had never colored her hair before, she didn't think the results could possibly turn out any worse than what she already had to start with. So she did it! She bought the kit and followed the instructions, and after washing and drying her hair she was pleasantly amazed. Almost as much as she had been when she had applied the makeup for the first time. Her hair not only had shiny golden highlights, but it also seemed to be fuller and have more body.

The following Monday at school two of the male teachers went out of their way to speak to her. And at lunch time she was sure two of them were talking about her. She still didn't have any of the other women as close friends, however some of them were now much friendlier than they used to be. But then she was much more outgoing than she used to be, too. Because she had more confidence.

When she left school that afternoon and was driving home, she passed a hair styling salon which catered to walk-ins. She remembered seeing advertisements for it on television. On a whim she turned into the parking lot and before she could lose her nerve, hurried into the shop. She knew that if they couldn't take her right at that very moment, her courage would vanish and she would leave. But they were able to take her. She was told that she had just barely beaten the after-school rush. She didn't know if she was glad or not.

Now filled with apprehension, she allowed the attractive stylist to escort her to one of the chairs. But when the stylist, who said her name was Orcid, asked how she wanted her hair, Justine was at a loss for words. She looked blankly at the stylist for a few seconds, realizing that she had no idea of what type of style she wanted. She heard herself saying, "I want to look glamorous, I want to look beautiful," and thought, in embarrassment, how stupid she must sound. She abruptly stopped speaking. Orcid didn't seem to think what she said was strange, and scrutinized her face for a minute.

"I don't want too much cut off," Justine said, as she untied the ribbon at her nape which held her hair in the ponytail. Then she spied a style on one of the posters on the wall. "Maybe something like that; what do you think?" The model's hair was streaky blond and cut in an uninhibited, wind-blown style, several inches below shoulder length.

Orcid continued to scrutinize her. Then said, "I think I have a pretty good idea of what would look good on you."

First, Orcid shampooed Justine's hair, then combed it out while wet. Next she took a pair of scissors and cut Justine's hair off, straight across, about four inches below her shoulders. After that, to Justine's horror, Orcid got out a straight razor.

"I don't do razor cuts very often, and the management doesn't really like us to do them, but in your case, with the texture and length of your hair, I think a razor cut would work best."

Justine closed her eyes, her hands desperately gripping the arms of the chair, and it was all she could do to keep from jumping up and running out of the salon. What on earth was she doing? She must have been out of her mind! Orcid tilted Justine's head upward and combed part of her hair over her face. Justine continued to keep her eyes closed when she felt the razor's slightly painful, pulling tug as it began to cut bangs. BANGS! She had never worn bangs! Not even as a child.

Her stomach balled itself into a knot, and she could feel herself beginning to get dizzy. She was hyperventilating. She forced herself to take slow, even breaths, and continued to keep her eyes closed while she prayed for it to be over quickly. She would just have to let her hair grow out again.

She didn't know if Orcid thought her behavior strange or not; by now she really didn't care. She just knew she couldn't bare to watch. It was almost as if she were having surgery. A part of her, which she'd had for almost as long as she could remember, was being severed from her body. She knew she was being ridiculous, but she couldn't help it.

After what seemed like hours, Justine felt a brush being run through her hair and heard the sound of a hair dryer. Then she felt the heat from the dryer against her cheek as Orcid began to style her hair while she dried it. But Justine still couldn't bear to open her eyes. Again, after what seemed like hours, she heard the dryer shut off.

"You can open your eyes now. The deed is done." Orcid laughed.

Justine's heart was pounding. She could feel her body drenched with sweat, almost as much as when she worked out. She took a deep breath, and when she opened her eyes she almost fell out of the chair. In fact, she was certain she would have if she hadn't still been gripping the chair arms so tightly. But the shock she experienced wasn't from horror; on the contrary, she couldn't believe it was actually *her* reflection she was looking at in the mirror.

It was Tina St. John! Rather, she looked like Tina St. John.

After she had been unable to find any information on Tina at the library, or anyplace else she could think of, she had convinced herself that there was no such person, and that the elaborate movies had all been nothing more than realistic dreams, including the Fantasy Channel. Now she realized that deep in her subconscious mind she had known all along what she could look like--what she could be like--if she would just have the courage to free herself to do it.

"Well, what do you think?" Orcid asked.

Justine swallowed. "I love it! Oh, yes! I love it! You did a beautiful job!" She still couldn't believe it. She continued to stare at herself, as if she was mesmerized by the person who was looking back at her. But SHE was that person!

Orcid unfastened the protective smock covering Justine and shook off the hair, and when Justine glanced down, she was astounded at the amount of hair lying on the floor. She hadn't realized how much had been cut off. But she didn't miss it! Not one bit! She felt lighter. Freer. She reached inside her wallet and pulled out a ten-dollar bill to leave for a tip. She knew it was probably too much, but she felt Orcid deserved it. If she had been able to have found a hundred-dollar bill in her wallet, she would have gladly left it as a tip. When she paid the bill it was fourteen dollars.

That evening, a Friday night, Justine looked forward to one of her Fantasy Channel movies. She didn't care if they were some supernatural phenomena, like something out of a Stephen King or Dean Koontz novel, or if she were dreaming them; she only knew that she was addicted to them.

She hit the magic numbers twice and nothing happened. She channel surfed for a while; then, with a feeling of dread, tried the magic numbers once more, and this time the handsome announcer appeared. As the movie began, she realized it was the same one she had watched the past weekend. But she didn't care, as she felt herself being drawn into the drama. This was a week when the announcer gave another number at the end of the movie. The fifth one-- which she promptly wrote on her check register along with the others, even though she still couldn't fathom what they could possibly mean.

The next day she sewed for several hours. She was making some very stylish clothes of which she was quite proud. Her mother had been nagging her lately to eat more, telling her she was skin and bones. But this was far from true. Although Justine had now trimmed down to an almost fashion model slenderness, she was muscular and lithe--hardly emaciated. She had replaced fat with muscle, and had never felt better in her life. Her mother had been shocked when she had first seen Justine's haircut, but had quickly agreed that it was much more becoming.

When Justine became tired of sewing, she decided to go to one of the malls and look around at the new spring fashions. She didn't intend to buy anything, but when she found herself looking in the windows of Victoria's Secret she couldn't resist going inside. What an absolutely wonderful store it was! She found some beautiful silk panties and bras, which she couldn't keep from buying. She had always only worn cotton before.

While paying for her items, she spied a provocative, white satin teddy which laced up the front, and she suddenly felt beautiful and erotic as she pictured herself wearing it. She thought clothes that laced up were sexy, and that the right man--someday, somewhere--would enjoy slowly and lovingly unlacing it to reveal her warm soft skin underneath.

Impulsively, she picked it up and added it to her purchases, feeling embarrassed as the clerk rang it up. What was she thinking? She would never wear it; she would never have anyone to wear it for.

When she got home she couldn't wait to try it on, and when she did, she looked every bit as alluring in it as she had thought she would--maybe even more so. She took it off but planned to sleep in it that night. She might as well get some good out of it. It had been too expensive to let it just lay uselessly in one of her dresser drawers.

That night she had no trouble finding the Fantasy Channel, punching it in with the remote control on her first try. It was the same movie. AGAIN!

The next weekend, when she was ready to go to bed she put on her new teddy, turned on the Fantasy Channel, and once more it was the same movie. What was happening? Oh, she enjoyed it all right, but why did the same one keep repeating? In it, she and the same beautiful man, after outrunning pirates, had been shipwrecked on a tropical beach. And following a romantic romp in the surf, their wet, naked bodies glistened--painted by the silvery moonlight-- as they began to make love. But that was where it always ended...just as they were about to consummate their love...which Justine was beginning to find extremely frustrating!

During the days, she continued to paint while listening to her favorite tapes on her Walkman as she created. The music inspired her--painting pictures in her mind--and she was extremely satisfied with some of her finished compositions. She also continued to do her exercise workout on a regular basis which had become part of her life. She knew she would never go back to the way she was before she had bought the little television set.

She added more blond streaks to her hair and sewed more clothes. She had begun watching *Style* on CNN each Saturday, and especially liked the clothes designed by Lacroix, Sui and Versace. She had also become skillful with using several different patterns on one outfit, creating and designing to suit her own taste, and was pleased with the results. Certainly, she no longer looked dowdy!

She had become used to being stared at by men, not only at school, but every place she went. At first it had bothered her, but now she was flattered and proud. After all, she had worked hard. She felt she had earned it. But her life was still boring. The few single men teachers she knew she found to be totally uninteresting. She didn't have the courage to go to a bar to meet men. Besides, she didn't think she would find the type of man she was looking for in a bar. She wasn't looking just for sex. She was looking for something to change her life; the problem was, she wasn't sure what it would be.

By the middle of May the weather had turned very warm with some truly hot days, and Justine felt like her emotions were in tune with the weather. Some days she felt as if she would melt from her inner heat. She knew she was too young for menopause. Besides, from what she had heard, what she was experiencing wasn't exactly like hot flashes.

Hers was a smoldering warmth--which exuded outward from all of her pores until it enveloped her body in a fiery passion that caused a dull ache in her heart, and she longed to meet the one who would be able to satiate her fire...before it totally consumed her. Sometimes she felt a deep despair that it would never happen. And often, at those times, she would have the wildly absurd impulse to eat candles--the way Tita had in *Like Water For Chocolate*--just to see what would happen: to see if she, too, could find the light. But she never actually did it; and, later would always feel foolish at having had such an idea.

She had come so far. And when the passion within her heart continued to cry out, she would try to lose herself in her art, her music, her clothing design, and her fantasy movie: for that is what it had become now, just that one movie. The same one, with the same man, but she was never able to remember what his face looked like afterwards.

School would be out in two more weeks and Justine dreaded the summer. She would have so much more time on her hands. Maybe she should travel, but she would feel guilty spending money so frivolously; besides, if she did travel, she wanted to go to Europe, and that she couldn't afford. As usual, on Saturday night she put on her white satin teddy (by now it had become a ritual) and turned on her movie. Only this time the movie didn't end as it usually did--when the lovemaking began; this time it continued. And Justine felt like she was being swept away.

It was the same man, the same beach, the same moonlight. But this time they were making love; and it was wonderful! It was like nothing she had ever experienced before. Her heart was pounding in synchronized rhythm with the crashing waves breaking against the shore, and when she reached the pinnacle of such a flood of passion that it seemed to flow as endlessly as the sea, she abruptly experienced the magical ecstasy of her first orgasm. Then, blessedly sweet contentment, followed by a deep and restful sleep.

When she awoke, there was the handsome announcer giving her another number, which she quickly wrote in her checkbook along with the others. Then, almost immediately, she was asleep again, and this time she didn't awaken until well after the sun was up.

On a restless whim that lovely Sunday in May, after she and her mother had eaten dinner and cleaned up the kitchen, she drove to the island beach. She parked well away from the usual crowd of happy beach goers--many of them teenagers, with a few young couples accompanied by small children, mixed in. Most of the "winter Texans" had, by now, returned to their homes in the northern states. She walked along the beach, but it bore little resemblance to the one on which she had been in her dream last night. However, it was soothing: the rushing sound of the surf, the coolness of the wet, gritty sand under her bare feet, and the warmth of the sun on her bare shoulders as the sea breeze whispered through her hair.

She sighed. Would she ever have the life she longed for? She was beginning to find it painful: the yearning--the longing. She thought she had determinedly resigned herself--a few years ago--to accepting her mundane existence; but, mistakenly, she hadn't. Her raging inner fire had merely lain dormant. Now she was almost sorry she had ever bought that television set. Maybe she had been better off before she had begun to dare to dream. But then again, maybe not. She felt so confused. She went back to her car, and on her way home she stopped at a Wal Mart and bought the latest paperback Dick Francis mystery.

That night, after her workout and her shower, she read until she was able to fall asleep, not turning on her television set. The following two nights she did the same. But she found she was consumed with such an insatiably restless energy that even the exercise couldn't dispel.

Wednesday morning on her way to school she noticed with irritation that her gas guage was on empty. "Damn!" She uttered, which shocked her. She never cursed, not even in her thoughts. Maybe she needed to see a shrink; maybe she needed some Valium--or Prozac...or something.

She stopped at a convenience store and filled her gas tank, but when she went inside to pay for the gas she had to stand in line, which agitated her further. Two people were ahead of her, taking their own sweet time in buying state lottery tickets, while she became increasingly more impatient.

"Fifty-seven million dollars. Yeah; I could use that," the man buying the tickets said to the clerk.

The woman standing in line behind him laughingly said, "Too bad you'll never get the chance to know what it's like, because I'm going to win it." And she bought ten tickets.

When Justine finally got to the clerk and opened her checkbook, she saw the numbers she had written down from the fantasy channel. Then, to her astonishment, heard herself saying, "I want one of those lottery tickets, too."

He gave her a slip on which to mark her numbers and asked, "just one?"

"Yes," she answered, as she filled it in with the numbers she had been compulsively writing down on her check register for the past nine months. When the clerk gave her the lottery ticket, she put it safely inside her wallet.

The school day seemed to drag by. Then at lunch time one of the married male teachers cornered her in the teachers lounge and told her he would really like to take her to dinner. She just stared at him--with such a look of disgust that he finally turned away with an embarrassed cough and a red face. What a sleaze, she thought. She knew his wife had given birth to their second child two months ago.

That evening she had no intention of watching television, but shortly before 10:00 P.M., when she remembered the lottery ticket, she got it out of her wallet. She turned on her television set, and at 9:59 P.M. she was avidly watching when the winning numbers were picked. She felt foolish. It was such nonsense, thinking that her one ticket would be the winner.

When the first number was picked it matched one of hers. Then the second and the third, which also matched. Her pulse quickened and her mouth became dry. The fourth number matched. And the fifth. By the time the sixth number was picked, Justine had such a roaring in her ears and so many little sparkley spots before her eyes--she wasn't sure what the announcer said it was. She didn't know whether or not it matched her last number! She thought it had been her number, but she couldn't be sure. She didn't know what to do.

She felt too weak to stand, so she just sat on her bed--in a daze--for at least an hour. Then she carefully put the ticket back into her wallet. She felt numb all over. She couldn't think. She put on her Walkman and did her exercises to the music of *Foreigner 4*. Then she took her shower and went to bed, still numb, and finally slept.

When she awoke the next morning it was just beginning to get daylight. She put on her robe and quickly went outside to get the newspaper. When she got back inside, she sat at the kitchen table and slowly opened the newspaper to the page where the winning number was printed. She was afraid to look. Maybe it had all been a dream, or even another one of her fantasies. Maybe she had, at last, reached the point where she could no longer distinguish fact from fantasy.

By now, she had the numbers on her ticket memorized. And when she looked at the winning number, her last number also matched. Not only did her numbers match, but they were even in the same sequence. She couldn't comprehend winning fifty-seven million dollars! Then again, there might be more winners besides herself. But even if the money had to be split with others there should still be plenty.

She turned on the TV to watch the early edition of the local news: the newscaster announced that there was one winning lottery ticket, which had been sold in Corpus Christi--the city where she lived. Justine felt faint and put her head down between her knees for a few minutes until the feeling passed.

As she got up to make coffee, the full meaning finally began to hit her. She was rich! She was free! She could do anything she wanted. She had just won fifty-seven million dollars! Even after taxes, she would have more left over than she could ever spend. She let out a whoop! Then another! Then a shriek! Her mother rushed into the small kitchen, clutching her robe tightly around her still rotund body.

"Justine? Are you all right?" She asked in alarm.

"Yes! I'm more than all right! You'd better sit down," she said, as she helped her mother into a chair. "I won the lottery, Mamma!"

"Oh, no, Justine; please don't tell me you gambled," her mother said, pleading with her eyes as well as with her voice.

"That's what I always found funny about you, Mamma. You play bingo all the time, but you consider the lottery gambling. Don't you realize, because I gambled, as you put it, that we're rich? Rich beyond our wildest dreams!"

Her mother began to explain, trying to justify herself. "Bingo is a harmless game, but the lottery is the devil's do. It causes people to spend their hard earned money on an impossibly small chance they might win. Bingo is totally different. Surely you can see that, Justine."

Justine bent over and kissed her mother. "It doesn't matter anyway, Mamma. It's over and done with; and I won. That means you can have anything you want, and I can have anything I want," she said, as she walked back down the hallway to her room. She still had to be at school on time, even if she was now a multimillionaire.

All day at school Justine felt like she was glowing again, and couldn't keep a smug little smile off her face. She knew the other teachers were looking at her strangely, but she didn't tell any of them about her good fortune. After school she went to claim her prize. She didn't allow any publicity or pictures. She wanted to retain as much of her anonymity as possible.

But at school the next day the word had gotten out. Many of the other teachers congratulated her--some with undisguised envy and awe plainly showing on their faces. After school she had a passport photo taken, then took it, along with her birth certificate, to the main post office where she filled out her passport application. She already knew what she was going to do.

She would find a cozy villa to buy. Probably in the South of France. Or possibly Greece, or Spain. Maybe even all three. But someplace on the Mediterranean. An open, airy house--with lots of windows to let in the warm golden sunshine of her days, and the cool silvery moonlight of her nights. She wanted to spend the rest of her life in the light, to never more have to be in the darkness. From now on, she would eat from the finest china and drink from delicate crystal goblets.

And she knew HE was out there somewhere. The tall, slender one with the soul of a poet. The one she would love. The one who would love her. She knew she would find him (or he would find her). She didn't know where or when, but she did know that her life would never again be boring!

Tomorrow she would shop for luggage!

...Tina and Royce riding on a horse together—wildly galloping like the wind...

SOARING

Here I stand . . .
Poised on the brink of the rest of my life.
With beseeching eyes
I raise my hands upward--
To the sky--
Eagerly awaiting

Adventures . . .
Of what is to be.
Of distant horizons across the sea,
Of beauty and mystery yet to seek.
Of art,
Of music,

And of great love
Yet To be felt . . . deep within my soul.
To taste,
To smell,
To touch,
To experience.

I am, at last, ready to take flight
To new heights;
To spread my wings and soar, knowing that,
Since being touched by the wonder of you,
I am now empowered
To be the best that I can be.

THE BEGINNING

As the last story ended, I continued to look into Schere's eyes. This time they were like pools of ebony--the same as they had been in the beginning. I blinked, to try to break the spell they seemed to hold on me; yet, in another way, I didn't want to break it. I felt deep sadness that there were no more stories.

She smiled her dreamy smile. "Michael, inside of most of us is another person whom we keep safely hidden away from the rest of the world. A sensitive, vulnerable person whom we mistakenly feel we must protect and insulate from risk of pain and ridicule--to protect from life's realities. But this inner person, the person we really are, is usually screaming to be freed...to experience life...if we will only listen and hear its plea.

"Justine found a way to liberate her inner person: to love herself enough to free herself to experience life--before it was too late--as each of us must learn to do in our own way. Michael; I hope you, too, will find the way to gain a new awareness of your inner self. That you will find a new wisdom born of sensitivity, along with a knowledge of your inner truths and spirituality, and that you will be able to learn to love yourself. Through my stories, I have shown you love in its different forms. And, most importantly, I hope I have given you the capacity to love and to be loved. You must also learn to trust--the way you have put your trust in me tonight while tied to my bed; for trust is a vital part of love.

I seemed to be unable to move. I blinked again...but the spell still remained. I swallowed, and was able to find my voice. "I've never had an experience like this before. I don't know what to say. I do feel different...but I feel so many things...I'm not even sure what all the emotions are." However, I did know that I still wanted her--now more than ever. But for some reason I was unable to tell her.

Her eyes continued to pull me in, only now they were dark green. I sighed and closed my eyes. Then I felt her arms around me. Her warm pliant body next to mine. Or was I dreaming? Was this yet another story? No. She said she had told me the last one.

Her heady Shalimar scent surrounded me as I felt her soft lips on mine--the gently probing, velvet tip of her tongue caressing the bottom edge of my upper front teeth. When I felt her begin to unfasten my clothes, passion flared inside of me: passion like I had never experienced before--or at least not in a very long time.

As our bodies joined, I gave myself to her freely; completely. But, in losing myself in her, I found myself; I felt like I had once again become a whole person. Like a part of me that had been missing up until this moment had, at last, returned.

She was making love to me; loving me. Her movements were soft and sensual, her hips rotating in a slow circular motion, fusing our bodies closer together, rather than the frantic thrusting I was used to.

I remembered what she had told me--about looking into the eyes of my beloved while we were joined in lovemaking. So I opened my eyes and looked into the fathoms of her eyes--their fervid green depth pulling me in--locking me to her. I felt as if we were floating together on a different plane from the rest of the world just before I experienced the intense explosions deep within by body--as if I were novaing into thousands of separate particles flying out to join stars in distant galaxies. Afterwards, content and exhausted, I lay wrapped in her arms and slept the deep restful sleep of a young innocent child.

When I awoke, she was sitting in a white damask slipper chair by the side of the bed...watching me. Watching me with those magic eyes, which were still deep green. Emeralds: the color of the sea. Her hair, no longer dark, now seemed to be a soft shade of brown with golden highlights. And in the glow of the candlelight, a strange, luminescent aura seemed to surround her face.

She smiled. "Did you have a good sleep, Michael?"

I still felt dazed, and as I sat up I noticed that the scarves which had previously bound me to the bed were now gone. I was fully clothed, only my shirt was unbuttoned. I was confused. Had she made love to me, or had I dreamed it? I cleared my throat. "Yes, I did. I dreamed that we made love; or was it a dream?"

"It is whatever you wish it to be, Michael," she said smiling. "I think you must go now. It is nearly daylight."

I sat on the edge of the bed and put on my shoes. I stood, and buttoned my shirt as I walked to her bathroom. After using the facilities, I again looked into the mirror over the sink. I didn't look any different. But I felt different. I felt like I had begun to find inner recesses of myself I hadn't even known existed. I smoothed my hair with my hands, then walked back into her bedroom. She rose from her chair, walked to me and took my hand, holding it in both of hers as she looked into my eyes.

"Michael, I hope you will always remember this night: that you will always remember what you have learned from the stories in my eyes. It has been a very special night for both of us."

I looked down at the floor, and again felt like an adolescent schoolboy with my first crush. A lump formed in my throat, making me unable to speak. I just stood there, nodding, then raised my head and looked into her magic eyes--for the last time. I still had that strange feeling like I might cry. The big, gruff defense attorney! But just in time, I regained my composure. Schere began walking, leading me by the hand down the hallway to her front door.

"Michael, you must grasp the reins of your life firmly in both hands and guide yourself to where you wish to go. If you accidentally choose a wrong road, you must go back and try again and again, as many times as it takes, until you at last find the right one. You must never allow yourself to just follow a road aimlessly along. You must choose and create your own destiny--or else you have wasted your life.

"Think of yourself as a mobile canvass, which is painted by your experiences. You can end up with a blank canvass, a pale and washed out composition, or one which is brilliant and vibrant. It is your choice. Always remember, our inner beauty is what is most important, as it is the reflection of our inner truths. Often, if we will only look deeply enough within ourselves, we will find that we already have the answers to most of our questions. Goodbye, Michael; if you hurry, you can watch the sunrise."

She released my hand, then opened the door. I meekly walked out into the hall, heard the door close behind me and the lock click. I wondered if I had fallen hopelessly in love with her. I didn't even know her last name.

Still feeling somewhat dazed, I walked to the elevator, rode to the main floor, then went to the bank of mailboxes where I looked up her apartment number. There was her name: Scheherazade Jamais. "Scheherazade!" The same name as the magical storyteller in the *Arabian Nights:* one of my favorite books when I was a child.

But she couldn't be. Scheherazade was a fictional character. Yet I continued to wonder exactly who or what she was. I no longer thought she was a witch or some type of sorceress. I didn't believe in witches or sorceresses. Maybe she was my guardian angel? But an angel would never look or behave the way she had...would she? Besides; I didn't believe in angels, either...or did I?

As I reluctantly walked outside, I hoped that someday I would know who she really was. However, regardless of who or what she was, I knew I would be eternally grateful to her for giving me this wondrous night. I took a deep breath; the air smelled fresh and clean. Another day. A rebirth. When I walked by an olive tree in full-bloom, one of the blossoms brushed against my cheek and I felt the wetness of the early morning dew--as if in symbolic baptism.

I sat in my car for a few moments as I reflected on the past night. Then, remembering her last words to me, I drove to the downtown beach where I parked and watched the sunrise--with all the eagerness of a child who was seeing its wonder for the first time.

Afterwards, I slowly drove home, then went to sleep on top of my bed, fully clothed. When I awoke at 10:00 A.M., I phoned my secretary and told her that I had the flu and wouldn't be coming in. Then I took my phone off the hook. I slept most of the weekend, dreaming of Schere and of her wonderful stories. I was still completely enchanted by her.

When I went to my office on Monday, I found it very difficult to concentrate. I wanted to phone Schere, but she didn't have a listing in the directory. I phoned directory assistance and was told she had a private number. That evening after work, I went to Anytime and asked Doug if he knew her. When he told me he didn't, I decided to go back to her apartment. If she was entertaining another guest, well, that was just a chance I would have to take.

I quickly drove to her building, but when I buzzed her apartment from the intercom outside the security gates, to my dismay no one answered. Next, I frantically buzzed the intercom number of the apartment across the hall from hers, and when an elderly female voice answered, I hastily explained that I was looking for Ms. Jamais.

The woman laughed. "Oh, Schere? She and that cat of hers left early yesterday morning for Europe. She travels back and forth a lot. She only stays here a few months at a time. Sorry."

I felt my heart fall. I mumbled my thanks to the woman, took several deep breaths, then stumbled back to my car. As I drove home, my eyes began to sting with unshed tears at the ominous feeling that I would never see Schere again. I began to think about our night together, and her captivating stories. The more I thought, the more it all began to seem like a dream.

As the days wore on, I felt changes in myself. My work was no longer my all consuming interest. I would often find myself daydreaming while looking out of my windows at the magnificent view of the bay which I had always before taken for granted. Frequently I found myself fascinated in watching the windsurfers.

Maybe I'd try it sometime, what the hell! I was amazed that I would ever have this thought. The "old Michael" never would have.

I also thought a lot about Joy. Several times I even drove by our old house on Del Mar, where once we had been so happy together--so eager for life, and I wondered how things had gotten so turned around.

On the following Saturday morning I woke up very early, and before I knew it I was in my car driving to Padre Island beach where I watched another beautiful sunrise, again experiencing that wonder and freshness of a newborn day. I thought of Schere, only this time with gratitude, rather than with longing, as I began to realize what a precious gift she had given to me: the gift of enabling me to find my spirituality; the gift of myself. And I thought of Joy, remembering how deeply in love we had once been--before our careers had taken over our lives, or, rather, before mine had taken over my life.

Joy had been committed too, but in a different way. I had lusted for prestige and glory. Joy had been looking for fulfillment of justice. How had we gotten so far apart in our dreams and goals?

I thought of Joy's warm softness--of how good she had felt in my arms--and I wanted her so desperately that the ache in my heart was so profound, I actually felt a stab of physical pain. I wanted her as my lover--my best friend--my companion--my soul mate. I could almost see her. Her slightly slanted eyes laughing up at me. Her stubborn mouth, her saucy turned-up nose.

For a while, I walked along the beach at the edge of the water, with that nearly unbearable emptiness in my heart, contemplating what Scherre had said about grasping the reins of my life in my hands and guiding myself to my chosen destiny. I breathed the clean fragrance of the sea and tasted the tang of salt on my lips from the faint morning mist. The new day's dazzling sunshine made the water sparkle--as if a giant had scattered handfuls of diamonds across the surface.

I stooped to pick up a sand dollar, and while marveling at its delicate markings I remembered that inside were five more tiny shells shaped like miniature doves in flight: symbols of peace and freedom. Once again, some of the words from the song "Nights in White Satin" abruptly flowed through my mind--the wisdom of their fundamental truth bringing a personal epiphany: a revealing awareness of *my* most intimate truths. And I realized that I, alone, was the true master of my own fate.

As I was consumed by another overwhelming yearning for Joy, I knew what a fool I had been. I hadn't recognized the most important thing in my life. I had let it slip away...unaware! But maybe it wasn't too late. I began to run back to my car. I could hardly wait to talk to Joy!

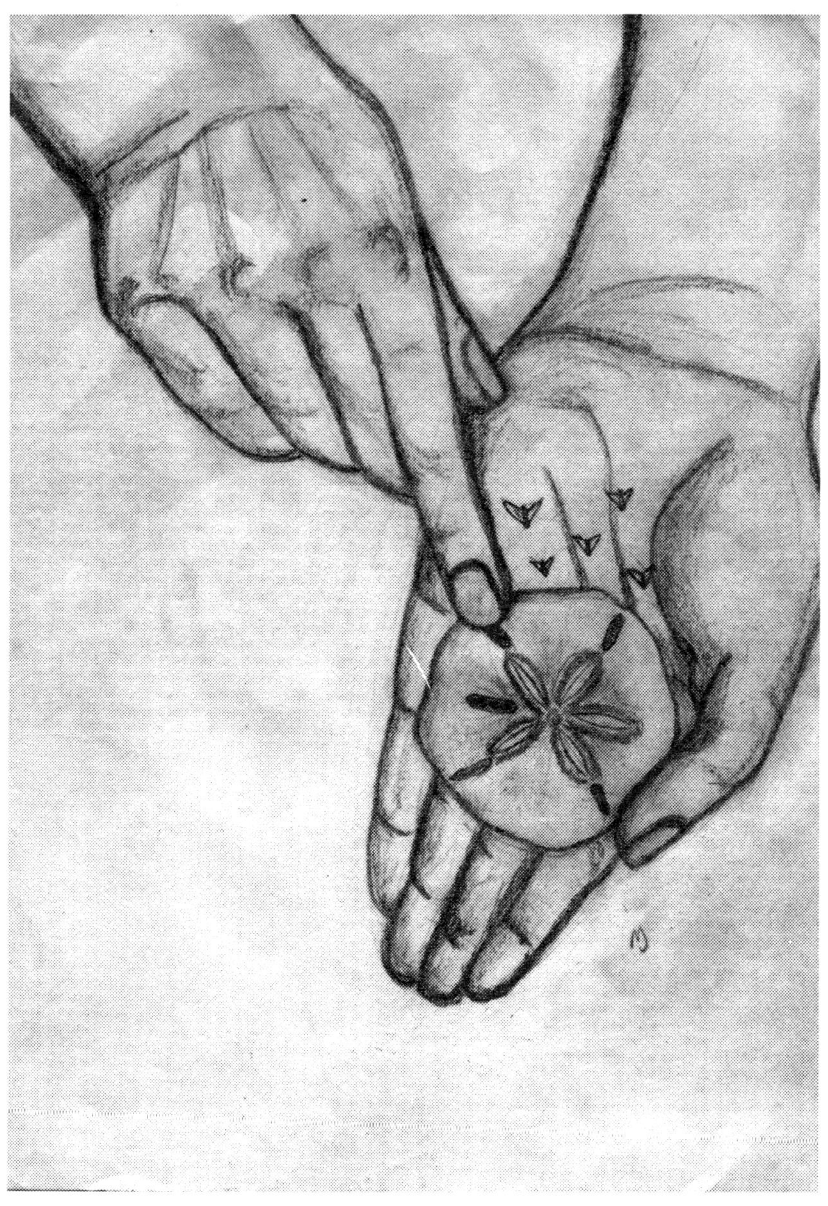

...inside were five more tiny shells shaped like miniature doves in flight: symbols of peace and freedom.